# YUPPIE SCUM

# SEAN BRECKENRIDGE

# YUPPIE SCUM

ST. MARTIN'S PRESS
NEW YORK

YUPPIE SCUM Copyright © 1993 by Sean Breckenridge. All rights reserved. Printed in the United States of America. No part of this book may be used or reproduced in any manner whatsoever without written permission except in the case of brief quotations embodied in critical articles or reviews. For information, address St. Martin's Press, 175 Fifth Avenue, New York, N.Y. 10010.

Library of Congress Cataloging-in-Publication Data

Breckenridge, Sean.
    Yuppie scum / Sean Breckenridge.
       p.   cm.
    "A Thomas Dunne book."
    ISBN 0-312-08928-7
    I. Title.
PS3552.R3625Y86   1993
813prm.54—dc20                                                      92-40819
                                                                             CIP

First Edition: April 1993

10  9  8  7  6  5  4  3  2  1

*"There's a lot less opportunity for anyone entering investment banking now. The smart people will be out looking for the new scam."*

—Brian Young, 32
Millionaire Investment Banker
*Fortune,* November 24, 1986

# PART ONE

**FRIDAY
AFTERNOON
JUNE 26, 1992**

# Prologue

The amber digits glowed tantalizingly on the computer screen before him. He paused for a short while, pressing his face within inches of the glossy glass surface of the monitor until the static electricity caused strands of his hair to levitate. Then he sat back in his chair and rotated a pair of ornamented Chinese meditation spheres in tight orbits in the sweaty palm of his hand. The inner chimes of the balls were therapeutic, soothing the tension some. But not completely.

The next transaction would be his twenty-third. Five more to go after this. *Hitting the homestretch.* He stole a glance at the clock on the VCR. Still had plenty of time before the end of the business day.

Mitch was playing with electric money. Lots of it.

Money that belonged to his friends and his clients.

He placed the metallic meditation balls off to the side. Time to get serious. His fingers burst into a brief flurry of keystrokes. In an almost instant response, strings of numbers began marching up the screen in a steady progression. Four-, five-, and six-digit figures. Sums that had already been transferred to an account controlled by him in the Cayman Islands. Occasionally, a seven-figure sum would scroll past his eyes, causing his heart to trip-hammer and the perspiration to darken the armpits of his pinpoint oxford shirt.

Jesus.

His eyes narrowed into watery slits as he drew another lungful of harsh smoke from the joint. The Rolling Stones were on the CD player in another part of the room: "Hot Rocks, 1964–1971." As he set about transferring the rest of his clients' liquid assets to himself, he sang along with Mick: "Please allow me to introduce myself, I'm a man of wealth and taste—"

He called up the command screen with the Microsoft mouse.

DO YOU WISH TO EXECUTE ANOTHER TRANSFER? (Y/N)
PRESS <F-1> TO CANCEL
PRESS <F-2> FOR HELP.

He typed Y and hit the ENTER key. The screen went blank for a moment. The software program then prompted him for information about the Spielvogel Children's Trust Account at the First Philadelphia Bank. Account number, the bank's ABA code, and the like. After roughly sixty seconds of data entry, the screen asked him to enter the telephone number of the Cayman Islands bank's dedicated line. He did so and thumbed the ENTER key.

The screen flashed PLEASE WAIT once more. A cartoon icon of a grinning bank robber winked at him while the computer's modem dialed up the bank. Whoever he was, the software's creator had had a warped sense of humor.

While waiting, he performed a C-section on the big-Grab-Size bag of Jumpin' Jack Cheese Doritos next to him and devoured the rest of the chips. Then he upended the bag and filled his mouth with the pulverized residue of salt, cheese powder, and crumbs. Eventually, the bank's mainframe computer on the other end of the line responded to the signals sent by the software—signals unintelligible to the human ear. Streams of binary numbers flickered past, causing the mainframe on the other end to bypass its own security procedure. Within moments, the funds were transferred cleanly to the Cayman Islands branch of the Hemisphere Bank of Exchange, Internationale.

He recalled how St. Germaine had pitched the software to him as an experimental prototype. The Saint had described it as sort of a skeleton key for computer-hackers. The software had a special algorithm embedded in its program code that rendered electronic fund transfer passwords useless. With this software, he realized no bank account in the world was safe.

Still, he had to be judicious in using it. Countless times, The Saint had stressed to him the importance of timing. In order for this scheme to work, St. Germaine had said, you had to move the money out of the accounts as close as possible to the end of business on Friday. Then, at the conclusion of it all, he was to send a predesigned computer virus timebomb through E-mail. A variation of the infamous Michelangelo virus, the code would muck up every proprietary databank, as of Sunday 12:00 noon.

If all worked as planned, it would be impossible for anyone to discover the missing funds until a week, two weeks after the fact.

By that time, of course, they'd be on a beach somewhere on the Italian Riviera, slathering each other with Coppertone.

The Saint was a total fucking genius.

Suddenly, the computer whirred and chirped with activity. The machine beeped and a new message flashed: **TRANSFER SUCCESSFUL. 15:43:15. JUN 26 – 92.** He shook his head in disbelief. It was all so easy. *So* easy. With just two keystrokes, he had embezzled $120,465.12 from the Spielvogel Children's Trust Account.

He thumped the ENTER button twice and the prompt returned: **TRANSFER FROM ANOTHER ACCOUNT? (Y/N).** He entered Y. **TYPE ACCOUNT NUMBER.** He consulted the log of his clients and their account numbers. He typed in the number of McPhillips' account.

**TYPE ACCOUNT NAME (LAST/FIRST).**

He typed: MCPHILLIPS/BRIAN.

Then he typed Y again at the execute prompt. The machine whirred into activity.

McPhillips had been a friend. In his cannabis haze, he smiled sadly and said, "Sorry, guy. I did it in the name of love."

But if McPhillips didn't understand, well, he could give a rat's ass, really. Sacrifices had to be made. And peer approval was hardly a priority at this stage of the game.

\* \* \*

He spent the next twenty minutes working through the rest of the list of his former friends and clients. When he had finished with the final electronic funds transfer, he rubbed his burning eyes with the heel of his hand. He stood up from the swivel chair where he had spent the last two and a half hours and allowed himself a luxurious stretch.

In the course of a few hours, he had become a very, very wealthy man.

No doubt about it, there would be holy hell to pay in the wake of this caper. Come next week, when the victims or the bank officials or whoever ultimately pieced together the scam, a shit-storm of fury would break loose. This was no penny-ante fraud. This one would make headlines from coast to coast. CNN and the NBC Nightly News with Brokaw. ABC, CBS. The *Wall Street Journal* would be all over it. Christ, C-span would probably be cluttered for months to come with congressional subcommittee hearings on the subject. Politicians scrambling over each other, each jockeying to get his legislation on the floor.

It was *that* big.

He disengaged himself from this reverie. No time to waste, he told himself.

Moving quickly now, he typed out the commands to send the file named VIRUS.XXX through E-mail to each one of the banks' mainframes.

Once this was completed, he exited the program and called DOS up on the screen.

At the C< prompt, he typed: **ERASE \*.\*.**

The computer responded: **ARE YOU SURE? (Y/N)**

"Of course I'm sure," he laughed, typing Y.

The hard drive of the computer then proceeded to lobotomize itself, wiping out all bits of information previously stored in its own memory, as well as any evidence of the crimes. He discharged the three-and-one-half-inch data disk from the drive and snapped it in two just as St. Germaine had instructed him to do. He tucked the fragments in his pocket and made a mental note to chuck them into the rubbish at the airport.

Then he picked up the phone and dialed the limo service. He

made arrangements with the dispatcher for the car to drive out and pick her up first, then return to Center City to get him.

Then he called her number.

She answered on the half-ring. In a voice that was all silk-and-cream, she cooed, "Tell me something good, loverboy."

A grin of delight came to his face. He told her something good, all right.

# PART TWO

**FRIDAY EVENING JUNE 26, 1992**

# 1

Slumped in the passenger seat of Mazzola's turbocharged Jaguar XJE, Charles Beekman III stewed silently, wondering how they were going to break the news to Jeff. Jeff was a pretty high-strung guy; he'd probably go absolutely ballistic over the news, totally apeshit. When you got right down to it, what red-blooded American male *wouldn't?*

So here they were, driving out to the suburbs to tell him in person. The prospect of this impending encounter with Jeff filled Beekman with misery. He hated being the bearer of bad news.

Still, despite his overwhelming sense of dread, he realized they were doing the right thing. Hearing it first from friends just might cushion the blow. At least a little. Then again, Chuck thought morosely, there were no magic words, no soft-pedaling the truth, to make this news bulletin completely painless to Jeff Wheaton.

As Mazzola jockeyed the Jag aggressively through the brisk flow of early evening traffic on the Schuylkill Expressway, he said, "Look, you want, I'll be the one to tell the Jeffster, all right?"

Beekman snapped upright. "Oh? You want to be the one to tell him?"

Mazzola shrugged. "If it's all the same to you." Mazzola paused. "Then again, if *you* want to be the one—"

"Well, okay, if you think it's best that you tell him, sure, fine," Beekman said hastily, straining to appear casual.

Inwardly, of course, Chuck Beekman was enormously relieved to have Mazzola offer to handle it. Truth be told, Bruce was simply superior to the average bear when it came to handling such high-pressure situations. The guy was perfect for the job, nerves of steel, having cut his teeth in junk-bond-fueled mergers and acquisitions on the Street during the anything-goes eighties. Bruce no longer worked in New York, but at that time and place, the ebb and flow of hundreds of millions of dollars were determined by instant electronic pulses amounting to mere fractions of a point. Mazz *had been there*, front-row center at the greatest financial revolution the world had ever witnessed. How often had he bragged of closing nine- and ten-figure junk-bond acquisitions during his six-year career with a variety of well-known bulge-bracket investment firms? Such deal-making was entirely unfathomable to Chuck. Chuck worked in the front office of his father's tristate Ford-Mazda dealership in Cherry Hill, New Jersey, where the height of his financial glory was scoring an occasional thirty-five-hundred-dollar markup over sticker on a Mazda Miata. Chuck Beekman would be the first to admit he was decidedly ill-equipped to contend with such high-stress confrontations as this Wheaton thing. Indeed, he made it a personal policy to defer them to the nearest Type-A person wherever possible. And Bruce wasn't just Type A; he was Type *triple A* plus. Mr. Take-Charge. Bruce frigging *thrived* in this type of situation. His seemingly effortless inner strength was just one of many reasons Chuck Beekman wished he were more like his friend Bruce Mazzola. Mazzola feared *nothing*.

"How are you gonna, y'know . . ." Beekman trailed off elliptically, fumbling for the words. "Like, uh, how do you plan to put it to him?"

Bruce Mazzola turned to his right and gave him a strabismic look, as if peering at an optical illusion. "How do you mean?"

"What are you gonna say?"

Mazzola poked a Dunhill cigar between his teeth, fired it up, and allowed himself an expansive lungful of smoke before responding. Chuck's eyes began stinging, but he held his tongue in check.

"You can't sugarcoat something like this," Mazzola said after a while. "You got to give him the straight dope right up front."

Beekman snorted a nervous laugh. "Now why didn't I think of that?" He felt like a fool for asking such a stupid question in the first place. "You got to be cruel to be kind, right?"

"Something like that."

"I gotcha."

They drove in rapt silence for a while, Chuck Beekman hypnotized by the white lines of the Schuylkill blurring by. Then Mazzola smirked and said, "You're not exactly looking forward to this, are you, Charlie Three-Sticks?"

"No," Chuck Beekman said. "Are *you?*"

"Man's gotta do what a man's gotta do. End of story."

"I guess," Beekman muttered. After a pause, Chuck summoned up the courage to say in a quiet voice, "Bruce, please don't call me that."

Of all the derogatory nicknames that had stuck to him over the years, he despised that one the most. *Charlie Three-Sticks.*

Five years ago, Jeff Wheaton had amassed a small fortune in a remarkably short period of time. He had started an instantly successful mail-order laptop computer business out of his living room—Wheat/Tech Computers. Virtually overnight, Wheaton had been crowned as something of a wunderkind by both the trade and mainstream media, a sensation in a highly competitive industry. His success story had been written up in a dozen national publications.

He was probably the most famous person Beekman knew— *and he used to be Chuck and Bruce's college roommate at Penn.* In college, Jeff had been an intense but relatively quiet guy who kept mostly to himself; his stellar success had blown away all those who had known him.

The thing about Jeff that struck Beekman the most was that he rarely indulged himself in yuppie status symbols. While Wheaton's three-story townhouse in Bryn Mawr was expensive, it was hardly lavish by anyone's standard. True to form, after he had banked his first million, Jeff had steadfastly refused to follow the lemming mentality of his generation, which dictated that young millionaires had to tool around in a BMW. When Beekman queried him why he didn't acquire a Beemer, Wheaton had replied that BMW was an acronym for "boring millionaire's wheels." Hey, you had to respect that. Success hadn't spoiled Jeff Wheaton. In the end, Wheaton wound up purchasing a previously owned 1988 Ford Bronco with eleven thousand miles on it from Beekman's father's dealership, hardly a typical multimillionaire yuppie's conceit. Ultimately, the only outward symbol of success that Jeff Wheaton paraded around in public was his trophy wife, Rachel.

Which happened to be part of the problem at hand.

They arrived at Jeff Wheaton's townhouse complex a few minutes before seven. The Ford Bronco was parked in the space in front of Wheaton's address. The poor bastard was home. As Mazzola pulled into the space near the all-terrain vehicle, Beekman experienced a harsh ejaculation of stomach acid that caused him to tense and nearly groan aloud.

Mazzola immediately detected the weakness. "You okay?"

"Yeah."

"You want to wait in the car?"

"No. No, c'mon. I want to be there."

Mazzola nodded. Without another word, he turned off the engine, opened the door, and alighted from the driver's seat. He dropped the smoldering cigar nub to the asphalt and casually crushed it out with a Bally-loafered foot. He walked toward the front steps. Beekman scrabbled out of the car and rushed to catch up with him.

Bruce knocked sharply on the door, the kind of no-nonsense rap a process-server might favor. Moisture collected in the hollow of Beekman's palms in the awful moments they waited for Jeff to appear. Finally, Jeff Wheaton answered the door in a purple pocket T-shirt from the Gap and chino shorts, a half-full bottle of citrus-flavored Gatorade in hand.

Wheaton blinked as it took a moment for his eyes to adjust to the waning sunlight; then a look of delighted surprise swept across his face when he recognized his college roommates darkening his doorstep. "Jeezzus!" he blurted. "Somebody slap me upside the head. Do my eyes deceive me or could it *really be*—Mazz and the Beeker? What the *hell* you chuckleheads doin' out here in the 'burbs?"

"Can we come in for a minute, Jeff?" Mazzola asked.

"For a minute? Hell, yeah, I think I could spare you guys a minute. Jesus. C'mon in." Wheaton cheerfully gestured them in with a beckoning motion of the bottle.

Mazzola and Beekman entered the foyer. Wheaton closed the door behind them and led them to the spacious living room. It was cluttered with a dozen or so Wheat/Tech laptop and notebook computers. Jeff burbled happily, "You guys really should have called ahead, I would've gotten a six-foot hero or pizzas or something. Shit, Mazz, had I known you were coming out to Bryn Mawr, I would've stocked the liquor cabinet accordingly." He laughed. "Bruce puts Jack Daniel's away like I drink Gatorade."

*Oh, no,* Beekman fretted. Jeff thought this was a social call, an impromptu boys' night out. Indeed, Wheaton's laughter was festive; the guy seemed to delight in having some surprise company drop by on what would otherwise have been a Friday night spent in solitude.

As Jeff disappeared into the kitchen to fetch a round of brews, his disembodied voice boomed out, "I gotta tell you, this is a treat, really. It's so rare that we get together these days. I mean, hell, I know we're all caught up in our own lives and all, but shit, we live within an hour's drive of each other. This is perfect, really good timing. Rachel's away for the weekend, visiting her mother and stepfather in Baltimore." He emerged from the kitchen with some cold St. Pauli Girls bunched together at the necks, proffering them to his guests. "You guys up for a night of five-card stud and some drunken stupidity or what?"

Bruce took the beer from him and, uncharacteristically, set it down on the coffee table without so much as a sip. His voice resonated with doomsday seriousness. "Jeff, I'm afraid this is not a pleasure visit."

The smile evaporated from Jeff Wheaton's face. "It's not?"

Mazzola shook his head. "No. I'm afraid we have some bad news. Some very bad news."

Wheaton blinked.

"Tell me," he said in a way that somehow caused Beekman to believe he had been expecting bad news for some time.

"Well," Bruce said. "It's like this—"

Then Mazzola dropped the bomb. . . .

Mitch Myerson had embezzled everyone's money and left the country.

And it appeared that he had taken Wheaton's wife, Rachel, with him.

An excruciating silence ensued. Then, as the news sank in, Wheaton's posture sagged and the color drained from his face. He literally staggered backward a few steps.

The reaction caused Beekman to think, *Oh, shit, maybe Bruce was too fucking direct this time.* Myerson had just run off with the poor guy's wife, for chrissake, and here Bruce was, breaking the news to him with all the sensitivity of a battering ram.

Wheaton's jaw moved soundlessly. When he regained his ability to speak, he said, hoarsely, "This can't be right. She told me she was going to Baltimore to visit her mother."

"Well," Mazzola said, "she lied."

"I can't believe this." Jeff's eyes flicked back and forth between the two men. "Are you absolutely positive?"

"Shit, what can we say, Jeff? We got it straight from the cops no more than an hour ago. They've been trying to get ahold of you themselves, but you've been out. I mean, Jeffster, it's not exactly the sort of news you leave on an answering machine."

Wheaton stared at the carpet, utterly dumbfounded.

Beekman cleared his throat and spoke for the first time. "Jeff, you're not the only victim. The police say that he somehow tapped into all the bank accounts of his clients with a computer and wiped them all out including all of *us.*"

"That's right," Mazzola nodded. "That mojo motherfucker, we trusted him with our hard-earned cash, and he bent us over and butt-fucked us bloody."

"He stole from all of us, Jeff. Took every penny."

Jeff Wheaton licked the corner of his mouth and ran a trembling hand through his hair. "But Rachel went with him, is that what you're saying?"

"That would appear to be the case." Mazzola nodded grimly.

"Jeff, we should point out that the cops aren't a hundred percent sure about that," Chuck Beekman added hastily. "It's a hunch."

"But it sure as hell looks that way," Mazzola said.

"I should have known," Wheaton muttered hollowly. "She gave me all the warning signs. I should've seen it coming."

"You don't mind my saying," Mazzola said gently, "I never much liked your wife."

That said, an ominous silence hung in the air. Beekman could hear the blood thumping loudly in his ears. Watching Jeff Wheaton endure this, the ultimate humiliation, caused him to squirm with discomfort. Poor bastard had not exactly had a banner year. First, Wheat/Tech Computers had teetered on the precipice of bankruptcy; now his gold-digging wife had dumped him in such an undecorous fashion. It occurred to Beekman that somehow the two events probably weren't unconnected and were, in fact, probably a classic example of cause and effect.

"Jeff, I'm sure you're not really up to it," Beekman said softly, "but the police need you to come back to Center City with us, to answer some questions. . . ." Chuck Beekman's voice trailed off as he watched Wheaton's expression darken. A firestorm of rage was gathering within his friend. "Hey, Jeff. Jeff, man, you okay?"

"He'll be all right," Mazzola said. "Just leave him alone."

But his fury abruptly broke surface, with nuclear intensity. He bellowed in a chilling primal scream of rage and anguish and sidearmed the beer bottle against the wall, where it exploded into shards. The splashback of cold fluid and fragments of glass rained down upon the three men.

"For Christ's sake, Jeff," Chuck Beekman squawked. "Don't!"

Oblivious to the others, Jeff Wheaton crossed the room to his golf bag, which was leaning against the mauve-colored wall. He kicked at it ferociously. The bag pitched over to the Oriental carpet with a heavy thump. Some of the clubs scattered askew, reminding Beekman, absurdly, of an open box of dry spaghetti he had dropped on his kitchen floor two nights before. Wheaton's face flushed an arterial purple as he delivered repeated kicks to the side of the fallen bag, his curses of Myerson rising alarmingly in pitch and volume—*"Cocksucker-sonuvafucking bitch. Took my money, took my wife"*—the curses were recited, two times, three times, four—over and over, until it became some sort of weird mantra of hatred. Then he spun away, dancing about the room with a wild-eyed expression signifying impending violence. Wheaton, a CPA and nationally renowned computer entrepreneur, randomly gathered up three golf clubs from the floor—a number one Callaway "Big Bertha" graphite driver, a number three Taylor-Made metal-wood, and a number two Tommy Armour 845 forged-steel-shafted iron—and stalked about the room in a mindless, bloodthirsty fury.

Beekman shouted, "Jeff!" and took a step forward to subdue his collegehood friend.

Mazzola restrained him with a firm grip of the shoulder that caused him to wince in pain.

"No," Mazzola hissed. "Let his anger run its course."

And, as Beekman had done so many times in the past, he deferred his judgment to that of Mazzola and he stood by, utterly immobile. The next hundred seconds would be ones that most people would forever regret, one hundred seconds whose agonizing details would be indelibly burned into the mind's eye to be replayed over and over in their totality with the clarity of a loop of Technicolor film. Jeff Wheaton swung the three clubs together as a single weapon, overhead in a vicious arc. The clubs made a whizzing sound in descent, and upon impact they demolished the glass coffee table in the center of the living room. The sound of shattering glass caused Beekman to flinch. Coasters scattered, two beer bottles catapulted a short distance across the room. A Waterford crystal vase with dried flowers tumbled to the floor, intact and undamaged among the broken shards.

By now, Beekman was cowed by the intensity of Wheaton's violent frenzy, too terrified to intervene. All he could do was to look on in paralyzed horror as Wheaton systematically destroyed his own living room with repeated blows of the golf clubs. The second swipe, on a horizontal plane, took out a row of picture frames, with shots of him and Rachel taken on their happy honeymoon in Tangiers, and the crystal Mikasa clock Beekman had given them as a wedding gift. The third bashed in the smoked doors of the ebony breakfront, shattering a display of the couple's

Limoges bone china. Another swing landed on the Italian leather couch like a tomahawk, cleaving a huge smile-shaped gash in the seat. The final blow took out the screen of the twenty-seven-inch Sony Trinitron. All throughout, the robotic chant: *"Took my money, took my wife—took my money, took my wife—"* To Beekman, watching this scene was like an out-of-body experience.

Finally, Chuck Beekman could endure no more. He summoned up the will to leap forward and stop the violence, but not in time to prevent the enraged CPA from heaving one of his laptop computers through the plate glass of the sliding door to the balcony. A tremendous crash of broken glass drowned out Beekman's cry as he tackled Wheaton. They tumbled to the floor in a writhing heap. A shard of glass from the coffee table sliced a gash in Beekman's left hand as they grappled. Eventually, Beekman managed to subdue Wheaton and quell the hysterics.

All at once, the rage bled out of Jeff; anguish flooded in in its wake. His face screwed into a pathetic mask of pain. "If he took all of my money, did he have to take *her* too?" Wheaton collapsed into a ball of agony, his body convulsing with sobs. Chuck Beekman cradled his onetime roommate from the University of Pennsylvania, whispering soothingly in his ear, "Man, I'm sorry. I'm so, so sorry."

When Chuck Beekman looked up at Bruce Mazzola standing there, he was mortified to see the slightest trace of a *smirk* on Mazzola's face. Mazzola with that trademark smirk of his! Was it possible that Bruce found this display amusing in some sick and twisted way? Had he actually *gotten off* just a *little bit* on Jeff's misfortune? No way possible, Beekman told himself, he had to be mistaken, that would just be too, too weird—

And, as if reading his thoughts, Mazzola blurred into motion and slammed his fist against the wall. "That bastard! That *bastard!* I'd give ten years off my life to have Myerson, right here, right now, so I could tear his balls off and *stuff 'em down his throat!"*

As Wheaton sobbed in his arms, Chuck Beekman felt a peculiar—but reassuring—sense of relief that he had misread Bruce's reaction. Mazzola could be downright cruel sometimes, sure, but no one could possibly be *that* cruel.

# 2

God, it was a magnificent night for major-league baseball. The night was clear, and the darkening sky was sprinkled with a galaxy of glittering stars. A balmy, early summer breeze drifted in from right field. Over the city of Philadelphia, the dusk had thickened into night; but here at Veterans Stadium, here at the ball game, scores of high-voltage klieg lights blazed brilliantly onto the playing field and into the stands. The diamond below and the outfield beyond it were a luminous emerald-green panorama spread before them in the artificial daylight. Night baseball, Brian McPhillips realized, was the last great innovation to the game. All the modern-day attempts to improve baseball since night games were invented had proven to be lamentable lapses of judgment on the part of the powers-that-be: artificial turf, designated hitters, domed stadiums, pay cable telecasts and free agency. This was a game that was born nearly perfect. Baseball required very few modifications.

McPhillips' young son Josh interrupted his reverie. "Look, Daddy! Look, look!" He was tugging at his father's shirt sleeve and pointing excitedly toward the third-base line.

"What is it, sport?"

"It's the big bird!" he trilled happily. It was, in fact, the Philly Phanatic, the Phillies official mascot, working the hometown crowd between innings, mocking the beer-bellied gait of the third-base umpire behind the ump's back. Josh squirmed with giggling pleasure, as the Phanatic turned his attention to the ballgirl, chasing her lasciviously toward left field. McPhillips wondered idly if they were perhaps getting it on. Hey, it *was* possible. He had heard that the Phanatic was actually quite a ladies' man in real life.

McPhillips removed his son's Phillies cap and ruffled his hand affectionately through Josh's white-blond mop. "Having a good time, Josh?"

Josh's eyes widened with sincerity as he blurted, "Oh, yeah!" The youngster waved his Phillies pennant with a child's exuberance. "The Phillies are gonna win the World Cereal," he said confidently.

"The World *Series*, Josh."

"Mmmm-hmmm," Josh murmured, ignoring his father's correction and filling his mouth with a tiny fistful of Cracker Jack.

McPhillips allowed himself a moment of paternal triumph. He had lobbied the law firm for these Friday-night seats for six months, all in anticipation of Josh's fourth birthday. Getting his hands on these tickets proved to be no cakewalk. Two nights ago, McPhillips locked horns with a junior partner to prevail over an eleventh-hour threat by some inactive B-list client who tried to glom onto them at the last minute. It might have cost McPhillips a few points in the standings in the never-ending game of partnership politics, but what the hell, is there any cause more noble than a son's birthday? If it came right down to it, his kid's happiness beat partnership status hands down.

These were good seats—check that: *great* seats, that's what they were. Eight rows behind home plate. Made all the difference in the world, being this close. You could hear the catcher chatting with the ump between hitters, the satisfying smack of the ball as it slammed into the catcher's mitt, the crack of the Louisville Slugger as it connected with Costa Rican horsehide.

As far back as McPhillips could remember, baseball had been a passion for him. Always. Baseball was a glorious American concoction, with no equal anywhere else on the planet. And while it was Josh's night to experience the wide-eyed excitement of a youngster at his first big-league ball game, it was an occasion for

McPhillips to cherish as well. Few of the innumerable joys of fatherhood compared to passing on the legacy of the nation's pastime to a firstborn son on the eve of his fourth birthday. Maybe watching him walk for the first time compared to this, or hearing him say "Daddy" clearly for the first time. . . .

Maybe.

Baseball was something father and son would always have in common, a bond that could bridge the chasm of any generation gap. Through the years, they would root for the hometown Phils, through good and bad seasons, cheering their postseason triumphs; discussing the wisdom of trades made by the front office; deriding the progressively more outrageous salaries ungrateful ballplayers commanded; assessing the promising rookies that cropped up through the farm system each season. McPhillips even treated himself to visions of his son's Little League heroics.

*Okay, okay.* He checked himself. Maybe he was oversentimentalizing the baseball thing a bit, but still, this was a night the kid would always remember. In that spirit, McPhillips spared no expense in lavishing Josh with mementos. Every time a vendor passed by hawking his wares, McPhillips flagged him down. Here it was, only the bottom of the third, and Josh was already juggling an official scorecard, Cracker Jacks, cola, a soft pretzel, a hot dog, a Phillies pennant, and the scarlet-red cap now perched precariously on the youngster's head.

The stadium announcer's voice boomed out: "Now batting for the Philadelphia Phillies, second baseman, Randy Ready."

Josh imitated the announcer in a loud voice, "Now batting, Randy Ready." The kid could name the Phillies line-up on command.

The Pittsburgh Pirates led, three to one. Randy Ready—a second baseman with a fabulous name for an athlete—drew a walk off the formidable Pirates' pitcher Doug Drabek on five pitches. On a two-to-nothing count, the next batter, centerfielder Lenny Dykstra, lashed a frozen rope into the left field. The Pirates' Bobby Bonds tracked the ball down and fired it to second base, but Dykstra's spectacular head-first slide beat the throw. The fans in the stadium erupted in cheers. The tying runs were now in scoring position. Josh was on his feet, yelling spiritedly for the home team.

McPhillips leaned over to his son and held up an open palm. "High five."

Josh slapped his palm and held out his own open hand at hip level. "Low five."

McPhillips tapped him a low five. It was part of their routine, part of their bonding. Father and son beamed; a home-team rally was brewing.

As the formidable clean-up hitter John Kruk stepped up to the plate, and the organist began playing the chords of the rally theme, the Pirates catcher signaled for an intentional walk. The stadium erupted in a chorus of boos. And it was at that moment that Brian McPhillips first noticed the two men in dark suits coming down the aisle toward their box seats. As they approached, McPhillips instinctively felt a twinge of uneasiness.

These two weren't here for the ball game.

His worst fear was confirmed when the two men approached his seat. One of them leaned over the railing toward McPhillips, peering at his seat number and consulting a slip of paper.

"Can I help you?" McPhillips said.

"You Mr. McPhillips?"

McPhillips drew back in surprise.

"Brian McPhillips?" the man elaborated.

"How'd you know my name?"

"Your law firm told us we would find you here."

"Very accommodating of them." He made a mental note to chew someone out Monday morning.

"We need to have a word with you, please."

"What for?" McPhillips bristled. "Who the hell are you guys?"

The second man stepped forward. "Mr. McPhillips, I'm Special Agent Jim Mracek, and this is Special Agent Ken Pennicola. We're with the financial crimes division of the Federal Bureau of Investigation. We need to speak with you in private."

*The Federal Bureau of Investigation!*

The coppery taste of fear leapt onto Brian McPhillips' palate; his stomach crushed into a knot of panic. Jesus Christ, what did they want with *him?* His first thought was that a case he had worked on at the firm had gone terribly awry and had somehow attracted the attention of the federal government, the Department of Justice, or something. But what, why? He was an ethical, aboveboard attorney . . . and he hadn't worked on any federal issues lately. . . . What the hell would they do? He conjured up a horrible vision of these dour-faced men slapping some cuffs on him and leading him out of the stadium enshackled before thirty-five thousand people and a television audience of millions. Oh, good Christ, here *in front of my son Josh*, on the eve of his fourth birthday. The prospect of this left him dizzy.

"Dad?"

McPhillips turned toward his son. "It's okay, Josh."

"What's wrong, Dad? Dad, what's wrong?"

"Everything's okay, sport. Just some men who have the wrong seats." McPhillips whirled back toward the two men and lowered his voice. "You guys show me something. Some IDs."

The men wordlessly produced their plasticized identification cards and displayed them discreetly. They looked embarrassed.

The IDs looked legit.

McPhillips nodded and sighed. "This better be good, fellas."

"We need to talk with you immediately on a highly confidential, but urgent matter," the one named Mracek said.

"Will I need an attorney?" McPhillips asked.

"Not to speak with us," Pennicola said.

"But I imagine you'll wish to consult one in due course," Mracek said.

McPhillips said icily, "Hey, listen, what is it with this cloak-and-dagger shit? I don't see you guys bearing any subpoena or a summons-and-notice from the proper judicial authority. If you've got to talk to me about a case or a client, it can wait until Monday morning. You obviously know where to find me. In the meantime, I'm with my young son here on his birthday and would like to enjoy my constitutional right to privacy."

Unexpectedly, Special Agent Mracek's face softened with compassion. "I'm afraid you've got it wrong, Mr. McPhillips," the agent said gently. "It's not you we're after. You've done nothing wrong. It's a highly personal and confidential matter that concerns you. Would you please step out into the aisle so we can talk? Just for a minute?" Mracek made a head motion indicating Josh, suggesting the matter should be discussed outside the youngster's earshot.

McPhillips squeezed the back of his son's neck and said, "Everything's fine, buddy. Just some business your Dad has to take care of."

McPhillips sidled out into the aisle and followed the men up a few rows to the edge of the ramp where they could speak in confidence.

"We apologize," Mracek said. "We were just trying to be discreet. For your sake. We didn't want to cause a scene."

"I appreciate that. Okay, so what's going on?"

Pennicola asked, "Do you know a Mitchell Foster Myerson?"

"Mitch?" Brian blinked. "Sure, I know him. Is he in trouble?"

"Do you know him as a business associate? A friend?"

"Both. He was one of my roommates at college, senior year."

"Have you had any contact with him in the last week?"

"As a matter of fact, yes. C'mon, guys, shoot me straight. What the fuck's going on?"

Special Agent Mracek said, "Mr. McPhillips, you're a victim of a highly sophisticated electronic wire fraud. It appears that funds have been completely depleted from two of your bank accounts."

McPhillips was stunned. "Omigod," he whispered. "No."

At that moment, the umpire behind the plate called a strike on a low-inside pitch at the knees, and the stadium was filled anew by boos and catcalls. When the noise subsided, Special Agent Mracek continued. "We believe that Myerson used a computer to obtain access to dozens of his clients' accounts."

"This is a major, major crime," Ken Pennicola added, "amounting to millions of dollars in stolen funds."

"You're just one of many victims."

McPhillips' mind was racing at full throttle. This just couldn't be happening, McPhillips thought. The down payment for their new house—was it really *gone?* Mitch Myerson wouldn't do such a thing to him, not to his friends, to his clients. *Would he?* "Are you positive of this?"

"We're afraid so," Pennicola said.

"Since you're acquainted with him, you may be able to provide some additional insight," Mracek said. "Will you please come with us?"

McPhillips drew in a breath through clenched teeth. "Of course. I need a minute with my son."

"Of course. We'll wait here."

As McPhillips descended the stairs to retrieve his son, he thought about his wife Lisa. Man-o-man. She was going to freak when she got wind of this. The new house had just gone poof.

McPhillips returned to the box seat and gently informed his son that they had to leave now. Daddy had something very, very important to attend to, something that had to do with work. Father apologized to son and promised that they would return to another baseball game. Maybe even tomorrow on his birthday. "But tonight, your Dad needs you to be a big boy tonight. Okay?"

The youngster nodded bravely and stood up to leave. " 'Kay, Dad."

"That's my boy. My big Josh." McPhillips held his hand out for the youngster, who took it.

McPhillips' heart was breaking: God, what an incredibly wonderful kid he had been blessed with! Bright and beautiful—that was the obvious stuff, but now he marveled at his son's display of unusual maturity and understanding for a child his age.

Hand in hand, Brian McPhillips and his son followed the FBI agents out of the stadium, solemnly winding their way down the ramps to ground level. Josh managed to hold back the tears until they heard the far-off crack of the bat against the ball and the thunderous roar of 35,371 fans that followed Dale Murphy's unseen, tie-breaking, grand-slam home run. At that moment, Josh's face twisted with misery, and he began to weep. The sight of it pierced his father's heart like a white-hot blade of anguish. He gathered the youngster into his arms and tried to soothe the pain of a ruined birthday.

*Mitch Myerson,* he thought balefully. *Say it ain't so, you pot-addicted scumbag.*

to envision this spectacle while he plotted his grand scam: feds and cops poring over his personal effects and papers in the aftermath, crawling about the minutiae of his apartment with all the painstaking scrutiny of an archaeological team at an ancient Egyptian excavation site.

Mracek glanced at something happening across the room and frowned. "Those assholes *still* at it?"

"Looks that way," Pennicola replied.

To McPhillips, Mracek said, "Wait here, I'm certain our superior will want to debrief you right away."

The two FBI agents then crossed the room to join a gaggle of law-enforcement officials locked in a heated squabble over who had the jurisdiction to take control of the crime scene. Two of the men—city detectives Conigliaro and Davies—argued that because the crime occurred in Philadelphia, the city's Technology Crime Bureau was in charge.

"Fuck you are," a G-man said calmly. "Interstate commerce is involved. Federal Computer Fraud and Abuse Act of 1986 controls. That means Secret Service and FBI secure the crime scene."

Outnumbered and outdressed, Detective Davies surrendered with a noise of disgust and waved the federal agents away dismissively. To his partner, he said, "Fuck 'em, Big Ed. They want it that bad, let 'em have it, you know? It's not like there's any cold meat involved." Davies and Conigliaro trudged to another room.

McPhillips turned his sights to the people in the room he actually knew, his onetime roommates who had shared a house on Spruce Street during their college days. Apparently, they too had been snookered by Mitch Myerson. Over at the wet bar, Bruce Mazzola was mixing himself a stiff vodka drink. That was vintage Mazz, boozing it up even at a time like this, as if life was little more than a perpetual bachelor party. At the other end of the room, Chuck Beekman was hunched over a computer terminal with a federal agent, peppering the fed with anxious questions. On Mitch's luxurious leather couch, another officer was seated facing a sallow-faced Jeff Wheaton and his Japanese-American business partner in the computer business—what was his name? Kamikaze, Kamikawe? Tommy something or other. A federal agent was quizzing Jeff, who responded to the questions with little more than a

# 3

Accompanied by the two FBI agents, McPhillips arrived at Mitch Myerson's penthouse apartment at approximately 8:45 P.M. Myerson had moved into the new digs last summer, but since McPhillips and his wife, Lisa, hadn't socialized much with the bachelor in the past year, this was the first time Brian saw where his former college chum had lived.

It was located on Rittenhouse Square, an address of old-money prestige that is to Philadelphia what Park Avenue is to New York. Gazing now at the luxury building, McPhillips experienced a sting of irritation. Mitch had certainly lived well off other people's money.

Mitch's apartment was the twelfth-floor penthouse. McPhillips followed Mracek and Pennicola into the elevator, which they rode wordlessly to the top floor. As they walked into Penthouse A, McPhillips glimpsed a crime scene teeming with life. It was a peculiar sphere of activity to be sure, an unlikely congregation of federal law-enforcement officials of every stripe, Philadelphia city detectives, a few of Mitch's victims, and—much to Brian's surprise—three of his college roommates from the University of Pennsylvania: Bruce, Chuck, and Jeff. Excluding himself, there were maybe a dozen people, all of whom were men. The air was presided by a code of authority. Taking in this real-life mise-en-scène, McPhillips wondered idly if Mitch himself had the foresight shell-shocked nod of the head. God, Wheaton seemed near-catatonic.

Bruce Mazzola was the first to notice him at the doorway. Mazzola strode over with his drink in hand, a freshly ignited cigar pinched between his two forefingers. He extended a dry hand to Brian and gave him the knuckle-numbing handshake that was the sine qua non of the circa 1986 investment banker. "Hell of a reason for a reunion, huh, McPhillips?" he said amiably. "How you been?"

"Been better."

"Haven't we all? Mitch threw us all one hell of a surprise party wouldn't you say?"

"Some party."

"You got that right. Hey, before the feds grab you, lemme show you something. See that?" Mazzola pointed his cocktail tumbler in the general direction of the sunken living room. "Over there, a Chippendale desk. On the breakfront, Limoges china, Baccarat crystal. Bauhaus chairs, Biedenmeyer couch. A Tizio reading lamp. Seems our beloved boy Mitch had a flair for knick-knacks and gimcracks. The coup de grace, of course, is that framed graphic over there. Above the VCR. That's a Keith Haring *original*. Not a print but the real goddam thing. Mitch possessed a quantum of class after all." Mazzola's tone was marveling.

"I disagree," McPhillips seethed. "I'd hardly call this a class act."

"Touché."

"Bruce, what the fuck *happened* here?"

Mazzola's tight smile resembled a grimace of pain. "What happened here, Bry, is that that back-stabbing crotchsucker wasn't content to simply screw each and every one of his best friends out of the modest sums we entrusted to him to invest for us. No, he had to access every one of our goddam bank accounts and clean out every fucking red cent."

McPhillips' eyebrows arched with incredulity. "How's such a thing possible?"

"The FBI says he used his home computer, of all things. Ironically, it was the one Wheaton gave him at cost. He had access to all that sensitive information about us, so he used a series of electronic wire transfers. Piece o' cake, if you know how it's done. That's what they tell me anyway."

McPhillips closed his eyes and clenched his fists, fighting to stem the rage collecting within. Mitch, a licensed investment adviser, a money manager with fiduciary responsibilities—he had turned out to be an embezzling thief! Despite Mitch's constant wheedling and promises of thirty and forty percent returns on investment, McPhillips had invested only $4,500 in Myerson's fledgling foreign currency exchange fund, Philly ForEx Fund. Brian held back because of his conviction that when money and friends were combined, both often ended up lost. Nevertheless, like several of his other college friends, he had thrown Mitch a small bone, more as a token of esteem for an old college chum. But if what Bruce was saying was accurate, if Mitch had indeed cracked the codes of his friends' bank accounts and embezzled everything, if it was true that Myerson had remorselessly screwed his friends and clients, then he was now on the lam with McPhillips' $107,000 nest egg.

As if reading his thoughts, Bruce asked, "How much he soak you for?"

"Over a hundred grand, including about $25,000 my parents just lent us for a new house. *Jesus Christ!* How about you?"

Bruce smiled fiercely and mouthed some words. *Two-point-one*, he seemed to be saying.

"Two hundred and ten thousand?"

Bruce shook his head and jerked his thumb skyward. "You misplaced the decimal point."

"You mean, two-point-one *million?*"

"Yep."

In spite of himself, McPhillips gasped aloud. "Bruce, over two million bucks?"

"All my base salary and bonuses from the days of wine and roses on Wall Street. My fuck-the-world, retire-at-thirty money. Poof. Gone like that."

"That's . . . that's a lot of money, Bruce."

"No shit, Dick Tracy. Everything I had." Mazzola nodded, smiled bitterly, and drank off half the vodka in a colossal gulp. "On my tombstone they'll put: 'Easy come, easy go.' "

McPhillips scarcely heard him; he was still reeling from the number Mazzola had just casually tossed out. Two-point-one million dollars! Before he'd even reached thirty! Good Christ, the junk-bond business had been very, very good to Mazzola. Brian came out of his reverie and said, "You seem to be taking it well."

Mazzola shrugged. "Actually," he said quite calmly, "if I fucking get my claws on that pencil-necked mongoloid, I'll personally gouge his eye out with my thumb and skullfuck him to death." Then his expression changed and he threw a comradely arm around McPhillips' shoulder. He whispered conspiratorially, "Oh, and by the by, this little soap opera gets *even* better. You see Wheaton over there?"

McPhillips glanced across the room at Jeff Wheaton, conversing with his business partner Tommy Kawakami. Wheaton's rheumy eyes were cast sightlessly to the ground as Kawakami spoke to him in a soothing, reassuring voice.

McPhillips nodded. "Yeah?"

Mazzola whispered it in Brian's ear: "Mitch made a hostile takeover of the Jeffster's wife to boot."

"No!" It jolted him like an electric shock. The night was becoming surrealistic. *"Rachel?* Ran off with *Mitch?"*

Mazzola nodded and drank off the rest of the vodka. "I never liked her, ever since she schemed to fuck up Jeff's bachelor party. I always thought she was a cast-iron cunt. Guy could eat raw road kill for her and, still, she'd throw him over for the first swinging dick with a fatter wallet. Capital C, capital UNT."

Having said his piece, he swaggered off to the wet bar to concoct himself another drink, leaving McPhillips there, trying to make sense of it all.

Presently, a battery of three federal agents and a Philadelphia cop came by to interrogate McPhillips.

Special Agents Ken Pennicola and Jim Mracek introduced McPhillips to their superior, Jack Newby, and Detective Eddie Conigliaro, representing the Philadelphia city police's technology crimes unit. Newby was a dark-skinned, barrel-chested man in his forties with salt-and-pepper hair, grayish-green eyes with an almost metallic cast, and a Patrician nose. He had the bland good looks of authority typical of a lifelong government agent. "I'm terribly sorry to meet you under these circumstances," Newby said, all soft-spoken sincerity.

"I appreciate that," McPhillips said.

"Yeah, damn shame," Conigliaro added. The Philadelphia dick had a face furrowed with heavy creases, reminding McPhillips of a surly sharpeii puppy.

"We'll need you to make a statement, of course," Newby continued. "And I imagine Billy Tibbens will have some questions for you. He's with the financial crimes unit of the Secret Service."

"Certainly." McPhillips pressed a finger to his lips. "You know, I have to admit, I wouldn't have expected the Secret Service to be involved here."

Conigliaro broke into a smarmy smirk and gave a *har-har* chuckle. "What, you thought all the Secret Service did was protect George Bush's ass so we don't have to call Dan Quayle 'Mr. President'?"

McPhillips decided he didn't like Conigliaro. "Not at all. I'm just surprised to learn that they have investigative powers for this sort of crime."

"Actually, the Secret Service is authorized by Congress to work hand in glove with the DOJ and the Department of the Treasury to investigate any incident involving the integrity of the nation's currency," Newby informed him. "That would include distribution of counterfeit bills or, as it happens, fraudulent electronic funds transfers through Fedwire."

"I see."

"Fact is, I wouldn't be surprised to see the SEC, the IRS, and the U.S. Attorney's office hopping into the fray in the next several days."

McPhillips nodded.

"Just a few questions, Mr. McPhillips," Newby said. "To help us get some background."

"Sure."

"You said Myerson was a friend of yours, correct?"

"Yes."

"Tell us about him."

McPhillips detailed how the five of them had attended Wharton undergrad together. Attended the same classes, became drinking buddies. Picked up coeds together at O'Hara's Fish House, Smokey Joe's. Senior year, they shared a house on Spruce Street. Their sixth roommate, a premed student by the name of Noam Benson, was killed in an automobile accident over Christmas break. It had brought the five of them closer together as friends. When they graduated, they got married, grew apart some over the next seven, eight years, as college friends are prone to do. Nevertheless, they stayed in touch regularly, attended all the homecoming functions. They had remained occasional friends who enjoyed each other's company and made reasonable efforts to stay in touch.

"Mitch had always liked the fact that I had gone to law school. I think he wanted to one-up me by enrolling in the joint M.B.A./J.D. program at Villanova law school. He was always that way. Competitive, even when it came to his friends."

Newby nodded. "Myerson was intelligent?"

"Sure. Real bright guy. But he was always looking for the shortcuts."

"How's that?"

"He applied for school loans he didn't need and put all the money into shares of IBM."

"Typical yuppie scumbag," Conigliaro muttered.

"Also, he exaggerated his law school grades to get a job at a large law firm." The grade switching had sounded innocuous enough at the time. In the context of the evening, however, McPhillips realized it was a prophecy foretold.

"You a lawyer, too?" Conigliaro asked pointedly.

"Yes, a bankruptcy lawyer. Why?"

Conigliaro shook his head, almost imperceptibly, but said nothing. It occurred to Brian that perhaps Conigliaro, like so many others, despised attorneys with a passion. Lawyer-bashing was an American pastime whose ever-rising popularity now rivaled that of NFL football. Some deserved to be bashed. Brian felt he didn't.

"That's enough, Detective," Newby said sternly. He picked up the line of questioning. "When's the last time you saw Myerson?"

"I'd played golf with him three, four weeks ago. Socially, that was really all we did together this past year, play golf. We'd kind of drifted apart. You know how it is. You get a family, two kids, mouths to feed—your priorities change. Mitch was still single and had different interests. We just kind of drifted apart. It happens."

"Did you know him to be patently dishonest?"

McPhillips shook his head. "Of course, he routinely lied about his golf scores, but that didn't suggest to me that he was going to steal from me."

Newby stroked his jaw. "All right, you made some investments with Mitchell Myerson's investment firm?"

"Yes. A little over four thousand dollars."

"What type of investment was it?"

"High risk. Foreign currency arbitrage. Mitch was supposedly a major player in it. After he left the practice of law, he joined a Philadelphia investment firm by the name of Carter-Rogers and Company where he traded in the firm's for-ex account."

"For-ex?"

"Foreign exchange. Currency futures."

"You got all that?" Newby asked Pennicola.

"Carter-Rogers. Got it."

"Please continue, Mr. McPhillips."

"I understand he made a lot of money for the firm. But about two years ago, he felt he got shortchanged on his bonus, so he struck out on his own. He started hounding me for more investment funds, but foreign exchange is too high-risk for my tastes. I kept it to a few thousand dollars, tops. Every other month, I'd receive statements bragging of twenty-five- to thirty-five-percent returns on my investment. There was one point where we'd racked up over a forty-percent return on our money. Mitch offered to send me checks commensurate with the returns he was bragging about, but, more often than not, I let him roll over the dividends into my principal."

"Yeah," Conigliaro said. "That's typical of this sort of confidence scam. No doubt he was just shaving off a piece of the capital you invested and giving it back to you to keep you thinking that you'd made a great investment, get you to put up more."

Newby shook his head. "I'm not certain that's what happened here. I get the impression that it was a fairly legit operation until the girl came into the picture."

McPhillips frowned. "I've heard you guys think Rachel Wheaton is involved. What makes you think that?"

"You might say it's some good old-fashioned detective work on the part of our people. Fortunately, Myerson has one of those high-tech phones with the redial function and a digital display." Newby pointed to Mitch's sleek telephone on the desk. "The last number dialed before he went on the lam was the Wheaton residence. At first, we thought Wheaton himself might have been involved. But he was eliminated from complicity after one of the limousine services reported picking up a woman at Wheaton's address, then a man at this address at 4:37 P.M. They were heading to the USAir terminal at the airport. The description the driver gave of the male passenger matches that of Myerson perfectly. Also, the female passenger matches the description of Rachel Wheaton. The driver claims to have gotten a good look at her."

"More than a good look," Conigliaro chuckled. "The driver watched them in the rearview mirror as they all but played hide-the-salami on the ride to the airport."

"That'll be quite enough, Detective Conigliaro," Newby warned.

"It's our theory that Rachel Wheaton and Mitch Myerson conspired to defraud a number of investors and leave the country together," Mracek said.

"Or at the very least, she's an accessory after the fact," Pennicola added.

"Well, I thank you for your time, Mr. McPhillips," Special Agent Jack Newby said. "Let me give you my card."

McPhillips accepted the card and glanced at it briefly. The regal FBI logo graced the top of the card.

"There are several numbers there, so you can call anytime, day or night," Jack Newby said. "Don't hesitate to give us a shout if something else occurs to you."

Mracek said, "I'm certain Billy Tibbens has a few questions for you."

Newby nodded. "Yes. Jim, why don't you take Mr. McPhillips over there to meet with him? I've got to call headquarters."

\* \* \*

As a prototypical computer-obsessed technonerd, Billy Tibbens was so engrossed in the glowing characters skittering across the monitor of the Wheat/Tech 486, he didn't bother to look up from the screen when Mracek introduced McPhillips to him. Tibbens struck Brian as one of those long-limbed, awkward geeks he used to see at the computer center at Penn, cerebral brainiacs who could solve complex calculus problems with little effort, but who could never effectively decipher the universal code of interfacing with other human beings.

Billy Tibbens was about twenty-three or twenty-four, with an eternally adolescent aura about him. He was flaxen-haired, cherry-lipped, pale, with colorless eyes magnified cruelly by thick glasses. A pencil-necked jughead—the kind of kid who must have been abused like a redheaded stepchild by high school classmates. But he was Mensa-brilliant, no doubt about that. A thoughtful observer would realize that this guy was the kind of progressive genius who could've gone either way: into the dark side of the electronic frontier, becoming a Phreak/Hacker tapping into the Department of Defense mainframes at the Pentagon and touching off World War III; or, as it happened, onto the side of the angels, unraveling complex computer crimes like this one for the financial crimes unit of the Secret Service. All in all, one was to be grateful that he chose to be in the employ of Uncle Sam. Guy like Billy Tibbens could wreak a lot of havoc if armed with a laptop, a modem, a telephone line, and a pissed-off attitude.

"McPhillips?" Tibbens squinted at the screen thoughtfully. "Brian, right?"

"Yeah," McPhillips and Mracek said at about the same time.

Billy Tibbens turned to his right and pulled a thick sheaf of printed pages from the crib of the humming HP Deskjet 500 printer. He leafed through the sheets and withdrew eleven consecutive pages.

"This stuff look at all familiar?" he asked, handing the papers to McPhillips.

McPhillips was astonished to find himself peering at a printout of his tax return for the last year.

"Your accountant filed your 1040 electronically, I presume?"

McPhillips nodded numbly.

Tibbens shrugged. "All he had to do was hack into the IRS database, download your file to disk, and print it in WordPerfect format."

McPhillips riffled through the pages and pages of sensitive financial information about himself: A credit report from EquiFax; an account statement from Charles Schwab reflecting the holdings in his stock portfolio; last month's statement on his checking and savings accounts at First Philadelphia Bank. Incredibly, he himself would have trouble getting access to all this private financial information on himself, yet Mitch Myerson, an interloper, had dipped into the computer banks from the comfort of *his living room* and had come up with a wealth of data. It was mind-boggling.

Handing it back to Tibbens, he said, "How'd he do it?"

"No mystery really. This here's your smoking gun." Tibbens patted the top of the Wheat/Tech 486 desktop computer. "A top-of-the-line IBM clone souped up with a ninety-six hundred–baud modem. All it takes is one hardwired PC with a telephone line and you can tap into virtually all the vital electronic streams of proprietary information available in this country." Tibbens swiveled around on the chair and peered at McPhillips with those magnified eyes. "You see, computer crime's where it's at these days. You can use computers to steal government secrets, pirate long-distance service, broker kidnapped children to pedophiles on electronic bulletin boards. All kinds of neat stuff."

Tibbens turned back to the terminal and continued talking while his fingers danced noisily about the keyboard. "You see, most bank robbers don't use guns anymore. Too dangerous, too unprofitable. These days, the computer's the weapon of choice. With a computer, the average take is about four hundred thousand. That's almost seventy-five times what some shithead with a gun gets pulling a stick-up."

"How's it going, Billy?" Mracek asked. "Any luck reviving the system?"

"Yeah. The guy tried to wipe out all the programs in the C-drive with a global delete command, but fortunately for us, he happens to have the new version of MS-DOS. I used the un-erase feature to restore *all* the files he attempted to delete."

The computerese was over McPhillips' head. They might as well have been speaking Chinese.

"You got a read on the guy's M.O. yet?" Mracek asked.

"Well," Tibbens said, making no effort to conceal the tone of admiration evident in his voice, "in my opinion, what we have here is truly a cutting-edge computer crime. Most elaborate I've ever heard of, much less worked on. I mean, the Nigerian scam was the most widespread operation, but that was very low-tech."

"The Nigerian scam?" McPhillips frowned.

"Yeah," Mracek said. "In that scheme, an individual purporting to be a member of the Nigerian government would contact an American corporation claiming that he wanted to smuggle fifty million dollars in government funds out of his country. The quote-unquote government official would imply that the American corporation could keep up to half of the illicit money if it permitted the Nigerian official to use its bank account as a haven for the embezzled funds. All the corporation had to do was provide its bank account number and wire transfer instructions on its letterhead to the Nigerian official. And, of course, the whole thing was a scam. The perpetrators would doctor up the letterhead to make it appear as if the corporation's CEO was authorizing the transfer of funds to the Nigerians. More often than not, the Nigerians siphoned off hundreds of thousands before the corporation wised up. It's amazing how many American corporations got burned in this scheme. Victims of their own greed, I suppose."

"Yeah, but this is a horse of a different color," Tibbens insisted. "This is a real, true-to-life, honest-to-gosh computer crime involving machine-to-machine transactions. You may or may not know that about eighty percent of computer thefts involving wire transfers are done by bank insiders or company treasurers who have access to the corporate money flow. Usually, it's some disgruntled employee who despises his boss or maybe your garden-variety embezzler. Here, you've got a *noninsider* who initiated maybe two dozen, maybe three, individual transfers in a twenty-four-hour period. Guy's gotta have balls this big." By way of illustration, Tibbens held aloft two peculiar-looking metallic spheres that chimed lightly. To McPhillips, he said, "Just out of curiosity, when you invested with your friend Mitch, did you fill out sheets of account information?"

"Sure."

"Gave your bank account numbers?"

"Yes."

"Did the form by chance ask you for your mother's maiden name."

"Yes, it did. Why?"

Tibbens nodded knowingly. "I thought so. That's generally the security code the banks ask for when you make a wire transfer over the phone or by computer. Even junior high school hacks have keyed into that little trick by now."

"Ah, Christ," McPhillips cursed softly.

"It's not that you did anything stupid. How were you to know? It's simply that we arrived at the information age and, with the prevalence of computers and the laziness of the powers-that-be, technology has far outpaced the law's ability to keep up with the scam artists. It's a big problem. Could be the next Geraldo show."

Chuck Beekman returned to the computer area with a glass of Diet Coke in hand. He gave McPhillips a melancholy greeting and said, "I still can't get over this. Friends don't do this to friends, do they?"

"You wouldn't say that if you were in my line of work," Mracek said.

"This guy had a lot of hair, all right," Billy Tibbens said, as he copied Mitch's software onto a backup disk. "Some computer criminals steal electronic money by what's known as the 'salami technique,' that is, they slice off a few dollars at a time from thousands of accounts so no one notices. This guy cleaned out everybody and everything in one fell swoop."

"From what we can tell so far," Mracek said, "Myerson scammed about two dozen accounts or more. He didn't play favorites. He stole from friends, widows, retirees. Took one woman's entire divorce settlement. We haven't even informed her yet."

"He appropriated a million-dollar trust fund from an orphan whose parents died in a plane crash," Pennicola chimed in. "Got some retirement money from senior citizens, too."

"And a six-million-dollar pension fund he was supposed to

invest in Treasuries for the employees of a corrugated box manufacturer, I think, from South Philadelphia."

"North Philly," Pennicola corrected.

"North Philly, right. In fact, the treasurer of that company was the one that alerted us to the crime this afternoon, after the bank notified him that one of the pension fund's checks didn't clear. Caught it just before the close of business. Otherwise, the scam would have gone unnoticed until Monday morning, just as Myerson probably planned."

"When the dust settles," Billy Tibbens said, "we might have a new world record for funds stolen by an attorney from his clients."

"How much?" McPhillips asked, holding his breath.

"The record's twenty million dollars. This is anywhere from thirteen to twenty-two million."

*As much as twenty-two million dollars!* Brian McPhillips felt his face go novocaine-numb. In a rare display of hostility, Chuck Beekman slammed his fist on the desk, startling the others. "How did all of this go undetected by the authorities?"

Billy Tibbens stared at him as if the question was preposterous. "There's maybe four hundred thousand wire transfers every day in this country, totaling one and a half trillion dollars. You tell me, how're you gonna police that kind of money flow? 'Scuse my French, but you start that shit, the goddam Federal Reserve would grind to a fucking halt."

"So where'd the money go?" McPhillips said.

Mracek gave a search-me shrug. "Anybody's guess."

"What's your guess?" McPhillips asked Tibbens. "Any possibility it's still in this country?"

Tibbens poked his glasses back up over the bridge of his nose and rolled his eyes thoughtfully. "It's possible. More possible than you might think. You see, if he was really smart, he would've had a dummy company set up in the North Antilles, the Seychelles Islands, the Bahamas, you know, one of those offshore banking havens. Then he just shuffles the money around, and it becomes pretty much untraceable.

"But some of these computer criminals get cocky and transfer the funds within the continental United States. Back in '88, for instance, seven people in Chicago fucked up a seventy-million-dollar wire transfer fraud from the Bank of Chicago by wiring it to New York *first* instead of directly to their dummy account in Australia. If it weren't for greed and stupidity, there'd be seven more multimillionaires jet-setting around the world right now, rather than seven more schmucks facing ten-to-twenty in the federal icebox."

"What are the odds?" Beekman asked.

"Hey, I'm no Jimmy The Greek. But possible? Yes. Likely? Probably not."

Pennicola and Crowley were called away for a conference with the other federal agents in the kitchen, leaving Beekman and McPhillips alone with Tibbens. Tibbens made a head motion indicating the other side of the room. "So that guy over there is Jeff Wheaton, the CEO of Wheat/Tech Computers?"

"One and the same, yes," McPhillips said.

"Friend of yours?"

"Yeah," Beekman said. "Went to college with him."

Tibbens clucked his tongue. "Too bad he's such a wreck right now. I'd *love* to talk to him. He's actually something of a hero of mine. Him, Bill Gates, Mitch Kapor, Michael Dell. Bloody superstars, those guys. Started the revolution."

McPhillips nodded distantly.

Tibbens' eyes narrowed. "Hey, you think he'd give me a deal on the new Wheat/Tech 486 laptop if I asked him?"

McPhillips couldn't believe the question. "Maybe now's not the time, okay?"

Billy Tibbens shrugged and immersed himself in his work.

# 4

The night eroded steadily. Another hour passed and it was now after ten o'clock. The federal agents had assured him that there was nothing more anyone could do. Thus, the night had taken on all the excitement of watching paint dry.

McPhillips was about to call it a night. He faced the awful task of returning home to inform his wife Lisa of their disastrous misfortune and to outline the few legal options available to them, most promising of which was suing their bank. It would result in some cumbersome, time-consuming, and expensive litigation, quite possibly unsuccessful. However, it was their only course of action at the moment.

Of course, the new home in Chestnut Hill was obviously eighty-sixed. No getting around that.

He walked over to the Biedenmeyer couch where Bruce and Chuck were swilling down much of Mitch's abandoned liquor and swapping Myerson stories. Most of the anecdotes focused on how Mitch Myerson had continually devised money-making schemes. Mazzola recounted the time Myerson had gone to Alaska with a companion and made a ton of sawbucks selling joints to the Eskimos. "Always looking for the golden gooses and the cash cows. Mr. Easy Street," Mazzola said.

"Remember when Mitch pretended to be a freelance travel writer so he could get free vacations at exotic resorts? I remember thinking that was so cool at the time." Chuck thought about this for a moment, then winced. "Good Lord! Maybe we should've known he was dangerous."

Bruce Mazzola, the handsome fraternity legend, party-boy-turned-Drexel-investment-banker, shook his head. "Let me give it to you short and sweet. Mitch was a loser with a capital L. Pathetic loser. On the Street, they woulda swallowed him whole for breakfast. Personally, the only reason I let him have any of my money was because he was supposedly a friend, and I wanted to be kind to a friend. But I fucked up, I broke a basic rule you learn on the Street. Kindness equals weakness. Bottom line: I fucked up."

"Jeez," Chuck said wistfully. "Nine, ten years ago, could we have even pictured that something like this would've happened? I mean, could we have even conceived that Mitch would've stolen our money?"

"Or Jeff Wheaton's wife?" McPhillips added.

"Her?" Mazzola made a dismissive wave. "No surprise there. I never liked Jeff's wife."

"Yeah." McPhillips felt now was the time to detach himself from Bruce and Chuck, bid them a melancholy goodnight, when a commotion fifteen feet away commanded his attention. It was Detective Davies, the craggy-faced cop with the horseshoe of prickly hair that ringed his balding pate, bursting out of the bedroom with a pop-eyed look of agitation. He hissed excitedly to his partner Conigliaro, who was tearing into a greasy cheesesteak sandwich that had just been delivered.

"Big Ed! You gotta see this, you *gotta* see this!"

"Whatcha got?" Conigliaro, with his mouth full, wiped his hands on his trousers and disappeared into the bedroom suite behind his partner.

"What do you suppose that's all about?" Chuck Beekman said.

"I don't know," Mazzola said, rising from the couch. "But I intend to find out."

McPhillips, Mazzola, and Beekman scurried into the bedroom. They found themselves in a huddle with the two Philadelphia cops. Davies was cackling with irrepressible glee. "I found me some crucial evidence here."

"Yeah?"

"Yeah. Get an eyeful a *this*—"

Davies aimed the remote at the VCR and thumbed a button. PLAY appeared in green letters in the top right portion of the still-blackened Mitsubishi thirty-five-inch screen, and then a picture flickered. The images were grainy, drenched in the hue of an orange popsicle; not enough light. But the automatic aperture of the camcorder presently adjusted; the image jumped a bit, then flooded into crisp focus. McPhillips could make out two people. Two people fucking.

Mitch . . . and Rachel.

Mitch, that lowlife, had recorded himself making love to Jeff's wife!

A strange admixture of sensations washed through McPhillips as he stared open-mouthed at the raw sexual act on the tube. On one level, he felt mortified for his poor friend Wheaton, betrayed by his wife and his friend. Jeff, the cuckolded husband whose wife was riding the flesh pony on Maxell videotape, the ultimate humiliation captured for posterity. But concurrently, McPhillips was unmistakably . . . *aroused*. He watched, transfixed, as Rachel, with her long, languorous body, gleaming, glistening with the sheen of her own wetness, entwined her tawny limbs around Mitch's frame as Mitch pumped in and out of her in full, luxurious strokes, their two bodies entangled, thrashing as one in the erotic dance of copulation. The taboo pleasure that overwhelmed him was accompanied by an iceberg of guilt, yet he could not tear his eyes away from the image.

"Motherfucker," Mazzola was saying softly next to him. "I can't believe my eyes."

"Hey, Big Ed," Davies trilled in a trembly voice. "How'd you like to strip-search *that* suspect?"

"Jesus H. Christ, who's the twist he's with?" Conigliaro muttered in awe.

"That," Davies said, "is the other guy's wife."

"Jesus God, I'm sorry, but she is the most beautiful creature I've ever seen in my life. Hey, honey, *I'd* steal fifteen mil for you too."

"Motherfucker," mouthed Mazzola again.

Even the unflappable Mazzola seemed genuinely appalled.

On screen, Mitch was talking porno to her, *do you like this, baby, do you like that?*—but Rachel was blissfully immersed in her own pleasure, her body bobbing softly to the rhythm of Mitch's thrusts, her face almost angelic in her mischievous pleasure. She hummed mellifluously with each stroke. When she turned her face to the camera and locked eyes coquettishly with the lens, it was as if she was inviting *him* next. She pursed her outrageous lips and blew the camera a kiss. The blood rushed to Brian's groin. He excoriated himself for his arousal over these images—*Stop. Stop it. Get a grip on yourself. Traitor. That's* Jeff's *wife! Stop.* Yet he could not look away; her bad-girl image was too captivating, her hair spilling about the sheets, a blond-and-honey-colored mane that cascaded about her face like a silken halo. God, but she was a sex kitten. In the midst of his guilt and arousal, he recalled the bizarre encounter he had had with Rachel Wheaton at that engagement party months ago, when he should have told Jeff—

The door opened. The lights went on, snapping the hypnotic trance like an ice-water enema. McPhillips and the others whirled around, blinking in the brightness of the high-intensity track lighting overhead. When his vision cleared, he was horrified to see Jeff, Newby, and Mracek standing there. Jeff's mouth twisted into a slash of horror when he saw the tape. He bolted from the room. McPhillips instantly felt dirty.

The full-color fornication continued apace on the picture tube. A vein bulged from Newby's forehead as he stalked over to the set and snapped off the power. Fixing the Philadelphia cops with a homicidal glare, he snarled, "I'm certain that your superior in the police department will be very interested to hear that his detectives' idea of investigating a crime scene is to watch sex tapes of the suspects that are in no way connected to the crime itself. Quite frankly, I find this unacceptably unprofessional—"

Mazzola, Beekman, and McPhillips, the private citizens in the room, quietly slipped away and regrouped in the living room.

"Wow," Chuck Beekman said, shaking it off. "Wow."

"I can't believe my fuckin' eyes," Mazzola said, shocked by what he had just witnessed.

"Jesus, I have to admit," Chuck Beekman said, "naked, she is really incredible. I mean really incredible."

Tommy Kawakami walked up to them, a stern look of disapproval on his face. "Very classy move, gentlemen. You get your rocks off?" Kawakami spoke to the men as if they had betrayed Wheaton as badly as Myerson had.

"We didn't know what was in the room," Beekman protested, lamely. "Not until we got there."

"Ah, Jesus," McPhillips said softly. "I'm going to talk to him. Where is he, Tommy?"

"I don't think he wants to see you," Kawakami said. "I think he wants to be alone."

"Tom, please. It's been a long night."

Tommy Kawakami glared at him for a moment, protective of his business partner with an almost canine loyalty. "All right, he's in the bathroom."

McPhillips disengaged himself from the group. He walked over to the bathroom where Jeff Wheaton had secluded himself. He gave a tentative knock on the door. "Jeff?"

Some hacking, throaty retching came from within. Brian waited a few seconds, then rapped again.

"Door's unlocked." The reply was weak.

McPhillips pushed the door open and slipped inside, securing it behind them. His nostrils burned from the acid stink of vomit. McPhillips faced Wheaton now, moved by the sight of the human mess huddled by the toilet. Jeff's eyes were bloodshot and rheumy; a thick cord of snot strung down from his face to the basin of the toilet. Wheaton was in the final shuddering throes of dry-heaving.

It was the precise reaction, McPhillips realized, that he would have had if it were Lisa on the receiving end of Mitch's pelvic thrusts in that video.

God, how he felt for this guy.

There was a soft knock at the door; then Tom Kawakami slipped in. He and McPhillips stood by silently as Jeff Wheaton shuffled uncertainly to the sink. He scooped cold water from the faucet to his face, rinsing the lingering effluvium and bile from his mouth. After a moment, Wheaton wiped his mouth with the back of his hand. "Every man who has ever met my wife," Wheaton

46

said, "has wanted to fuck her. Every man. Even you guys, I'd bet."

"Not me, Jeff," Kawakami said.

McPhillips remained silent.

"At first I thought that it was the sexiest thing in the world," Wheaton said. "Forget about starting your own company, being your own boss. No, I always thought it was the greatest accomplishment to marry a woman that every man desired. But you know, I've since learned the truth: it inevitably winds up killing you. Mitch will learn that soon enough. She'll do to him what she did to me. I don't even think she can help herself."

Stumbling for words, any words, McPhillips said, feebly, "Maybe you're better off, Jeff."

The words caused Wheaton to cry quietly. "I can't believe I can feel this much pain," he sobbed softly. "God, it hurts so much; it feels like I'm gonna die."

McPhillips wanted to say something—*anything*—to ease the pain. "You know, the FBI's going to do their best."

"C'mon, don't jerk my chain, Brian. They're not going to catch them."

McPhillips was surprised to hear himself say, "Well, then, maybe we could go after them."

Tommy Kawakami turned to him with a scowl. Yet it was this statement that instantly ended Wheaton's sobs. "What do you mean?" Jeff asked.

McPhillips was so gratified to see Wheaton's suffering receding before his very eyes, he forged ahead. "Well—Jeff, I don't know. I was talking to Tibbens, and he seems to think there's a chance they're still in the country. He says, it's been known to happen in this type of crime. The suspect gets overconfident, complacent. Gets sloppy. Thinks he's too smart to get caught. It's been known to happen."

"Tibbens told you that?"

"Yeah. Said that it's a possibility. I mean, realistically, it's only been a few hours. They couldn't have gotten too far. Maybe they're in New York, taking a breather before they get out of the country."

"New York!" Light returned to Wheaton's lifeless pupils. "You're right! Rachel *loves* New York. She wouldn't leave the country without first spending a weekend there, shopping for clothes."

"Okay. So maybe we could go to Manhattan, take a look for them there."

"Oh, my god! Tommy, what do you think?"

"I don't know," Kawakami said gently. "I suppose there's a possibility. I don't know—"

"Oh, man, I'm ready, Jesus, I'm all ready." Jeff Wheaton was imbued with a renewed sense of purpose. "Brian, what do you say? Let's go after that cocksucker tonight. *Let's get Mitch!*"

"Not tonight, Jeff," McPhillips said quietly. "There's nothing we can do about it now. If they're in New York now, they're in a hotel room somewhere, crashing. International flights don't leave New York until mid-afternoon, right? Let's all get a good night's sleep and do it first thing tomorrow."

"You're right, you're right. Tomorrow's better. Oh, Jesus, maybe we can find them. Do you think we can find them, Brian?"

"It's possible," McPhillips said, giving him an encouraging shrug. The rest of his thoughts on the matter were left unspoken. Anything's possible, of course. But likely? Not likely.

McPhillips was suddenly aware that Tommy Kamakawi was staring at him, his face a Kabuki mask of chilly disapproval.

# PART THREE

### SATURDAY MORNING
### JUNE 27, 1992

# 5

On Saturday morning, ex-investment adviser Mitchell Myerson awoke in an unfamiliar bed at an unusually early hour. Though he typically required eight hours of sleep each night, he now came out of a placid, pot- and sex-induced slumber of just over five hours, feeling exceptionally clearheaded, invigorated, and elated. He sat upright against the headboard, vigorously scrubbing his sleep-puffened face with his fingertips. He blinked several times until his vision cleared and adjusted to the soft light of the new morning.

The pale sunlight filtered in around the drawn blackout blinds like the corona of a solar eclipse. In the glow of daybreak, he could discern the delicious contours of Rachel Wheaton's slender body beneath the sheets as she dozed next to him, irrefutable proof that the events of the previous twenty-four hours were not a product of his imagination. Rachel, sweet Rachel. She was his trophy, his prize for possessing uncommon brilliance and audacity. She was his lifemate now.

And quite suddenly, the gravity of his accomplishment washed over him, and all the emotion rushed in at once. He had pulled it off, by Jesus, hadn't he? Oh yes, yes he had. He had pulled off what was, in all likelihood, the crime of the fucking century. Throughout it all, he had performed flawlessly. Myerson the Iceman. Mr. Smooth. Gets the money and the girl.

As for the anticipated guilt he was certain would accompany taking money from his clients, Myerson was mildly surprised to discover that he was not troubled in the least. While it was true that he had stolen from his collegehood friends and people who had trusted him as both an attorney and an investment adviser, it wasn't as if Mitch had *killed* anyone. We're only talking about money here. No biggie. Take Chuckie Beekman, for example. All Charlie Three-Sticks had to do was track down Charlie Two-Sticks on the fourteenth hole of Upper Merion and get him to replenish the discretionary trust fund with a nice fat check. Obladi, oblada, life goes on, right?

Guilt feelings? Quite the opposite. The thought of what lay ahead for him and his new companion caused a lush shiver of euphoria to course through Myerson's body. He reached beneath the covers and fondled himself with a cupped palm, enjoying the erotic charge of the moment.

Mitch Myerson delicately slipped out of the king-size bed so as not to wake Rachel. She stirred, however, issuing a soft murmur that reminded him of an appreciative sound she often made during their lovemaking. Rachel shifted, her limbs moving in a brief swimming motion, a sort of breaststroke amidst the tangle of bedsheets. But she presently resumed the tranquil rhythm of her breathing, her slumber unbroken.

Myerson padded barefoot across the plush carpet of the hotel room, still clutching his genitals. He eased open the door of the ServoBar and withdrew an Evian. The hotel would hose him royally for this modest six-ounce refreshment, probably charge his room tab somewhere in the neighborhood of four or five bucks. That was beaucoup bucks, even if it was Alpine snowmelt delivered to his door by Concorde. It was only *water,* for Chrissakes. Under normal circumstances, Myerson would never tolerate such an outrageous ripoff, but these were *not* normal circumstances, of course, and with a fresh fortune of perhaps twenty million dollars in the bank, Myerson thought himself entitled to something better than Manhattan tap water.

Sitting in the easy chair and filling his mouth with the chilled liquid, he gazed at his companion as she slept. She was so heartbreakingly beautiful, he sighed with gratitude every time he cast his eyes upon her. Last night, she had commemorated his cunning financial coup with a marathon lovemaking session some three hours in duration. He turned over the previous evening's chain of events in his mind. Shortly after they had arrived in the room and begun their now-familiar ritual of undressing one another, they went at it like cannibals, tearing first at each other's clothes, then at each other's flesh. Sexual savages, they were, going at it with teeth bared, sinking teeth into naked flesh. He let her take command, and she did so with the resolve of a woman who wanted to use her expertise in sex as the instrumentality for conveying a gratitude beyond words. And she went at it for hours, taking her time, teasing him, allowing him to feel the heat and the hunger and the intensity, pumping him with velvet strokes of her hand, taking him into her mouth from time to time, letting him approach the first crest of climax, but never quite letting him get all the way there.

Finally, when it seemed he could take no more, she mounted him, wrapping her creamy legs tightly around him and pulling him into her, oh, sweet penetration at long last. He surrendered himself fully to her, as the muscles of her thighs and her belly flexed rhythmically above him, surging, rocking him toward orgasm. While she worked above him, he feathered his fingers through the silky tangles of her streaming curtain of hair, traced the soft curve of her cheekbones, brushed his fingertips over those pouting lips, then down the slope of her neck, her skin slick with perspiration, and around the lush swell of her full breasts, his tour of her magnificent physique slowing at her nipples, which were thick and erect with lust and excitement. Then he moved his hands along the hollow of her flat, heaving belly, and—as he felt the steadily tightening coil of a powerful climax building in his loins—he brought them around to cup the gentle curves of her ass. She instinctively sensed he was close, and her steady thrusts took on a new intensity. She gently squeezed his balls in her hand and wet-kissed him flush on his mouth as the first ripple of the orgasm tore through his body. He jerked and shuddered inside her with a forceful explosion, six, seven waves in all, and in the midst of it, she whispered in his ear with urgent sincerity, "I love you, Mitch"—only the second time she had told him that.

It had been far and away the most erotic night of his life. Just thinking about it, he felt himself stiffen.

Wanting to intensify his natural euphoria, Mitch Myerson walked to the bathroom and extracted a fat, torpedo-shaped joint from the baggie he had stashed in his toilet kit. He returned to the easy chair and ignited it. *Wake and bake,* he said to himself. Myerson had smoked pot since he was thirteen and, at thirty years of age, could no sooner resist the demon weed than he could the force of gravity. Not that he would ever want to quit smoking dope. Over the years, marijuana had been very, very good to him, earning him plenty of beer money at Penn, for one thing. And then there was the time, after his first year of law school, when he spent a summer in Alaska with a classmate named Shane Wicker, purchasing several pounds of marijuana in Anchorage and selling them off in the Eskimo villages, joint by joint. What a pisser that had been. A pound of pot at that time went for twenty-five hundred dollars in the city, a rather modest investment. When all was said and done, he and Shane cleared twenty grand on each pound: roughly sixty thousand dollars for their trouble. More to the point, he *enjoyed* smoking pot. *Just say no, my ass,* he thought, allowing himself a luxurious hit of cannabis smoke followed by a refreshing chaser of French glacier water.

A year around the world. That was what Rachel had wanted, her ultimate fantasy, the fantasy Jeff Wheaton had steadfastly refused to make a reality for her. Stupid, stupid Jeff. Too wrapped up in himself and his failing mail-order computer company to see he was losing her. Earth to Jeff, earth to Jeff. Fuck the company. Pay some attention to your wife! But of course, that was all water under the bridge anyhow. Rachel had been Jeff's true treasure, and it wasn't Mitch's fault that Jeff's myopia had caused him to neglect her, to deny her the earthly riches she deserved. Rachel was a woman of uncommon magnificence, a woman you never said no to. As an investor in the futures markets, Mitch Myerson considered Jeff's wife in the context of his livelihood: she was a precious commodity, not unlike gold. The laws of the marketplace were such that she would inevitably wind up in the hands of the bidder who placed the highest value on her. Myerson was that bidder. He had been willing to steal twenty million dollars for the privilege of possessing her.

It had been his idea for them to run off together. It was a totally out-of-left-field impulse, on one level preposterous and silly, and yet, the more he thought about it, the more he came to believe it was actually an inspired and romantic notion. Fugitives of love, that's what they were. Moreover, after five weeks of sneaking around behind his ex-college roommate's back, he realized that blowing out of town was an inevitability.

So during lunch at Old Original Bookbinder's on Walnut Street one glorious April afternoon, Mitch casually slipped the prospect in as a non sequitur to their light conversation about Rachel's modeling career. "Rachel, I've been thinking. Why don't you and me pack our bags and start a fresh life together in some other part of the planet?"

To which she responded, "I'd love to."

Mitch Myerson would never forget the excitement sparkling in her metallic-blue eyes as she agreed to throw over her husband for a lifetime with him.

He worked feverishly over the following weeks, plotting the scam in meticulous detail. He got the appropriate signatures for powers of attorney from those of his clients who were willing and artfully forged some others. He made the proper arrangements at the banks for wire-transfer capability for the target accounts. All the while, he carefully avoided any conduct that might raise suspicion among his clients and the bankers.

Then, through an incredibly good stroke of luck, Rachel recalled a friend of a friend of a friend who was chummy with a high-profile British banker by the name of Raoul St. Germaine, who provided private-banking services to England's aristocracy. At first, Myerson was highly skeptical of involving a third party. However, at their first meeting, Mitch found himself captivated by the sheer charisma of "The Saint," as he liked to be called. The Saint took the Concorde from London on several occasions to meet with Myerson and, in one instance, arranged for Myerson to jet to London for a meeting at his spectacular offices there. The final version of the scheme actually came together during the last of their face-to-face sessions, over brunch at the Four Seasons, when

St. Germaine described a new, underground computer program that could electronically access all of his clients' bank accounts. As the British banker described it to him in his clipped accent, Myerson was blown away. Theoretically, the software program placed tens of millions of dollars in liquid assets within Myerson's reach. Without it, the haul would have amounted to a paltry two or three million dollars, scarcely worth the trouble of embezzling his clients' funds at all.

Instead, the haul was in the neighborhood of $20 million, a neighborhood Mitch was euphoric about moving into.

St. Germaine had made him wealthy beyond comprehension.

Now he and Rachel were in New York, the fugitives of love, running from the law. Not that being on the lam would be so unendurable, mind you. They would travel to every great metropolis the planet had to offer: Paris, Tunis, Berlin, Capri, St. Moritz, Positano, Budapest, Belgrade, Cap Ferrat, Biarritz, Venice, Athens, Istanbul, Moscow, Estoril, London, Bombay, Calcutta, Tangiers. Life would be a whirl of yachts in the bluest of oceans and summers in the lush greenery of Provence. New friendships would be struck with jet setters of international renown and perhaps even of royal blood. Mitch would shower his new bride with the gifts and luxuries for which she had hungered so long—alpine-white diamonds and pigeon-blood rubies. They would make love on the most exotic beaches on earth, beaches made of sand as white and fine as sugar, with the roiling surf licking at their feet. . . .

The millions that made up their new fortune were already overseas, patiently awaiting their arrival. Mitch wondered where the money was at this instant. Australia? Switzerland? France? Ah, that was St. Germaine's concern—to bounce it around the globe to a number of internationally connected banks to throw off the authorities. Even now, a fortune was beaming around the globe, bouncing off satellites and pulsing through underwater cables in the form of some electric surge of energy that would come to rest at a bank in Rome in the form of twenty million dollars in hard currency. St. Germaine was a genius and would see that it went without a hitch. The whole thing was indescribably fantastic—and so pathetically easy.

With a sigh of contentment, Myerson rose and walked over to

the window. He edged the shade back with a forefinger and gazed out upon the new day. At 5:47 A.M., the sun was climbing above the river to the east. Sunlight reflected off the steel-and-glass towers along Fifty-seventh Street, bathing the cityscape of Manhattan in a beautifully golden apricot glow. He spit a gob of saliva on his fingers and extinguished the joint, turning his thoughts to the business at hand. There was but one task to complete on American soil, namely, getting his hands on a sizable advance of the money from a St. Germaine–controlled bank in New York. Scoring some traveling money.

Then he and Rachel could begin their majestic intercontinental adventures together.

# 6

Ninety miles to the south of Manhattan, Brian McPhillips methodically dissected the morning papers strewn about on the kitchen table. A molten anxiety roiled through his duodenum as he searched the pages for a mention of his name.

Predictably, he had been unable to sleep after returning from Mitch's place last night. He had tossed and turned pretty much the entire night. When dawn finally broke, he had arisen and bolted down to the Wawa at Twenty-first and Hamilton streets to pick up that morning's *Inquirer* and *Daily News*. He had feared the worst, worrying how his colleagues at the firm would react when they read the news of his financial tribulation. It took no great stretch of the imagination to envision the senior partners gathering behind closed doors come Monday morning. The perpetually bow-tied managing partner, Chic Spencer, would call McPhillips' prudency into question in the wake of the Myerson fiasco. "How can an attorney so irresponsible with his own assets be entrusted to handle client matters with millions of dollars at stake?" Chic Spencer would ask in that doomsday Orson Wellesian voice of his. McPhillips' lack of complicity in the scheme would be immaterial. Far lesser indiscretions had knocked many a better man from the partnership track at the law firm.

However, for all the trepidation he had had that morning, a thorough search through the *Inky* and the *News* turned up nothing about the crime. McPhillips surmised that it broke too late to make the Saturday early edition. Terrific. It would hit the Sunday *Inquirer* when the circulation jumped to over a million readers.

For a long while, McPhillips sat alone at the blondwood kitchen table, absently massaging the stubble of his jaw with the heel of his hand and staring into space. A neglected bowl of Cap'n Crunch's Crunch Berries grew soggy before him. Only when the compressor unit of the refrigerator clicked on, its motor humming and rattling noisily, did he snap out of his early morning reverie. *How the hell could this have happened?* he wondered.

He walked to the living room, opened the credenza, and retrieved the photo album with ten-year-old snapshots from his college days. On the occasion of his thirtieth birthday, some five months before, Lisa had surprised him with a thick scrapbook of photos, clippings, and other memorabilia Brian had collected over the years, the bulk of which were from his undergraduate days at Penn. Lisa's labor of love was all the more impressive considering that she had not attended the University of Pennsylvania and therefore had not witnessed firsthand the camaraderie of which her husband had often spoken with equal measures of awe, nostalgia, and reverence. In spite of this, she had managed to fashion a remarkable road map of his collegiate days in something largely resembling chronological order.

Back at the kitchen table, he cracked open the book and submerged himself in a parade of nostalgia.

It opened with a section on his college days at U Penn. Photos of McPhillips from a time when life was a four-year party of free-flowing draft beer and dizzy coeds with names like Sippy, Heather, and Cricket. There he was at a Smokey Joe's Super Bowl Party, a Delta Phi frat party, the Spring Fling outdoor concert, the Senior Week pub-crawl. Shots of him at Troy's, Abner's Cheesesteaks, O'Hara's. There were even photographs of him with Mazzola and Myerson among the mobs of people in downtown Philadelphia the night the Phillies last won a World Series. The ecstatic mob of Phillies fans celebrated with a riot that tore up six square blocks around City Hall. There were many photographs of McPhillips with his collegiate sweetheart of three years, Chelsea Robbins. That Lisa had not played censor here with the Polaroids of his old flame was a telling statement of her character. To be sure, Chelsea Robbins was a girl whose beauty frequently intimidated other women. In between heated arguments, Chelsea and McPhillips would talk about marriage and children together. But it was not meant to be. And there were many, many photos of McPhillips, Myerson, and the rest of his roommates at the house on Spruce Street, most of the pictures taken while the subjects were in inebriated states. Judging from this particular collection of photos, one could easily draw the conclusion that college was basically four years of drinking and screwing with an occasional literature class wedged in amid the nonstop hedonism. . . .

The next segment of the scrapbook was devoted to a sort of where-are-they-now of McPhillips' circle of friends from Penn. A 1987 *Wall Street Journal* article mentioning Bruce as a participant in the junk-bond offering to fund a major hostile takeover artist's bid for a public company . . . a clipping from *Wall Street Letter* with the scoop that Bruce Mazzola had landed on his feet after the demise of Drexel Burnham by launching a hot new LBO boutique called FYM Group . . . a blurb from *Philadelphia Business Journal* announcing the formation of Mitch Myerson's new foreign-exchange investment firm . . . the two-page spread in *Inc.* magazine featuring a color photograph of a confident-looking Jeff Wheaton at his factory in Yardley, Pennsylvania, with the headline "Is Jeff Wheaton the Next Steven Jobs?"

His friends all went on to become fabulously successful, prototypical yuppies thriving in the you-could-be-the-next-millionaire eighties.

His eyes lingered on a snapshot of the youthful Mitch Myerson. Hard to believe the twenty-year-old in this picture became the thirty-year-old thief who pilfered his life savings.

Brian McPhillips closed the scrapbook. He had had his fill of reminiscing.

Adulthood had just begun to make sense to him; then the events of last night turned his world upside down. Until last night, Brian McPhillips was pleased enough with his station in life. He was comfortable with young adulthood. No longer did he fantasize about making a living as a rock-'n'-roll star, perhaps the most certain sign he had finally grown up.

Indeed, he was now accustomed to the thin layer of tallow that now coated the washboard muscles of his abdomen and the unfamiliar new aches in his joints that would accompany weekend athletics. He was startled to find one day that he preferred reading the *Wall Street Journal* to *Rolling Stone*, and favored Tchaikovsky over the Doors. On some Sunday mornings, he and Lisa would lie in bed late, playfully picking out the gray strands multiplying in each other's hair until the kids woke up and demanded their attention.

Both he and Lisa had fully embraced the responsibilities of parenthood in recent years with great enthusiasm. The emphasis of their daily lives had shifted from self-indulgence and creature comforts to providing a nurturing support system for their two children, Josh and Ashley. When children entered the equation, they changed your life completely, of course. They became the gravitational center of your universe.

When Lisa became pregnant with their first child, they vowed to each other not to be the sort of people who wore their parenthood like a yuppie status symbol. They disdained the behavior of their contemporaries who acted as if their newly born offspring presented them with the opportunity to set new worldwide standards in proper childrearing. They vowed not to overdress their children in loud pastels from Baby Gap, not to have their infants record the outgoing message on their answering machine, not to fall into the predictable trap of believing that *their* progeny were developing intellectually at a far greater pace than other children their age. They promised not to babble on to childless friends and relatives how bringing up a youngster had changed the course of their lives completely, but, oh *how worthwhile it all was.*

Of course, all that went out the window the moment McPhillips cradled his newborn son in the crook of his arm that first time. From that moment on, parenthood had proven far more rewarding than anything else he and Lisa had ever previously experienced.

Just last week, the not-yet-four-years-old Josh had asked his father if the hole in the ozone existed as a passageway for dead souls to get to heaven. McPhillips was too stunned to frame any sort of fatherly reply to this query. A few weeks before that, Josh had self-assuredly informed him, "Daddy, the difference between dragons and dinosaurs is that dinosaurs were real and dragons weren't." Upon hearing that, McPhillips was moved to ask Lisa how old one had to be to qualify for Mensa. He posed the question in a jocular manner, but he was actually quite serious. He thoroughly believed his child was on the genius track.

Parenthood was extremely satisfying to Brian and Lisa. In some great measure, it made them appreciate just how shallow and meaningless the party years of the eighties had truly been.

Generally speaking, McPhillips was largely a creature of virtuous habits. In that sense, the old saying applied: The apple didn't fall too far from the tree. His father, who had been an executive at a grocery-store chain, had instilled certain values in him that even now had a profound influence on his conduct. Although he drank a bit socially, he hadn't been excessive about it since the party years of undergraduate school. He neither smoked nor consumed drugs. In addition, his father had influenced him considerably with regard to the importance of setting aside a portion of one's wages for a long-term goal. Even during that agonizing first year of law school, McPhillips scraped up a few dollars meticulously typing briefs, memoranda, and journal articles for his classmates at a dollar a page. Unlike the wealthy Main Line prep-school brats whose lawyerly arrogance had developed into second nature during their boarding-school years, McPhillips worked to put himself through school, even though he didn't have to. Some of the money he had earned from his late-night labors was squirreled away in his mutual fund accounts: Twentieth Century Ultra, Janus Fund, T. Rowe Price International. In time, his extracurricular enterprise permitted him to accumulate a modestly impressive sum, but he fell alarmingly behind in some classes, most notably Property and Torts. Thus, while his colleagues spent their Christmas and spring breaks schussing down the slopes of Colorado or cultivating carcinoma in the Florida sun, McPhillips spent his lone-wolfing it in the Biddle Law Library, bolting down smuggled cups of coffee and thickening up his class outlines.

His uncommon diligence that first year paid off handsomely. He graded onto the *Law Review,* thereby capturing the elusive Holy Grail of all first-year law students. *Law Review* status at an

Ivy League school guaranteed Brian McPhillips lifelong employability in the lucrative profession of the law, no matter how severe the economic downturn was. "Set for life," a jealous classmate named Siegel said, upon hearing the news.

True to form, McPhillips landed a prestigious plum of an entry-level job at a prominent white-shoe Philadelphia law firm after graduation. He vowed to funnel ten thousand dollars a year into his savings account for the next five years, a challenging goal notwithstanding his considerable first-year associate's salary of $42,500.

Shortly before he married Lisa in 1987, McPhillips had developed into something of a wunderkind when it came to personal investing. He subscribed to all the industry bibles and oracles—*WSJ*, *Barron's*, *Money*, and a slew of pricey newsletters. He consumed the weekly tables of mutual funds in *Barron's* with the same schoolboy zeal he once reserved for poring over the Sunday paper's compilation of major-league statistics as a kid. With all the loyalty of a mercenary, he abandoned funds at the first hint of trouble, switching to the red-hot sector funds and up-and-coming international mutuals. Through frugality, discipline, and the power of reinvested dividends, Brian accumulated over seventy-eight thousand dollars in his mutual fund accounts over that five-year period. His achievement astonished his friends and acquaintances, who were hopelessly ensnared in the materialistic feeding-frenzy of the credit-card-driven eighties.

And now, his expanding family had all but outgrown this two-bedroom rental in a complex six blocks from the art museum. There was scarcely room for all four of them in the kitchen at mealtime. There was no bedroom for Ashley in the apartment; her crib was next to Brian and Lisa's queen-size bed and had become a significant impediment to their once-lively sex life. All signals clearly indicated that the time had come to purchase a home of their own, thereby making the transition from yuppies (Young Urban Professionals) to *smacks* (Suburban Middle-Aged Couple with Kids).

For several months, he and Lisa had combed the suburbs with surly realtors, looking for the Perfect House. Nothing grabbed them. Nothing, that is, until six weeks ago, when they found the domicile of their dreams. It was a spacious four-bedroom Tudor on a half-acre lot. It had neatly manicured lawns in the front and back and was located off Germantown Avenue in the bucolic Chestnut Hill area with good schools nearby. The asking price was ridiculous, of course. Over a quarter of a million dollars. But Brian engaged in some shrewd negotiations with the overly optimistic owners and succeeded in encouraging them to shave thirty thousand off their price. McPhillips and his wife signed a binder, and closing was set for August 1, at which time the McPhillipses would put up a fifty percent down payment.

But Myerson had killed their dream. In the course of a single afternoon, the bastard siphoned off eight years of their sweat and thrift. For that, McPhillips despised him with as much cold and black hatred as his heart could conjure. Yet he could do no more than curse and fume and sputter, having no outlet to vent his mind-numbing rage.

The phone rang; he knew immediately who it was. He scooped up the receiver before the first ring finished. "Jeff?"

"Morning, Bri. I hope it's not too early to call."

"Jesus, Jeff. *Of course* it's too early. It's a Saturday morning, for chrissake."

"I know, I know. Look, I'm sorry, but I've got to know if we're still on for New York."

"Of course we are."

"Well, Mazzola's not."

"He's not? Why not?"

"I don't know," Jeff said, making no effort to conceal his exasperation. "Bruce is giving me all sorts of static, saying they're already out of the country. I'm not counting on him."

"All right."

"I just needed to know if you were still committed."

"Yeah, I'm still good to go."

"Super. That's great. Thanks, Brian."

"Don't worry about it."

"One other thing. Jacket and tie required."

"What?"

"Bring a jacket and tie to change into at the hotel."

"You serious?" Brian frowned into the phone.

"Dead serious. We need to look credible."

"All right. I will."

"Great. Be at Thirtieth Street Station at nine sharp, all right? Don't bother with tickets, I'll have them in hand."

They rang off. Brian nibbled a fingernail. It was madness, really. Going to New York City on a desperate lark, hoping to find Bonnie and Clyde. Not just a needle in a haystack, a needle in a *hay field*. It occurred to McPhillips that perhaps his weekend would be better spent in the bowels of the law firm's library, boning up on the current trends in banking law to see whether there was some precedent to compel the FDIC to indemnify them for their losses. But Wheaton was so pathetically out of sorts. Certainly, he could spare half a day to help a friend, even if it was merely to humor him.

He could hear Lisa stirring upstairs. Being a light sleeper, she undoubtedly had been awakened by the ringing of the phone.

In a few minutes, she came downstairs into the kitchen. Their six-month-old daughter, Ashley, was snuggled over her shoulder, and Lisa made small soothing circles on the baby's back with the flat of her hand. Even at her early-morning worst, Lisa was attractive in a fresh-scrubbed, homecoming-queen sort of way. It was over six years since they had met on the Starship gondola at Stratton Mountain, since he first watched her graceful form gliding down the slopes, yet Brian never tired of looking at her. She seemed especially beautiful to him when she held their baby daughter.

"Morning, beautiful," McPhillips said.

"Who was that?" she asked around a yawn.

"Jeff."

"Mmm. Poor Jeff."

"Yeah, I feel for the guy. Coffee?"

"Yes, please."

Brian poured his wife some coffee in a mug of unknown origin that said HOME OF THE NEVER-ENDING COFFEE POT. Then he got some apple juice from the refrigerator for the baby. He placed the mug on the table, and she murmured a sleepy thanks.

After a moment, Lisa said, "The house in Chestnut Hill was

such a beautiful place, Brian. It was perfect for us. You realize that, don't you?"

"Yes."

"It had a rolling green lawn and plenty of space for the kids to grow up. It had great schools, and it was close to the train station. And the neighbors were wonderful people, Brian. People our age. We would have been so happy there."

What did she want him to say? "C'mon, Lisa," he said gently. "Why torture ourselves?"

"I know. It's just such a shame, especially after all that mortgage broker put us through." She seemed to wince at the thought. After a time, she noticed the cereal. "Brian, what are you eating?" she asked.

"Cap'n Crunch's Crunch Berries."

"Why?"

"I don't know," he said. "I had a craving for something sweet. Needed a sugar fix or something. Want some?"

She made a face of distaste. "Yuck."

"That's a pretty forceful denouncement of a product we feed our older child on a daily basis."

"Hmm. That's some food for thought."

"Pardon the pun," Brian smiled. "Want a warmer for your coffee?"

"No. Would you take the baby?"

McPhillips took Ashley into his arms. It never ceased to amaze him how perfectly crafted Ashley's features were. Her glowing pink face was flawless. Her mother's features, he knew. She'd grow up to be a world-class heartbreaker. "How's Josh holding up?" he asked.

Lisa's eyebrow arched. "Needless to say, you have one unhappy young boy upstairs. He cried himself to sleep last night."

"Needless to say, I feel positively horrible about that."

"On his *birthday*, Brian." She shook her head as if to say, *tsk-tsk*.

McPhillips was annoyed. "Spare me the extra helping of guilt, Lisa. It wasn't my fault that Mitch screwed me."

"I suppose not entirely."

"What's that supposed to mean? 'Not entirely'? "

"Just that you shouldn't have entrusted any money to him."

"Thanks for the advice, Lisa. You'd make a terrific Monday-morning quarterback."

Lisa looked at him with sleepy eyes and smiled. "Thank you. I think."

Brian sighed. "Look, I'll make it up to Josh. There's a doubleheader against the Mets next Saturday. I'll just pressure the firm to cough up another set of tickets."

Lisa sat upright. "Next week? Brian, what's the matter with *today?* It's his birthday today, you know."

McPhillips felt the sheepish look on his face. He placed Ashley in her high chair before he spoke again. "Lisa, I can't. Not today. We're going to New York."

"To New York? What on earth for?"

"To look for Mitch and Rachel. Jeff Wheaton has this hunch his wife is still in this country. In New York, namely. We're going to take the train up there and look around a few of the hotels."

"I know Jeff must be all but hysterical, but that's an exercise in futility if there ever was one. Can't you talk him out of it?"

"Uh, I doubt it. Especially in light of the fact that it was my idea."

"*Your* idea?"

"Yes."

"You must be joking," Lisa said. "New York's a city of what, nine million people?"

"Eight million in the latest census."

"Whatever. Goodness, Brian, can't you disabuse him of the notion that his wife is still in the United States? I mean, you recognize that, don't you?"

"Jeff says Rachel has an obsession with New York City. He thinks it's impossible for her to leave the country for an extended period of time without a farewell stay in Manhattan."

Lisa rolled her eyes in exasperation.

"As you know," he continued, "Rachel's something of a princess. Jeff seems to believe that there's only a dozen or so world-class hotels worthy of Rachel's exacting standards. We simply start at The Plaza and work our way down the list."

"And this was your bright idea?"

"Yes."

"And what about Josh? Will you be home in time for his birthday dinner?"

"I don't know."

Lisa turned angry. "Brian—"

"Lisa, I don't know. Jeff knows his wife's mind. It's worth a shot; it's perfectly conceivable that—"

"Do *you* have to go? On your son's birthday?"

Brian spoke softly. "Lisa, we lost over a hundred thousand dollars in this scam. Quite frankly, I think it's a risk worth taking. It'll probably amount to nothing but. . . ." His voice trailed off, and he made a gesture of disgust. "I'm going to New York. Period."

Lisa sighed. She stared sightlessly at the table, combing her hair with her fingers, stewing in her private thoughts. After a while, she said, "You know, I'm not surprised Mitch and Rachel ended up together. You ask me, they're pups from the same litter. Mitch always rubbed me the wrong way. Every time he saw me, he'd say something slimy, like he was coming on to me. Like his pistol was always loaded. Call me crazy, but I've never ever trusted anyone who's tanned the whole year round." She sipped her coffee and furrowed her brow. "And Rachel, she reminded me of some sleazy little . . . Siamese cat. Something about her, always so calculating and manipulative. Always with that blow-job pout on her lips." Lisa did a fairly credible imitation of Rachel's pout. "Like she was going to take on every male within a radius of five square miles. You ever notice that?"

"Not really." McPhillips was mildly surprised to hear his wife use the phrase *blow-job pout* to describe another woman.

"The French have a term for her type: *la beauté du diable*—the beauty of the devil."

"That's a good turn of phrase."

Lisa turned to him then and fixed him with an inquisitive squint. "Be honest with me," she demanded. "You found Rachel very attractive didn't you?"

Why did wives always have to ask questions like this? McPhillips could hardly plead the fifth, so he lied. "No," he said, with his best *Who—me?* expression. He dropped his eyes to his watch: goodness, look at the time. Pushing away from the table, he said,

"I've got to get to Thirtieth Street Station by nine. I'm going upstairs to talk with Josh." He kissed the top of his wife's head and his baby's cheek, then edged sideways through the narrowness of the cramped kitchen.

At the stairs, he heard the baby begin to beep and squawk to her mother, signaling she was ready for her breakfast.

# 7

It is often said that Philadelphia's Thirtieth Street Station is everything a train station ought to be. At once cavernous and ornate, glorious and nostalgic, the station remains a neoclassical monument of a bygone era, a time when the once-mighty Pennsylvania Railroad of the thirties and forties was the supreme mode of transportation for the northeast corridor.

The station's history is as distinguished as its appearance. The structure is the work of the late Wellington Jarvis Schaefer of the Chicago architectural firm of Graham, Anderson, Probst and White. City officials considered over 130 plans submitted by competing architects before settling on Schaefer's submission. Construction of the architectural masterpiece was completed in 1934. Not only was it an instant hit, but it proved to be an enduring marvel as well, an edifice widely admired and studied by contemporary scholars of architecture.

With over fifty thousand commuters per day—3.5 million per year—Thirtieth Street Station is second only to New York's Pennsylvania Station as the busiest train terminal in the country. As the most baroque train terminal in America, Thirtieth Street recalls a time long before airborne shuttles, when the railway was the predominant means of shuffling travelers between Boston, New York, Philadelphia, Baltimore, and Washington. Today, even the most jaded passenger cannot ignore the majesty of Thirtieth Street Station, which was fully refurbished in 1991. While rushing to make, say, the Metroliner to Baltimore, one is given pause by a single glimpse of the coffered ceiling some six stories high, painted in an awe-inspiring red and cream and gold motif. Five stories of windows allow the natural light to spill in, brilliantly illuminating the full expanse of the structure. Swirled-marble Corinthian columns support the coffered ceiling, and cylindrical Art Deco chandeliers dangle grandly overhead. Quite encouragingly, many things have remained unchanged: the old-fashioned, Roman-numeraled clock still sits atop the central information booth; the train information still flutters on the schedule board in its digit-counter format; and the original wooden benches of the 1930s still provide passengers with a place to rest while waiting for their connection.

Nonetheless, it is undeniable that time has taken its toll on some of the station's original grandeur. The Horn & Hardart, for example, has gone the way of the redcaps, as have virtually all of the mom-and-pop-run tobacco shops and newsstands. Today, slick franchise outlets thrive in their place—Hertz, McDonald's, Häagen-Dazs. The glaring neon of their signs is incongruous against the dignity of the rest of this palace, reminding one of the inevitability of change. Yet the essential ambience remains. Only a few of Thirtieth Street's contemporaries may be mentioned in the same breath—Grand Central in New York, the Union Stations of Chicago and Washington, Union Terminal in Los Angeles. All are monuments to a grand era gone by.

*They certainly don't build 'em like this anymore*, McPhillips thought appreciatively as he walked through the central concourse. In spite of his anxiety about the Myerson thing, he felt a slight charge of exhilaration. It was always something of a pleasure to be in this marble palace, regardless of the reason his business brought him here. His footfalls echoed sharply in the cavernous expanse.

He found the others at McDonald's in the southeast corner of the concourse. Wheaton and Beekman were there as expected, and so was Mazzola, who had apparently had a last-minute change of heart and decided to accompany them. The half-eaten remains of their McBreakfast and wadded-up wrappers were scattered before them on the table. Jeff Wheaton was simultaneously consulting a narrow blue-covered book and a color photocopy of a street map of Manhattan while typing the information into a black-hulled Wheat/Tech 486 laptop computer. Bruce Mazzola was leaning toward Chuck Beekman, emphasizing whatever point he was making with a white coffee-stirrer.

"Good morning, guys," Brian said. "How're you doing?"

"Feeling like we could bite the ass off a bear," Mazzola replied smartly. "How're *you* doing?"

"I thought you weren't coming, Mazz."

He shrugged. "Changed my mind. Hey, that slimebucket took three million bucks from me. I've gotta at least give it a shot."

Wheaton looked up from his computer screen. "You still have time for breakfast, you want."

"No thanks." McPhillips patted his stomach lightly. "I had already."

Wheaton nodded. "Take a seat. We've got about fifteen until the train leaves." He resumed tapping at the keyboard.

"Hey, McPhillips," Mazzola said. "What do you call an Ethiopian with buck teeth?"

McPhillips shrugged.

"A rake." Mazzola smirked.

"Very amusing, Bruce. Is that a Wall Street yuk?"

"I suppose you could say that. Any off-color humor at the expense of Ethiopians, Iranians, Helen Keller, Gary Hart, blondes or the Bhopal disaster may properly be classified as such."

"Charming."

"This guy is on a roll," Beekman enthused. "Tell him the one you just told me about the leper."

"How do you circumcise a leper?"

"How?" Beekman chimed in, playing straight man.

"You shake him."

Beekman guffawed.

"Why don't pygmies use tampons? They keep tripping over the string."

McPhillips squinted at him.

"Two more," Mazzola said. "What's green and smells like pork? Kermit's finger. . . . What's the first thing a blonde says after sex? 'You guys all on the same football team?'. . . . What's Helen Keller's favorite color? Corduroy."

"That's *three*, Bruce," Wheaton said, not looking up from his work.

"So sue me." Mazzola chewed on his coffee-stirrer.

Beekman snorted appreciatively. "Hey, I got one. What does *yuppie* stand for these days?"

Mazzola shrugged, not bothering to feign interest.

"Young, Unemployed, Previously Prosperous, Indicted Executive."

"Not funny," Mazzola razzed him. "Two thumbs down."

"Oh, excuse me, Mr. Comedy. We can't all be witty enough to create half the space-shuttle jokes in America the day the *Challenger* exploded." Chuck Beekman jerked a thumb toward Mazzola and said to McPhillips, "Did you know that, Brian? Did you know that when Bruce was a young pup on Wall Street, he was the one who started the joke about the teacher onboard the space shuttle?"

"I don't think I know which joke you're talking about."

"Oh, you know the one," Beekman insisted. " 'What color were Christa McAuliffe's eyes? Answer: Blue. One blew this way, one blew that way.' You remember that one?"

"Unfortunately, yes."

"Bruce dreamed that one up."

Mazzola wriggled his eyebrows in acknowledgment.

McPhillips smiled mischievously. "Hear any good Mike Milken jokes lately?"

Mazzola frowned. "Now *that* is nothing to joke about."

Chuck Beekman rolled his eyes. "Look out below, here comes Bruce Mazzola's impassioned speech about the great genius, Michael Milken."

"Go ahead and laugh, smart guy," Mazzola said, wagging the stirring stick at Beekman. "But you should be proud you graduated from the same school as Milken did. For my money, he was the greatest genius of the twentieth century. Even more so than that frizzy-headed faggot, Einstein."

Beekman rolled his eyes. "Aw, c'mon."

"I'm serious."

"A bigger genius than *Einstein?*"

"I worked with the man. I witnessed his greatness firsthand."

McPhillips shook his head. "Whoa, time out. Let me get this straight. You're saying Milken was more of a genius than Einstein?"

"Fuckin'-ay right. Greatest genius America ever produced." Beekman pshawed and gave Mazzola a dismissive wave.

McPhillips said: "Bruce, how can you say that with a straight face?"

"Because it's true. Look at the facts. All Einstein ever gave the world was the technology to exterminate every human being on the planet. But Mike Milken single-handedly built an empire that shook the earth. He created trillions in wealth—*out of nothing.* He did so much more good for the world than Einstein. I don't think there's any comparison actually."

Beekman laughed and started to chant, "Free Milken. Free Milken."

"Don't laugh. If the government hadn't conspired to put Mike away, we wouldn't have any of these problems in the high-yield market today. It's true, when they free Mike Milken, a lot of the problems the government caused will be solved virtually overnight."

"Seems to me that's the same argument Jim Bakker's attorneys tried," McPhillips said.

"Ah, fuck you, McPhillips. You're just like the rest. Understanding the greater picture is beyond your realm of comprehension."

McPhillips shook his head. "Bruce, the guy put the whole country in hock. My firm's done enough bankruptcy work last couple of years, enough savings and loan cleanups, that I simply can't agree with you. This savings and loan thing, that's Milken's doing. Not all of it, but a lot of it."

"That's bullshit!" Mazzola said heatedly. "Unadulterated bullshit." He leaned toward Brian, narrowed his eyes, and pointed the coffee-stirrer at him. "I'm disappointed in you, McPhillips, buying into that brainless media propaganda. What's the matter? You think it should be against the law to make that kind of money?"

"No. Just that it should be against the law to break the law."

Mazzola started to say something, then waved him off dismissively. McPhillips, for his part, kept his tongue in check to keep the debate from flaring up into a full-fledged conflagration, the direction in which it was most certainly heading. Having been enriched by the great Michael Milken during his years at Drexel's Beverly Hills office, Mazzola was simply too myopic to objectively consider the widespread economic damage the securities firm wrought when it ruled Wall Street in the eighties. But McPhillips' firm was there to mop up some of the mess left in the aftermath, filing Chapter 11s for once-solid companies now slowly choking to death on debt. McPhillips had seen enough in the last few years to consider the last decade a horrifying abomination. Contrary to Bruce's apologist declarations, Milken's greatest accomplishment was to suck two billion dollars out of the American economy as his own salary for commandeering a game of musical chairs involving the ruination en masse of the nation's best-run corporations. True, the Milken machine spouted geysers of gold for hundreds of investment bankers, securities attorneys, and hostile raiders. But McPhillips firmly believed that M&A artists were the greatest alchemists of all time, turning paper to gold. Meanwhile, the entire junk market was no more than a fraudulent Ponzi scheme that impoverished the country and permitted the Japanese to forge ahead as the preeminent economic superpower on the face of the planet. But try telling that to one of Milken's minions. God, how Bruce had changed. McPhillips inwardly lamented the loss of his onetime college buddy and glanced at the stranger facing him.

After an awkward silence, Jeff Wheaton intervened. "Hey, fellas, can't we change the subject here? I'm getting an Excedrin headache, huh?"

Bruce simmered for only a moment longer before the trademark smile of mischief reappeared on his face. "All right, all right, while we're on the subject of Wall Street, that reminds me of a war story from the early days. You wanna hear this? It's great, you'll love this, Jeff. Even you'll find it funny, McPhillips. Jeff, put that fuckin' computer away. You could use a laugh."

Wheaton, eager to keep the peace, mumbled, "Just a second, let me save this file." He punched the F-7 key, shut down the system, and slipped the laptop into its padded carrying case. "Awright, I'm all ears."

"All right." Mazzola looked around the table to be certain he had everyone's rapt attention before he began.

"Back in '85, I was transferred to the Beverly Hills branch of Drexel to train with Michael Milken—" (here, Mazzola crossed himself in reverence at the mention of his mentor's name, *possibly just to piss me off*, McPhillips thought) "—and it was a fuckin' furious pace. I mean, you had to hit the ground runnin' to keep up with *these* stallions. These were the true thoroughbreds of the Street. Anyways, I got used to runnin' on three, four hours of sleep a night, chasin' deals seven days a week and lovin' it, abso-fucking-lutely lovin' it. Everything was about closin' deals, closin' the deals at all costs. And on the Street, we were the champions; we closed 'em like nobody's business.

"It was deal after deal after deal." Bruce snapped his fingers in quick succession. "They were fucking great times, those days, the best imaginable for a guy in his mid-twenties. Adrenaline was always pumpin'. Anyhow, I'll never forget, I had this client, name of Broadhurst, some big fat fuck who was a director of Greenhills Savings and Loan in Maine. I think he's serving a sentence now at Club Fed for embezzlement or something, but that had nothing to do with us. Anyway, this director fancies himself to be some real macho type, and I'm on the phone schmoozing with him one day in October when he says, 'Bruce, you know, we do tens of millions of dollars worth of business a year, and yet we've never met face to face.' I go, 'Yeah, that's a damn shame. We oughtta hook up some time. Whyn't you come out to Beverly Hills, and I'll take you to some pussy shows?' But he says, 'I got a better idea. Whyn't you and Trenton come out to Maine for the weekend, and we'll do some duck hunting at my cabin.'

"Well now, I'm not into this *Field and Stream* crap, but the guy's a major client, he's bought a ton of high-yield product from me, so I go, 'Sure, why not.' And he tells me don't worry about the airfare, that it's all taken care of, which I assume to mean it's been charged to the bank. Whatever. Well, Sam Trenton and I get the green light from the powers-that-be—anything for the fuckin' client, of course—and we end up at this guy's cabin somewhere in God's country, the fucking backwater woods of Maine. It's me,

Trenton, Broadhurst, another director by the name of Ed Gathers, and Trenton's faithful golden retriever, Scout.

"Now, you gotta understand Broadhurst. All week long, he's this milquetoast director of some piss-squirt savings and loan. Come Friday, he's some macho kind of weekend warrior with the big swinging schlong. He's gonna show these boys from Drexel what kind of bad-ass dude he is. At dawn, he rolls our asses outta bed, sets us up with all the hunting gear, gives us shotguns, and next thing you know, we're all set to go out and bag us some ducks, when Broadhurst says, 'Wait a minute.' He pulls out some sticks of long-fused dynamite from a crate he has in the closet."

"Dynamite? What for?" Beekman asked.

"Well, that's what Trenton asks. 'What the fuck you need that for?' he goes. And Broadhurst—I'll never forget the look on his face—Broadhurst gets this shit-eating grin from ear to ear and says, 'That's to flush out the bashful ones.' And we shrug, okay, fine, whatever, and think no more of it. And we go out.

"And we're out there in the marshes, trudgin' around in our knee-high boots for an hour. Nothin'. Two hours go by. Nothin', not a bird in sight. Three hours and I'm thinkin' they all headed to Florida already and I'm ready to say fuck this, boys, let's go back to the cabin and watch some college football with a bunch of cold ones. Then suddenly, Broadhurst pulls up short and puts a finger to his lips." Bruce imitated the director, putting a finger to his lips. "He points to a thicket in the bushes about seventy-five yards away. Whispers: there's a flock of 'em in there. Then, next thing you know, he's whippin' out the dynamite, and I'm thinkin', 'Oh, fuck, what's this shithead gonna do now?' Well, sure enough, he pulls out an Ohio blue-tip and lights this six-inch fuse and just like in the cartoons with Wile E. Coyote, the fuse starts to spit and sizzle, and Broadhurst leans back and heaves the dynamite toward the thicket with everything he's got. It sails out a good sixty yards, landin' just shy of where the fuckin' birds are. There's one problem, though."

Beekman frowned. "The fuse went out?"

Mazzola shook his head. "The dog."

"The dog?"

Mazzola leaned forward with a wild-eyed look. In a hissing

whisper: "The fucking dog chases after the stick of dynamite. He thinks Broadhurst is playing fetch with him!"

"Holy shit," McPhillips heard himself say.

"So what happened?" Beekman said, scarcely containing himself.

"So what happens is that the dog runs out towards it, and Broadhurst is screamin', 'No Scout! No! No!' What the fuck, *all of us* are screamin' and yellin', 'No! Bad dog! No!' But Scout won't listen. He scoops up the dynamite in his mouth, his tail waggin', and he starts runnin' back to where we're squatting. We're yellin' and yellin', but that just encourages the fucking dog, and he starts runnin' faster. I can still see it in my mind, the fuse burnin', sparks shooting out of the side of his mouth, and everybody's thinkin', 'Holy shit, we're *all* gonna die.' And the dog's comin', comin'—fifty yards, forty, thirty-five. . . ." Bruce let his voice trail off.

Beekman was visibly agitated. "And?"

Mazzola relished this moment. "What happened next is that I said, 'Fuck this,' and I leveled my shotgun at the mutt and—*bang!*—I turned him into puppy chow. O'course, then we turned tail and ran for our fucking lives when suddenly—KABLOOEY!—the dynamite explodes. Bits of golden retriever rain down on our heads. It takes us all a minute or two after that to recover, to gain back our senses."

The other three stared at Mazzola in silence.

"Then Broadhurst, that big macho fuckwad, breaks down and starts bawlin' like a chick. 'Scout, Scout, my poor poor Scout. I can't believe it!' Just cryin' and cryin'.

"So I put my arm around the guy and say, 'There, there. Look on the bright side. At least you don't gotta bury him!'" Bruce Mazzola punctuated his own punch line with thunderous laughter.

The other three stared at him for a long while before Chuck Beekman said in a hushed tone, "Mazzola, you're a twisted motherfucker."

Mazzola took this as a compliment. "I know."

Jeff Wheaton stood up and slung the carrying bags over his shoulder. "C'mon," he said, checking his watch. "Our train's boarding."

# 8

Not unlike death and taxes, one could always count on the *New York Post* to fully chronicle the previous day's tales of madness and carnage in its inimitable fashion, replete with excruciatingly lurid details and screaming ninety-point Helvetica bold headlines.

According to the *Post*, Friday, June 26, had been especially harsh to the children of New York. Let's see . . . a four-year-old was killed in a hail of bullets while walking on the streets of the Bronx with his mother, the innocent victim of a crack deal gone sour. . . . A two-month-old infant in Brooklyn met an infinitely more grisly demise at the hands of her parents, who, annoyed with the newborn's crying at all hours of the night, had chopped her into bite-sized pieces and fed the pieces to their pet Rottweiler. . . . In Bensonhurst, a former father-of-the-year was jailed on charges that he systematically sodomized his twelve adopted children, boys and girls between the ages of four and fifteen, and had encouraged them to have sex with one another.

But children were not the only victims in the city on Friday. A serial killer was putting bullets in the brains of the cabbies at the pace of two a week, and the police had no suspects, no leads. Not that the cops were always on your side in New York. EMS was accusing two of New York's finest of looting the decapitated body of a Manhattan accident victim, stealing $128 from his wallet and the diamond ring from his partially severed forefinger. Generally speaking, the *Post* reported, race relations had deteriorated to an all-time low, and sex-and-bribe scandals among local government officials were at epidemic proportions; but the good news was that Mayor Dinkins managed to squeeze in six hours of tennis in Queens yesterday.

Good God, if one were to accept the premise that the Saturday, June 27, issue of the *Post* was a reliable snapshot of the state of affairs in the city at that moment in time, well then, you'd have to be a mental patient to want to live there. *Thank Christ we're out of this urban toilet by 11:15 tomorrow morning,* Mitch Myerson thought to himself. He turned to the sports pages, an oasis in this desert of man's inhumanity to man. Phillies beat the Pirates, six to three, on Dale Murphy's third-inning grand slam. . . .

"Honey?" Rachel called out.

Myerson looked up from the paper. He caught sight of Rachel Fairweather Wheaton gliding up to him with a positively luminescent smile lighting up her face. She sported sexy aquamarine aviator-style sunglasses, which tipped midway down the narrow bridge of her upturned nose. She looked *très* European today. Myerson was crazy about her.

"Have you been waiting for me for a long time?" she asked sweetly.

"Only all my life," he replied, with a smarmy smile.

She flopped down into the seat next to him. "Honey," she purred in her buttery voice. "I've got fabulous news."

"What is it, Nuffy?"

"I know you think it's silly, but I just had to call and find out what our horoscopes were. You know, for luck."

"Nuffy, I don't think it's silly."

"Yes you do and it's sweet of you to deny it. But it's really *wild!* You won't *be*-lieve how in sync our horoscopes are today. It's *in*-credible!"

"Tell me."

"Are you really interested?"

"Of course."

"Okay. Only if you really want to hear it." She produced a scratch pad with Le Parker Meridien logo. Mitch could see that she had copiously written down the information from Jeane Dixon's 900 number in a meticulous schoolgirl's hand. "For Leo—" She looked up at Mitch and arched her eyebrow mischievously. "That's you. Leo the *Lion*."

Mitch beamed. *The Lion*. He liked that. "What's it say?"

"For Leo: 'At the risk of opening some wounds among old friends, you must take an aggressive stance and flatly refuse to be talked down or intimidated by colleagues or business associates. A major reorganization of personal money matters is about to take place!'" She slapped the pad down on her lap and cocked her head. "Isn't that un-*bee*-lievable?"

Mitch nodded.

"Want me to go on?"

Again he nodded.

And she read aloud her own horoscope for Sagittarius, but Mitch lost track of her words. He was simply too mesmerized by his companion's effortless charisma to follow what she was saying precisely; he was so enchanted by her capacity to captivate him with the simplest of gestures, of expressions. He watched her radiant face as she spoke to him in her honey-buttered voice, so euphonious to his ears, drinking in her beauty, ecstatic that *he* had what it took to possess this woman, to make her his.

When she finished reading, she leaned over to Mitch as if to share a confidence with him. "Of course, I don't believe in all that stuff," she giggled melodiously. "It's just silly fun."

Mitch nodded happily and kissed her. Then he sat back and took in the atmosphere around them. They were on the garden level of the Trump Tower on Fifth Avenue off Fifty-seventh Street, brunching on buttery almond croissants with imported fruit preserves and exotic coffees at a modest little restaurant called, simply, Bistro. They were just killing time, enjoying the first few moments of their new life together, the fugitives of love. He was distracted by the elegance of Trump Tower's interior, with its burnt-orange Italian marble and *faux* gold trim. Near their table, a three-story waterfall tumbled into a large reflecting pool with a refreshing slap-and-gurgle sound. Soft classical music drifted from the speakers; Mitch recognized the piece as Boccherini's *Minuet*. So this was Trump Tower, Mitch thought. The Donald's pride and joy. Donald Trump happened to be a hero to Mitch Myerson. A role model. Well, this morning's *Post* just said Mr. Trump was on the verge of personal bankruptcy. Mitch felt smug. Trump had a negative net worth and some no-name bimboid from Georgia. That meant Mitch had more money than Donald Trump and a classier piece of ass to boot. The student surpasses the teacher. Who would've thought—

"Penny for your thoughts, babe," Rachel said.

"Is that all they're worth to you?" he chided.

"Tell me what they are, and maybe I'll up my offer."

"I was just thinking . . . how easy it turned out to be. I had this incredible excitement while I was putting this plan together, and when I saw it could work, well, it was an unbelievable high. But in the back of my mind, I thought I was going to feel, you know, a lot of guilt after it was all over. You know, taking money from some people who used to be friends." Mitch looked at her evenly and went on: "And I thought I'd feel a little guilty about taking you away from your husband."

Her eyes held his without a blink. "And do you?"

"No." A smile spread over Mitch's lips. "Much to my surprise, not at all."

She leaned forward and whispered conspiratorially. "And how did it feel when you knew you'd pulled it all off? When you got both the bucks *and* the babe?"

"Great, fabulous. It felt better than sex." He leered at her. "Well, maybe not better than *that*."

She giggled her melodious giggle.

"Oh, I've got good news," Mitch said. "I got us tickets to *Miss Saigon*."

"*Omigod!*" she gasped. "Mitchell, you don't understand! I am *dying* to see this play! How did you get tickets?"

"When you've got twenty mil net worth, it's a fingersnap."

"No, really!"

Myerson shrugged. "The concierge hooked us up while you were upstairs dressing. They cost me a little bit more than face, but, hey, I think maybe you're worth it."

"Have you made dinner plans for us yet?"

"Yes. French food at Maurice at six-thirty. French food is your favorite, *non?*"

"Mmm, yes. French food is *orgasmic.*"

"Now, Nuffy, I've got to TCOB for an hour or so." TCOB was an acronym for 'taking care of business'—their code word in reference to the computer scheme itself. "It's better that I go alone. St. Germaine said so."

Rachel pouted. "What am I supposed to do with myself while you TCOB?"

"Nuffy, *you* wanted to come to New York. There must be a thousand things."

"Let's see. I could get a facial at Georgette Klinger. Or a body-wrap in Japanese seaweed at Christine Valmy." She rose from her chair, stepped over to him and poured herself onto his lap. "I want to do something to make myself more beautiful for you."

Mitch Myerson laughed. "Impossible!"

"Or . . ." Rachel's voice trailed off, and she bit her lower lip playfully. She looked like some little Daddy's girl, a mischievous princess who was used to getting her way just by sugarcoating her requests with a dollop of feminine charm. "Or, I could do a tiny bit of shopping."

"That's perfect, Nuffy. Bloomingdale's is maybe eight or nine blocks from here—"

"Six."

Mitch laughed. *Of course* she would know precisely where Bloomingdale's would be. "Six blocks. Go shopping, then, whatever makes you happy."

"You," she cooed.

"Me?"

"You're what makes me happy."

"And you make me happy. That's why we're together now." Fugitives of love.

She lifted her silken leg and straddled him on the chair, so that their faces were almost touching. He could feel the heat from her creamy skin. She laced her arms about his neck. "In fact, I've never been so happy," she whispered. "So fulfilled. So *sexually* fulfilled."

Mitch felt the blood rushing to his loins and the accompanying twitch in his groin. He wasn't expecting to feel her hand there, but there it was, causing him to moan involuntarily. She worked her hand expertly, squeezing, stroking, pushing. His eyes fluttered shut, his breathing became labored.

"I love the things you do for me, Mitchell," she murmured. "Do you realize that?"

"Yes. Oh, yes."

"Do you like how I show my gratitude to you?"

"Yes-s-s. Very much so."

She undid his zipper. He sucked in a full breath in anticipation and held it in his lungs, not daring to exhale. She reached her hand inside his trousers, peeled back his underwear, and clasped her hand around his stiffening member. He groaned aloud when she pumped him gently. Were people watching them? He didn't care. Not now. Let them watch. . . .

Her voice came to him as if in a dream: "I know this is right, Mitchell. It was fate for us to be together."

"Mmm."

"I love you."

"I . . . love . . . you. . . ." He could feel the sweet pressure building in his abdomen.

She worked him like that for a while and his trance deepened.

But abruptly: she stopped.

Withdrew her hand, adjusted his underwear, zipped him back up.

He nearly whimpered with disappointment. He blinked repeatedly, as if he had just awakened from an erotic coma. As a consolation prize, she threw her arms around him and kissed him full on the lips. "Let's save it for later, baby," she murmured, cupping his cheek in her palm.

Mitch nodded. "Right, we'll save it for later."

She rolled off his lap and slipped into the chair next to him.

Mitch kneaded his groin, hoping to relieve the throbbing pain. Blueballs.

Rachel watched him and smiled secretly. Men were oh-so predictable. Malleable, like Play-Doh. The best way to a man's heart was always through his cock. She pulled out her gold cigarette case, put a Dunhill to her bee-stung lips, fired it up, and inhaled exquisitely. Her eyes narrowed. "Honey?"

"Yes?" Mitch said hoarsely.

"I'll need some money." Then she smiled sweetly. "For shopping."

# 9

The nine-twenty train to New York was scheduled to arrive at Penn Station at ten-fifty. Their car was a little more than half-filled. Mazzola took a window seat, and Beekman sat next to him; across the aisle, it was Wheaton who had the window, McPhillips beside him. Before the train had even lurched into motion, Jeff Wheaton had unsheathed his computer and was already clacking away at a furious pace.

McPhillips could contain his curiosity no longer.

"Looks like you're rolling out the big guns on this one." McPhillips pointed to the laptop.

"Uh huh. All the big guns," Jeff replied distractedly.

"What's the computer for?"

"Battle plans."

"Battle plans?"

"Yeah, it's how we're going to do this thing. I've got a pretty comprehensive plan of attack. You'll see when we get to New York."

Brian nodded. Wheaton's preoccupation with the laptop reminded McPhillips of the computer geek from the Secret Service they met last night. What was the guy's name? Oh yeah. *Tibbens.*

"How're you holding up?" McPhillips asked solicitously.

"Fine. And you?"

"Well, quite frankly, Jeff, I hope you're not, uh, getting your hopes up . . ."

Jeff Wheaton looked up from his work and sighed. "*Et tu, Brian?*"

"What do you mean by that?"

"I've already been through this with Bruce. He's flat out told me he thinks this is a mission doomed to fail from the get-go. All but tried to talk me out of it. Said you lawyers have a term for this sort of thing. I believe he called it a 'fishing expedition.' "

"Yeah. That's a term we use."

"What about you, Brian? You think we're on a fishing expedition?"

"I don't know, Jeff. I mean, there *is* a pretty good chance they're already out of the country—"

"Right. But there's also a chance they're still *in* this country, too. No matter how slim that chance is, it's a chance. And if they are, they're in New York City. I know it. I know Rachel, and I know Mitch—a little bit at least—and I think we can find 'em if they're there. Look, what else are we supposed to do? Sit around with our thumbs up our sphincters, waiting for the FBI to give us hourly bulletins? Brian, you lost a lot of money. That should be enough for you to do whatever it takes to hunt him down like a dog. You guys have nothing to lose—*I'm* paying for the tickets and the hotel room in New York. Just promise me that you'll follow my game plan when we get there, all right?"

Brian nodded. "Sure."

Jeff returned to his computer and was quickly consumed by his work. For his part, McPhillips opened his briefcase and withdrew a copy of the Matthew Bender treatise on banking law, hoping to find an answer to the question of FDIC indemnification. As he thumbed through the section related to electronic fund transfers, he was aware of Bruce Mazzola's resonant voice as it carried from the other side of the car. He was regaling Chuck Beekman with more tales of high adventure from the glory days when junk bonds ruled the world. It was as if Mazzola was stuck in a time warp. Like most people, McPhillips was sick and tired of hearing of the rollicking eighties. Still, he had to wonder why it was that

Mazzola never spoke of his post-Drexel days. What *exactly* did Bruce do for a living for the last three years, anyway?

The first half of the trip was uneventful. Wheaton, exhausted from a lack of sleep the previous night, had nodded off and dozed lightly in the window seat. McPhillips closed his book and yawned. After forty minutes with the Bender treatise, his inquiry into whether FDIC money was available under this scenario was inconclusive. Such was the nebulous nature of the law. He slipped the book back into the briefcase, balled up his fists, and stretched.

Chuck Beekman came over to his seat. He spoke softly so as not to disturb the slumbering Wheaton. "I thought he would never stop talking about junk bonds and hostile takeovers."

McPhillips smiled knowingly.

A look of concern crossed Beekman's face. "Hey, Brian, can I talk to you for a few minutes?"

For the first time, Brian noticed that Beekman was anxious. The guy was literally wringing his hands.

"Sure," Brian said. "What's up?"

"I need someone to talk to about this—this matter, and you've always seemed to be someone—" Beekman bit his lower lip.

"Of course."

"It's highly personal, actually."

"All right. You want to go—"

"Let's go to the cafe car. I'll buy you a cup of coffee or something. Okay?"

The Amtrak cafe car was located four units toward the front of the train. There, they found one table seat left. McPhillips waited alone at the table while Beekman purchased some food. The window at their table was huge, nearly half the height of the side of the car. McPhillips squinted out on the view blurring past him. It was the junkscape of industrial-ugly New Jersey hurtling by, a rolling progression of rotted piles of unused lumber and the rusting carcasses of abandoned vehicles. Of course, what did he expect, the scenic route? After all, they didn't exactly lay train tracks on prime commercial real estate.

He turned his gaze to the customers about the cafe car. Started people-watching. At the table next to him, he could hear snippets of conversation between a talent agent and a blue-collar type of character actor whose face he had seen in perhaps a half-dozen motion pictures. The where and the who eluded him. (Mobster pictures? James somebody?) Another table, another character: some self-tortured punk rocker with a truckload of bad attitude, stretched out on his seat, sucking on a clove cigarette. His head was cleanshaven and was tattooed with a blue-green serpent. His skin was an unhealthy-looking fish-belly white. He glared back at McPhillips with a snarling expression that threatened impending violence: right here, right now. McPhillips' gaze dropped to the punk's black T-shirt with huge white letters: DIE YUPPIE SCUM. McPhillips wondered: Does that message refer to *me?* This scumbag wants *me* to die?

Beekman's return derailed his train of thought. "Hey, buddy," Chuck said with a weak smile. "All I got are hundreds." He thumbed open his wallet and held it out to McPhillips as proof. Inside were eight crisp one-hundred-dollar bills and nothing else. "You mind spotting me ten? I'll square us away at lunch when we get to the Apple."

McPhillips slid a sawbuck across the table to him.

Beekman paid and brought the coffee and pastries over. "A buck-fifty for a cup of coffee!" he exclaimed. "A buck-fifty. When I asked the guy why it was so expensive, he told me, 'Because it's imported.' It just now hit me: *All coffee's imported.* That sonuvabitch!"

He made no attempt to give McPhillips the change, nor did Brian demand it. They sat in silence for a minute, noshing, sipping. The coffee was harsh enough to strip varnish from a picnic table, and the turnover had the metallic taste of too many preservatives, but neither voiced a complaint aloud. The table swayed with the motion of the train; coffee sloshed out over the side of the ALL ABOARD AMERICA cup and onto the Formica tabletop. The pitch and yaw of the train, normally soothing, was a definite liability in the cafe car. As Brian mopped up the coffee with a wad of napkins, he spoke first. "What's on your mind, Beek? You okay?"

"No. Actually I'm not." Beekman stared out the window. "Actually, I'm screwed in a big way."

"You want to talk about it?"

Beekman shrugged. "Ah, everything sucks."

"I think I know how you're feeling. This Myerson thing has thrown us all for a loop—"

"Nah, it's not just that. Don't get me wrong. That's a lot of it, of course. But my whole life just plain sucks." Beekman sulked back into his pensive silence.

McPhillips studied his college roommate. Beekman wore a white golf shirt with BEEKMAN FORD-MAZDA embroidered at nipple level. He sported a golf cap emblazoned with the same block-letter logo. A Mickey Mouse watch encircled his wrist. Time was not treating the Beek too kindly. His curly hair was receding with unnatural speed and an unflattering bald pate was emerging. Beekman's eyes were sunken, and, although they always had been, even in college, the crow's-feet and dark circles made him look five or six years older than he actually was. Life sucked, that's what Beekman had said, but really, how bad could it be for a guy who was being groomed to take over Beekman Ford-Mazda, the seventh-most-profitable automobile dealership in the Northeast? McPhillips pointed this out to him.

"That's just it," Chuck Beekman cried. "I haven't told my old man that I got wiped out by Mitch. Not yet. Brian, I'm scared shitless to tell him about it."

"Chuck," McPhillips said soothingly, "we all got dicked over by Mitch. It wasn't your fault, it wasn't anyone's fault—"

"You don't understand. That's beside the point. My old man is gonna see it in the papers, and he's gonna bust a coronary, I swear it."

"Did you lose a lot of money?"

"Of course I did. But you're not getting it, Brian. This will be the last straw. I can see it now. He's gonna call me into his office on Monday, and he's gonna do it over the house phone so everyone knows he wants to see me. Then he's gonna say, 'You goddam shithead, you goddam shithead. I buy you the best education money can buy, and you go and get *dumber.*' He's gonna say, '*My* father never put *me* through college, and yet you're dumber than me! Dumb, dumb, dumb!' " As he played out this exchange, Chuck Beekman gently cradled his head in his fingertips as if it were going to crack open.

"Chuck, if you want, we'll all talk to him—"

"That wouldn't help, Bri. You see, this is just the excuse he's been waiting for to turn over control of the dealership to Michael!"

Michael Beekman was Chuck's younger brother, three years his junior. Whether justified or not, Chuck had long harbored a paranoia that Charles Beekman II favored the youngest son, who was more handsome, more athletic, more self-assured, more like Charlie II, than his eldest son Chuck. Such was the price paid when one invoked the privilege of nepotism to provide his lifelong livelihood.

"Sibling rivalry sucks, Brian. It's hell. I mean, I can see my father using his mastery of the mind-fuck to motivate his salesmen, but why does he have to pit me against Michael all the time? What is it with this winner-take-all shit, anyway?"

"You're right," McPhillips nodded. "It isn't fair. Maybe you should have a talk with him about that."

"Ha! That's a laugh. Talk to him, *right?* That'll just show him I'm weak! No, when he gets wind of this, I'm finished. Michael wins. End of story. *Goddammit!*"

"There's got to be something—" But McPhillips saw the futility in finishing the thought.

There ensued a long period where neither of the men spoke. The clatter of the tracks beneath the train drowned out the conversation of the character actor and his agent next to them. McPhillips stole a peek at the punk and realized the punk was scowling maliciously in their general direction. Die yuppie scum.

Chuck finally spoke. "That's not the only thing bothering me, Brian."

"What else, buddy?"

Chuck Beekman drew in a deep breath and sighed it out in a series of short pops. "We've known each other a long time, Brian, haven't we?"

"Of course."

"Gone through good times and bad together?"

"Good times and bad."

"And we can talk honestly? Man to man, right?"

"Chuck, you know that's true." *Just get on with it, man.*

"I'm going to ask you a question, and I want the honest-to-God truth, all right?"

"I'll do my best."

"You ever fuck around behind Lisa's back?"

McPhillips stiffened. "Hey, what kind of lousy question is that?"

Chuck Beekman drew back and put his hands up defensively. "If that's an out-of-bounds question, all you got to do is say so—"

"It's not necessarily out of bounds, Chuck, it's just—Jesus, the way you *phrased* it."

"Okay. Well, anyway, you know what I meant."

Brian frowned. "What is this anyway? Truth or Dare?"

"Are you saying 'Dare'?"

"No."

"So, then. The truth?"

"The answer to your question is no. I've never cheated on Lisa."

"Hmm. Let me ask you another question then. Have you ever *come close* to being with a woman other than your wife?"

" 'Come close.' What exactly does that mean?"

Beekman rolled his eyes in exasperation. "Just like a lawyer. Evading the issue by screwing with semantics. Brian, yes or no, have you ever come close to banging another chick, your secretary or even just some skirt you met on the street?"

"No. No. And no."

"Do you ever fantasize about it?"

Brian hesitated just a moment too long. "Not really."

"I don't believe you, Bri. Not completely, anyway. I happened to see how you reacted to that video of Jeff's wife getting it on with Mitch. I hope I'm not speakin' out of school here, but I do believe you popped a one-eyed meat puppet right then 'n' there."

"Gee, Chuck," McPhillips said drolly. "I didn't know you took such a personal interest in my erections."

Beekman ignored this and pushed forth, his eyes taking on a feral, liquid glint as he spoke. "Let me tell you what happened to me the other day. It'll blow your mind. This sweet young piece of cheesecake from California came into the office. Her name was Cheri Richmond. She's blond and blue-eyed, wearing this red, tight, short-cut number that rides right up her crack. She's got these creamy legs and a perfect ass—two round handfuls." Beekman cupped his hands for illustrative purposes. "Well, she wants to cut a deal for a Mazda Miata. She's throwing out all these numbers, but all I'm thinking is how badly I want to nail this babe. I flirt a little bit with her, a double entendre or two, and then something really weird happens. I realize she's turned on; she's hot for *me!* Brian, you know the heat between two people who suddenly realize at the same time that they want to fuck each other like wild animals? Well, that's what was going down between us, Bry. It was all I could do to keep myself from pulling her into the storage area and reaming her senseless."

"But you didn't."

"No, I didn't. I don't know why. Maybe it's—I don't know. I don't know why I didn't do it. But I did get her telephone number and I'm . . . I'm *obsessed* with this Cheri Richmond, but not Cheri Richmond herself, rather, the *idea* of having intercourse with another woman! Brian, for chrissake, I need your advice."

"My advice?"

"Yeah, what would *you* do, if you were me?"

Brian shrugged. "I can't really say. Maybe you should talk to a counselor about it."

"A shrink? Of course I'm talking about it to a shrink. Some guy in Center City, twice a week. Get this: He tells me I *should* go for it. Says it would be good for our marriage."

"Sounds to me like you need a new shrink."

"Brian, I'm obsessed with the idea of having an affair. Is that normal for guys our age?"

Suddenly, Bruce Mazzola appeared from nowhere and slid into the seat next to Chuck, startling both of them. "Do my ears deceive me, sports fans, or could it really be true? The Beeker is tempted by the fruits of another?"

"C'mon, Bruce." McPhillips shook his head.

Mazzola turned to Beekman. "Now, Chuck, you come clean with Uncle Bruce. You a little tired of eating home cooking every night?"

"If you must know, yes. My wife and I are having some problems . . . there's a woman I've met. . . ." Beekman shrugged. "And I'm . . . attracted to her."

"Full steam ahead, boyo," Mazzola said, pushing his index finger through an "o" of his thumb and forefinger on the other hand. "What's the hitch?"

"I don't want anyone getting hurt."

Mazzola pshawed. "A little cheating, so what? You keep it to yourself, it's a victimless crime."

McPhillips shook his head. "It's hardly a victimless crime, Bruce."

Mazzola gazed at him evenly. "Always the lawyer. God forbid you should say something's all right every once in a while. Jeeeezus. C'mon, big Bri, stop being such a boy scout. We're talkin' human nature here. Don't you ever get the urge to fuck someone other than your wife? And spare me the crap about how you couldn't 'cause you love her too much. You and I both know love's got nothing to do with it. It's got to do with basic primal instincts. Man is a hunter. Always was, always will be."

"You're a bachelor, Bruce. You have a constitutional right to be promiscuous."

"Well, we're talking about *you* right now, McPhillips. Riddle me this, boy wonder: if you had the chance to nail Kim Basinger, Sharon Stone, Michelle Pfeiffer, or Madonna in the privacy of a hotel room with no chance of anybody in the world finding out about it, including Lisa, *especially* Lisa, you tellin' me you wouldn't think twice about it?"

"Yes. I would definitely think twice about it. And then I wouldn't do it."

Even Beekman snorted in contempt. "Right, Bri."

"You've got to be yankin' my chain here," Mazzola said in mock exasperation. "I'd pay big bucks to be in the same room with Michelle Pfeiffer's *pap smear*, let alone the real thing."

"Amen," Chuck Beekman laughed.

"I don't know, Chuck," Mazzola said, as if McPhillips wasn't present. "I'd say there's three possibilities here. Brian's either a liar, a faggot, or—" Mazzola turned to Brian to finish the sentence—"he has no dick."

McPhillips froze, enraged. Suddenly, he was odd man out of this conversation. Was he really such a boy scout? Were he and Lisa *really* just a remote desert island of matrimony set amidst a boiling sea of temptation and infidelity? He had long believed that the first extramarital affair in a marriage was not merely a *fling*. No, it was far less innocuous than that. It was more like a cancerous tumor of deceit that took root and, nourished by temptation and weakness, would, in time, grow uncontrollably until it killed off the marriage. In its wake would be enormous pain for everyone, fractured relationships, the emotional toll on the children. It was the ultimate end to one's innocence. But then, it was also something else entirely: It would be a personal failure he would have to live with the rest of his life, regardless of whether or not Lisa ever found out about it. As his law school classmate Siegel was fond of saying, "A man simply can't let the little head do the thinking for the big head." So true.

But still, that didn't mean he wasn't tempted from time to time. Any red-blooded male was. Even now, Brian was still haunted by the nakedness of Jeff's wife on that videotape. Even now, McPhillips had a vision of Rachel, writhing in sweaty pleasure, a vision he could not shake from his head. And he was haunted by a bizarre encounter he had once had almost two years ago while Lisa was home with the children. . . .

McPhillips rose from the table. He said cheerfully, "Well, I'll leave it to you two to hash this one out between yourselves. But Beek, I ask you to keep five words in mind, just five."

Chuck Beekman gave him a blank look. "And what, pray tell, are those five words?"

" 'Half of everything you own.' " McPhillips looked at Bruce. "Oh, and Mazzola? Fuck you and your lousy attitude."

"Likewise, I'm sure." Mazzola shrugged.

Brian McPhillips made his way back down the aisle to his car. He collapsed into his seat, closing his eyes and pinching the bridge of his nose. Next to him, Jeff Wheaton muttered as if he were talking in his sleep, "Twenty more minutes 'til arrival." For McPhillips, those twenty minutes couldn't pass quickly enough.

# 10

With a calamitous squealing of brakes and the acrid stink of smoking rubber, the Yankee Clipper lurched to a halt at the platform of Track 15 in New York's Penn Station. It came in at 10:48 A.M., a full two minutes ahead of schedule.

Well before the train had come to a full stop, Jeff Wheaton was on his feet, gathering his belongings. He moved about with a newfound sense of purpose and dispatch. "C'mon, boys, let's go," he implored his companions. "Not a moment to waste."

But while the train settled amidst a burst of sizzling steam clouds and a mechanical clattering, the doors to their car remained closed. Impatiently, Jeff bounced around the doorway, rocking on the balls of his feet with the pent-up energy of a caged animal awaiting liberation. It was as if he'd had a shot of adrenaline.

Finally, the doors parted with a pneumatic whoosh.

"C'mon, guys, shake a leg," he barked over his shoulder before surging onto the platform and into the crush of passengers herding toward the stairs.

"That's fucking great, just fucking great," Mazzola grumbled as he slung his weekender bag over his shoulder. "Now Wheaton's gone and turned military on us."

The thick swarms of passengers made for slow passage through the terminal. As they wended their way toward the West Thirty-first Street exit, a slick-haired Jamaican con artist in a cowboy outfit beckoned from a cluster of pay phones, hawking some poor schmuck's AT&T calling card number for five bucks. Near the Pizza Hut emporium, a one-eyed vagabond with jaundiced skin and snot yo-yo'ing from his nose screamed repeatedly, "I have *so much hate*, I have *so much hate!*" Then he met Beekman's stare with his own rheumy eye and spat sardonically, "Have a *nice day*, sir!" Clearly rattled, Beekman averted eye contact and hastened his pace.

They ascended the stairs leading to the street level. There was a WELCOME TO NEW YORK sign of sorts for the benefit of the incredibly naive: DO NOT RELINQUISH YOUR BAGGAGE TO ANYONE OTHER THAN AN AUTHORIZED AMTRAK RED CAP IN UNIFORM. Passing beneath it, they emerged outside on the corner of West Thirty-first Street and Eighth Avenue. They were instantly assaulted by the cacophonous noise of the metropolis. The air resonated with the dull roar of combustion engines, the bleating of angry horns, the grinding of garbage trucks, the metallic rattle from nearby construction sites, urgent police sirens, and car alarms.

Mazzola beat his breast triumphantly in the midst of the urban pandemonium. "*Man*-hattan! Good to be back in the greatest fucking city in the world." By contrast, Beekman plugged his ears until he could acclimate to the din.

As they queued up to the yellow cab stand on Joe Louis Plaza, the ninety-degree heat, the oppressive humidity, and carbon monoxide enveloped them. Within minutes, they were dripping with sweat. *This must be what it's like to move around in dog's breath*, McPhillips imagined. He cast his eyes to the slate-gray heavens beyond the spires of the skyscrapers. Looked like rain.

A cab pulled up after only a brief wait. While the other three tumbled into the back, Wheaton slid into the front seat next to the driver. According to the photo ID on the dashboard, the driver's name possessed thirty letters, nearly all of them consonants. McPhillips was hard pressed to discern which was the first name and which was the surname.

"The Grand Hyatt, please, as quickly as you can," Wheaton said.

The turban-headed cabbie issued a grunt of acknowledgment and wheeled away from the curb, melding into the turgid four-lane flow of northbound traffic on Eighth Avenue. Their progress was halted by a red light at West Thirty-fifth Street.

On the sidewalk outside, two Hispanic men engaged in a violent shouting match in Spanish in the doorway of a seamy adult bookstore. The cabbie turned up the music to drown them out. However, the music was more unpleasant than the altercation outside; it was an eerie twing-twanging of dueling sitars against an irregular backbeat. The vocalist screamed out nonsensical syllables in a tuneless fashion that brought to mind the sound one would make at having white-hot coals applied to the bottom of one's bare feet.

"Do you by chance have any Billy Joel?" Chuck Beekman asked hopefully.

"Beeyee Choal?" the driver responded uncomprehendingly.

"Skip it," Beekman said.

The interior of the cab reeked of curry and body odor.

"Excuse me?" Bruce said irritably.

The cabdriver ignored him.

"Excuse me, *sir?*" Bruce spoke in a belligerent tone universally understood by even the most hardened of New Yorkers. "You *mind* if we get some air-conditioning back here?"

The driver gesticulated wildly. "Ees brucking."

"It's *what?*"

"He said it's broken," Wheaton said, interpreting from the front seat.

"Yeah? So's his fucking English."

Wheaton turned and gave Mazzola an annoyed look. "Lighten up, Bruce. It's only another eight blocks."

"Fine," Mazzola spat. He cranked the handle to the window. The glass stopped less than half the way down and wouldn't budge, a safety measure required of all cabs in New York City. The open window only made things worse, however, as dense, superheated city air and fumes from spent fossil fuels rolled into the cab.

On Forty-second Street, they hit a bad-luck streak of four consecutive red lights. That was followed by three city blocks of one-lane traffic, due to construction and steam pipes spiking up from the pavement. Finally, at East Forty-second Street and Lexington Avenue, the cabbie made a U-turn and braked to a halt at the entrance of the Grand Hyatt. The fare was $4.75; Wheaton handed the driver six dollars and told him to keep it.

A dapper, red-jacketed doorman named Carlos opened the back door to the cab. Wheaton, Beekman, Mazzola, and McPhillips gathered their gear and piled out of the cab. To no one in particular, Mazzola made a face and said, "Someone should break the news to that cabbie that dog food is not suitable for use as a breath-freshener."

Carlos retained the stone-faced expression of a totem pole.

The four men entered the hotel through the revolving doors and rode up a short escalator into the magnificent lobby, which was bustling with activity, with luggage carts wheeling past and international businessmen chatting in foreign tongues. McPhillips' nostrils filled with the enticing smell of rich coffees and expensive perfumes, interspersed occasionally with the mossy scents emanating from the palm trees and other tropical plants. The Grand Hyatt was justifiably proud of its status as one of the handful of New York's ultraelite hotels for business travelers. Located directly above Grand Central Station, it was often home away from home for the professional teams that came to play the Mets, Yankees, Knicks, Rangers, Jets, or Giants. Jeff Wheaton had selected it as their base because it was arguably the most centrally located hotel in the city and, therefore, best suited for their purposes.

"Okay, you guys hang here," Wheaton said. "I'm going to check us in."

McPhillips fished out a fifty-dollar bill from his wallet. "Here."

"I won't accept that," Wheaton said, backing away as if he were being offered a subpoena. Jeff walked away to join the line at the front desk.

"That's peculiar," McPhillips said, speaking his thought aloud.

"Yeah," Beekman said. "Must cost a fortune to stay here." Brian noticed the obvious look of relief on Chuck's face. For all his family's wealth, Chuck Beekman had something of a reputation as a schnorrer among his circle.

Bruce Mazzola excused himself to go to the pay phone to

retrieve messages on his answering machine at home. Beekman and McPhillips stayed near the elevator banks, keeping watch over their belongings and admiring the tranquillity of the lobby. The expansive confluence of space and air of the lobby reminded McPhillips of a casino, but the similarities ended there. The Hyatt was a seamless blend of cosmopolitan chic and continental charm. Its decor was drenched in subtle elegance, with brass banisters, marble floors, smoked mirrors, all bathed in subdued lighting. Lush tropical flora sprouted at every turn, and multitiered curtains of water tumbled down walls of glossy marble. Suspended from the center of the vaulted ceiling of the lobby was an intriguing symmetrical mobile constructed of thin copper tubes nearly two stories in size. The melancholy tinkling of a piano from the open-air cocktail lounge, the Crystal Fountain, wafted over to them.

In a short while Mazzola returned.

"No messages," he said, shrugging. Squinting in the direction of the piano player, he said, "I could certainly use a drink. I don't suppose the bar's open for business yet, is it?"

"Don't think so," Beekman said.

Mazzola frowned. Then he leaned forward and lowered his voice to a traitorous tone, as if he were about to propose mutiny. "Just between us girls, this's really just a colossal waste of time. I mean really, what are we doing here? We're just a posse—a posse for his pussy." Mazzola paused to allow himself a boyish smile at his own wordplay. "Whatta you say we go through the motions—for Jeff's sake—then raise a little hell while we're here in N.Y.C.?"

McPhillips bristled at Mazzola's condescending attitude. "We promised Jeff that we were going to—"

Mazzola cut him off. "Listen to yourself talk, McP. You sound like a *wuss*. 'We promised Jeff.' You *heard* what the FBI said last night. That peckerhead is *out of the country*. All *we're* doin' is jerkin' each other off. Either we tip a few cocktails later or we write off this whole excursion as a friggin' waste."

"Mazzola, you know what? You're a—"

"Sh-sh-sh," Bruce hissed. "Here comes Jeff."

In the next instant, Jeff Wheaton walked up. "All right, we're all set." He dealt copies of the VeloCard magnetic key cards to each one of them with the efficiency of a Vegas blackjack dealer. "Let's rock 'n' roll."

"Yeah, let's rock 'n' roll," Bruce Mazzola said, winking conspiratorially at the others.

Upon entering Suite 2704, each man had the same priority: emptying his bladder. But while the other three took their turns jetting loudly into the commode, Jeff ignored the call of nature and concentrated on setting up for their brainstorming session. He opened the blinds to let in more light, revealing the suite's disappointingly poor view. Then Wheaton booted up his Wheat/Tech 486 laptop with the 80MB hard-drive and the internal modem. Using the portable 2.5-pound Kodak Diconix printer he had brought along, he spun out several copies of the document he had been readying on the train. Then he recruited McPhillips to help him move the oblong table to the center of the master suite. Four chairs were placed around the table. At each seat, Jeff Wheaton placed a thick manila envelope. Each envelope had a different designation on its face, carefully written in black letters. EAST SIDE, WEST SIDE, MIDTOWN, and JFK AIRPORT, they said respectively.

While Wheaton tended the hard copy sprouting from the portable printer, McPhillips picked up the phone to call his wife on his MCI card. Wheaton cleared his throat politely and requested that he hold off on the call until after their meeting was concluded, that is, if it could wait. McPhillips agreed that it could. In the back of his mind, though, he thought the entire affair had taken on the no-nonsense air of an executive business meeting. Perhaps Jeff was going a bit overboard.

"I'll get the others," Wheaton said, crossing over to the adjoining suite. "Watch the printout."

Wheaton ducked his head into the junior suite where Mazzola and Beekman were unpacking their toilet kits. "All right, if you guys have basically settled in, let's get the show on the road, huh?"

"In a New York minute," Mazzola said.

Wheaton disappeared back into the master suite. Mazzola withdrew a cigar from his briefcase, unwrapped it, and lit it with a matchbook sporting the Grand Hyatt's logo. Then he gathered up the remote control, snapped on the television and shuffled through the spectrum of channels with the sound muted. Channel 28 was Showtime.

"Sonuvabitch!" Mazzola said, lighting up with excitement. "*City Slickers* is on Showtime! It must've just started."

"Maybe we should be getting into the other room, Bruce."

Bruce Mazzola puffed his cigar haughtily and cursed. Defiantly, he did not shut off the power to the television. Instead, he lowered the volume. Then he crossed over the threshold into the master suite and flopped down at the empty seat where the Midtown packet lay untouched. The sound of the movie from the other room was plainly audible. "Go with your friends to Wyoming," Patricia Wettig was imploring Billy Crystal. "Go and find your smile."

Jeff Wheaton eyed Mazzola evenly. "Bruce, turn the television off."

"It's not disturbing anyone. Fellas, is it bothering you?"

"You should turn it off, Bruce," McPhillips said.

Jeff Wheaton was glaring at Mazzola with wordless fury. If looks were heat, Bruce Mazzola would have vaporized instantly, McPhillips said to himself.

The words came from Wheaton in a low volume, but the tone was at once deliberate and menacing. "I said . . . turn it off."

Mazzola eyed him for some time, sizing him up. Then his face flushed with scorn. "Psheeeezus," he spat. He made a show of pushing away from the table disgustedly, bolting upright. The chair toppled over. Mazzola tromped childishly into the other room and snapped off the set. McPhillips and Beekman exchanged astonished glances. Wheaton stared heatedly in the direction of the junior suite.

Presently, Mazzola returned to the table and dropped into his chair like a leaden weight. His posture was a contemptuous slouch; he drummed his fingers impatiently on the table. His eyes darted about the room, seeing nothing, until he was unnerved by the silence. He looked directly across the table and locked eyes with Wheaton. Wheaton was staring back expressionlessly.

Mazzola began, "Look, if you want *my* opinion—"

"Get out of here," Wheaton said coldly.

Shock was Mazzola's first reaction; then his brow furrowed with outrage. "You're talkin' to *me*, in *that tone?*"

Wheaton's fury then exploded in a gale-force rage.

"*Get out of here, Mazzola!* Just catch *the next fucking train back to Philadelphia!*"

The unexpected eruption straightened Mazzola's posture. He sat up in ramrod-straight rigidity.

Wheaton yelled, "We don't *need* your nonstop negative bullshit. We *know* this is a long shot; we don't need you to constantly remind us of that. If you think we're just jerking ourselves off, well then, *go*, get the fuck outta my face. McPhillips and I will split your goddamn list!"

Lockjaw-mute, Bruce Mazzola was clearly poleaxed by the unexpected intensity of Wheaton's fury. After a long beat, he finally spoke. "Let's all just calm down," he said hoarsely. "That sonuvabitch took *my* money too. I want him as bad as anybody at this table."

Wheaton fired a threatening finger at him. "Then shut your blowhole and pull your weight."

Mazzola muttered, "Right, fine."

"And put out that god-awful cigar. This ain't no fuckin' bachelor party, pal."

Mazzola did as he was told, stubbing out the stogie in the nearby ashtray.

McPhillips suppressed the urge to applaud. Mazzola needed to be read the riot act. He'd been acting like an asshole all along.

An awkward silence prevailed. Distant traffic noises from twenty-seven floors below were the only sounds in the room. Jeff Wheaton massaged his temples fiercely, struggling to regain his composure. Across the table, Bruce Mazzola blinked repeatedly, slowly recovering from the tongue-lashing he had just endured. It was then that Chuck Beekman cleared his throat and came up with the line of the day.

"Look on the bright side," he said to Bruce. "Just be glad he didn't have a *golf club* handy."

In spite of himself, Mazzola snorted a laugh. "You're right. Guy woulda bashed my lights out."

Then, Wheaton's chilly demeanor thawed, and a smile spread

across his lips. He shook his head at the memory of yesterday's irrational violence. "Yeah. I can do some damage with a golf club, all right."

"That's what I hear," McPhillips said with a grin.

Jeff Wheaton nodded and laughed at his own expense.

The wisecrack had caused the tension in the room to all but evaporate.

"I apologize, Bruce," Jeff Wheaton said cordially. "That wasn't me there, you know. I'm just on edge. You know?" He sighed with a measure of regret. "I'm sorry." Wheaton extended his hand in the spirit of friendship.

"Ah, fah geddaboudit," Bruce mumbled, pumping Wheaton's hand in a ballsy investment-banker clasp. "But Jesus, if you weren't such a close friend, I would've had to shatter your jawbone, talking to me that way." He said this with a laugh.

*Glasnost* accomplished, the strategy session began.

# 11

"There's a few things I need to say before we get down to brass tacks," Wheaton told them. "First thing I want to say is thanks for all the support you guys have given me, emotional and otherwise, for the last fifteen hours or so. Obviously, this has been a terrible personal tragedy for me, and you've been a great bunch of friends, the best a guy could ask for. That each of you agreed to accompany me here to New York, well, I'm especially grateful for that. Thanks a lot.

"Second thing is also very important. Let me tell every one of you that I'm going to insist on bearing the entire expense of this trip, and I won't hear another word about it."

McPhillips piped up. "Jeff, that's really beyond the call of duty here. There's no reason for it."

Wheaton held up his hand in a silencing gesture. "As I said, it's important to me. I've got my reasons for it, which I won't go into right now."

McPhillips did some quick mental calculations. The round-trip Amtrak tickets were forty-nine dollars apiece—that meant two hundred dollars just for the four of them to get there. The hotel was probably another three hundred or so. Hot pursuit wasn't going to come cheap.

Jeff Wheaton had brought two briefcases along. One was made of leather, the other of aluminum. Now he placed the leather briefcase on the table and snapped it open. "As you're painfully aware, we have to make one leap in logic to justify our efforts here. We have to assume that they're in New York City at this very moment."

"How do you figure New York?" Chuck Beekman asked.

"Two reasons. To take a jet to anywhere else in the world, you usually have to do it from New York. Secondly, my wife, Rachel, loves Manhattan. If she were going to leave the country for an extended period of time, she would insist on spending a weekend in New York first. That's just the way her mind works."

"But still," McPhillips said, "wouldn't Mitch be an idiot to stay in the country for a few days with the FBI hunting him down?"

"Yes, but you see, he *doesn't know* the FBI's onto him, not yet. He's all but certain the theft won't be discovered until Monday morning. And he would've been right, if it weren't for that fluke."

"What fluke?" Beekman asked.

"The fluke of that pension fund's check bouncing late yesterday afternoon. Otherwise, he would've had a full weekend to lose himself in New York City."

"Which is what he thinks he has right now," Brian said.

"Right."

McPhillips nodded. It *was* plausible that Mitch had gotten overconfident and sloppy. It would be entirely consistent with his character.

"Okay, now let's consider my wife, Rachel, for a minute," Wheaton said. "I speak from firsthand experience when I tell you that Rachel's a bit of a prima donna. When it comes to accommodations, for example, she's like a little Leona Helmsley. No Motel-6 for her."

The others laughed at the preposterous notion of Rachel at a Motel-6.

"Since she stays only at the truly five-star hotels, I've been able to narrow down the field quite considerably. Brian?"

On cue, McPhillips distributed the fresh copies of the document that the printer had issued a few minutes before. It was a list of luxury hotels in Manhattan, broken up into three categories:

| EAST SIDE | MIDTOWN | WEST SIDE |
|---|---|---|
| The Carlyle | Stanhope | Le Parker Meridien |
| Doral | Royalton | Helmsley Park Lane |
| Dorset | Ritz-Carlton | Wyndham |
| Mayfair Regent | Sherry Netherland | New York Vista |
| Grand Bay | Westbury | St. Moritz-on-the-Park |
| Pierre | Waldorf-Astoria | Omni Berkshire Place |
| Lowell | Peninsula | New York Helmsley |
| Regency | The Plaza | Inter-Continental |
| Helmsley Palace | Grand Hyatt | New York |
| U.N. Plaza | | |

"Wow," Mazzola enthused. "Jeff, babe, this is some piece of work."

"Where'd you get this list?" Beekman asked.

"Tommy Kawakami gave me a hand with this thing. He knows New York backward and forward. Took about an hour to whip this thing together from a copy of Zagat's and a New York Bureau of Tourism guide last night."

"Mutt-san and Jeff." Mazzola smiled.

"Way I figure it, we split these up into three bite-sized pieces, if you will. East Side, West Side, and Midtown. Between the three of us, we can canvass all of the major luxury hotels within three or four hours."

Chuck Beekman cleared his throat. "Jeff, my packet says JFK."

"Right. The fourth man has to canvass the airport."

"Canvass the airport? That sounds like shitwork to me."

"On the contrary, Chuck. That's the most important role. But if you'll hold that thought, I'll come to it shortly. Let me finish the hotels first, all right?"

Beekman nodded, but he had a sour look on his face.

Bruce Mazzola then spoke up. "Jeff?"

"Yes?"

"I see that you gave Brian the West Side and myself Midtown. If it's all the same to Bri, I'd like to swap with him and take the West Side. When I worked for Drexel, I stayed at most of these hotels on the West Side list, like Le Parker Meridien and the St. Moritz. I bet I still know most of the personnel at these places."

"Brian?" Jeff said.

"Doesn't much matter to me," McPhillips shrugged. "I'll take Midtown."

"Fine," Jeff Wheaton said. "Then why don't you guys switch?"

They did.

Then Wheaton said, "Okay, let's open up the packets now."

Each man unclasped his envelope and shook out its contents: a colorful map clipped to a manila envelope.

"On the top is a color photocopy of a street map of Manhattan," Jeff Wheaton said. "You'll note that I've highlighted in hot pink the most direct route to follow in covering the eight or nine hotels assigned to you. Most of the five-star hotels are clustered together, so it should be no more than five to ten minutes' walking distance between locations. You follow?

"Now, there's another manila envelope attached to the top sheet. Go ahead and open that."

McPhillips unclasped his second envelope and let the papers inside tumble out onto the table. There were twelve collated sets of three color photographs, enlarged on glossy photocopy paper, each set bound by a paper clip.

"We have a Canon color copier at the office," Wheaton explained. "Kawakami'll probably have a conniption when I tell him on Monday that I made four hundred color copies over the weekend, but what the hell. It's not like it's gonna push the company into Chapter 11."

McPhillips leafed through the photocopies. They were remarkably crisp reproductions of the original photographs. The top two photos of each set were of Rachel Wheaton; the third was of Mitch Myerson. At the top of each page was the legend: Rachel Wheaton/Mitch Myerson—$10,000 Reward for Info Leading to Their Whereabouts—(212) 959-9768.

The first photograph of Rachel was an alluring head-and-shoulders shot taken a little over a year before, when Rachel was feverishly pursuing a career in modeling. She had cheekbones to break your heart and bedroom eyes that gazed at the camera in a smoky, seductive way. The second photograph captured her standing astride a ten-speed bicycle on an autumn day in Fairmount Park. She wore a gleaming bicycling outfit that form-fit her like a second skin. A wisp of her blond hair spilled over one eye. Her smile was dazzling, and she seemed flushed with contentment. Brian guesstimated that the shot was taken less than a year ago, in the happier times before she made up her mind to run off with another man.

The third photograph of the set was a two-shot of both Jeff Wheaton and Mitch Myerson at the Bala Cynwyd Country Club. McPhillips had seen it several times before, once in the Wharton alumni newsletter a few years ago. It was a photograph taken of them the day Jeff shot a hole-in-one at the ninth hole. Both men were beaming broadly in this picture. In one hand, Jeff held the prized golf ball aloft; in the other, the eight iron he had used to accomplish the feat. Next to him, Mitch held up a single finger to indicate Jeff's ace and a placard stating: WHEATON ACES 9TH HOLE, BALA CYNWYD C.C., 7-15-89. Despite the outward appearance of pride for his golfing companion, McPhillips was convinced that at the time, the bastard was probably dying inside that Jeff had scored the ace and not *him*. Mitch Myerson was a notorious practitioner of schadenfreude.

Then McPhillips felt a twinge of depression when he realized how much happiness was embodied by these photographs. The happiness they conveyed stood in stark incongruity to the grim resolve of the task at hand.

"All right, now listen up," Jeff said. "Here's the game plan. What you'll do at each hotel is you'll first approach the concierge. You'll grease the palm. Slip him a twenty."

"Slip him a twenty?" Mazzola said.

Without a word, Jeff Wheaton withdrew from the leather briefcase two thick packets of white envelopes bound by rubber bands. He tossed them casually. They made slapping noises when they landed on the table.

"That part's covered," Wheaton said softly.

Mazzola opened one of the packets. "Jesus Christ!" he cried out.

Each envelope was stuffed with tens and twenties.

"How much is in here?"

"About four hundred dollars. A twenty and two tens for each hotel. I don't like to think of it as a bribe, per se. I prefer to think of it as incentive money."

McPhillips thumbed through the crisp bills in his white envelope and wondered if Jeff Wheaton had taken leave of his senses.

Jeff continued, "So you give him a twenty. Then you'll show him the photos. Tell him you're looking for these two people, ask if he's seen them. Rachel, at least, tends to make an impression, and maybe he'll recognize her immediately when he sees a photo. You might also try to jog his memory. Ask him if these two people spoke to him about tickets to a Broadway show, a restaurant, a museum, whatever. If he remembers seeing them, call the cops immediately and call me. If he has no recollection of them, then urge him to keep his eyes opened. They may come into the hotel some time during his shift.

"Then, move over to the registration area. Give ten dollars apiece to the front desk personnel. Ask them the same questions. Ask them to check the register. Maybe they're under Rachel's maiden name, Fairweather. Maybe they're under one of our names. That may sound ludicrous, but often a con artist will use the name of one of his victims as an alias.

"Leave everyone with a set of photographs, there's plenty to go around. And always, always—remind them of the ten-thousand-dollar reward."

Jeff Wheaton looked about the table to see if everyone was following him. Then he said, "What we'll do after we wrap up here is go downstairs to the guest services desk of the Grand Hyatt, and I'll show you how I think it should be handled. Any questions?"

There were none.

"Okay, then, one last thing before we turn to canvassing the airports. Communications."

Wheaton placed the aluminum briefcase up on the table. He opened it up. Cradled inside was a Bell Atlantic self-contained cellular telephone.

"You can reach me at any time from any pay phone on this," Jeff told them.

Beekman whistled in awe. "With the computers and the portable phones, this really is a high-tech manhunt."

"Fuckin' James Bond, that's what he is," Mazzola snorted in amusement. Yet even he seemed impressed.

Then Wheaton withdrew what looked like three cheap plastic watches and handed one to each of the men. "Take this and put it on your wrist."

McPhillips strapped it on and inspected it. Its face bore the Motorola logo.

Wheaton said, "This is a wristwatch pager. Brand-new gadget that Motorola just came out with. If something happens on my end, I'll beep you guys immediately from the cellular phone. If you need to get ahold of me, the phone's been assigned a number with the New York area code, (212) 959-9768. The number is on a sticker affixed to the band of your wristwatch pager, and it appears on each copy of the photographs you've been given."

"Out-fucking-rageous," Mazzola said, shaking his head in utter amazement. "James Bond meets Dick Tracy."

Chuck Beekman could barely contain his excitement. "Hey, wouldn't that be fucking wild, man? Wouldn't it be wild if we really did catch those guys here in New York? We'd wind up *nationally famous*. Celebrities!"

Brian McPhillips drew in a deep breath. While Chuck's optimism was buoyant, his was guarded. Wheaton had done his homework, that was for certain, and they were fired up some, each man prepared to a man to give it the old college try. If Mitch and Rachel *were* in New York, maybe, just maybe, they could get lucky and nail 'em. Okay, it was still a long shot, but hell, Wheaton had decreased the odds as much as possible. The rest was up to them.

McPhillips exhaled anxiously.

The Motorola wristwatch pager indicated that it was now almost noon.

*All we need now is a fucking miracle*, McPhillips said to himself.

# PART FOUR

### SATURDAY AFTERNOON
### JUNE 27, 1992

# 12

Five time zones away, a man known affectionately among his intimates as "The Saint" sat in the comfortable chill of his lavish fifty-first-floor office in a London skyscraper. His face was a frown of concentration, awash in the ghostly light emitted by the nine computer monitors arranged in a high-tech honeycomb before him.

Accumulating vast quantities of information was an obsession for The Saint; computer databases were unquestionably the most efficient, up-to-the-second means to this end. The screens flickered with activity: news stories and archival retrievals from Reuters, Dow Jones, NEXIS, Associated Press . . . various graphs of the previous week's market movements in currency, commodity, and equities marketplaces around the globe. So many exchanges to follow: the PHLX in Philadelphia, the London and New York Exchanges, the Merc in Chicago, the SIMEX in Singapore, the MATIF in Paris . . .

His gray-flecked pupils flitted from screen to screen as he tracked the never-ending moneystream. Billions of pounds coursing electronically about the planet before his very eyes. He could watch the screens for hours. He often did: The Saint needed only three or four hours of sleep, which permitted him to keep vigil throughout the night. It was a passion.

His concentration was broken by a series of sharp beeps from one of the computers. It was the alarm function of a time-management program, preset for 5:00 P.M. each afternoon. The alarm reminded the banker that it was time for his twice-daily medication. He silenced the alarm by poking the ESC key with a ring finger, on which he wore a 1983 World Series championship ring bestudded with diamonds. The Saint had obtained the artifact from a down-on-his-luck ex–big leaguer in the U.S. It was a surefire conversation piece The Saint wore everywhere.

Raoul St. Germaine withdrew a bottle of Volvic from the refrigerator beneath the bar and filled a Fleur Tokey–designed goblet until it was brimming. He withdrew six plastic bottles containing powders of various exotic minerals and natural extracts. There were two amino acids—phenylalanine and selegiline (1-deprenyl). There was ephedra, an herb from China reputed to have medicinal powers; ginkgobiloba, an extract from the bark of the ginkgo tree. Also, a vitamin-B complex. The sixth receptacle held lemon-flavored Crystal Lite, to make the concoction more palatable.

St. Germaine spooned equal measures of the ingredients into the goblet and stirred briskly until all had dissolved into a yellowish formula. Then he inserted three prescription tablets into his mouth—L-Arginine, an anti–Alzheimer's disease prescription ordered by mail from Switzerland; Piracetam, a supposed memory enhancer available in Europe only; and Hydergine, an extract of ergot approved in the United States as a remedy for Alzheimer's disease—and washed them down with a few swallows of his elixir.

Instantly, The Saint experienced a rush of energy and a surge in clarity. It was as if a high-intensity light had snapped on in his cerebrum.

For two years now, Raoul St. Germaine had been a vigorous proponent of these so-called "smart drugs," compounds that allegedly boosted memory, perception, and intelligence. St. Germaine swore by them. Not that he especially needed smart drugs. He possessed an IQ of 172, spoke eight languages fluently, and was legendary in high society for his near-photographic recall of names and faces. Perhaps he didn't *need* the extra 10 IQ points the smart drugs conferred upon him, but he always found good use for his enhanced intelligence.

Refreshed, St. Germaine took the opportunity to stretch a bit. He strode over to the glass wall of his office with its commanding view of South London. The Canary Wharf development project was less than half a kilometer away. St. Germaine gazed upon the hulking, half-completed shell that doomed the Reichmann brothers' global empire and had in the process killed off many a lesser bank. The Hemisphere Bank of Exchange, Internationale, had purchased three million pounds of Canary Wharf debt in the secondary market and had lost nearly all of it. Yet St. Germaine still considered it a good investment. Ironically, to be mentioned in the same breath as the Bank of Toronto, the Bank of England, and Citibank USA in connection with such a highly publicized financial debacle was a welcome turn of events. It gave The Saint's bank the imprimatur of legitimacy. Diverted unwanted attention away from its lesser-known but more lucrative operations.

As Raoul paced the expanse of his office, the sound-absorbing plushness of the carpeting cushioned his footfalls. St. Germaine's workspace was spectacularly appointed. It had to be. His prospective clientele consisted largely of British aristocracy and European financiers from around the continent. The office boasted a fully functional bar on the one side, the impressive formation of computer monitors on the other. The gilded mahogany desk that dominated the room had been handcrafted from non-rainforest materials by the celebrated British designer Nicholas Pryke. The walls were taken up by an awe-inspiring collection of masterworks by nineteenth-century American Impressionists. The Saint was supremely confident that these works had been wildly undervalued by collectors and would at least triple in value when Japanese investors returned to the marketplace. The banker had an 1886 Long Island seascape by William Merritt Chase, a portrait of a dour-faced aristocrat by John Singer Sargent, and an early work by Edwin Church. His mansion in Highgate contained a half dozen others.

Movie star–handsome, The Saint was always deeply tanned and athletically trim. He had Paul McCartney eyebrows that made him appear eternally inquisitive and a cupid's-bow pout to his lips. He looked quite a bit younger than his thirty-nine years, which was attributable in no small part to his enthusiasm for cosmetic surgery. St. Germaine believed the proper scalpel-wielding surgeon could effortlessly erase facial imperfections that would otherwise hinder one's self-esteem. Cosmetic surgery clearly worked for The Saint. Most everyone acquainted with him agreed he exuded a positively royal demeanor.

His father had been a successful banker before him, so St. Germaine had firm roots in the privileged upper-class of British society. He had attended the Balliol prep school with Robert Maxwell's children, Ian and Kevin. He graduated Oxford with honors and then the London School of Economics where he was second in his class. He had taken scrupulous care to marry properly, having courted and won the hand of much-sought-after socialite Miss Amanda Yearwood-Courage.

From all outward appearances, their marriage seemed sturdy. The couple divided their time between a mansion in Highgate, a weekend place in Wiltshire, and a flat in Knightsbridge. At the annual Hemisphere Bank affair in the South of France, it was always Amanda St. Germaine who was the darling of the event, chirping, *"So* lovely to see you, dear" to the pampered clients. She was the hostess with the mostest, the lady who emptied every hothouse within a 15-kilometer radius to see to it that her guests' quarters were overflowing with flowers. It was Amanda who at last year's lavish function had placed the baby-blue velvet pouch on everyone's plate, the one with the solid-gold ingot secreted inside.

Contrary to appearances, however, the St. Germaines had by mutual consent separated. Theirs had become a marriage of convenience. In keeping with the Bank's best interests, Amanda never breathed a word of their estrangement to a soul in return for the weekend place, the flat in Knightsbridge, and a most generous stipend. Perhaps against his better reason, Raoul indulged himself a bit much in his newfound bachelorhood, diddling several of his estranged wife's socialite friends. But when word reached him that Amanda was seen consorting with Lord Nigel Dunkirk-Sexsmith, a proper wanker with a cheeky attitude, The Saint was furious. Raoul had retaliated in kind by seducing Lady Dunkirk-Sexsmith at the Ritz-Carlton, introducing her to a very close friend of his by the name of John Thomas. Her Ladyship made the most peculiar noises while under the influence of the Big O, an observation he shared with Lord Nigel one afternoon at an especially competitive cricket match.

The moment he had inherited the banking empire at the untimely death of his father, Raoul had set about building the business into an intercontinental financial powerhouse. In doing so, St. Germaine called upon his prodigious wealth of charms, building a network of the powerful and the influential that was astounding in its breadth. He took colossal pride in his personal relationships with numerous MPs—Members of Parliament—with both the Tory and Labor parties as well as his vast contacts within the Westminster lobbying community and on Fleet Street. The *London Observer* named him to its most recent list of the Twenty-five Most Influential Men in Britain, calling St. Germaine "a charismatic, brash, and street-savvy private-banker in the tradition of Edward Safra."

Most gratifying to St. Germaine, however, was his ability to combine his passion for sport with his appetite to build a truly global bank. A major coup came when he wangled a coveted invitation to join the Cambridge Old Merchant Taylors' cricket team in London's celebrity league. The celebrity league was packed with moguls and movie stars. St. Germaine promptly established himself as the team's premiere batsman and a bloody good long-stop. In the first season, The Saint powered his team to victories over such formidable opponents as the Marlborough Blues, The Earl of Carnarvon's XI, the Hottentots, and the Lavinia Duchess of Norfolk XI. Next season, St. Germaine was elevated to captain by unanimous vote.

One Sunday afternoon, the Old Merchant Taylors were scheduled to play Bunbury's, a team studded with ale-swizzling rock stars: Bill Wyman, Simon LeBon, Ronnie Wood, and Eric Clapton. Early on, St. Germaine cracked a ball off the thick of his wicket that struck Clapton squarely on his guitar hand. Clapton howled and sprinted to the side of the pitch to submerge his throbbing hand in ice water, all the while fretting that his upcoming tour of Japan was in serious jeopardy. True to form, St. Germaine seized the moment to sell Clapton on the personalized banking services *only Hemisphere* could provide. . . .

\* \* \*

Raoul St. Germaine took immense delight in the irony of his sobriquet.

For he was hardly a saint.

He was, in fact, quite the opposite.

While it was true that most of his bank's funds came from wealthy individuals who valued St. Germaine's personal approach to their private banking needs, he had another source of revenue. This source provided business that was far more lucrative than that for which he was renowned.

It was the sort of business St. Germaine could not publicize.

In recent years, he had quietly cultivated a reputation for himself as the man to call if you needed to bankroll your covert operation.

He was extremely aggressive in this arena. He took no moral high ground when it came to the political, moral, or religious objectives of the group seeking funding. No, he was not an ideologue in any sense of the word.

He cared only that the client was ready, willing, and able to pay the spread he demanded.

Conveniently enough, payment could be tendered in oil, gold, or other natural resources. He had set up a shell corporation in Luxembourg for the purpose of bartering the futures contracts of such commodities on the various futures exchanges around the world. His fees were high, of course, but not excessively so, considering he was engaging in bloody dangerous business and was often the only source to turn to.

He had begun by bankrolling minor-league terrorists in the Middle East and armed insurgencies in highly unstable Latin American countries. From there, sales of sophisticated weaponry to Third World countries was the logical progression and a very remunerative avenue for The Saint. Wars and national drug crises proved to be big business for him. Indeed, he had played a crucial role in financing some events that made headlines on the front pages of newspapers around the world.

His secret list of clients included the Contras and the rebels of Afghanistan. He had played matchmaker with West German chemical experts and Third World generals who dreamed of nuclear capabilities as a means of erasing their historical enemies. He provided short-term capital and extensive money-laundering services for the Cali cartel in its ambitious plan to expand its crack-cocaine operations into Germany, France, and the rest of the European Community, a plan that had been executed with great success.

Working through third-party operatives, he had arranged for Middle East mercenaries to create a military camp for training bodyguards for Colombian drug billionaires. He provided financing for a settlement hastily erected in the occupied West Bank. He counted the CIA among his clients and was chagrined that the KGB had not approached him before the fall of the Soviet Union. He enjoyed the company of and had mastered the customs and etiquette of Middle Eastern cultures, which had opened up a vast wealth of opportunities for his operation. When the Iranians needed a middleman, they knew who to call in the dead of the night.

One of his specialties was assisting dictators in absconding with billions of dollars looted from national treasuries of poor countries. With a network of banks spread around the globe, he effortlessly set up an intricate shell game that concealed the money trail. On behalf of one dictator, he purchased $125 million in New York City real estate and collectible works of seventeenth-century Dutch masters. He skimmed a good portion of this for himself.

Of the utmost importance in his line of work was knowing when to say no. When Iraqi emissaries desperately sought an audience with him to plead for assistance in securing arms during the final weeks of the Persian Gulf War, St. Germaine turned a deaf ear. Such an operation was too hot to handle. U.S. intelligence could have found him out, which would have brought his empire crashing down.

That was the fate of his major competitor, the mighty Bank of Credit and Commerce International. When BCCI collapsed and its myriad of sins and scandals came light in late 1990, St. Germaine nearly trembled with ambition. He was amused by the international press' outrage over what had happened at BCCI. If only they knew the whole of it! BCCI was just the tip of the iceberg. What would they print if they knew of *his* operations?

Now that the titanic BCCI had fallen to a heap of rubble, a

power vacuum existed in this particular sphere of financial influence. The Saint was poised to step in.

But he had to be cautious. There was always the temptation to a man of The Saint's ambition to rush right in. He prided himself on having the patience of, well, a saint. A low profile was key. Mustn't act capriciously; mustn't take unnecessary risks. If he continued apace, he was the heir apparent to much of the business once handled by BCCI.

Now this American embezzlement thing was something of a snack to The Saint—an $18.7-million electronic scam that he had orchestrated on behalf of an American and his lover out of Philadelphia, Pennsylvania. A complete no-brainer. All he had to do was marshal the stolen funds among the various banks he controlled throughout the globe until no investigator could possibly discern where they went. For this, he was to personally receive a fee of two million U.S. dollars.

Not bad for a weekend's worth of work.

But the fee was one thing; the enticement of this challenge was quite another. This American thing was a dry run for a much broader scheme—a series of massive computer frauds on a global scale. If this one worked, The Saint would engineer similar scams at the world's largest banks. Next time it would be *hundreds* of millions. The funds would eventually settle in dummy accounts in banks The Saint outright owned or otherwise influenced.

It never ceased to amaze The Saint how billions of pounds in electronic money could be made to disappear within a matter of minutes only to reappear elsewhere without a trace. This sort of scheme, he predicted, would be the instrumentality for the greatest crimes between now and the end of the century. Billions would switch hands.

The Saint peered out of the window on the fifty-first floor, looking out over the sprawl of construction sites at Canary Wharf. Sporadic bursts of light from a welding torch captured his attention for a moment. It was like an S.O.S. in Morse code.

Time to ring up the bank and see if the pot-addled Yank named Myerson had been by for his bundle. St. Germaine picked up the telephone and put in a transcontinental call to Mr. Mahmood, his man on American soil.

# 13

There must be some mistake. . . .

Mitch Myerson looked again at the address on the piece of paper he held in his hands. He read it aloud. "Forty-six East Sixty-eighth Street."

Then he peered at the address on the brass plate of the three-story brownstone. 46 East Sixty-eighth Street.

They were one and the same.

Couldn't be, Myerson thought to himself. A bank in a brownstone? A wave of panic washed over him as it occurred to him that St. Germaine had provided the wrong address.

Myerson stepped back from the building and into the street. A welcome breeze whipped up, tousling his hair. Myerson jammed his hands in the pockets of his chinos, and he casually glanced up and down the block. There were Mercedes and BMW cars parked along both sides of this section of Sixty-eighth Street, virtually all of them bearing either diplomatic or MD license plates. Two long black limos idled patiently across the street.

Located two blocks east of Central Park, between Park and Madison Avenues, this stretch of East Sixty-eighth Street was pristine and peaceful, a secluded respite from the insanity typical of New York City. The neighborhood was residential in nature, populated mostly by diplomats and consulate generals, assigned by the governments of their homelands to represent them at the

United Nations. With the exception of the medical offices of a few prominent plastic surgeons, there appeared to be no commercial establishments located on this block, much less a bank.

Nor did the brownstone at 46 East Sixty-eighth Street resemble anything like a bank branch. It was a handsome structure, nestled between the consulate general of South Africa and that of the Dominican Republic. The entryway of the brownstone had two huge cherrywood doors, carved in an intricate bas-relief. It was protected by an imposing black wrought-iron gate with sharp metal spikes atop the posts. All in all, this was an elegant fortress. A home fit for a diplomat certainly. But for a bank? Mitch Myerson didn't think so.

Myerson stepped down the six speckled-cement stairs to the double door to take one last look. It was only then that he noticed the unassuming three-by-five-inch brass plate on the side of the entryway, affixed there as if it was someone's afterthought: THE HEMISPHERE BANK OF EXCHANGE, INTERNATIONALE.

The discovery made Myerson smile. Leave it to St. Germaine to come up with some discreet, clandestine operation far off the beaten track to launder Mitch's dirty money. *No CitiBank for The Saint, uh-uh.*

It was then that Myerson noticed not one security camera trained on him—not two—but *three*. One peered at him from the left side, another from the right. The third one scanned him from behind the dark crescent-shaped glass above the doors. They were big, ugly cameras, sinister in size and appearance, unblinkingly recording his likeness in a technically intricate setup perfectly suited for a network sitcom production. A cord the girth of a swamp snake tailed out of the back of each black oblong box and into the exterior wall of the brownstone.

Myerson stabbed a finger at the button beneath the nameplate. He heard the distant sound of the buzzer from deep within the brownstone.

An electronic voice crackled through the speaker. "Identify yourself, please."

"Richard Positano," Mitch replied, in a voice so loud he startled himself.

"Hold, please."

Despite the electronic distortion of the voice, Mitch detected the trace of an accent.

The voice returned. "Please state your account number, Mr. Positano."

"I have no account with you."

"Sorry, repeat please."

"I don't have an account with this bank."

A pause. Then: "State your business, please."

"I am a client of Raoul St. Germaine. He sent me here."

The mere mention of St. Germaine's name was like a magic phrase, the illicit banker's equivalent of "open sesame." A harsh buzzer sounded, and, concurrently, Myerson heard a solid click within the lock of the metal grating. The grating receded mechanically into a recess in the doorjamb. Myerson stepped forward and turned the knob to one of the cherrywood doors. It opened with a squeal of the hinges, and Mitch walked into a dark, narrow corridor about eight feet long, the end of which was sealed off by another, more formidable double door constructed of forged steel. This doorway seemed as impenetrable as a bank vault.

Presently, the steel doors opened from within. A dark-skinned man of enormous girth appeared. He had a neatly trimmed beard and wore an Italian suit that appeared to be straining at the seams. The man was of Middle Eastern descent. Arabic, Israeli, Egyptian . . . Myerson was unable to discern which. Mitch ventured a guess at the man's weight: two hundred-fifty, two-seventy-five pounds. He had black, foreboding eyes beneath a single continuous eyebrow thick as a mustache. His oily black hair was combed back into a slick ponytail. His Neanderthal demeanor suggested a propensity for engaging in unspeakable violence.

"Please do not be offended," the man said in a voice that was no more than a whisper, shocking Mitch with its softness. Mitch noticed an unusual instrument in the man's hand, a thin tube of metal fashioned into the shape of a six-inch loop. When the man swept the instrument over Myerson's person, Mitch realized it was a metal detector.

The detector sounded with a shrill siren.

The man whispered, "Have you any metal concealed in your clothes?"

"Are you asking me if I am carrying a gun?"

"Any metal at all, please." The security man produced a plastic tray from a nearby credenza. Mitch placed his spare change, his Cross pen, his new Baume and Mercier watch, and his keys on the tray. The loud jangle caused by the keys echoed in the confines of the narrow corridor, and Mitch found himself staring at them for a few seconds. He realized with some amazement that he would never have a use for any of them ever again. Their usefulness ended the moment his new life began. It was truly a symbol that he and Rachel had the unshackled freedom to do whatever the hell they wanted from this day forward. . . .

The man swept over Myerson again with the device. This final inspection resulted in only a few amplified clicks that reminded Mitch of a Geiger counter. Satisfied that the customer posed no potential breach to the bank's security, the man returned Mitch's personal effects. "Thank you for your cooperation, sir," the behemoth whispered. "Please, if you would be so kind as to follow me."

The security man showed Myerson into the lobby and told him that an officer would attend to him momentarily. Then the hulking security official disappeared into an elevator. Alone, Mitch Myerson settled comfortably into the cushions of a plush couch and looked around at the lobby of the Hemisphere Bank of Exchange, Internationale.

Conspicuously missing was any sort of Cirrus cash machine or an area for filling out deposit and withdrawal slips, the staples of the conventional neighborhood bank. For the most part, however, the interior *did* resemble a legitimate bank. The lobby was well appointed and pleasing to the eye, decorated tastefully with fine prints and sculptures from contemporary artists. An exquisite grandfather clock stood in a corner like a reliable sentinel, ticking metronomically. There was a lavish Turkish rug running the full expanse of the floor and antique lamps on the burnished walnut furniture.

The other side of the room was commanded by a chest-level marble counter designed to serve customers, although it was considerably smaller in size than that of a typical commercial bank. It seemed to Myerson that the counter could accommodate only one teller at a time. Beyond the counter, a large brass plate bore the Helvetica logo of Hemisphere Bank of Exchange, Internationale. On the counter itself, there was a modest, stand-up placard that announced ASK ABOUT OUR EXCHANGE RATE FOR RUSSIAN RUBLES. Myerson knew that, generally speaking, rubles were not traded by legitimate international banks. In addition to the placard, there were four full-color posters touting Hemisphere Bank's preoccupation with exchanging foreign currency for its customers. Each poster was illustrated with photographs of dozens of foreign currency notes and was emblazoned with a bold legend at the top that stated: LET US EXCHANGE YOUR FOREIGN CURRENCY. In small print was the proviso: $10,000 MINIMUM

Finally, Myerson's eyes rested on a large electronic toteboard on the wall to his right. In glowing neon red digits, the board displayed the bank's current rates of exchange for francs, marks, pounds, lira, guilders, yen, pesetas, kronas, schillings, shekels, pesos, and drachmas. Myerson committed the rate for Italian lira to memory: WE BUY AT 000750. WE SELL AT 000834.

Instinctively, Mitch Myerson knew this operation was not legit. After all, St. Germaine would not have sent him here if it were. The clandestine aura shrouding this bank caused his imagination to run freely. Did Hemisphere Bank of Exchange finance international terrorists? Gunrunners? Dictators? Drug rings? The Contras? The CIA? The KGB? What type of front-page headlines would result if this bank were seized by the federal government? Mitch suspected that a "60 Minutes" exposé of Hemisphere would spell the demise of scores of diplomats, drug czars, and politicians. He made a mental note to bring it up with St. Germaine when they reconnoitered in Paris in late July to toast their twenty-million-dollar triumph.

The bell to the elevator pealed softly, and the doors opened. An elegant Middle Eastern gentleman in his mid-thirties stepped out, accompanied by a striking, dark-skinned woman in black haute couture fashion. He carried about him an air of international intrigue and self-confidence; on first impression, one would take him for either the son of Middle Eastern royalty or a handsome, refined terrorist. He had dark eyes and a finely groomed mustache, a fleshy face with a disarming smile. His hair, like the first man's, was swept back into a ponytail, where it dangled like a comma. The woman was slim and elegant, her shiny blue-black hair pulled back in a bun. She had three strands of cultured pearls about her neck and Bulgari rings on the majority of her dark, slender fingers. Her lips were a smear of suggestive, brilliant red lipstick. A world-class ice princess. She reminded Myerson of the women in that Robert Palmer video on MTV, "Simply Irresistible." The woman appeared cryptic, aloof, and untouchable.

"Mr. Positano," the man said, offering his hand as he approached.

Myerson stood up. "Yes." They shook hands.

"We have been expecting you," the man said. "Welcome to the Hemisphere Bank of Exchange. My name is Mr. Mahmood."

Mahmood spoke perfect English, with an almost imperceptible trace of an accent. St. Germaine had told him that Mahmood was strictly Ivy League-educated, Yale undergrad, Harvard M.B.A.

"It is a pleasure," Myerson said.

"Permit me to apologize once again for any inconvenience you might have endured as a result of our extensive security measures."

"You owe me no apology, Mr. Mahmood."

"As you may know, the professional services we offer our clients are considered quite, shall we say, *unconventional* by American banking standards. It is best not to involve the authorities in our business. Thus, imposing the most strict security measures possible is imperative."

"So I see," Myerson said. "In fact, you've done such a commendable job keeping this bank secluded, it's nearly impossible to find."

Mahmood chuckled, merriment playing in his dark eyes. "We have no need to be located on a busy corner in the center of New York, Mr. Positano. Quite the contrary, this is the perfect location to serve our international clientele. They know precisely where to find us."

It occurred to Mitch Myerson that on a per-transaction basis, the Hemisphere Bank of Exchange, Internationale could be the most lucrative banking institution in all of New York.

"Would you care for some coffee, Mr. Positano? We have an especially fine brew for the pleasure of our clients."

"Please."

He turned to the woman and said, "Anya, a cup of our finest roast for Mr. Positano." The woman nodded formally and disappeared. Something caused Myerson to believe that Anya and Mr. Mahmood were doing the nasty thing, some nonverbal signal he had intercepted.

Mr. Mahmood beckoned. "Come with me, Mr. Positano, please."

Mitch Myerson followed Mahmood into the elevator. As they rode to the fourth floor, Mahmood casually told Myerson, "The stairwell is constructed entirely of highly conductive steel. At night, it is electrified with a high-voltage charge to repel any intruders."

Myerson nodded, expressing fascination. He was uncertain as to how he was expected to react to this nugget of trivia.

They arrived on the fourth floor, where all pretenses of legitimacy had been dropped in the design. Each room was spartan and windowless, the center of which was dominated by long tables. Each table had a state-of-the-art money-counting machine and a currency-bundling device on it. Myerson peered casually into each room as he followed Mahmood down the corridor. They passed a room with an open door. The sound of men conversing jovially in Mandarin Chinese intrigued Myerson, causing him to look inside. He glimpsed several Chinese men smoking filterless cigarettes amidst a thick haze of blue smoke. Some of them were feeding money into counting machines. Mitch lingered in front of the open door, staring at the table, mesmerized by all the money there. One of the Chinese men noticed him and locked eyes with Mitch. A feral expression of crazed violence contorted his face, but before the Chinese man could rise up from his seat to strike Mitch, Mahmood stepped between them and closed the door. "This way, please." Mahmood's tone was polite, but firm.

Mahmood led him to a back office that had a mahogany desk. He motioned for Myerson to take the seat facing the desk. Mahmood walked around the expanse of the desk and slipped into the oversized leather chair. Mitch noticed that the desk was completely free of papers.

"You may wonder why a man of Faheed's size speaks with the whisper of a child," Mahmood said. "A few years ago, you see, was a very dark time for his country. He was abducted off the street by political revolutionaries. When they accused him of not coming forth with all that he knew, they took two steel bars"—Mahmood used two pencils to demonstrate—"and pressed them against his neck, like a vise. They did that for several days, for many hours at a time. He nearly died, of course. It was terrible there. All the wealthy fled for their lives, left their mansions behind and came to America." Mahmood shrugged. "Faheed left his voice behind." After a pregnant pause, he provided the moral of the story. "Americans, they take so much for granted living in such a free country."

Myerson nodded reverently, but said to himself, *Shut up and gimme the cash already.*

"Tell me," Mahmood said, brightening, "how is our good friend Raoul St. Germaine?"

"Quite well," Myerson said simply. In fact, he scarcely knew the man. He had met St. Germaine on only a handful of occasions—for two secret breakfast meetings a month apart at the Four Seasons Hotel in Philadelphia and once in London.

"Please send my warmest regards, and, if you speak with him before I do, thank him for the lovely Fabergé egg. It was a most thoughtful birthday gift."

"I will do so," Mitch assured him. But at the moment, Myerson was less concerned about conveying pleasantries to his secretive banker than he was about getting his hands on the one hundred thousand dollars' worth of Italian currency he was here to receive. "Now, let's talk about the business at hand—I assume everything is in order?"

Mahmood met Myerson's impatience with a smile. "You may put your mind at ease, sir. We have followed the instructions in Mr. St. Germaine's communiqué to the letter. As always." Mr. Mahmood opened the top drawer of the desk and withdrew a legal pad with some writing on the front page. "That notwithstanding, I must beg your patience, Mr. Positano. I have some supplemental questions to ask. Questions that are meant to ensure a safe passage to your destination without interference from inquisitive United States Customs officials."

Myerson nodded. "By all means."

At that moment, the elevator door opened, and the woman named Anya appeared with a tray full of Limoges china and a selection of sweets. Mahmood waited. On the tray was a sterling silver decanter of steaming coffee, an elegant matching cup and saucer, a small pitcher of chilled cream, a sugar bowl and an arrangement of fancy cookies and fruit tarts. As Anya bowed to place the tray on the low table next to Myerson, he could feel her warm breath on his cheek. Her business finished, she wordlessly disappeared from the room.

Mr. Mahmood put on a pair of reading glasses and scanned the sheet. "Do you have any familiarity with the American customs laws regarding currency brought in and out of the United States on international flights?"

"Only a passing familiarity. Any amount of cash over ten thousand dollars is supposed to be declared, right?"

"That is correct. You are by law required to file a formal notice with the Treasury Department at the airport before you depart. This is something that I assume you wish to avoid?"

Mitch Myerson hesitated. He wasn't certain he liked the question. "Of course," he said finally.

"The purpose of which, I assume, is to avoid any contact whatsoever with any law-enforcement authorities when you leave the country?"

Mitch bristled at this inquiry. "I don't see the point of your question," he said brusquely. "Are you asking if I'm a fugitive from the law?"

Mahmood hastened to reassure him. "Please, Mr. Positano. Any information you give me is held in the utmost confidence. If this were not so, Raoul St. Germaine most certainly would not have sent you to me. I am here to *help* you. Please."

The mention of St. Germaine's name soothed Mitch some. It was true: St. Germaine himself placed the highest trust in Mahmood. He *had to be* reliable. "Okay, yes. That's a correct statement. I don't want any unnecessary attention."

Mahmood nodded and fingered his mustache thoughtfully.

"As you probably know, the U.S. Customs officials have become quite clever over the last decade. It has become increasingly difficult to elude their scrutiny. You understand, they have caught on to almost every currency-smuggling method imaginable. They have learned that children are frequently used as couriers, with money stuffed into their teddy bears and soiled diapers. They have discovered money being smuggled in portable computers, undergarments, shoes, even—most distastefully—in one's private orifices." Mahmood leaned forward to hammer home his point. "As such, Customs has been given the absolute lawful discretion to peer into your asshole with a flashlight if they damn well please and for that reason alone, I cannot emphasize enough the potential danger to you and your companion. You will be carrying almost eighty million Italian lira in your belongings."

The gravity of this weighed in on Mitch for the first time. Smuggling one hundred thousand dollars in currency onto an international flight, it seemed, would be no cakewalk. They could get caught—

Mr. Mahmood continued. "It is my understanding that you are bound for Europe?"

"Yes."

"That is good. Very good. U.S. Customs has limited resources, and most of its manpower is devoted to Colombians, South Americans, and Latin Americans who are entering or leaving the country. Blacks and Hispanics who fit what the authorities call 'the drug courier profile.' Your companion, is she black or Hispanic?"

"Neither."

"Good. Now, your luggage, is it soft-sided or hard-sided?"

"Soft-sided."

"Good."

Mitch Myerson was mystified. "Why is that good?"

"Customs has the time and the personnel to make only selective searches of luggage. It is well known that false bottoms and false sides are most easily created in the hard-sided suitcases, so nine times out of ten, Customs officials are more likely to seize that type of bag in a random search."

Myerson nodded. You learn something new every day.

"In addition," Mahmood said, "you must have tags affixed to your luggage. Even if you use an assumed name and false address. Baggage without name tags is automatically suspicious to Customs officials. Do you have tags on your luggage?"

"No, but now that you've mentioned it, I'll do that at JFK."

"Very good." Mr. Mahmood placed the pad back in the top drawer of the desk. "That is the last of the questions I have for you."

Mitch Myerson leaned forward. "Actually, I have a question for you."

"Please."

"St. Germaine tells me that the biggest problem at JFK is a dog." The Saint had spoken of a U.S. Customs currency-sniffing hound, a short-haired black Afghan named Bear, that was frequently turned loose on the luggage before it was loaded onto the airplanes. Indeed, Bear had been so successful that the Medellín cartel was said to have placed him on its hit list. "Do you know what I'm talking about?"

"Yes, I am aware of this dog Customs has," Mahmood said.

"He said you could take care of that."

"Mr. Positano, contrary to widespread belief, this dog is not able to smell out *money*. He smells the residue of *drugs* on the money."

"I am aware of that, Mr. Mahmood," Myerson said. He paused. "Mr. St. Germaine said there might be some residue of drugs on the money you give me."

Mr. Mahmood considered this for a moment. After a while, he said, "Yes, I cannot say this is not possible." He smiled. "In any event, that is of no consequence. The dog will not be able to find *this* money with merely his nose, no matter how great his sense of smell."

Mr. Mahmood rose from his chair and walked a few steps to the wall on his left. There was a small gunmetal-gray safe built into it. Abboud deftly glided the combination knob to its code numbers, cracked it open, and withdrew two items: a small leather bag and a small black box roughly the size of two decks of cards. He brought the items back to the desk, placing them in front of him.

Up close, Myerson saw that the leather bag was large, elegant and Gucci.

Without speaking, Mahmood removed the items from the bag: a can of Gillette Foamy shaving cream, a white plastic container of Mennen talcum powder, an economy-size tube of Ben Gay, a bottle of lemon-creme flavored liquid Maalox, a green fifteen-ounce bottle of Prell shampoo, Crest tartar-control toothpaste. In all, there were ten articles of personal hygiene products inside the Gucci bag.

"These are Korean-made replicas of popular American brands," Mahmood explained. He picked up the can of Gillette Foamy and untwisted the top portion. The top screwed off smoothly. Mahmood slid the can and the lid across the desk to Mitch.

Myerson looked into the can and saw only shaving cream. "Where's the money?"

Mahmood smiled. "It is secreted in a chamber beneath the shaving cream. You'll note that the can is specially counterbalanced to give whoever is handling it the impression that he is holding nothing more than a harmless can of shaving cream. Go ahead and screw the top back on."

Mitch did as he was told.

"Now push the button," Abboud said.

Shaving cream flowed out and puffed up into a small creamy teardrop-shaped dollop in the palm of Myerson's hand.

"That's good," Mitch said. "Real good." He wiped the shaving cream into the red cloth napkin Anya had brought with his coffee.

"And this," Mahmood said, sliding the black box over to within Mitch's purview. "This is a German-made Film-Safe X travel-box. It is lead-lined, designed to shield four rolls of 35-millimeter film from X-ray scrutiny." Mahmood flipped open the top, revealing the innocuous-looking rolls of yellow-labeled Kodak Ektachrome film. "The rest of your money is inside the fake rolls of film, which no Customs person would dare expose."

Mahmood sat back in his chair, quite self-satisfied.

Mitch pursed his lips and nodded. "I'm most impressed, Mr. Mahmood. And I thank your staff for the thoughtful courtesy of secreting the money in advance for me; that was most kind. But, of course, I would like to see the money for myself."

The smile slipped from Mahmood's face. He cleared his throat. "It would be a most unpleasant task for us to remove the money from its hiding places now. Not to mention a time-consuming one."

Mitch Myerson shrugged. "Not to worry. I have the time."

Mahmood was about to protest further, but Mitch cut him off.

"I'm afraid I must insist," Myerson said.

Mr. Mahmood fingered his moustache and narrowed his eyes. "But of course," he said in a cordial tone. "As you wish."

# 14

At 12:37 P.M., Bruce Mazzola found himself in a crowd of astonished spectators at Forty-second Street and Fifth Avenue, diagonally across from the New York Public Library. He stared at one of the most bizarre spectacles he had ever encountered.

There, on the sidewalk, was a midget/quadruple-amputee on a portable hospital bed, playing the "Star-Spangled Banner" on a Casio keyboard with her tongue.

Mazzola looked on with morbid fascination as the woman's swollen tongue snaked out, striking each key with a musical precision. He had never seen anything quite like it. The woman's eyes stared sightlessly ahead, bulging from her head as if to burst loose. Mazzola stood transfixed, watching that tongue—a tube of parched and discolored muscle, really—as it worked to make a living for this limbless lump of flesh.

Some clown in the crowd began to sing the lyrics. Within moments, almost everyone except Mazzola had joined in. The chorus grew in volume as the amputee played the final strains of the anthem with inspired bravado. Before the last note faded, the crowd erupted into spirited applause and showered her collection box with coins and bills. Mazzola walked away, shaking his head at all the suckers. Unlike them, he felt no compulsion to pay a cover charge for some freak show. In fact, as far as he was concerned, *all* of Forty-second Street was a godforsaken freak show.

When Bruce Mazzola lived in New York City, he was fond of telling out-of-town acquaintances that Forty-second Street was the asshole of Manhattan. Every day, twenty-four hours a day, the sidewalks of this thoroughfare were jammed with beggars, grifters, freaks, dopers, perverts, crackheads, whackadoos, thugs, and creeps. Degenerates of every stripe. Oh, yes, and *tourists*. Plenty of tourists. Foreigners with video cameras who didn't know any better or who simply had to have a glimpse of this slimy human soup for themselves.

This afternoon, the street scene was alive with surrealistic activity. Bruce Mazzola took it all in, like the omnipresent smells of charred soft pretzels and fermented piss. To his right, drug deals were being conducted brazenly in the stark light of midday in the doorways of rotted structures with decade-old Store for Rent signs. All around him, panhandlers stumbled about, an army of lobotomized zombies, their upturned palms thrust forward for handouts. Several distraught souls carried signs that said things like HUNGRY AND HOPELESS, PLEASE HELP. Mazzola brushed past them as if they were invisible. At the corner, a homeless man held a sign that said, GIMME MONEY SO I CAN BUY MORE BEER. Finally, a guy who shoots straight, Mazzola thought, flipping the guy two bits.

The gold-toothed con artists were out in force as well, peering around nervously for police while they hawked counterfeit Rolexes or suckered out-of-towners at a game of three-card monte. In a display window, an ancient fortune-teller named Anna beckoned from her booth, promising to foretell Mazzola's future by a mere reading of his palm. "Read this," he said to Anna, giving her the finger.

Walking further west, Mazzola caught a snippet of dialogue from some cherubic-faced Holy Roller who had managed to corner a crack-addled prostitute. The Holy Roller was on the verge of tears, pleading with the indifferent whore: "Please, please go toward His holy light, go to church. Do not ignore His holy light. Accept Jesus Christ in your life." Perhaps by way of response, the whore wheezed ominously and hocked up a brown oyster of phlegm which she deposited on the filth-encrusted sidewalk. A few strides up the block, a gaggle of South African radicals garbed in red, yellow, and green robes and headgear beseeched a small gathering with a bullhorn: "Avenge Rodney King! Riot *today* against the United Racists of America, mah *brothers!* You have the *right to* remain . . . violent." Mazzola surged past the demonstration, encountering a homeless man huddled in a ragged sleeping bag underneath a cash machine. The man was masturbating. A tortured look of agony twisted his whiskered face.

Mazzola plunged deeper into the asshole of Manhattan. Past Broadway, past Times Square, into a netherworld where human despair gave way to sexual perversion. He moved westward past the blackened rubble of demolished buildings, abandoned by disheartened developers in mid-construction. He moved past the dirtbag hotels with the names of dead presidents, where a room could be had for an hour or for a lifetime. Past the Fun City Twenty-five-Cent Peep Shows and the colorful arcade of hardcore porn theaters with their triple-X features like *Wet Suck 3*, *Sweater Meat*, and *Tripod*. Past the live twenty-four-hour hard-core homo S & M shows that promised *Kocks Around the Klock*. The totality of this atmosphere represented the true essence of Forty-second Street, making it the Rodeo Drive of sicko titillation. What greed and money were to Wall Street, lust and fuckfilms were to Forty-second Street.

Mazzola made his way through the milling crowd of dazed perverts. Crossing Eighth Avenue, he took a left, walking past the Port Authority Bus Terminal. It dawned on Mazzola that he was still carrying the thick manila folder of photographs Jeff Wheaton had given him. The thought filled him with contempt. *Those guys aren't gonna find doodly-squat*, he thought. *A bunch of limpdicks running around New York's hotels like a band of trick-or-treaters.* He estimated that their sorry crosstown charade would be said and done within maybe five hours. Plenty of time.

He found a waste receptacle, where he tore the envelope and its contents into even quarters and slipped the pieces into the rubbish. From his front pants pocket, he withdrew the fat envelope of cash Wheaton had supplied him with to bribe hotel employees. He extracted the bills and crumpled the envelope. The envelope joined the rest of the trash; the money disappeared into his pocket.

He noticed an exotic-looking Puerto Rican prostitute watching him. She eyed the money hungrily as he slipped it into his pocket. Even from a distance, he could tell the hooker had a lot of mileage on her odometer. Skanky face. She lit up a Marlboro and sucked on it suggestively, tossing him her best seductive look. He gazed back at her with disinterest. He had no intention of paying for it. She read the message on his face and turned away, already searching the terminal for another trick.

A beefy Port Authority cop approached her then, tapping a nightstick on the meat of his palm. The cop had a touch of gray at the temples and a belly bloated by decades of doughnut consumption. Bruce could hear the cop say, "Cupcake, now y'know I can't let you hang out at the Port Awt'ority Terminal to look for tricks." She eyed him for a lazy moment, exhaling her smoke slowly. Then she sauntered up to him in a saucy manner until her face was inches from his. In a sleepy voice, she said: "What're you gone do 'boud it, Misser *Po*-liceman? You gone arress me? You gone put me in *han'cuffs?*" She brazenly kissed the cop on the lips, stepped back and blew the rest of her smoke in his face. Rather than angering the cop, though, this act of defiance left him aroused. His voice went husky, "Oh now you'd like that, woon'-cha? You'd like me to slap the cuffs on ya. Woon'cha?" He stepped forward and returned her kiss.

Mazzola walked away from the exchange. He patted the cash in his pocket like an old friend and headed down Eighth Avenue.

The strip joint was three blocks away. It was called Sugar-Cane's. He sauntered through the front entrance, paid the five-dollar cover charge and descended the steps two at a time. It took a few moments for his sights to adjust to the smokey gauze that hung in the air.

Then he saw him. Guy had put on some weight, but it was definitely him.

Mazzola grinned and walked up behind the man, who was swilling his draft and looking around nervously. Mazzola gave the guy a reverse bear hug. The man was so startled, he knocked over his beer, sending a fat tongue of liquid across the surface of the table.

The man turned around. Seeing Mazzola, he shook his head and smiled. "Rebel, rebel."

"Sam the Man," Mazzola said. "Sam the Man Trenton. How's it hangin'?"

"It's hanging, it's hanging." Sam Trenton clapped his old friend on the shoulder. "I must say, I was totally blown away to get a phone call from you. What're you doing here in New York? Aren't you in Philly these days?"

Mazzola made a capsicum face. "It's a long story. The upshot of it is that somebody embezzled a bunch of money from me and my friends."

"Oh no."

"One of the guys thinks he's in New York."

"Any chance you'll find him?"

"You kiddin' me? In *New York?* A snowman's chances in hell, maybe."

"I'm sorry to hear it."

Mazzola waved him off the subject. "Sammy, you're looking great. What say, lemme buy you a fresh one and let's enjoy the shoe show." While at Drexel, he and Sam had called strip tease acts "shoe shows" because that was virtually all the girls wound up wearing at SugarCane's.

The beers came quickly. *This is gonna be good*, Mazzola thought. Killing time with Sam would get his mind off unpleasant things.

"Cheers," he said, hoisting his drink to the heavens.

# 15

Rachel Fairweather Wheaton stood at the lip of the lower level of Bloomingdale's, where she enjoyed a commanding view of the entire floor. The panorama spread out before her caused her heart to flutter. . . .

It was a minimall of world-class beautifying products from Princess Marcella Borghese, Estée Lauder, Lancôme, Clarins, and oh-so-many others, all clustered together in one concentrated nucleus. She lingered there for some time, watching the scores of impassioned shoppers coursing through the aisles. It was part of the ritual, a prelude as natural to her as the national anthem before a baseball game.

She was checking out the competition.

Attractive women were everywhere. (*Of course*—this *was* Bloomingdale's, after all.) Rachel watched these ladies, searching out the most attractive ones. She appraised them with a critical eye: their skin, their faces, their bodies. After a while, she permitted herself a satisfied smile.

Of all the beautiful women here, not one was as beautiful as she.

With the warm glow of superiority, Rachel Wheaton went shopping.

On Rachel's list of life's pleasures, shopping was a passion right up there with sex. Indeed, Rachel was fond of metaphorically linking the experience of shopping to the act of copulation. Just think about it, she would say to anyone who would listen. Imagine a Max Mara dress to absolutely die for. Well, that was like *flirtation:* the garment catching the eye of a beautiful girl, demanding her attention. And picking it up, taking it off the rack, that was like flirting back, right? If the touch and feel of the dress set off sparks in you, if it sent a current of warm electric excitement zipping through your body, it was like *foreplay*. Then you'd try it on, give it a chance to see if you would go *all the way*. And if, by chance, the fit was perfect, if it flattered you and enhanced your loveliness, you came to the moment when you knew: *you had to have it*. That was *lust*. Taking it up to the counter, well, that was where the sweet *anticipation* built, when you could sense it was really going to happen. Then when the clerk took it from you, you knew, there was no turning back now. That was like that first surge of *penetration*, the flush of pleasure that came from knowing it was *yours*. The next phase occurred when the salesclerk handed you the shopping bag filled with your purchase, and you experienced the full weight of it in your hands. That was, quite simply, *orgasmic*. Leaving the store with that Max Mara dress in hand, and you, absolutely in love with it, that gave you an afterglow rivaling that of a string of multiple orgasms.

Good Lord, if shopping were sex, she'd be a nymphomaniac.

And here she was at Bloomingdale's. Bloomie's was an absolutely fabulous confection, a dazzling, gleaming monument in celebration of feminine beauty. It was a full city block of the finest in fashions and fragrances and cosmetics, a store without equal anywhere else in the world. There were floor-to-ceiling mirrors and brilliant lights everywhere—neon, fluorescent, incandescent. Feel-good music throbbing through the speakers: "Walkin' on Sunshine." The sounds: the click of ladies' heels beating at a fast clip against the hardwood floor; the swishing sound people made passing each other in the aisles; the ringing peal of rich women's delighted laughter. And the smells: of perfumes and colognes and, occasionally, of butter-drenched croissants and muffins. Was there any other place on earth with so many fabulous fragrances?

She loved the intoxicating ambience of Bloomie's. It made her feel positively regal, like a movie star. Yes, she was a material girl, all right, and she made no apologies for it. A girl had to make the most of what mother nature gave her before Father Time took it away.

*That's* why they invented Bloomingdale's, after all.

She rode the escalator to the fourth floor. The ladies' department was virtually sensory overload to Rachel. *Everything* competed for the privilege of her attention. A Tahari silk jacket in size four, simply orgasmic, $286. A yummy Donna Karan cotton bodysuit, perfect for the airplane, $375. A Nicole Miller evening dress in a multicolored flower pattern, suitable for a romantic night at an oceanside restaurant in Positano, $475. The new Christian LaCroix collection was out, and it was simply to die for, simply to die for—but the least expensive piece had a $425 price tag. A sleek H20 purple one-piece bathing suit that would look simply delicious wrapped around her tight little body—$175. Even a pair of suede and leather pumps by Sam and Libby—$200!

As she moved past the displays of Betsey Johnson, Norma Kamali, and Sonia Rykiel, she felt her agony grow. Quality fashion didn't come cheap. Yet Mitchell had given her just $180. One hundred eighty dollars! To shop *Bloomingdale's*, if you can imagine! The price tags were depressing.

Over breakfast at Trump Tower, she had protested the pittance he had offered her, telling him she *needed* things, and $180 wasn't enough. She reminded Mitchell that he had rushed them out of Philadelphia in such a hurry she had no time to pack her makeup and things. And, God, she didn't have enough clothes for a *week*, let alone an entire year. Mitchell was apologetic, of course, but said the $180 was all they had at the moment.

So there she was, stuck in Bloomingdale's without enough money to buy so much as a *schmatte*. She was in hell.

In a funk, she took the down escalator to the lower level, hoping to find some affordable items in La Parfumerie. Attractive salesclerks were calling to her from every corner, trying to entice her with freebies.

"Wonderful gift set today with any purchase of Molto Missoni, Miss, beautiful gift set."

"It's Clinique bonus time, Clinique bonus time."

"Free clutch purse for ladies when you buy a ten-ounce Kelemata vegetal extract."

She ignored them and plunged resolutely into the maze of counters. There were a thousand exotic products that promised to tone, firm, hydrate, nourish, enhance, and protect her natural beauty—a thousand things she burned to have for her own. A Princess Marcella Borghese colore bellezza collection. La Prairie Switzerland skin caviar and cellular eye complex. Clarins Botanical Purifying Plant facial masque, Gel Nettuyant Purifant, and Lait Auto Bronzant. Elancyl ToniCompact HP 24 Body Profiling Concentrate with one hundred thousand microparticles. Rene Furterer Gelee de Structure Traitant. The truth was, she needed all these things.

She moved past the Germaine Monteil booth and approached the Clinique counter. She was determined to purchase only the absolute essentials and no more. The salesgirl in the antiseptic white lab coat greeted her cheerfully. "How can I help you today, Miss?"

Rachel instructed her to select only the smallest of sizes in soap, moisturizing lotion, seven-day scrub creme, beauty emergency masque, and exfoliating scrub. Just the essentials.

"Will that be everything today?" the girl asked.

"Yes, I believe so."

As the salesgirl rang up the purchase, Rachel prayed it wouldn't be over $200.

"That will be $221.53, ma'am," the salesgirl said sweetly.

*Ouch.* Rachel bit her lip.

She dipped her hand into her purse for the cash. She snapped open her wallet and let her eyes fall on the credit cards. *Credit cards.* The sight of them caused Rachel to experience a delicious rush of endorphins. She still had her husband's Visa Gold card! With a ten-thousand-dollar limit! Oh, how Jeffrey used to go ballistic on her when he opened those monthly Visa bills. How she hated those arguments!

What a nice farewell next month's Visa bill could make. A sort of have-a-nice-life-oh-and-P.S.-*fuck-you*. The idea of it sent a thrill rippling through her, wicked and luscious.

The salesgirl asked, "And how will you be paying today? Cash or charge?"

Rachel gave her a sugary smile. "Charge," she said, sliding Jeff Wheaton's Visa Gold card across the glasstop counter.

# 16

When the chief concierge informed Roberto Esperanza of his plans to take a two-week vacation in Sicily, Esperanza welcomed the news. It meant that he, Roberto, would serve as the full-time concierge at the United Nations Plaza Hotel for a fortnight. More importantly, it also meant some additional money for Berto and his young family.

Roberto Esperanza was a thirty-four-year-old Argentinean who worked at the U.N. Plaza as a junior concierge, putting himself through the night program at St. John's Law School. Juggling both a career and graduate school was grueling, of course. The demands of classes, studies, and making a living left precious little time to spend with his pretty young wife and two-year-old daughter at their home in Sheepshead Bay, Brooklyn. Fortunately, Esperanza was one of those people blessed with the wondrous ability to get by on just five hours of sleep, which was all he got when school was in session.

Roberto assured Mario Fabrizzi, the chief concierge at the U.N. Plaza, that he had nothing to worry about. The chief's precious ship would be in capable hands during his absence. Indeed, Fabrizzi often remarked that Roberto possessed all the requisite virtues to someday become a full-fledged member of Les Clefs d'Or. Not only did Esperanza speak five languages, he also had an impeccable manner, infinite patience, a quick mind, a dry wit, fortitude, and creativity. On innumerable occasions, Fabrizzi had lamented Roberto's lawyerly aspirations aloud. What use did the world have for yet another litigator? Indeed, there would be one million lawyers in the U.S. by the year 2000, but almost certainly not a million jobs for them all. The world all but cried out for another concierge worthy of the gold crossed-key lapel pin of Les Clefs d'Or. As an elegant gentleman who took enormous pride in the nobility of his profession, Fabrizzi was pained to see Roberto's potential squandered in a *law school.*

In the days prior to his departure, Mario Fabrizzi became more anxious. After all, the guests who frequented the U.N. Plaza Hotel were diplomats, chargés d'affaires, and officials from foreign governments the world over. They were notoriously demanding—accustomed to having the most outlandish requests filled. It posed a challenge to test even the most highly skilled of concierges. Moreover, the services Mario Fabrizzi provided for the guests were synonymous with the hotel's very reputation *itself*. How could he in good conscience place this herculean responsibility on the shoulders of a young assistant no matter how capable the assistant was?

So as his date of departure drew near, Mario Fabrizzi mercilessly drilled Roberto. Fabrizzi lectured him on his personal standards of excellence until the assistant could recite them like a creed. A seemingly endless series of lists was prepared to anticipate any emergency. Mario Fabrizzi fussed and fretted.

To Roberto Esperanza, his superior's fastidiousness was utterly unnecessary. Esperanza would handle himself just fine. He was comfortable offering suggestions as to any fine restaurant in the city, whether it was Petrossian or Planet Hollywood. He knew the strings he could pull, the resources he could tap. He felt confident that he could face any contingency.

When the taxicab finally dragged the reluctant Fabrizzi off to make his flight at JFK, Esperanza was relieved to have him out of the way.

In the eight straight days Roberto Esperanza had manned the mirrored concierge desk at the U.N. Plaza, things had gone smoothly. Guests presented him with a steady flow of the usual requests: Broadway tickets, restaurant suggestions, transportation arrangements, offbeat tours of the city, faxing documents. He fielded several unusual demands that week as well.

On Monday, a panicked German industrialist who spoke no English appeared at his vestibule. He spoke only German and explained that he had inadvertently left all his business cards in Stuttgart. Could Roberto find a way to get five hundred business cards printed up—in *less than an hour?* (Yes; mission accomplished with twelve minutes to spare.)

Wednesday morning, the entourage of a prince from some obscure South Pacific nation requested to have His Highness' king-size bed in the Presidential Suite sprinkled with rose petals before he turned in each evening. Piece of cake.

Thursday, the coup de grace: He managed to get both a marriage license and a minister within hours to accommodate two lovebirds from upstate who were seized by a spontaneous impulse to unite in holy matrimony. He even managed to get the wedding cake in time from L'Eclair on First Avenue at Fifty-fourth Street.

And earlier this morning, Saturday, he had orchestrated a customized tour of Harlem for a group of Japanese real estate moguls. The Japanese were apparently intrigued by the culture of black Americans, life on the streets, the source of inspiration for rap music. Esperanza's itinerary concluded with a dinner of corn bread, black-eyed peas, fried chicken, collard greens, and ribs at Sylvia's Soul Food Restaurant in the heart of Harlem.

Roberto was justifiably pleased with how capably he had handled the challenges so far. The German businessman had even fired off a note of gratitude to the hotel management on his behalf. (Albeit, in German.) When Fabrizzi returned, he would, no doubt, nominate him for a Silver Plume award (the American concierge society's equivalent of an Oscar) and, for the hundredth time, attempt to talk him out of a law degree.

Roberto Esperanza permitted himself a smile.

Shortly after two o'clock that afternoon, a man in a blazer approached his desk. "Pardon me."

Roberto Esperanza looked up from his paperwork. The man standing before him had a haggard look, as if he hadn't had much sleep. "Good afternoon," Esperanza said. "How may I assist you today?"

"I'm looking for someone."

"I beg your pardon."

"I'm looking for my wife," the man said, "and I need your help."

The man in the blazer extended his hand and introduced himself as Jeffrey Wheaton, the founder and chief executive officer of a national computer retailer based near Philadelphia. He struck Esperanza as an especially young man to have attained such success, but Esperanza knew that in the computer industry, fortunes had been made by men even younger than this Mr. Wheaton.

Esperanza nodded and said, "Please call me Roberto." Fabrizzi would have disapproved of the first-name-basis approach, thinking it undignified, but Esperanza thought it more intimate.

Jeff Wheaton produced a trio of photographs—color photocopies of photographs, actually—and slipped them across the desk to Esperanza.

"This is what she looks like," Wheaton said. "I'm offering a ten-thousand-dollar reward for any information leading to my finding her."

"I see." The woman in the picture was exquisitely beautiful. She had sparkling eyes and an angelic expression. "What is your wife's name?"

"Her name is Rachel. We've been married for almost two years. She left home last night with another man. I believe she's in New York right now. She's mixed up in some very ugly business. The FBI's involved—"

Esperanza formed a steeple with his fingers and touched the tips to his chin in a thoughtful pose. "Perhaps we should take this up with the hotel's security. If you're willing to give me a moment, I would be pleased to ring them for you?"

Mr. Wheaton shook his head. "No. Please, no hotel security. It's *you* I need to speak with. Security wouldn't have had contact with her. *You* might have. She would have checked in late yesterday afternoon. Were you in the hotel?"

"Yes. I was on duty until midnight."

"Well, then, perhaps she came up to your desk, asked you about a restaurant—?"

"I'm sorry, sir," Esperanza said gently. "For reasons I'm

certain you appreciate, I cannot speak on matters that could compromise the privacy or security of the hotel's guests."

Mr. Wheaton held up his hand in a placating gesture. "Roberto, let me assure you—I fully appreciate the hotel's policy regarding the privacy of its guests. And certainly, I don't wish to put you in a precarious situation with your superiors. But *dammit.*" He sighed in frustration. "Roberto, you married?"

"Yes, I am."

"Put yourself in my shoes for a minute. Imagine my pain. Good Christ, I'm just an ordinary guy, like you, making an honest living, paying my taxes. I'm not a threat to the hotel's security—I'm a jilted husband in search of the truth. I need *closure*, a reason *why*. That's all. I'm begging you, man to man, to *help me.*"

Because the nature of Roberto Esperanza's calling was to *accommodate* people, not to *rebuff* them, he felt an impulse to help this devastated man from Philadelphia despite the hotel's rules. The concierge was to cut through the red tape, to bend the rules, to do whatever was necessary to make one's life more livable. His impulse to help, coupled with the man's tormented look, worked to topple his resistance.

"Very well," Esperanza said, adjusting his reading glasses. "Let's have another look."

"Thank you, Roberto." Mr. Wheaton pushed the pictures closer.

Esperanza peered at the images before him. "She's a very beautiful woman, Mr. Wheaton."

"Yes, she is," he said miserably. "Have you seen her in the hotel?"

Esperanza shook his head. "I have not. I wish I could say otherwise."

Wheaton pursed his lips. "All right, then, let me show you a picture of the snake that made off with her." He laid down a third photograph. To Esperanza's surprise, Wheaton himself was in it. He and a companion at some golf course, both of the men with broad smiles on their faces.

"This man," Jeff said, barely suppressing the rage, "this man stole my wife. A man I trusted as a close friend and business associate. Took all my money too." His voice dropped a register.

"Put yourself in my place, Roberto. Can you imagine the pain I'm feeling?"

Esperanza said nothing. If someone ran off with his wife, Marisol . . . he would hunt the skunk down and personally relieve him of his *cojones*.

Wheaton exhaled. "Perhaps they asked you for directions or asked you to recommend a restaurant. Tell me, have you seen either of them?"

"I'm very sorry, Mr. Wheaton. I am certain I have not."

Wheaton nodded and sighed dejectedly. "Well, I appreciate your time," he said.

"Perhaps they have checked into another hotel?"

"Yes. I've been to six of them so far. You're next to last on my list."

Esperanza felt a compulsion to help, to not give up the fight. "Mr. Wheaton, may I hold on to the pictures? If by chance they check in this afternoon or go to the Ambassador Grill for drinks." Esperanza shrugged.

Wheaton's face lit up a bit. "Please. By all means, hold on to them. I've put a phone number at the top. You can reach me night or day."

"Very good, sir."

"You've been most kind, Roberto," Jeff said. Suddenly, a crisp new twenty-dollar bill materialized before Esperanza on the top of the desk.

"No, please. That is absolutely not necessary." Esperanza spoke firmly, pushing the bill back to Wheaton. "I cannot accept it."

Mr. Wheaton appeared mildly surprised by the concierge's rejection of the gratuity. He replaced the bill in his pocket. As he gathered up his briefcase, Wheaton said, "Finding the two of them means more to me than I can possibly express. Thank you for your help."

The two men shook hands, as if forging a pact.

When Jeffrey Wheaton of Philadelphia was gone, Roberto Esperanza took one last glance at the pictures. The two photos of the woman Rachel: He had known that type of woman in his lifetime. The glowing face of an angel, the black heart of a demon.

The last shot, a picture of the back-stabbing weasel with the *cojones* who thought nothing of stealing another man's wife. Roberto's eyes lingered on the photos for a moment longer, their images burning into his mind's eye.

Then a call came in from the guest in Room 1714. Could he recommend a fine Vietnamese restaurant? "I believe Indochine would be a superb choice, madame. . . ."

# 17

"Remember, gentlemen, only tips 'n' gratuities will get you nudity," the DJ's amplified voice boomed out from behind the glass-encased booth at SugarCane's, as the anemic-looking redheaded stripper finished her set and stepped off the stage. The DJ was a grizzle-bearded, 300-plus-pound fat slob by the name of Lewis, who wore cheap sunglasses. His voice was a sandpaper-monotone, rough-hewn by years of abusing whiskey and cigarettes. "Let's hear it out there for Ginger. Ginger, gentlemen, *Gingerrrrrrr.*"

The twenty or so patrons of SugarCane's provided intermittent applause for Ginger. She waded into the audience to solicit ten-dollar table dances.

Like most other strip joints in the West Forties, SugarCane's seemed to revel in the seediness of its atmosphere, where poor illumination was supposed to pass for ambience. The whole place reeked of stale beer, perfume, and the awful desperation of lifelong losers who bused into the nearby Port Authority for an afternoon of erotic titillation in Times Square. The draft beers at Sugar-Cane's were invariably lukewarm, flat, and outrageously over-priced. Moreover, Bruce Mazzola had always judged the girls at SugarCane's to be so-so at best. On the upside, however, they were far more approachable than the ice-cold babes of, say, Stringfellow's or Pure Platinum. The clincher was the strict house policy that permitted patrons to massage the dancers' breasts during a lap dance for an extra five bucks. For twenty bucks, some girls would even unzip your pants for you and grind their bare tushies against your stiffened blue-veined porksword. Mazzola and his one-time cohorts from the Street had had many a good time here, too many beer-soaked three-hour lunches to remember.

In that sense, SugarCane's struck Mazzola as the ideal backdrop to reconnoiter with his old buddy Sam Trenton for the first time in two years. The plan was just to shoot the shit about their days together on Wall Street in the 1980s, a common experience about which only a privileged few could boast.

Whereas many of the young men of their fathers' generation had fought battles in Korea and in Vietnam, Bruce and Sam had waged an entirely different sort of war. They had served side-by-side as soldiers of fortune in the great financial revolution of the mid- to late-eighties. It was a glorious time, where swashbuckling corporate raiders had declared civil war on the fat, overpaid captains of American industry. The raiders had enlisted sharp, young, Ivy League–educated soldiers like Bruce and Sam to do battle on the front lines. And for a time, no corporate officer was able to sleep well at night.

One of the spoils of war for Bruce, Sam, and thousands of other investment bankers was the enormous geyser of wealth that erupted, generous tributaries of which streamed through their own pockets. Another perk was the concurrent aura of charisma previously reserved for rock stars. The investment banker was, for all intents and purposes, a modern day version of *Elvis*, for chrissakes.

When one segment of industry becomes a conduit to so much of a nation's wealth, it becomes impossible to elude the scrutiny of the media for any length of time. Thus, the media wound up playing an integral role in amplifying the mystique of the young investment bankers who were freshly minted from the elite **MBA** mills. Financial reporters had difficulty understanding precisely what it was they *did* for a living, so they resorted to likening under-thirty Wall Streeters to mythical figures straight out of folklore and fable: warriors, swashbucklers, knights. The public bought into this notion in a big way.

Bruce Mazzola had expertly played the role of the larger-than-life investment banker. He wasted no opportunity to maximize his braggadocio or promote his own brand of take-no-prisoners machismo. Mazzola was *always* the mastermind behind the impromptu weekend-warrior excursions via helicopter to Killington or to some little-known resort in the Canadian Rockies for killer skiing. One especially notorious story had Mazzola and some traders getting together over drinks at Flutie's at the Seaport to form a high-stakes pool for the 1987 Super Bowl. The cost was $10,000 a box. An A.V.P. from Morgan taunted Mazzola, "Hey, Brucie, hope this ain't too rich for *your blood.*" Instantly, Mazzola whipped out his checkbook and bellowed, "Put me down for the ten boxes in the middle row and tell me who the fuck I make the check out to."

News of that incident traveled fast among people on the Street. Next thing you knew, people were trading Mazzola's-so-macho one-liners at Harry's and Delmonico's. A particularly popular line went: "Mazzola's so macho, he jogged home after his vasectomy."

Mazzola's self-confidence and aura of wealth was an especially useful factor in his ability to effortlessly pick up the eager young women who flocked to Friday afternoon happy hours at the South Street Seaport in search of the wealthiest of New York's wealthy yuppies. In those days, an Ivy League investment banker in an Armani suit and Paul Stuart braces was walking aphrodisiac to the big-city babes. Casually slipping your Wall Street affiliation into your rap with some Ford model at Odeon almost automatically meant getting your nookie card punched. Mazzola proved to be a silk-smooth master at getting the fashion models out of their panties. He notched 126 sexual conquests in that time, the names of whom he kept in a coded section of his Filofax.

After the demise of Drexel Burnham Lambert and the outrageous multi-billion-dollar LBO of RJR Nabisco, the media reversed course. Suddenly, cover stories in major magazines vilified *all* of Wall Street for the alleged excesses of the decade. The S & L scandal mushroomed. The economy turned sour. Overleveraged companies slashed personnel. Unemployment figures soared to record highs. Scapegoats were sought. Michael Milken was nominated as a symbol of the decade's unchecked greed and embraced by the public as such. Suddenly, the kinder, gentler 1990s were looking like mop-up time for the financial and environmental excesses of the 1980s. In the end, the unemployable thirty-year-old M & A specialist became the media's most tiresome cliché.

But for many of those who had Been There . . . for those who had actually participated in the financial revolution . . . for those who had defended themselves on the Phil Donahue show . . . for those who religiously attended the annual Drexel alumni bashes year after year . . . for these people the past was a source of enormous pride and achievement. Mazzola was one of them and he was positively thrilled to find himself speedrapping about those times with his former cohort Sam Trenton. He spoke with the exhilaration of an all-American quarterback reliving a four-season dynasty of consecutive national championships.

"Hey, Trent, you remember that time we cashed our bonus checks on Friday and took the Concorde to Paris for forty-eight hours?" Mazzola burbled. "We wound up at the Bois de Boulogne, that city park with a thousand prostitutes?"

Trenton nodded distantly.

"Jesus, it was a total sexual bazaar," Mazzola said, slapping the table. "Every nationality had its own section in the park. Chicks from Peru, Colombia, Argentina. Remember when Brendon Ross wound up with that transsexual from Ecuador? You remember how we almost tore our stomachs open laughing over that?" Mazzola grinned at the memory of it.

Sam Trenton leaned back in his chair, a weak smile coming to his lips. "Yeah, Bruce. That was a lot of fun, that weekend."

"Jefe, we had some fast times, you 'n' me."

"Fast times. That's for sure."

"Sam, I promise you, real soon, I'm gonna sit down behind a word processor on some tropical island and I'm gonna grind out the *real story* of the eighties. The ultimate tell-all, you know what I mean?"

Trenton shifted in his chair uncomfortably, cleared his throat. "Don't you think people have heard enough of the eighties?"

"No," Mazzola replied. "I don't. Especially since the *real* story hasn't been told yet."

Trenton pressed a forefinger thoughtfully to his lower lip and nodded. He cast his eyes down to the table and stared at the five interlocking rings of liquid his glass of beer had left on the surface. They resembled the Olympic logo.

*What the fuck is eating him?* Mazzola wondered. Guy had been a sullen spoilsport right from the get-go. It was no fun reminiscing without the give-and-take he craved from this reunion. He could take Trenton's passivity no longer.

"Hey, Sam," Mazzola said pointedly. "What's with the fucking hangdog look?"

Sam shrugged.

"Talk to me," Bruce implored.

"It's just that—I dunno, sometimes I look back on recent history and—"

Mazzola waited.

"Sometimes I don't feel very good about some of the stuff we did, Bruce."

"Oh?" Mazzola cocked an eyebrow. "Like what stuff in particular?"

"The whole M & A thing. I mean, sure, you and I made truckloads of greenbacks. But I mean, it was kind of like . . . I don't know. When you look at the big picture, what did we really *do?*"

"We only changed the course of financial history, that's all."

"But was it for the *better?* I don't know if what we did was anything special."

"Sam, is this really *you* talking? Listen to yourself, how you're selling yourself short. We were Masters of the Universe, pal, the best there ever was—"

"Bruce, c'mon. We happened to be at the right place at the right time. Any garden-variety fuzznut out of b-school willing to put in eighty hours a week could have done what we did. We had access to hundreds of millions of dollars in firm capital and a huge institutional customer base. It was a no-lose situation. I mean, pardon me for saying this, but from what I remember, you *despised* math, didn't you?"

"I never pretended to be a star in math," Mazzola replied. "But I was very, very good with numbers." He grinned.

Trenton sighed. "Sometimes I feel a little guilty about what we did. Looking back on it, I think we pissed on the federal securities laws from time to time."

Mazzola shrugged.

"We didn't *produce* anything," Trenton continued. "There was no real social utility to what we did."

"What about the shareholders?" Mazzola pointed out. "We helped the little guy."

"Yeah," Trenton said with a melancholy smile, "I used to toe that line too. That was our standard response at cocktail parties. 'Look at what Drexel did for MCI. We raised a billion ducats for MCI so they could tear down the Ma Bell monopoly.' Great American success story, creating something out of nothing. But somewhere, we lost our religion, Bruce. I guess it was just too tempting to help the sharks in the feeding frenzy on Corporate America. Too much money was at stake. Next thing we knew, we found ourselves justifying the cannibalization of once-strong American companies. We became totally desensitized to the damage we were doing.

"Sure, some small shareholders benefited from the takeover plays. But look at all the union guys we put out of work. I was listening to an all-news station yesterday and they said that America dropped from the greatest industrial power on the planet in 1980 to *fifth* in 1990."

Mazzola drew back in disbelief. "You attribute that to what *we* did?"

"Yeah. Yeah, Bruce, I do. We piled all that debt on hostile takeover targets and now, after monthly debt service, there's nothing left for research and development. R & D is no longer a fixed expense. It's now categorized as a 'variable overhead expense.' That means it's the first place companies cut when they run into trouble. Guess who the top three holders of new patents in the U.S. were last year? *Not* G.E., IBM or AT&T. They were *Toshiba, Mitsubishi, and Hitachi.* While we shuffled the papers that permitted the slicing and dicing of Corporate America, the Japanese were putting their twenty-five-year strategic plans into effect."

"You don't mind my saying so, Trent," Mazzola growled, "you're starting to drone on like some born-again asshole."

The DJ's raspy voice intruded, booming out, "Mo' honey for yo' money at SugarCane's, my friends. Put your hands together for Melika, up on the main stage, *Melikaaaaaaaa.*"

Sam Trenton rolled the empty beer glass between his hands and sighed. "At one point, I was making more money in a single year than my old man had made *in an entire lifetime.* That kind of money does something to your head, Bruce. You start to believe your own shit. I guess we all knew the party had to come to an end eventually. Congress was gonna step in and change the tax law or something. Instead, it was Rudy Giuliani. Whatever. What we always underestimated, I think, is how far we had to fall. The crushing reality of it was, we were making five hundred thou and *still* we were no better off than Joe Average in Peoria, Illinois. We too were always just a few paychecks away from being tossed out on the street.

"Personal bankruptcy was a major reality check for me, Bruce. I lost my penthouse overlooking Gramercy Park, lost my BMW convertible. I learned the hard way that despite being Harvard-educated, there was no place on the Street for me anymore. I was *fungible*. Whenever I went down to the Claims Office to reapply for unemployment, I was always bumping into classmates from Harvard who were in T-shirts and Levi's, waiting in the same lines. Did you hear that six months after he was out of work, Brendon Ross applied for and got a job with the City Sanitation Department? Instead of working *on* Wall Street, the guy ended up *sweeping* it."

Mazzola had tuned him out. He was distracted by the sight of a tremendously obese man from New Jersey waddling up to the lip of the stage. Another loser buying into the fantasy of *hey, maybe she does want me after all.* Guy had to be four hundred, five hundred pounds easy, though once you hit that kind of tonnage it became increasingly difficult to put a number on it with any accuracy. The stripper had overdone the mascara thing a bit, having caked on so much beneath her eyes that she resembled a raccoon. She paused in mid-grind to let the guy slide a crisp five-spot into her lacy thigh garter. Guy's breathing was labored from the effort of moving fifteen feet. *Right piece of trim could send this porker off to heart attack country,* Mazzola thought.

When Mazzola tuned back in to Trenton's rhetoric, he heard him say "—so after a few years of doing essentially nothing, I pleaded and begged and worked my way back on to the Street this spring."

Mazzola felt a stab of jealousy. "Doing what?" *Bending over a desk for an MD?*

"IPOs. Can you believe that?" Trenton laughed at the irony.

Mazzola frowned. Initial public offerings? That was just the opposite of leveraged buy-outs. No gonzo at all in that kind of work.

Sam said, "So I'm specializing in the capitalization of emerging companies. It's a big growth area. Our economists just issued a report on the re-equitization of America. In the eighties, there were twenty-nine straight quarters of equity being retired due to M & As and LBOs. That figure amounted to $486 billion in just eight years. The economists predict it'll take thirteen years just to re-equitize the fucking country, to get back to where we were in 1980."

Mazzola made a point of yawning dramatically, but it did nothing to discourage Trenton. Guy was on a statistic-spouting roll. This was fucking psychotherapy for him, confession being good for the soul, or whatever.

"Wall Street's a real different place these days, nothing like when we were there. You can tell it from the way people dress. There's still Hermès ties everywhere, I guess there always will be. But the traders and brokers wear only white and blue shirts. No pinstripes. Rolexes are now passé. Round watches with white faces and Roman numerals are all the rage. Leather straps only, no gold. Wearing suspenders would get you laughed off the Street. Oh, and Italian-cut suits have gone the way of the Quotron."

Mazzola shrugged. If that was Wall Street now, he wanted no part of it.

"The real play on Wall Street these days is in the arena of derivative products. Know what DPs are?"

"I know all about derivative products," Mazzola lied.

"Swaps, hybrid instruments, complex options, 'swaptions.'

They're essentially synthetic transcontinental plays on an underlying stock or portfolio of securities. The DP specialists are the real geniuses on the Street. Our guys have this product, a contingent premium option, that hedges an investor's downside risk of an unfavorable price spike with an embedded put feature. The put feature knocks out at a prespecified strike price—"

Thankfully, Sam's boring discourse on derivatives was drowned out by a loud electric squeal of earsplitting feedback, as the DJ burbled, "Money, money, money, money, money. You take care of the ladies and they will take care of *you*. And don't forget to take care of your barkeeps, people."

Mazzola had had enough. He was out of here.

At that moment, Trenton grinned a cheesy grin and said, "Did I tell you I'm getting engaged?"

"You don't say." Mazzola smiled fiercely. "Who's the lucky gal?"

"Name's Belinda Foster. Graduated a year behind me at Harvard b-school, Barnard undergrad. She's a two-year analyst with Goldman's IMD. Her family's from Greenwich and her father's a partner at Cravath."

Mazzola nodded tersely at the girl's credentials, which sounded like a typically self-indulgent wedding announcement right out of the Sunday *New York Times* society pages. Then Mazzola smirked. "I'm real happy for you, Trent. Got this warm, shiny feeling all over."

The blissful look fled Trenton's face. "What's *that* supposed to mean?"

"What's what supposed to mean?"

"Why are you being so goddamed *sarcastic?*"

"Sarcastic?"

"That's right, sarcastic. You turned into a real douchebag all of a sudden."

Mazzola stared at his companion calmly. "Sam, my man, there's ten things I despise about the nineties. They are as follows." He ticked each one off on a finger. "Ten: political correctness. Nine: non-alcoholic beer. Eight: nesting. Seven: anti-smoking activists. Six: yuppies who think their own rug-rats are the greatest thing since sliced bread. Five: rap music. Four:

country music. Three: safe sex. Two: the shift from cocaine to *Rogaine* as our generation's drug of choice." He lowered his voice. "But the number one thing I hate most of all is *reformed investment bankers* who apologize for their past. You, boyo, fall into the latter category."

Trenton stared at him. "You're like a hippie stuck in some sixties time warp, you know that? It's 1993, Bruce."

"And *you're* like some recently converted born-again Christian. You and me, my old friend, have nothing in common any more."

After a pause, Sam Trenton nodded gravely. "You've always been one to come straight to the point, Bruce. And I suppose I have to agree with you."

Mazzola stared at him. What a disaster this get-together turned out to be.

"We've shared a lot of great times, Bruce," Trenton said gently. He offered his hand for Mazzola to shake. "Still friends?"

"Fuck that," Mazzola spat, pushing away from the table. "What's in it for me?"

Trenton glared at him. "I know what you're going through, Bruce. You're terrified that maybe, just maybe, those days were as good as life is going to get for us. You're scared that maybe the rest of our lives will be one big downhill slide from here on out. That's some heavy shit."

"Spare me the psychoanalysis," Mazzola said. "Far as I'm concerned, those days were just a prologue to the big time. You have a nice life, hear?"

As Mazzola stalked across the room toward the exit, Sam Trenton shook his head and hunched into a remorseful cocoon of regret. Mazzola brushed past the strippers, who called out to him with offers to dance, just for him. From the corner of his eye, he caught a glimpse of the vanilla-skinned stripper named Ginger. She threw him a smoky look, pursing her lips in a puckered circle of shiny red meant to make him think of a specific sex act. Instead, it reminded Bruce of the Japanese fighting fish he used to have in his office.

He approached her, pressed a twenty-dollar bill into her palm. "Ginger, my friend's name is Sam. Needs a lap dance real bad.

You tell him it's a wedding gift from his Uncle Bruce." He whispered in her ear. "Tell him it's for old times' sake."

"Okay," she said enthusiastically. Ginger primped her frizzy red hair and sauntered over to the table to throw a one-on-one bachelor party for the dejected Sam Trenton. Bruce Mazzola, meanwhile, left SugarCane's without looking back. On the sidewalk, he thought about how his encounter with Sam would play as a chapter in his tell-all book.

Then his thoughts turned to a steaming hot shower back at the hotel.

# 18

From the waiting area of Gate 35, he watched as yet another Alitalia Airlines jetliner climbed the sky bound for Italy. He crossed Flight 657 off the list and the sense of utter futility crept over him once more. In over four hours of surveillance at John F. Kennedy International Airport, Chuck Beekman had swept his eyes over a veritable sea of faces.

No Mitch. No Rachel.

Hours ago, what little hope he clung to had all but slipped away. Sure, he thought they had an outside shot after Jeff Wheaton's optimistic pep talk at the Grand Hyatt. And Jeff *had* done his homework, there was no doubt about that. He had supplied Beekman with a list of *all* the flights to Italy out of JFK that day—in chronological order of departure.

Why Italy? Beekman had asked him.

Because, Wheaton had explained, Rachel was obsessed with the fantasy of taking a year out of their lives to travel the world. Inevitably, that fantasy involved a definite itinerary that started in Rome, went to Florence, then Milan, then Genoa, then Positano and the entire Amalfi Coast before moving on to France. Rachel had even gone so far as to work out the details with a travel agent and pressure Wheaton to dip into his corporate funds at a time when Wheat/Tech was shaky. Her wheedling was a source of constant friction.

It was Wheaton's theory that if Rachel was going to leave the country for some time, she'd follow her Italy itinerary to the letter.

Sounded good in theory.

And so Chuck took a helicopter service to the airport. . . .

But no dice. He had crisscrossed the length and width of the godforsaken airport, going to the ticket counters, asking baggage handlers, scoping out the waiting lounges in the international terminal. But nothing. No sighting.

Feeling discouraged, Beekman walked away from Gate 35, craving food. He had another twelve minutes before the next flight to Italy took off—TWA Flight 169 to Rome at Gate 52. Might as well kill a few minutes with a quick nosh. As he melded into the flow of travelers pushing through the concourse, his eyes fell on a particularly pretty co-ed with a Walkman plugged into her ears. She must've been no more than nineteen, twenty. She looked sporty in a clinging USC T-shirt and a baggy Sergio Tacchini warm-up suit, a Prince tennis racquet tucked under her arm. Beekman ogled her backside as she hurried past him. She had a delicious little body that curved neatly into the lush swell of her behind. A California girl.

*Hubba hubba, you little slice of cheesecake you.*

He meandered through the airport in search of food, humming the melody to "Misty" to himself over and over and over. It was the first snippet of Muzak he had heard when he arrived at JFK and now, maddeningly, he could not get the horrid tune out of his head.

Chuck angled over to the food court. He approached the counter at Nathan's and ordered the lunch special. Hot dog, root beer, and cheese fries, $6.75. He took a small table and tore into the dog greedily, washing the mouthful down with a frosty gulp of root beer. *I'm a lot hungrier than I thought.* Over the public-address system, an authoritative voice interrupted the Muzak version of Elton John's "Your Song" to announce: "Mr. Yass to the courtesy desk please. Mr. Harry Yass."

Beekman nearly spat out a wad of chewed-up frankfurter in his laughter. Harry Yass. Very clever. For a moment, he toyed with the idea of having Mr. Mike Hock paged.

Then and there, a titanic wave of depression crushed his spirits.

Chuck Beekman was a desperately unhappy soul. It had gotten so bad, even his psychotherapist was unable to provide relief as of late. For one thing, his relationship with Phoebe, his nagging wife, continued to deteriorate with each passing day. Phoebe was afflicted by Seasonal Affective Disorder—or SAD—a mysterious ailment that affected as much as four percent of the population. It meant that Phoebe suffered from chronic depression related to a particular season, usually the whole of winter. It had something to do with diminished sunlight and photovoltaic deficiency or something. Whatever, she experienced crazy swings in her moods and her weight. She slept fourteen hours a day and lounged in bed for up to a week at a time. The bizarre twist was that now she suffered from SAD in the *summer.* She was on a maximum dosage of Prozac, but the upshot of it was that she stayed huddled in a fetal position in bed, surrounded by a dozen high-intensity lamps, stuffing her ballooning face with chocolate-covered ice cream Bon Bons and watching the yenta shows all day long. Oprah. Donahue. Montel Williams. Cripes, Phoebe *herself* was a primo candidate for one of those freaking shows. *"Hypochondriac Wives Who Lie in Bed All Day and Refuse Their Husbands' Sexual Needs"*—on *the next Geraldo!*

Beekman hadn't made love to his wife in over two months. God, a man had *needs.* Couldn't berate a married guy in his shoes for wanting to jump someone else's bones.

But McPhillips had been right on the mark, of course. The complications that would accompany an affair would be onerous. Divorce. Alimony. Worst of all, his irrational ex-wife would control a big chunk of Beekman Ford-Mazda. What would his father say about his oldest son *then?* Oy. The mere thought of it caused him to squinch his eyes tightly in dread.

The bottom line was that he feared his father more than anyone else he knew. The man was a cold fish. Chuck's face blazed with humiliation as he recalled the day he graduated from Penn, which started out as one of the happiest times of his life. His euphoria vaporized when his father handed him a "statement" for $785,673.55 over dinner at Bookbinder's. Beekman peered at it, asked his father what it was for. "It's important for you to know," Charles the Second told his namesake, "what you're getting into financially when you decide to have children."

Solving the cryptic meaning of that episode was a recurring objective of Chuck's psychotherapy sessions in the years following the incident. The son of a bitch had actually calculated it to the *penny*. Hey, it wasn't as if the event of Chuck's birth had forced Charles Beekman II to clip food coupons from the newspaper or anything.

It seemed Chuck was always fighting for his father's approval, yet somehow always falling short. Most recently, Chuck had approached his father with the idea that the fall clearance sale should be publicized extensively on "The Howard Stern Show" on WYSP-FM. A big fan of the show, Chuck was certain Howard and Robin could really do it up right, generate some excitement. Hell, even Baba Booey and Stutterin' John could make an appearance! It would be great!

Naturally, his old man blew the idea right out of the water. Instead, he opted to go with his younger brother Mike's plan to target all the local country & western stations and emphasize the deals on last year's model of Ford pickup trucks.

That latest incident only reinforced Chuck's conviction that his father liked Mike best.

And now *this*.

Come Monday, he was going to have to come clean with his old man. *Dad, Mitch Myerson wiped out my trust fund*. His old man would go apeshit, of course. Beekman imagined the inevitable ignominy: full control of the family dealership going to his younger brother, Michael. The thought decimated him. What was it going to be like, working as an underling to his younger brother? The ultimate sibling rivalry nightmare! Christ, he'd rather have white-hot knitting needles shoved into his eyes than have his younger brother as a boss and endure the abusiveness of Mike's Attila the Hun complex.

What would he do? What *could* he do?

*Quit*, that's what he'd do.

Beekman gasped at the thought that had just leapt into his mind. *Quit?* The notion was astonishing to him, foreign. But it *was* an option of course! He'd just tell his old man to take the dealership and *shove it*. The prospect of it gave him a liberating thrill. Nevertheless, he was stuck by the thorny problem of making a living. What could he do? Open up a Subway franchise? Buy a bar in Center City? Run a 7-Eleven in the burbs? Nah, the only thing he knew was the car business. Making an overstocked inventory of new and used Mazdas and Ford trucks *move*, blowing 'em out of the lot, that's what he knew and *all* he knew.

That's when his brainchild was born. *Screw 'em all! I'll open my own dealership!*

It was a true masterstroke of genius! Why not? If the old man and his brother conspired to freeze him out, he'd simply apply to Ford for his own franchise. He knew the ins and outs of applying for one's own dealership. He could pull it off. The head of the body shop was a totally cool, forty-year-old black guy by the name of Whitey. Chuck and Whitey got along *famously*. Maybe he could have a serious *tête-a-tête* with Whitey and entice him to apply as the lead partner in the franchise. A minority applicant would cut through years of red tape like a razor-sharp knife, vault the application to the top of the waiting list. The Big Three were dying to do some affirmative action after years of lining the pockets of white country clubbers like Chuck's dad. And Bruce Mazzola could work out the finances—selling junk bonds or stock to the investing public, arranging a limited partnership. Hell, maybe Bruce would even consent to being a silent partner in the new venture.

Beekman found his enthusiasm progressing steadily to euphoria. Somehow, a bright and shiny vision of a new wife, one like Cheri Richmond, came into the picture of his sparkling new life.... *Trading up to a brand new model to replace the used one he currently owned*, so to speak.

They wanted to futz with him? He'd show them *all*.

His wristwatch pager went off. He swallowed his mouthful of food and glanced down at the number: 359-9768.

A bank of phones awaited him two gates down. He dodged around the flow of passengers, maneuvering toward the only open phone. He used the Sprint card Wheaton had given him, calling Jeff's cellular phone.

Jeff Wheaton picked up on the half-ring. "Chuck?"

"Yeah."

"Any good news to report?"

"Negatory," he sighed. "Not a single sighting."

Wheaton let out a sound on the other end. When he spoke, his voice was thick with disappointment: "Ah, well, it was a longshot at best, I guess. Why don't you take a car service back to the hotel now?"

"Really?" He couldn't believe Jeff was packing it in already. "Are you sure? A TWA flight leaves in another, uh . . ." Beekman looked at the watch. "Another four minutes."

"Well, okay. Fine. But after that, come on back."

Wheaton hung up, disconnecting them. Beekman stared at the phone for a moment, pitying Jeff Wheaton. After all was said and done, everyone else would get on with their lives, but Jeff's life was completely shattered. How could you ever recover from having a best friend steal all your money *and* your wife too?

With some effort, Beekman was able to push it out of his mind, turning his thoughts instead to the more pleasant business of planning his own automobile dealership. He felt an electric thrill. He'd have to hash out the financing options with Mazzola over drinks later that night, but it was definitely doable.

*Chuck Beekman Ford-Mazda.* Jesus, he liked the ring of *that.*

# 19

His feet aching, his head pounding, Brian walked along Fifth Avenue, past Bergdorf Goodman on Fifty-seventh Street and F.A.O. Schwarz on 58th. When he arrived at The Plaza, it was 4:51 P.M. Since leaving the Grand Hyatt, he had already been to the Stanhope, the Royalton, the Ritz-Carlton, the Sherry Netherland, the Westbury, the Waldorf-Astoria, and the Peninsula. The Plaza was the last destination on his list.

McPhillips had gone oh-for-seven so far in the hunt for Mitch and Rachel. Accordingly, his hope was just about running on empty. Indeed, he had to agree with his wife and Mazzola. This had been as much a waste as they had both predicted.

Nevertheless, The Plaza represented the last best shot at finding Mitch and Rachel. The Plaza was at the top of everybody's list of New York's most luxurious hotels and was perhaps best suited to satisfying Rachel's voracious appetite for extravagance. Brian summoned up his last reserve of optimism and wended his way through three lanes of slow-moving Fleetwood limos and yellow cabs, as he walked up to the entrance of the immense eighteen-story French Renaissance structure.

He lingered at the entrance, pausing to read a plaque near the brass revolving door. It informed him that The Plaza, designed by Henry J. Hardenbergh, was an instant success the moment its doors opened on October 1, 1907. The Plaza became famous as the playhouse of American aristocracy, a home and stomping ground to heirs of the Vanderbilt, Gould, and Harriman fortunes as well as a favorite hangout of George M. Cohan, F. Scott Fitzgerald and even The Beatles. The greatest compliment ever paid to The Plaza came from the renowned American architect Frank Lloyd Wright. The founding father of modern architecture often kept a suite in the Plaza, and admiringly called it the only structure *not* designed by him that he admired.

McPhillips allowed himself a small smile. As usual, the plaque neglected to reveal the *full* story. The real dope on The Plaza came to him by way of Ruth Wycoff, a fellow member of Philadelphia's bankruptcy bar. She told him that the sparkle of The Plaza name had been tarnished when Donald Trump plunked down $390 million for the privilege of owning it in 1988. Apparently, The Donald had momentarily forgotten the art of the deal and had vastly overpaid for the property. To compound his folly, he immediately commenced hundreds of millions of dollars' worth of renovations at The Plaza. Ruth described a crunching debt burden that had the bankruptcy bar in New York drooling. Money was so tight, Ruth said gleefully, The Plaza's kitchen staff had been instructed to segregate beer and soda cans from the rest of the garbage to recoup their five-cent recycling value. Some of the more heartless wags went so far as to say that The Donald had had Ivana making beds to save a buck or two on staff.

Now that was Marla's job.

Brian pushed through the revolving door of The Plaza. He was instantly impressed. You wouldn't guess The Plaza had any money troubles from a cursory glance at the lobby. The opulence here was otherworldly. A gorgeous crystal chandelier hung before him, reflecting its own light in a thousand glittering sparkles. The rich, blood-red carpet crushed softly beneath his shoes, like walking on a cloud.

No time to admire the glitz, he reminded himself. He moved quickly past the dining area, where a wedding reception was in full swing. He could hear the soft clatter of utensils against china and the murmurs of the attendees over gentle chamber music. All too predictably, it was Pachelbel's Canon. The smell of fresh-baked bread and friesia greeted him. Turning right, he walked through the large archway into the main reception area.

To reach the concierge's desk, McPhillips had to move around an impressive arrangement of friesia that dominated the middle of the lobby. There were two people on duty behind the concierge's desk. Brian addressed the more senior-looking of the two. "Pardon me."

The concierge had snow-white hair, wire-rimmed glasses, and a kindly disposition. He looked up at McPhillips brightly, his eyes twinkling. "Yes?"

McPhillips took in a breath and let it out. At least this would be the last time he'd have to go through this rigmarole. "I know this will sound somewhat irregular, but . . . I'm looking for two people. It's very important that I find them."

"Are you a guest of the hotel, sir?"

"No, I'm not. But it's my belief, *our* belief really, that the two people in these pictures might be guests. If I could just show them to you, perhaps you could tell me where they are. I'm willing to pay you for your time."

The concierge held his gaze for a long moment before responding. Then, before McPhillips could demur, the concierge summoned a large man in a suit who was standing near the registration desk. McPhillips could tell immediately that the man was hotel security. He had a flesh-colored earplug secreted in his left ear; a flesh-colored wire looped out of the earpiece and disappeared into the jacket of his cheap suit.

"All such requests must be cleared through hotel security, sir," the concierge explained politely.

McPhillips nodded, though he hadn't wanted to get hotel security involved. Could mire things up.

The barrel-waisted security man approached in stiff, stick-up-his-wazoo strides. He carried the self-important air typical of the palace guard. He had a thick mustache, a heavy jaw marred by pockmarks, and cold steely eyes. The guy was about twenty pounds overweight, from his steady diet of red meat and Budweiser, and his black hair fell limply over a receding pate. McPhillips was reminded of G. Gordon Liddy, the legendary iceman who masterminded the Watergate break-in. Potentially lethal.

"S'up?" he asked the concierge in a gravelly voice.

The concierge made a mannerly gesture indicating McPhillips. "This gentleman is looking for two people he believes are guests of the hotel."

The security person turned to Brian as if acknowledging his existence for the first time. "Help you?" he asked curtly.

"My name is Brian McPhillips."

"Scagnetti. Joe."

They shook hands. Scagnetti's hand was cold but dry.

McPhillips explained things to Scagnetti in an abridged version. Scagnetti scarcely nodded as he listened to the details.

"Let's see the pictures," the security person said, making a quick beckoning motion that annoyed McPhillips.

Brian handed them over, expecting absolutely nothing to happen. To McPhillips' surprise, something did.

The security man's eyebrows climbed his forehead. "I've seen the woman," Scagnetti said with conviction.

McPhillips' eyes went wide. "You *have?* You've *seen* her?"

"Yeah, definitely," Scagnetti said, tapping the photo with a beefy knuckle. "You don't forget a face like that." He looked at McPhillips and smiled with yellow teeth. "In my line of work, I mean."

McPhillips could barely contain his excitement. "Have you seen her recently?"

"This afternoon. In fact, I believe she might be registered in the hotel."

McPhillips slapped a hand to his forehead. "Incredible. This is amazing." He paced around in a tight circle, trying to think. He had to call Jeff immediately. "You think she's still here? I mean, can you find out? If I give you her name—"

Scagnetti held up a hand as if to say *whoa there.* "I don't know. Why don't you come to my office for a cup a joe, and we'll put our heads together on this."

"This is unreal," McPhillips murmured. "I need to make a phone call."

"You can make it from my office," Scagnetti said, accommodatingly. "C'mon, it's just down the hall."

They strode briskly past the great hall with the wedding

reception in full force. Past the hotel-owned shop that sold nothing but mementos emblazoned with The Plaza crest. "You have no idea what this means to me and my friends," McPhillips burbled.

"Yeah, I'm sure," Scagnetti said, somewhat distractedly. From his suit jacket, he withdrew a walkie-talkie with a stubby rubber-coated antenna and raised it to his lips. "Goldwater, drop what you're doing and get to I-room two." Then Scagnetti jammed the radio back into the inside pocket of his jacket.

They walked for a considerable period of time, winding their way down a seemingly endless series of hallways. Eventually, they arrived at a room secluded somewhere deep in the bowels of the hotel. Scagnetti opened the door and switched on the lights. Inside, it was decidedly un-Plaza-like. Dim and spartan, it stank of stale tobacco smoke. There was only a conference table, several uncomfortable-looking chairs and a telephone. An entire wall was made up of a dark glass mirror. It appeared to be a meeting room of some sort.

The man Scagnetti had paged—Goldwater—entered the room right behind them. Goldwater was a hulking gorilla, also with bad skin, but even more bald than Scagnetti. McPhillips expected an introduction, but Scagnetti merely looked at Goldwater and, in an unimpressed tone, said, "That was fast."

Goldwater shrugged and said nothing.

Then, unexpectedly, Scagnetti slammed the door shut with a rifle-shot crack, startling McPhillips.

"Have a seat, sir," Scagnetti commanded in a peremptory tone.

*Oh, shit*. McPhillips' stomach sank. "You haven't actually seen her, have you?"

"Have a seat, *sir*," Scagnetti growled, pulling one out from under the table for him. "The sooner you cooperate, the sooner all of us can get out of here and get on with our lives."

McPhillips cursed under his breath and sat down heavily. *Great!* Now these two jamoches were planning to get their rocks off playing Gestapo with him. "You've got it all wrong," he said, amazed at how *lame* that sounded.

Scagnetti ignored him and lit a cigarette. "By law, I've got to inform you that we're videotaping this entire conversation on tape-delay closed-circuit television." He indicated the mirrored wall. "It may eventually be admissible as evidence."

"Oh Christ," McPhillips moaned in disbelief. "You're *mirandizing* me? You're not even a *real* cop."

"Like I said," Scagnetti told him, "this conversation is being recorded."

McPhillips wasn't entirely certain that they could legally do this, but he wasn't about to make a federal case out of it. Not now.

Scagnetti addressed Goldwater. "Gordo, this guy's waving these photos around, harassing our people with probing questions about hotel guests."

Gordon Goldwater laced his fingers across the bulging stomach of his mutton-shaped body and slowly shook his head from side to side. McPhillips half expected him to say *tsk-tsk*. Instead, he said to Brian, "What're you doing that for, mister? Are you a private detective?"

"No. I'm an attorney," McPhillips said.

Scagnetti made a sour face. "You tryin' to serve some papers on one of our guests, counselor? We don't go for that—lawyers hassling our guests with legal papers—"

McPhillips waved him off. "It has nothing to do with that. I already told you why I'm here. The guy in that picture embezzled millions of dollars. That woman is believed to be an accomplice. She's the wife of a friend of mine."

"Yeah? That right?" Scagnetti issued a throaty chuckle of disbelief. "Don't know what it is, but I got a bad feeling about you, Mister Attorney." He dragged on his cigarette and fired Brian a malicious glare. "Yessir, a bad feeling."

"Lemme see the pictures," Gordon Goldwater said.

Scagnetti gave them to Goldwater, who looked them over.

"Y'know, we get a lot of troublemakers hanging out at this hotel," Scagnetti informed Brian. "Con artists, flimflammers, male prostitutes, firebugs, luggage thieves. Even mental patients. So I'm askin' you to shoot me straight. What's your game?"

"I don't have a game," McPhillips sighed irritably. "I'm personally out of pocket to the tune of one hundred thousand dollars, and I'm motivated to get it back. That's all. You know,

I've schlepped around to every other luxury hotel in midtown, and not *one* has jerked my chain around like *you* guys have—"

Unmoved by this revelation, Scagnetti glared at McPhillips in venomous silence. "What do you think, Gordo?"

"Nice looking bird," Goldwater said. "Got real nice gams."

"I was talkin' about this guy," Scagnetti said in mock exasperation. But he was actually smiling; Goldwater had known full well who he was referring to.

Goldwater shrugged. "Hard to say."

"Call me tone-deaf," Goldwater said, turning back to McPhillips, "but something' don't ring right to me. You're not FBI, are you?"

McPhillips sighed again. "No."

"CIA?"

"No. I'm *nobody*."

"If that's some other guy's wife in the photos, what do you care?"

"I told you already," McPhillips said, unable to hide his irritation. "The guy who's with her took all my money too. Check it out with the FBI if you want. It's the Myerson case."

Holding his gaze, Scagnetti said, "I suppose I could ring up DeBalducci. He's a friend of mine at the Bureau. Run this cock'n'bull story up a flagpole, and see if anyone there salutes it."

Gordon Goldwater spoke up. "Could take hours, this bein' a Saturday."

Scagnetti shrugged. "Why should I care? I'm on the clock. Just means time-and-a-half for me." He chuckled. "I don't know if our attorney friend gets paid by the hour. Which happens to remind me, Gordo, how does a lawyer say 'screw you'?"

"How?"

" 'Here's the bill for my services.' "

*Har-de-har. What a pair of tools.*

Fed up, McPhillips said, "All right, give me back the pictures, and I'll just get out of your hair, all right?"

Scagnetti ignored him. "You know what my theory is," Scagnetti said to Goldwater. "I think Mr. Attorney's after the hardbody in this snapshot."

"You mean a *Fatal Attraction* kind of thing?" Goldwater said.

"Yeah. Mr. Attorney here has a puppy-dog crush on some other guy's tomato, and he's trackin' her down."

"That's totally absurd," McPhillips said. He felt his face burn with humiliation. "Why're you guys bustin' my hump?"

Scagnetti leaned in so close, McPhillips could tell he had been avoiding regular dental checkups for years. " 'Cause I don't like sleazebag sharpsters like *you* asking probin' questions about the guests in *my* hotel." Scagnetti leaned back. "They pay me to worry about that."

McPhillips' eyes settled on Scagnetti's hair. "Not enough, judging by the quality of that toupee."

A lethal silence prevailed. Unable to smother his amusement at the put-down of his colleague, Goldwater snorted with glee. But Scagnetti's face blazed a stop-sign red. "You got a real smart mouth. You want to play hardball? All right, we'll play hardball, you mutt."

McPhillips leaned forward and snarled, "Scagnetti, you really wanna fuck with a lawyer? You ever hear the words *'false imprisonment'?* 'Unlawful restraint of an individual's personal liberty or freedom of locomotion'? You know all about false imprisonment, don't you, Scagnetti? Multimillion-dollar punitive damages and all that? Didn't they teach you that in rent-a-cop school?"

Scagnetti stared at him for a moment. "You threatenin' me with a lawsuit, counselor?"

McPhillips snarled back, "You bet your momma's tail I am." Brian pointed at the two-way mirror. "And I'm gonna subpoena that fucking tape as evidence. You think Donald Trump has money problems *now*, you just wait 'til his ass gets dragged into federal court—"

For several moments, Scagnetti and Goldwater swapped uncertain looks. Then McPhillips' wristwatch pager went off.

"Jesus, what's that?" Goldwater said.

"It's my pager," McPhillips said. "I need the phone."

"Be my guest," Scagnetti said sarcastically.

McPhillips punched up the number displayed on the face of the pager, 359-9768. Jeff picked up after a single ring. "Brian?"

"Yeah, it's me. I'm just chewing the fat with the friendly folks who work Plaza security."

"Real smart mouth," Scagnetti hissed.

Jeff Wheaton was in ill-humor. "Well, old buddy, looks like it's a wash. Nobody's seen nothing."

The disappointment in Wheaton's voice tugged at McPhillips' heartstrings. He didn't know what to say. "Well, we did our best, Jeff."

"Yeah, that we did. That we did. Everybody's getting together at the Hyatt, and then we're gonna go out and have a pity party or something. So, I'll see you in a half-hour, okay?"

"Yeah. Sure."

"Good. Oh, and Brian?"

"Yeah?"

"Thanks for coming along. I appreciate it."

"Forget it."

Wheaton hung up.

McPhillips gently replaced the phone on the cradle and stared at the floor. After a long silence, he looked up at his captors and said, "If you guys have gotten your badass rocks off, am I free to go?"

"Ah, get the hell out of here," Scagnetti grumbled, waving him away.

McPhillips fired a frosty glare at Scagnetti on the way out, but the security chief avoided his eyes.

# 20

At that moment, three men were possessed with thoughts of Rachel Wheaton, one of whom was her jilted husband Jeff. . . .

On Saturday afternoons especially, the open-air AT&T InfoQuest Atrium on Madison and Fifty-fifth Street was a popular hangout for romance-novel readers, unpublished writers, kibbitzers, and loiterers alike. That afternoon, all forty of the tables in the high-ceilinged atrium were occupied. At several tables, elderly Jewish retirees spoke in excited Yiddish about the Ivy League schools their grandchildren were attending. In other seats, homeless men in grime-coated winter jackets dozed. Near the entrance of the building, a spirited game of chess between two middle-aged men had drawn a fascinated crowd and considerable betting activity among the spectators. But several of the people loitering around in the public area of Park Avenue Plaza craned their necks to catch a glimpse of the real oddball among them that afternoon: some guy sitting by himself and surrounded by a half dozen electronic gadgets and gizmos.

Jeff Wheaton sat at the table, knowing he was being stared at, not giving a damn. His laptop computer was humming before him, pulling up the names of the hotels and the people with whom he spoke from his database software. His cellular phone was connected to the computer's RS-232C serial port and he was able to dial each number simply by entering a command into the computer. He called each hotel on the printout, asking if anyone had seen anything in the interim.

Of course, no one had.

His thoughts were dominated by those of his wife. He shuffled through his memory bank, trying to find the missing piece to the puzzle: *How did this happen?*

*They'd met at a Center City health club. She was working the StairMaster with such ferocity that a crowd of men had gathered to watch. Wheaton found it highly exotic the way she jounced up and down on the levers of the whining machine with the rhythm and resolve of a piston. Her body was tight and well-sculpted; her movements were feline-graceful. Her face flushed with a rosy glow from the exertion and perspiration; she gave off a magnetic heat that drew him and the others in an attraction that was purely animal. When she turned to him—him!—and flashed a tentative smile, Wheaton felt his knees buckle.*

*Some steroid-addled jerk with a World Gym T-shirt said to his companion, "Man-oh-man, what I wouldn't give to make soup out of her tights."*

*Among them, only Jeff Wheaton worked up the hair to approach her. He expected it to be a total kamikaze move; a girl as attractive as this one must have had to fend off literally thousands of unwanted, "Anyone ever tell you you're beautiful?" solicitations from gold-chained Guidos in her time. So when Wheaton tried to strike up a conversation with her at the water fountain, he fully expected to crash and burn.*

*However, he was delighted to find that she was not a stuck-up bitch-on-a-pedestal, as one might think. Rather, she was friendly and accessible. She told him her name was Rachel Fairweather.*

*"My name is Jeff," he said. "Jeff Wheaton."*

*Her eyes sparkled. "I know."*

*"You do?"*

*"Sure. You own the computer company, don't you?"*

*"That's right," he said, puzzled. "How did you know that?"*

"*Everyone at the club knows that.*" Her smile broadened.

As far as Wheaton was concerned, there could be such a thing as too much beauty in a woman. The type frequently appeared in Revlon commercials and on the cover of Cosmopolitan. Such a woman was so beautiful as to appear utterly untouchable, as cold as Freon and as responsive as a mannequin. This type of beauty rendered the woman otherworldly; for all intents and purposes, she was an alien.

But Rachel Fairweather was not that way at all. For although she was breathtakingly beautiful, there was something about her that was warm and inviting. She had a gift for making the give-and-take of male-female conversation effortless. She liberally sprinkled compliments of his physical appearance in the talk, touched his arm lightly to emphasize key points, engaged his eyes with hers. She struck Wheaton as that rarest of creatures—the most beautiful cheerleader in your high school who was humble enough to talk to you and to share a laugh with you even if you weren't the starting quarterback of the football team, even if you had the misfortune of being born with an aptitude for mathematics.

And what was it she had said to him just now? You own the computer company.

Well, whatever. If a woman this stunning was willing to give him the time of day simply because he founded a computer company with $13.4 million in annual sales, that was fine with him. Wheaton himself was not exactly a Mel Gibson, but he was good-looking in a pleasant, yuppie sort of way, and he was comfortable with the opposite sex. He had *built a multimillion-dollar business from squat, after all, and why shouldn't he be entitled to a beautiful girlfriend like Rachel Fairweather?*

In fact, that was his very thought as he asked her to join him for dinner. She instantly accepted. He couldn't believe his luck.

That weekend, they made love for the first time. Making love with Rachel was as phenomenal as he had expected it to be. She was a spirited and inventive partner, willing to put his pleasure before her own time after time. She took maximizing his every orgasm with incredible seriousness, as if each one presented an opportunity for her to prove her superiority in bed over all his past and future lovers. Though Wheaton had never been one to confuse great sex with love, Rachel's passion in bed was something he had never before encountered. It was such that he became instantly obsessed with her.

He found he craved her companionship constantly. She had a way of making him feel as if he were the only one on the face of the earth she talked to in this manner. She could effortlessly have him believe that his sense of humor was the best she had ever encountered. She was all poise, charm, and charisma; like the way she would laugh in ringing peals at his most effortless attempts at humor; like the way she would lock his eyes up in hers and brush his forearm lightly with her fingertips when she was making a point; like the way she would drop her silken voice to a sweet whisper when she shared an intimacy with him. As Wheaton would describe Rachel to his friends, she had a way of making a man feel like a man. He found it impossible to resist a woman like this once she turned her charms on him unremittingly.

Nevertheless, the speed with which their relationship gathered velocity was alarming to Jeff's many friends and employees. Rachel's beauty was never in dispute, but many thought she had a saccharine-sweet phoniness about her. For her part, Rachel was unable to get along with anyone of her gender; her cool air of control and confidence was off-putting to women. "She's after his money," was a cynicism heard from more than one of Wheaton's female acquaintances.

Jeff Wheaton didn't believe this for a moment. Of course, he wasn't naive enough to deny that his instant success was a part of his appeal to her. Indeed, he often joked that keeping her in the style to which she had grown accustomed burned more cash than his entire research and development department did at Wheat/Tech. But he was confident that his money and his reputation as one of America's most prominent under-thirty entrepreneurs were only small components of his attractiveness to her. They were compatible on so many levels that he was certain she was in it for love *and* money, not simply one or the other.

But then, as the old cliché goes, he spoiled a good thing and married her.

*It wasn't long after the honeymoon that Rachel dropped her carefully crafted facade, and Wheaton began learning new peccadilloes about his new wife. For one thing, she was seriously addicted to shopping. Moreover, he learned that flirtation was an impossible habit for her to break. He frequently observed her catching the eye of men they would pass on the street. She enjoyed her talent of causing a man's heart to flutter simply by giving him a smokey look with her bedroom eyes; the fact that she was now married was not enough incentive for her to cease her indulgence in this sport. Wheaton found it maddening.*

*The largest source of contention in their marriage proved to be Rachel's inability to make a career out of modeling. Truth be told, Philadelphia is hardly a boomtown when it comes to providing livelihoods for models and actresses. On the other hand, New York was simply ninety miles to the north, and it was the center of the universe for the modeling profession. So Rachel set her sights on a move to New York and began to work on Jeff to relocate his computer operations. Wheaton wouldn't hear of it. New York City was too expensive, he told her. The taxes would choke a small business to death. The cost of rent alone would be mind-boggling. Cost of labor. Unions. Besides which, he had already invested capital in a factory outside of Philly; to move that operation would be plain foolhardy. No, he told her. New York was out of the question.*

*After his rejection of this proposal, she blamed him for anchoring her to a city that had no opportunities for models. She declared him an obstacle to her career. She accused him of being sexist, as well; perhaps he would be happier having a no-brain wife who was barefoot, pregnant, and in the kitchen, fetching him beers whenever he yelled for one. Wheaton told her she was spoiled, which did nothing to soothe the growing hostility between them. Rachel often sought vengeance by engaging in gargantuan shopping sprees that left Wheaton staggered by the monthly Visa bills that came in their wake.*

*When Rachel cut him off from sex, he grew despondent and began contacting marriage counselors, hoping to repair their crumbling marriage. But then a different catastrophe took him away from his noble efforts: Wheaton's business plunged into a severe tailspin.*

It wasn't his fault. His company was a victim of the computer industry's most treacherous reality: Today's technology is instantly doomed to be yesterday's technology. Wheat/Tech had succeeded in carving out a niche for itself in the booming laptop computer marketplace with a simple tripartite approach: quality that was comparable to the Japanese; prices that undercut the Japanese; and customer service that blew the Japanese away. This was an incredibly successful formula for several years. In fact, Wheaton's company had always received high marks from PC magazine and Computer Shopper for its ability to keep up with the breakthroughs that occurred in personal computer technology, reacting swiftly to the changes and demands of the marketplace.

But not long ago, the company was full steam ahead on production of the 286-chip laptops when, suddenly, 386-chip machines became all the rage. By the time Wheat/Tech's research and development team had configured a new line of 386 machines, the 486-chip generation was born. Next thing one knew, laptops were passé; notebooks were the thing. Then palmtops became hot. If you were in the business of manufacturing personal computers, it was impossible not to get killed during this incredible revolution. The misfortunes of the industry were compounded by a killer recession that decimated corporate-level sales. The fortune Jeff Wheaton had won overnight was now being lost as quickly. The next chapter in the story of Wheat/Tech Computers looked like Chapter 11.

Life was hard, but business was murder.

While he huddled with slews of expensive attorneys and accountants to salvage the business he had worked to create from nothing, his marriage was sliding irreversibly. His wife's loyalty to him dissipated proportionately with his net worth. When he asked her to scale back on her shopping, she took it as a personal affront. She stepped up her spending. She became antagonistic and more critical of his appearance and mannerisms. She took to staying out late at night with "friends," and made mysterious phone calls, talking in soft whispers in front of him.

*Finally, the beginning of the end came a few months ago, when she abruptly announced, "I want to take acting lessons in New York."*

"In New York? Wait a minute, time out. Run that by me again?"

*She rolled her eyes and sighed bitterly. "I said I'm going to take acting lessons in New York."*

"Acting lessons? Why would you want to take acting lessons?"

"I want to have something to fall back on in case the modeling career doesn't work out."

"Acting?" *Jeff Wheaton was genuinely perplexed.* "You mean to say that's going to be your fallback career?"

"Modeling is very competitive, and you can do it only until you're thirty. Acting is a career that you can do for the rest of your life."

"Rachel," *he said,* "acting is very difficult to break into. Kind of like hitting the lottery."

"I'm aware of that," *she snapped.* "That's why I want to enroll in this class in New York. It's taught by Sandra Seacatt, and she's the finest acting coach in the city. All the top stars take lessons from her."

"Uh-huh. And how much will it cost? Including train tickets?"

*Her voice was coated with equal measures of contempt and sarcasm.* "Oh, I know we can't afford it. So don't worry about it, I'll pay for it myself. I just wanted to let you know."

"How are you going to pay for it, Rachel?"

"I'll manage."

"Rachel, it's very expensive. There's headshots, videotapes, résumés, agents—"

"I said, I'll manage."

"And acting, Rachel. I mean, there's a million pretty aspiring actresses waiting tables in New York—"

"Yes, Jeffrey. I'm painfully aware of how little you believe in me—"

"That's not the point."

"It most certainly *is the point. Of course, it's* too much *of an investment for us to make in* my *career. You've done everything you possibly can to sabotage* my *modeling career. Everything we do is for you and* your *work. Never for* my *work."*

*Jeff Wheaton was powerless to keep his frustrations from surging past the boiling point. "Work? You call* that *work? Forgive me, honey-baby, but parading down a catwalk in Paris in next season's designer fashions is* not *work.* Work *is getting up at quarter to six every morning;* work *is dealing with a shitstorm in the office every day;* work *is doing everything you can to meet a payroll until your stomach burns a fucking hole in itself. That, you spoiled princess, is* work*."*

*Unaccountably, her lips parted in a cryptic smile. Then she narrowed her eyes into hateful slits and said, "You make me want to go out and fuck somebody else. You know that?"*

*"You don't need me for that," he hissed. "That's second nature to you."*

*They stared at each other for a long while. They had, quite simply, become strangers to each other.*

*Then she said, "You've already lost me, Jeffrey. I'm already gone."*

*She left the townhouse, slamming the front door behind her. His stomach boiling with rage and anguish, Jeff Wheaton wondered if she had made up the whole thing about the acting class, intentionally provoking a fight so that she could go out for the evening without his questioning her. . . .*

*She didn't come home that night. As the early morning hours crawled by, Wheaton flipped about restlessly, unable to slip into the membrane of sleep. He was certain his wife was in the arms of another man at that very moment, and a fire raged in his brainpan. He agonized over excruciatingly painful questions: Who was she with? What was he like? Was she doing for the other guy what she used to do for him?*

*And now, to find that the other man was his old college roommate, Mitch Myerson.*

*Well, guess what. Mitch could have her. Good luck, farewell, and amen to them both. They deserved each other. Yet he burned with an inarticulate desire for some closure, to bring things full circle. Jeff briefly fantasized about finding them, con-*

*fronting them. What would he do if that happened? Though he had never before felt this way, he was fairly certain he would kill Mitch with his bare hands. As for Rachel, his first impulse was to strike her as well—but no, no he couldn't do that to her. He had loved her too much, too recently. Instead, perhaps he could utter some Bogartesque phrase that would haunt her forever. No, actually, on second thought, he just wanted to stop them from getting away with millions of dollars of pensioners' and orphans' money. He wanted them to rot in the slam for, say, ten to twenty years of their lives.*

*It was a fantasy.*

*And it looked like that was all it ever would be. . . .*

On the way out of The Plaza Hotel, McPhillips showed the pictures to several staffers. None recognized either Rachel or Mitch as guests of the hotel. That was par for the course. Dejected, Brian left with nothing more than another Plaza anecdote to tell Ruth Wycoff at the next meeting of the city bankruptcy bar.

Outside, he was instantly beset by several men in ridiculous costumes who beseeched him to take a ride in their horse-drawn carriages. He waved them away. He crossed the street to the wide plaza that faced the hotel and he rested on the edge of the large fountain there, taking care to avoid the fresh bird droppings. Pigeons seemed to be everywhere. Brash and bloated, they strutted fearlessly among the people on the plaza. Delighted Japanese tourists took photos of the filthy birds and fed them bits of soft pretzels, fortifying New York's exploding pest population. McPhillips watched without interest as a film crew worked industriously to set up the next shot for a movie at the exterior of the Oak Room. Brian wasn't entirely certain, but he thought he spotted the character actor he had seen on the train, standing at the chow line. . . .

*It's my fault this all happened,* McPhillips said to himself miserably. *None of this would've happened if I'd done the right thing. I should've told Jeff right away.* Yes, indeed, it was McPhillips who had had the last clear shot at preventing this from happening. He groaned aloud, lamenting his failure to act some two years ago.

\* \* \*

*Jeff Wheaton popped the question to Rachel Fairweather after just three months of dating. He proposed to her at the Harry Connick, Jr., concert in Philadelphia. Connick, who happened to be an acquaintance of Wheaton's younger brother, graciously arranged to have two front-row-center seats reserved for Jeff and Rachel at the show. An hour into the performance, Jeff was brought up onstage, where he got on his knees and proposed to her before fourteen thousand delighted spectators. When Rachel said "yes," the hall erupted in cheers, and Connick himself played an especially spirited version of "It Had To Be You" in honor of the happy couple. Jeff Wheaton's circle of acquaintances was abuzz for weeks afterward. Who was this girl that had cast such a spell on the Jeffster?*

*Shortly after the Connick concert, Jeff and Rachel threw an engagement party for some fifty guests at Jeff's spacious townhouse in Bryn Mawr. Although McPhillips, for one, had met Rachel on perhaps four or five previous occasions, the party would mark the first time many of Jeff's friends met the mysterious woman.*

*The night of the engagement party, Josh McPhillips was ill with the flu, bedridden with nausea and dizziness. McPhillips was torn and told Lisa they should beg off the engagement party entirely, but Lisa insisted that Brian put in an appearance for both of them. Reluctantly, Brian came to agree that it was the right thing to do, but he promised to make it an early night.*

*The night of the party, he called ahead to Wheaton's and offered to lend a hand, and Jeff invited him out a half-hour before the other guests were expected to arrive.*

*When Brian arrived shortly before seven-thirty, Jeff's car wasn't there. His new fiancée answered the door. McPhillips was astonished when he saw how beautiful she was. Rachel Fairweather wore a Louis Dell'ori silk crepe de chine strapless party dress that revealed as much of her body as it concealed. She lingered there for a moment as if presenting herself for Jeff's friend's approval. "Hello, Brian," she said in cheerful singsong.*

*"Good to see you, Rachel," he said, bussing her cheek. "As*

*you know, Lisa sends her regrets. She's just feeling under the weather."*

"Of course," Rachel said, her eyes twinkling. "Well, it was good of you to come without your wife." As she said this, she flashed him a dazzling movie-star smile. "Do come in."

"Thank you." He stepped inside and closed the door behind him. "Where's the groom-to-be?"

"You just *missed* him. He went to Super Fresh to buy some more snacks and club soda." She clicked her tongue and rolled her eyes in mock exasperation. "You know Jeffrey. Too much is just enough." That maxim obviously applied to his choice of fiancées as well. What a piece of eye candy!

"Well, congratulations to you both," McPhillips said. He presented her with a chilled bottle of Perrier-Jouet champagne with a fleur-de-lis hand-painted on its face and the matching hand-painted champagne flutes as well.

"Oh, aren't you a babe," she cooed, accepting the gifts.

"Lisa and I will be sending you an engagement gift next week. Now tell me, how can I put myself to use?"

"Really, Brian. There's no need to concern yourself. Everything is quite in hand." She arched an inquisitive eyebrow. "Can I buy you a drink perhaps?"

"Club soda for openers would be perfect, thanks."

*Instead, she brought him a J & B and water. Since it was his usual drink, he made no protest. He sipped it.*

"How is it?" *she asked, biting her lip.*

"Strong."

"Good," she said. "Oh, and may I be so bold as to make a suggestion?"

*He blinked.* "Of course."

*Then she surprised him by stepping forward, close enough so that he could feel the heat of her breath on his face.* "Loosen up, Mr. Attorney," *she teased him, tugging loose the Windsor knot of his Burberry's red and blue striped rep tie.* "It's a party for god's sake!"

"That it is," he said awkwardly. *God, she was very easy on the eyes, Jeff's fiancée. He was ashamed to admit to himself that* he'd been slightly aroused by her act of yanking his tie. "When Jeff gets back, I'd like to make a toast to the two of you."

She didn't respond to this. Instead, she just gazed at him for a while as if she were committing his features to memory. A half smile played on her cherry-red lips. "Come sit with me on the sofa."

She put some Kenny G music on the Yamaha stereo. An alarm went off in his brain. Jeff's fiancée was flirting with him, if not downright coming on to him. He dismissed the thought as preposterous. But what did he really know about this girl? Not that much. She had attended Boston University, liberal arts major; her family's wealth had come from developing shopping malls upstate; she loved to party. Things had happened so quickly between her and Jeff; he wondered how much he knew about her.

He tried to make conversation. "I understand you do some modeling."

"Some." She rolled her eyes modestly.

"How's that going for you?"

She was capable of turning a simple shrug into some elegant gesture. "Philadelphia's not exactly where it's at. New York is where I'll be eventually, where we will be, I mean." She smiled. McPhillips nodded and had another sip of his scotch. Rachel was one of the ten most beautiful women he had ever spoken to this closely. "Your fiancé's a very lucky man to have such a beautiful woman."

Her eyes took on a liquid glint. "Do you really think so?"

"Sure," he drank off some of the scotch. "Jeffrey's a lucky guy. And you're a lucky woman."

She rolled her eyes modestly and laughed, a lilting melodic giggle. "No, I mean, do you think I'm beautiful, Brian?"

He chose his words carefully, so as not to come off as suggestive. "I think you're attractive, yes, if that's what you mean. You're a model, after all. Don't you think you are?"

"Of course. I'd just like to hear you say it." She playfully swept her slim fingers through her shiny blond hair. "Another drink, Brian?"

He looked down at the drink in his hands. To his surprise, he had finished it off. Before he could respond, she was up and *making him another.* McPhillips looked at his watch. What the hell was keeping Jeff?

She brought him a fresh cocktail. He thanked her.

"So, how do you like married life?" she asked him.

"It's wonderful. I highly recommend it."

"Uh-huh," she said, looking at him sideways, as if she were skeptical of this claim. She watched him with those eyes, and a slight smile playing on her face, like she didn't quite believe him.

"What is it?" he said after a while.

"Don't you ever get tired of, you know?" She rolled her eyes and laughed, acting as if she was uncomfortable asking him this. "Don't you ever think of being with another person, ever?"

What's going on inside her head? "No," he blurted a little too quickly. Oh, how she loved to play big-time headgames with him. That's all it was. Maybe she'd been something of a tease all her life, and she was just doing what came naturally. Just for the sport of it, purely innocuous. But he realized he was trembling some.

"You know, you are a very handsome man, Brian McPhillips," she said. "I just know you broke a lot of girls' hearts in your time."

"Why are you telling me this?"

She feigned hurt feelings. "Is it wrong for me to tell you that I find myself attracted to you?"

"Yes. It doesn't sound . . . right, Rachel."

She moved closer to him and brushed a thin wisp of blond hair from her eye. "But it's true."

"I'm one of your fiancé's best friends." How lame *that* sounded!

"So? That doesn't make you any less handsome than you already are."

"It's *not* appropriate."

She giggled. "I'm *not* married yet."

"I am!" Pull away Brian, *he thought.* Get up and leave, Brian. But he did neither.

She sighed. "Don't you think I'm sexy?" she teased him in a childlike voice.

"C'mon, Rachel. Stop it." It sounded feeble.

*"Make me," she teased. "Tell me to go away."*

*"Why are you doing this?" he whispered.*

*"Because I'm a bitch," she said cheerfully. "But I'm a very, very beautiful bitch. That means I can have whatever I want."* Her hand caressed his thigh lightly. His flesh tingled with sparks where she had touched him. God, her seductive powers were incredible and—he feared—irresistible. She had such beautiful eyes, warm and uninhibited, green and blue with flecks of gold. This wasn't happening; this wasn't happening. She grabbed him by his tie and pulled herself closer to him, her bee-stung lips just inches away from his. Then she put the fingertips of her right hand to his face and lightly raked his cheeks, his chin, his jaw with her nails. When she moved her mouth toward his, he realized that the unimaginable was very imaginable, was about to become real, and he felt himself anticipating the sensation of her lips pressed against his. She was so very, very beautiful, and although it was his close friend's engagement party, for chrissake, and although he had a wife at home with a sick little boy . . . he was utterly powerless. It was unstoppable. She kissed him.

She pulled away and touched a finger to his lips. With a serene smile, she said, "Jeffrey must never know." Then she rose from the couch and disappeared into the kitchen, leaving Brian to wallow in his arousal, guilt, and humiliation.

After that, of course, McPhillips had a miserable time. Jeff's townhouse was filled with young professionals of every description—a metropolitan staff writer for the Metro section of the Inquirer, a young V.P. who worked the front office of the Flyers hockey team, a ghostwriter of famous people's bios, a book-jacket photographer, and several young executives from Cigna, where Jeff had once worked. Even Mitch Myerson made an appearance, though he showed up with a hideous, gum-chewing date from Camden, New Jersey. Tellingly, Rachel's only invitee was her sister from Baltimore. The party was conspicuously bereft of any friends of hers.

It was time to leave when Jeff pulled him aside and said, "Bri, what's the matter with you? You haven't said a word to anyone all night."

"Ah, I'm sorry, Jeff. You know, I feel guilty that Lisa's home by herself with the kids. I think I should leave."

Jeff nodded sympathetically. "Nobody'll think you're an uncouth slob if you go home to look after your children. And if they do?" He shrugged. "Screw 'em."

On the way out the door, Rachel stuck her tongue out at him, a gesture only he witnessed. Jeffrey must never know. *Her words haunted him.*

*That night, while he slept next to his wife, Brian McPhillips' graphic sex dreams wove in and out of his coil of sleep. He awoke in the morning, feeling a fire of guilt in his belly. It was the closest he had ever come to infidelity.* Don't be so kind to yourself, *he thought.* It *was* infidelity.

He should've told Jeff. He should've just tossed the facts on the table and let Jeff make the call for himself. God, he should've come clean with Rachel.

Easy to say that now.

It was one of those moments one devoutly wishes to have over. But now, Jeff's wife was gone; Brian's money was gone, and so was the money of twenty-eight other innocent people.

He plodded dejectedly in the direction of the Grand Hyatt, his conscience nagging him, saying, *I told you so.*

After consummating the transaction, Mitch took a walk to gather his faculties. He found himself under the expanse of a deciduous tree somewhere in the middle of Central Park. The Park functioned as something of a demilitarized zone, a DMZ, to the crime and madness of the City. Mitch strolled toward the small rowboat lake in the Cherry Hill area of the park. Red-breasted orioles twittered musically in the poplar tress above. Mitch drew up to a lamppost between two park landmarks, Bow Bridge and the Bethesda Fountain. He peered in both directions to be certain the coast was clear.

A bald woman of Amazonian proportions glided by on Rollerblades, the icy expression of an Easter Island icon on her face. Mitch waited until she passed until he lit up the joint. *Mustn't make a stupid stupid mistake now,* he reminded himself. He was toting a Gucci bag full of Italian currency. Still, he was clearly entitled to a celebratory toke or two.

His lungs filled to capacity with pot smoke, his thoughts turned to the woman that made all this possible. Rachel, sweet Rachel. . . .

*He recalled the day these dizzying events first went into motion. It was just over three months ago today that Rachel Wheaton had come to Myerson's office in Center City. He could remember it as clearly as if it had been a religious vision; he would always remember every nuance.*

*She came to him at about three o'clock on a Friday afternoon when he happened to have taken one of the bloodiest business beatings ever. The irony of it all brought a nostalgic smile to his lips.*

*Rachel Wheaton had called his office earlier that morning. Said she needed to see him that afternoon. It was a personal matter, she'd said. His curiosity piqued, he agreed.*

*When his secretary Sophie buzzed him on the intercom to announce Rachel's arrival, he found himself sniffing his armpit to see if he stank; pulling out the rowing machine from behind his desk to impress her. Though she was the wife of a friend, there was something about the magnificence of Rachel Wheaton that made a man feel like a man.*

*Mitch shooed Sophie away. It was just the two of them now.*

*God, Rachel was so breathtakingly beautiful that afternoon. But she looked so fragile, so vulnerable. Like a woman whose heart had been shattered. A protective impulse swept over him.*

*"Thank you for seeing me, Mitchell," she had said in a voice that was almost a whisper.*

*"Of course. Anything for a friend. Can I get you something, Rachel? A drink?"*

*"Do you have a sparkling water?"*

*"Saratoga okay?"*

*"Please." Then she shook her head and made a dismissive wave. "Perhaps I should make that a real drink. Have you any Gordon's?"*

"I do."

"With tonic then."

He fixed her the drink from the wet bar, his mind racing with the intrigue of this peculiar encounter. He handed it to her and sat on the edge of his desk, his hands jingling the change in his pockets.

"I do hate so to bother you, Mitchell," she said with a sad smile. "It's just that I didn't know where else to turn."

"Don't concern yourself, Rachel."

"I mean, you really know Jeff. You both were friends from college, and I thought maybe you could help me...." She let her voice trail off.

Mitch cocked his head and peered at her. "Rachel, is everything all right with you and Jeff?"

She bit her lip. "No," she said finally.

Then she just opened up her soul to him and let the juicy, intimate details of her crumbling marriage spill forth in a torrent of emotion. He let her talk and talk for fifteen minutes, uncomfortably sometimes, as she confessed that Jeff's computer company was in serious trouble.

Mitch Myerson felt a naughty thrill rising up in him at these words. He had always been somewhat jealous of his college roommate's nationally publicized business successes and his beautiful wife. To hear that Jeff Wheaton was possibly losing both his company and his wife filled Myerson with a delicious measure of schadenfreude. He couldn't help himself. "How is Wheat/Tech in trouble, Rachel?" he asked, with a mask of concern.

Well, she explained, the competition was severely undercutting Wheat/Tech Computers in price. Dell, AST, Gateway, Southgate—all were shoring up their market share at the expense of Jeff Wheaton's company. On top of that, the Koreans were building incredibly cheap machines that Jeff couldn't compete with. Wheat/Tech's cash flow was hemorrhaging; money put up for research and development was thrown down the drain as the technology outpaced the company's ability to bring a new product to market. And Jeff—he was a basket case, neglecting Rachel, making her feel second-class. They were fighting constantly. Sex *had always been good with Jeffrey, but now they weren't even making love. It had gotten to the point where Rachel no longer felt she was attractive.*

*Mitch Myerson licked his lips and plunged in. "That's not true, Rachel. You're very beautiful."*

*"No I'm not," she said, weeping.*

*"Oh, yes you are. I've always thought Jeff was a lucky man." Too lucky, he thought.*

*"Do you really mean that?" she asked.*

*"Of course." He had always found Jeff's wife to be gorgeous. Why, if she hadn't been married to Jeff, he would have . . . what? What would he have done? He would have taken her for himself, that's what he would have done.*

*"You know how to make me feel special," she said then.*

*"You are special."*

*"I've been feeling so empty lately."*

*"I can see that, Rachel."*

*"I'm in a lot of pain."*

*"I know. You don't deserve that."*

*"Would you hold me?" she asked.*

*"What?" The request took him by surprise.*

*A bashful look came over her face. "You don't have to if you don't want to. I understand. You're Jeff's friend—you'd feel funny about it—"*

*"—Well, that's right. You're Jeff's—" He found himself stammering like an awkward schoolboy.*

*"You're right," she said, standing up to leave. "Maybe I should go."*

*"Wait," he blurted. "I'm sorry. I didn't mean to—"*

*"It's okay. Really. I should go now."*

*"Please. What I meant to say," Mitch Myerson said, "is that I would hold you, if it would make you feel better."*

*She smiled then—and to Myerson, at that moment, she looked like a movie star from a wet dream.*

*"Yes, it would make me feel better."*

*He nodded and let her come to him.*

*She threw herself into his arms and wrapped herself around him with surprising ardor. The breath rushed out of Mitch Myer-*

son all at once. Her face over his shoulder, she sighed contentedly. "Ohhhh, God," she murmured. "I've craved the feel of you for the longest time."

Myerson's heart nearly burst with joy. "Me?"

"Yes. I've always watched you from afar, wondering what it would be like, to be together with you."

"I've got to confess something myself, Rachel," he sighed. "I've always felt the same way."

She broke their embrace so she could see his face. She smiled and whispered, "I know." After a pregnant pause, she asked, "Can you lock the door?"

He became lightheaded with desire. "Here?"

"Yes."

"Not here. I can't do it here."

"Please," she murmured. "I need it from you."

"Please. Can we wait?" His mind was throbbing. "Let's get a room," he croaked, cotton-mouthed.

They left together, taking a hotel room in Culver City.

With that, Mitchell Myerson had plunged headlong into the forbidden zone—a secret affair with the wife of a college friend. That night, while Jeff worked late at the factory to save his company, Myerson surged into Rachel Wheaton with repeated thrusts. She moaned melodically. After it was over, they lay together on sheets soaked with sweat, and she said that making love with Mitch was everything she had fantasized it would be. She told him she thought they fit together like two pieces of a puzzle—a description Myerson found unspeakably erotic.

When Mitch Myerson arrived at the office on Monday morning, he found a dozen ties from Brooks Brothers awaiting him. "We belong together," the card said, making his blood jump.

And so it was, they were at the point of no return. . . .

He finished off the joint and tossed it aside. They had so much to look forward to.

He wouldn't trade places with anyone else on the planet.

Mitch walked off toward Fifty-ninth Street, tingling with the anticipation of being with her, now and forever.

# PART FIVE

## SATURDAY NIGHT
## JUNE 27, 1992

# 21

McPhillips returned to the Grand Hyatt suite at six-fifteen. He was in a black mood.

Walking into the junior suite, he encountered Mazzola, who was toweling himself dry from a shower. Mazzola whistled the tune to "Roxanne." Spying McPhillips, he said, "Hey, buddy, how'd it go in Midtown? Turn up anything?"

McPhillips rubbed his eyes and sighed. "A big fat goose egg. I even got detained by the hotel security at The Plaza, if you can believe it."

Mazzola's eyebrows arched. "You don't say?"

Brian made a dismissive wave as if to say, *don't even get me started*. Then he asked, "Any luck with you?"

"Nah. The whole day was a total abortion. We were just spinnin' our wheels out there, Brian. I guess we all got to face the music now. Those two are *long gone.*"

"I suppose you're right," McPhillips said, glumly.

Mazzola vigorously shook a can of Paul Mitchell styling mousse. He upended it and dispensed an egg-shaped puff of foam into the palm of his hand, then massaged it into his scalp. "Now I'm not the type to say I told you so, but Jesus, it didn't seem likely we were going to find 'em, you know?"

Changing the subject, McPhillips asked, "Where're the others?"

"Ah, let's see . . . Beekman's on his way from JFK via car service. Hopefully, he'll be here any minute. Wheaton, well—" He trailed off and shook his head. "The Jeffster refuses to give up the ghost. He's still poking around some of the hotels."

"Really?"

"Yeah. Man's got to know when to cut his losses, you know what I mean?"

"What time is it?" McPhillips asked.

"It's early."

"Do we have the timetable for Amtrak here in the room, or does Jeff have it?"

"Hey, listen, McPhillips," Bruce said softly. "I got something to say."

McPhillips crossed his arms. "Yeah?"

"I guess I've been something of a primo asshole this weekend. I don't know, I guess I'm just out of sorts. I mean. . . ." He shrugged and gave Brian an embarrassed grin. "Call me sensitive, but when I lose two million dollars in an eye-blink, I have this tendency to turn into a real bastard. You know what I mean?"

"Yeah," McPhillips said. "I know exactly what you mean."

Bruce laughed. "Yeah, I know you know what I mean. Anyway, I thought we could let bygones be bygones and call a truce. What do you say?"

Brian was more than willing to smoke the peace pipe. "All right by me."

"Splendid," Bruce burbled. "What do you say you let me buy you a drink at some formerly hip and trendy bar before we bolt this town. Maybe Harry's or the Surf Club or Bamboo Bernie's. . . ." Mazzola dropped the towel from his body and wriggled into a pair of bikini underwear.

"Uh, I'll have to take a rain check on that, Bruce," McPhillips sighed. "It's my kid's birthday today, and I really should—"

"*C'mon*, chief." Mazzola launched into the hard sell. "What's another hour in the grand scheme of things? I thought we'd do a little male-bonding while we got the boys together. Just picture it: we could, a) wax nostalgic about the old days at Penn, b) assassinate Mitch Myerson's character, and maybe even c) figure out the meaning of life." Mazzola splashed Clinique for Men scruffing lotion onto his face as he spoke.

"Mighty tempting," McPhillips said, without much zeal.

"Christ, it'll all be on *my* expense account. What more could you want?"

Maybe Mazzola had proposed a capital idea, after all. As it was, McPhillips could have used a stiff drink right about then. Perhaps reliving the old glory days of Locust Walk *would* do them some good, take the edge off their communal misery. "All right, I'm game."

"Yabba grabba brew!" Mazzola yelled in Flintstonian exuberance, pumping his fist.

"You want to grab a drink at the hotel bar?"

"No can do." Bruce Mazzola made a face of disapproval. "No atmosphere. Just some jerkweed tinkling the ivories and singing 'Feelings.' *For*-gedda-boudit." Shaking his hairbrush for emphasis, he added. "This calls for a bar. A *real* bar."

"What about Jeff?"

"Jeff told us to go ahead without him. Promised to hook up with us later."

"Fine," McPhillips said.

Mazzola grinned impishly. "Oh, and while we're throwing back a few on my tab, I thought maybe you and Beekman could give me some feedback on the ideas I have for my M & A memoirs. I'm thinking of calling it *Soldier of Fortune*. Bitchin' title, no?"

McPhillips nodded. "Yeah. Catchy."

Mazzola switched his blow-dryer on full blast.

When Beekman returned from the airport a few minutes later, he also professed to be in the mood for some heavy drinking. After some deliberation, everyone agreed on Cafe Iguana, a bar some twenty-odd blocks south of the hotel. As a trendy Tex-Mex meat-market, Iguana met Mazzola's threshold requirement of hip and happening. McPhillips was not hung up on the "hip" prerequisite, but thought it was a satisfactory choice because of its relatively close proximity to the Grand Hyatt. Brian planned to pack up in an hour or so and catch an eight o'clock Metroliner back to Philadelphia.

After leaving a note for Jeff, they took a cab downtown to Nineteenth Street and Park Avenue South.

At quarter to seven on a Saturday night, Cafe Iguana was sparsely populated. There were perhaps eleven or twelve other patrons on the lower level. It was early yet, Mazzola told them. The place would be packed to the rafters in another two hours. At the bar, they commandeered a trio of stools directly beneath the giant crystal lizard. Bruce got the bartender's attention and slapped down a twenty. "A pitcher of kamikazes," he told him. "And make it industrial strength." To his companions, Bruce gave a twenty-tooth smile and said, "Tonic for the troops."

Inwardly, McPhillips groaned. Broadway Bruce, forever the party boy. Getting his friends wasted was Job One.

Over the next half-hour, the kamikazes anesthetized their misery to some degree. McPhillips felt his face grow more numb by the minute. The alcohol provided little solace to his dread of returning home later that night. Brian slumped over his drink, his misery shrouding him like a black cocoon. He slipped into a melancholy silence.

By contrast, the alcohol had a positive effect on his companions. While not exactly exuberant, Chuck and Bruce conversed spiritedly. Chuck babbled excitedly about some hot new business proposition he had for Mazzola, something about a new automobile dealership. But Bruce showed no interest in Beekman's proposal. Instead, he talked incessantly of his soon-to-be-written memoirs. After some time, the subject reached a more neutral ground. The topic was the first female each of them had ever wanted to fuck.

Without hesitating, Beekman said, "Definitely the Catwoman from 'Batman.' That's the first chick I ever wanted to bang."

"The Catwoman, ay?" Mazzola squinted at him, nodding with approval.

"Julie Newmar in that skin-tight black outfit and the mask? *Mee*-yow, baby!" Beekman was clearly aroused by this childhood memory. "I was eight years old then, and it was the first time I realized that my pee-pee had a greater purpose in life than just passing water."

"For me," Bruce said, "it was *Ginger* from 'Gilligan's Island.'"

"Oooo," Beekman said by way of approval.

"You think about it, the whole show centered around the prototypical male fantasy of having a movie starlet alone on a desert island. I imagined that after a while, Ginger would've gotten so horny she'd be begging *Gilligan* for a hot-beef injection. Sherwood Schwartz was a genius, really. That show was a hotbed of sexual tension."

"*Absolutely*," Beekman agreed, scooping up some hot salsa sauce with a tortilla chip. "Sherwood Schwartz is the most underrated giant in the history of television."

"How about 'The Brady Bunch'?" Mazzola asked him. "Who would you have done there?"

"I would've sexed up Marsha and Jan. And Cindy on the occasion of her sixteenth birthday."

"Not Mrs. Brady?"

"Nahh." Beekman paused and reconsidered it. "Well, maybe. Depends."

"Alice the housekeeper?"

"Hey, a guy's gotta draw the line somewhere," Beekman laughed.

Bruce Mazzola turned to McPhillips. "How about you, McPhillips? Who was your first fantasy babe?"

"Susan Dey on 'The Partridge Family,'" he responded without much enthusiasm.

"Ooo-la-la," Beekman said, making a pained face and drumming his hands on the edge of the bar. "I would've poked her in a big way."

Mazzola squinted at Beekman. "You're pretty horny for a married guy, Beeker."

"What can I say? My pistol's always loaded. Hey, how about another round of poison, guys? Whattaya say? Huh?"

They put in their order with the bartender, who, for no apparent reason, informed them apologetically that he was in reality an up-and-coming soap-opera actor. The drinks were brought promptly: a Long Island iced tea for Beekman, a Stoli-rocks for Mazzola, a J & B–water for McPhillips. A fresh basket of tortilla chips was placed before them as well.

Beekman absently scarfed down a handful of chips. A

thoughtful look came over his face. "You know, Cindy Crawford signed a copy of her new swimsuit calendar for me at Encore Books last October. Maybe I should a had her autograph my *Schwantz* in indelible ink, huh?"

"Hmm," Mazzola said thoughtfully. "Perhaps in your case she could've just initialed it."

It took Chuck Beekman a split second to realize his manhood had been slammed. With a loopy grin, he muttered, "Ah, fuck you, ya bastard."

Mazzola laughed heartily and swallowed almost a third of his Stoli. "How about Betty Rubble? Would you have done her?"

"*Defi*ni*tely!*" Beekman bellowed. "That Barney Rubble was a lucky guy."

"Agreed. Unlike Wilma Flintstone, Betty Rubble had real eyes, not dots of ink. Speaking of Wilma Flintstone, would you do the nasty with her?"

Beekman considered this for a moment. "Pass."

"How about Pebbles Flintstone?"

"Pebbles?" Beekman looked around, confused, a look of alarm on his face. "Isn't that child molestation?"

"No, you *twit!*" Mazzola said with a smirk. "I'm talking about the later Hanna-Barbera spinoff, when Pebbles and Bam-Bam were teenagers. Remember?"

"Oh. Yeah. Well, if I had my druthers, I'd rather have Judy Jetson over Pebbles Flintstone."

"I'll drink to that," Bruce Mazzola said, hoisting his glass. "She's no Penelope Pitstop, of course, but she's eminently doable."

McPhillips emerged from his solipsistic silence. "I can't believe this," he moaned. "Each one of us just had his life savings wiped out, and you two are carrying on about having sex with *cartoon characters. Jesus!*"

Chuck Beekman and Bruce Mazzola contemplated this observation.

Then Bruce said, "McPhillips, my chum, you're *right* of course. But there tain't nuttin' I can do about it. I made a fortune; I lost a fortune." Mazzola shrugged. "I'll make another fortune.

I'm still young." He drank off the rest of his Stoli and ordered another round for the group.

McPhillips sighed. He wished he had the same optimism. It was going to take him years to replace the money. Ah, Christ. He didn't even want to think about it.

The bar talk resumed with Mazzola's favorite topic: his Drexel memoirs. Bruce spoke animatedly about the tell-all book he intended to write, the angle no one had bothered to cover yet, especially not that *pussy* book, *Liar's Poker,* written by that guy from Salomon who wasn't even on the *Street*, for chrissake; he was in *London!* No, Bruce's book was going to be a blockbuster, telling The Story the way it really was—the mind-blowing bonuses, the colorful personalities, the sex on the trading floor, the young Masters of the Universe at work and at play, the jealous members of the press who besmirched the firm, and the real story behind the politically-ambitious prosecutor who couldn't stand to see the free-enterprise system working so well under Mike Milken—

McPhillips sighed and stared at his drink, concealing his annoyance by watching the ice cubes melting. *Here he goes again—*

—and then he was suddenly aware that Mazzola was saying, "Hey, *McPhillips!* I'm *talkin'* to *you!*"

Brian broke the surface of his contemplative solitude. "What?" he managed, genuinely surprised.

"You got a *problem?*"

Mazzola's hostility unsettled him.

"I don't . . . I *really* don't understand what you're talking about, Bruce."

"You think I don't *notice* that every time I mention the word 'Drexel,' you get this prissy look on your face like, 'oh, no, here he goes again.' "

"I do?"

"Yeah, *you do,*" Mazzola snarled. "And it fuckin' gets under my skin every time you do it!"

"Bruce, I'm sor—" McPhillips cut off his own apology. Why was *he* apologizing? *Mazzola* was the boor who monopolized every conversation with his unhealthy obsession about past glories. Brian said gently, "Mazz, it's just that you work Drexel into the conversation *all* the goddam time. It's like, you *never* talk about the present. What *do* you do for a living these days? I don't even *know*."

Mazzola's glare was as lethal as atomic waste. "I was a part of *history*, buddy. Never before were so many so richly rewarded for their talents. And for some reason that *pisses* you off!"

*God, what a warped sense of reality Bruce has!* "No, it doesn't piss me off, Bruce." He sighed testily.

Beekman cut in. "Fellas, fellas, let's just take it easy here, huh? We're all *friends*, for chrissake—" His peacemaking efforts were feeble at best.

Mazzola fired a finger at McPhillips. "It so happens that Drexel was the greatest place in the fucking universe to work at, do you realize that?"

McPhillips didn't bother to suppress his smile. "That sounds suspiciously similar to what the young mafiosos say about organized crime."

This put Mazzola over the precipice. *"Organized crime,* huh?" he roared. "Is that what you think it was?"

"Fellas!" Beekman cried. *"Please!"*

"No," McPhillips said. "Chuck's right. I take that back. And apologize. Now can we drop this, Bruce?"

*"No! You* drew *first blood,* asshole!"

"I'd rather we not get into this—"

"I'd rather we *did*, you pussy. That is, unless you left your *balls* at home with your wife!"

Brian McPhillips wiped his mouth with the back of his hand. It was completely against his nature to back down from a challenge of this sort. He had been insulted, pushed to the brink; but there was no telling what could happen if he opened *this* Pandora's box. Rolling the dice, he decided to forge ahead. In a rational, coolheaded tone, he said: "I don't agree with a lot of what you guys on Wall Street did, that's all."

"Maybe you got an inferiority complex," Mazzola challenged. "Maybe you got something against someone else makin' a lot of money."

"Bruce, you guys made money out of *thin air*. You printed up phony money and sold it to the public as junk bonds. I *know* personally, because I'm cleaning up the mess as a bankruptcy attorney. There's carcasses of savings and loans and overleveraged companies all over the place."

Chuck Beekman joked, "Then maybe you should be *thanking* Bruce for making work for you lawyers, huh?"

"None a this would've happened," Mazzola said firmly, "if a politically-ambitious prosecutor by the name of Guiliani didn't put a gun to our firm's head and threaten to pull the trigger if we didn't do it ourselves. *He's* the bad guy; *he* mucked up the self-regulating forces of the free-market system. It was total McCarthyism—"

"Bullshit!" McPhillips bellowed. "You guys fucked up the *country!* The eighties were just some out-of-control penis-measuring contest to you guys. You took *billions* out of the marketplace for yourselves and laid waste to thousands of good American businesses. And you put thousands of people out of work!"

"Is that so?" Mazzola sputtered.

"Yeah, that's so! The eighties were a *crucial* time for the future of this country. Wall Street *should've* been out finding capital for research and development and new technologies so America could compete on a global basis. Instead, it squandered billions in capital on useless hostile takeovers which treated companies like trading cards—"

"Hey, Drexel wasn't doing *anything* that anybody else on the Street wasn't doing—"

"Let me finish, *goddammit!*" Incensed, McPhillips pushed on. "It's gonna take the rest of this *decade* to untangle this stinking mess, and by that time, the Japanese, the European community—hell, even the goddam *Koreans*—will have overtaken us completely. America will be reduced to begging for scraps of foreign investment, German-owned factories, whatever. Bruce, face it. You guys *fucked up America!*"

Following McPhillips' impassioned speech, Bruce Mazzola sat in seething silence. He was all but radioactive with enmity. Finally, he said, lamely, "You think being a *lawyer* is any higher up on the food chain of morality? *Everybody* knows what pond scum attorneys are—"

"Don't waste your breath," McPhillips said, coolly, taking a swallow of his J & B. "I don't get bent out of shape over knee-jerk lawyer-bashing. I can sleep at night with what I do for a living."

"*I can sleep at night too, cocksucker!*" Mazzola screamed.

His outburst turned heads. The barkeep gazed dully in their direction.

Suddenly, Mazzola's mouth twisted into a ferocious grin. He hushed his voice. "Well, I never told you this before, buddy boy, but you 'n' me got more in common than just our monograms, y'know—"

The mock-chummy tone of his voice filled McPhillips with a dread he could not identify. He looked away.

"Yeah," Mazzola said, "it seems we both sampled the same poontang, you 'n' me."

McPhillips glanced at Beekman for possible enlightenment. Beekman returned with an unknowing shrug. "What're you talking about?" Brian asked Bruce, point-blank.

"You remember Chelsea Robbins, buddy?" Bruce shot him a lewd wink.

Chelsea Robbins. Chelsea Robbins. Chelsea, pronounced Chel-see-*ya*. Oh yes, he remembered her. The mere mention of the name conjured up a hundred sweet memories in McPhillips' mind, not the least of which was her creamy, porcelain-smooth angel's face. She used to stand there, her head cocked slightly to the side, her mouth drawn into an irresistible pout, giving him that *look*, a wisp of her sunwashed blond hair falling over one of her green eyes like a comma. She could melt his heart instantly with just a single shot of The Look. Brian McPhillips and Chelsea Robbins had been an item on the Penn campus for almost four years. They had met in freshman lit early in their first year. At that time, they both were just discovering that college in the eighties was nothing if not a place where a student entered a hands-on apprenticeship in sex education. Moreover, college was a place where you learned how to fall in love with someone. By Thanksgiving break, it seemed everyone on campus was scrambling to pair off with a suitable partner. So it was with Brian and Chelsea. By Christmas, they were deeply in love with each other. For each of them, it was the first time either had experienced the sensation. They lived together. They endured a very intense up-and-down relationship. They'd nearly gotten married. But she had emotional problems. She'd been abused as a child. In the end, he couldn't save her from her demons and the relationship self-destructed. While he loved Lisa with every ounce of his heart, a special place existed for his memories of Chelsea.

*Of course* he remembered Chelsea Robbins.
*So what about her?*

"Enough years have passed, I guess the story can now be told," Mazzola said with his no-soul smirk. "Remember early sophomore year, you were away for the weekend, visiting one of your old high school friends at Cornell? Well, so happens, I'm at an ATO party that Saturday night and it's a hoppin' time—you know how those ATO parties could get. Well, right around midnight, I'm shootin' pool in the basement when who should come up to me, but Chelsea Robbins. Turns out some dweeb ATO brother who wanted to get into her pants slipped a couple a crushed up 'ludes in her beer. So she's comin' up to me, wired-out-of-her-brain wasted, buddy boy. Not that she didn't know what she was doing—"

"Bruce, don't do this," Chuck Beekman pleaded with his eyes closed, as if in prayer. *Beekman had heard this story before!*

McPhillips was paralyzed, quaking with horror and rage. *He's lying. He's lying. The fuck is lying*, Brian told himself. Mindfucking him.

"Well, she's practically throwing her fuzzbasket at me, creaming herself over me right then and there. So I ask you, Bry, what could I do? I did what any guy with a tube of meat hanging between his legs would've done—" Bruce Mazzola lowered his voice to almost a whisper "—and I took her back to my dorm and I reamed her all . . . night . . . long. Until she was *too sore* to take any more—"

"Bruce!" Beekman wailed in agony.

McPhillips felt the rage envelop him, his brain shutting down, his consciousness slipping away from him. Intense colors exploded behind his eyes, popping like fireworks. It was like an out-of-body experience, as if he were across the room watching this scene unfold from afar.

Mazzola pushed his face within a few inches of Brian's and, leering, he whispered the punchline: "And Sunday night, when you came back from Ithaca, wanting to make love to your girlfriend, it was *my spooge* in her cunt that made it so easy for you to slip your cock in—"

Brian McPhillips was powerless to stop himself from what happened next. He grabbed a fistful of Bruce Mazzola's shirt in his left hand and thrashed his right arm quickly, violently, smashing a tightly clenched fist against Mazzola's jaw—*once, twice, three times*—only vaguely aware of the wet slapping noise his knuckles made against the flesh and bone of Mazzola's smug face. The force of the third blow sent Bruce Mazzola toppling over backwards in a spill that took out three stools. Dazed and confused, Brian stood there for a short while—it was impossible for him to gauge how long—breathing heavily, his knuckles reddened and throbbing. Chuck Beekman was yelling something at him. But he couldn't understand a word; the thumping in his brain drowned out every word. The paging device hung limply from his wrist, shattered and useless.

Through no volition of his own, Brian McPhillips somehow turned his back on the scene and began walking. He walked outside the bar, onto Park Avenue South.

It was raining. Fat droplets splattered down on him, bathing him in a cold and sobering baptism.

And after a short while, it finally began to hit him, what had transpired in there. Bruce—the bullyboy with the cashmere baritone, the unstoppable ladykiller—had owned up to seducing Brian's college girlfriend. McPhillips couldn't shake the image of it from his mind's eye. He ran blindly down the sidewalk.

He flagged down the first cab that came by, which screeched to a rocking halt at the curb. When he grasped the handle of the door, he was alarmed to find that he was shaking uncontrollably. With some difficulty, he opened the door, twisted himself into the backseat, and reached behind him to slam it shut. He told the cabbie to just drive, just keep going. Where was not of concern. As long as some miles were put between him and the numbing ugliness he had encountered minutes ago.

# 22

There were more than a few of Jeff Wheaton's friends and colleagues who had disapproved of his decision to sell a 49.1 percent stake in Wheat/Tech Computers to the Kawakami family last year.

Then there were those in the trade press who criticized the deal. To sell such a large equity stake in one of America's largest direct-order personal computer firms to the Japanese was, in their view, tantamount to striking a Mephistophelian bargain with the devil himself.

Jeff Wheaton had heard this talk before. His response: That's pure racism.

In fact, any attempt to convert Wheaton to the masses of Japanese bashers would have been futile, no matter how fashionable it had become of late. He bristled at talk of a Japanese conspiracy to take over the world. Now that the Russians had abruptly quit the Cold War, it seemed as if Americans needed a surrogate adversary, a new enemy to the integrity of democracy. The press did its part. It played up the Yellow Menace myth for all it was worth with headlines designed to whip the American public into a Pearl Harbor–like frenzy. Extra, extra, read all about it:

THE JAPANESE BUY COLUMBIA PICTURES.
THE JAPANESE BUY PEBBLE BEACH.

THE JAPANESE BUY ROCKEFELLER CENTER.

It was as if *every* Japanese citizen had in some way conspired to get a piece of the U.S. for his or her very own.

That perception, Wheaton insisted, was racist.

Worse, the xenophobic zeitgeist of the day was dangerously counterproductive from a long-term perspective. Anti-Japanese hysteria impeded interest in a nation that could provide valuable lessons to the corporate and social cultures of America. Jeff Wheaton knew that from first-hand experience.

Akito Kawakami had made Jeff an offer he could not refuse. Mr. Kawakami had a controlling stake in a computer parts importing company in Tokyo that produced LCD backlit screens, math co-processors and microchips for laptop machines. He was seeking a strategic partnership with an established computer manufacturer in the U.S. After being rebuffed by Michael Dell of Dell Computers, Mr. Kawakami approached Wheat/Tech Computers with the same offer. Cash-starved and on the precipice of Chapter 11, Jeff snapped up the opportunity.

It was a natural synergy. With Kawakami Industries as a partner, Wheat/Tech received a much-needed cash infusion that shored up the company's balance sheet and provided some extra funds for R & D. The deal had also cut the per-unit cost of production substantially and made Wheat/Tech a player in the personal computer marketplace again. Kawakami contacts in Japan also made the sale of Wheat/Tech laptops in that country a possibility for the first time, which would leave Dell, Compaq, and Northgate salivating on the sidelines. Akito Kawakami even permitted the company to retain its good name and asked that Jeff stay on as Chief Executive Officer.

But Wheaton was decidedly uncomfortable when Akito insisted on installing his twenty-eight-year-old son Tommy as president of the restructured company.

Jeff's concerns over the division of power, however, proved to be short-lived. Tommy Kawakami was an unmitigated computer genius. Tommy had graduated from Princeton in three years and had gone on for a graduate degree in computer science from MIT. Wheaton was cheered to learn that it was Tommy Kawakami's idea to court Wheat/Tech for the strategic alliance.

Also, Jeff was thrilled to discover that he and Tommy Kawakami were both complete gadget freaks, obsessed with new technology. They shared a compulsion to load the latest models of Wheat/Tech computers with more bells and whistles than the competition. As such, future generations of Wheat/Tech computers would operate by light pens and would have voice-recognition technology.

Happily, their bond went beyond business. Tommy had proven himself as more than just an equity partner. He had become a friend and a confidant as well. Mutt and Jeff, as their employees called them.

Yentified dollars had saved Jeff's company. For that, he made no apologies.

To be sure, Jeff agreed that the Japanese had to drop their give-an-inch-take-a-mile approach to international trade reform, but they most certainly couldn't be faulted for their long-term approach to manufacturing. It was a global marketplace now. The rest of the world had to get with the program. Heal thyself, America.

From his table at the AT&T Building on Fifty-sixth and Madison, Jeff Wheaton dialed the home office of Wheat/Tech Computers in Philadelphia. He used a brand-new AT&T VideoPhone 2400 which Wheat/Tech had installed throughout the company earlier that month. It was their latest high-tech toy.

Tommy Kawakami picked up after two rings.

"Tommy, it's Jeff. I'm on VideoPhone."

"Let me switch mine on." A moment later, the image of Kawakami's face appeared in three-inch miniature on the liquid-crystal screen of the VideoPhone. "Jeff, how are you?" His tone shifted when he saw the melancholy expression on his partner's face. "Have you turned up anything in New York?"

"Sore subject. Let's pause for a commercial message first. Have the second-quarter sales figures printed yet?"

"They have."

"You've got a copy in front of you?"

"Right here."

"So, don't keep me in suspense. How'd we do?"

"Pretty damn good, boss," Kawakami said brightly. "We're up forty-two percent overall in gross revenues versus same sales period last year. All product lines saw double-digit growth with the exception of desktops, which saw a modest increase of just below five percent. With those kinds of figures, we've taken a healthy bite out of Dell's market share and Northgate's got no place to hide. That's more or less the skinny."

*Finally*, Wheaton thought. *Some good news for a change.* "I attribute the last quarter's success to you, Tommy."

"Please," Kawakami responded modestly. "That's much too charitable."

"I mean it. The new sell-through discount to college students was a brilliant idea. And you arranged for DAMARK and Combco to take a truckload of the old 386s off our hands. A job well done."

Tommy Kawakami was never comfortable with compliments. He changed the subject. "No sign of 'em, there, huh?"

"Nope. I mean, I *did* see Paula Abdul and Emilio Estevez walking together down Broadway. And Morley Safer, you know, one of the guys from 'Sixty Minutes'? Saw him on Fifty-seventh Street. But no sign of Mitch and . . . my wife."

"Any stones left unturned?"

"We've combed the goddamn city, Tommy. I've called every hotel in the city, followed up. But according to the progress reports from the troops in the field, nothing. Big fat goose egg."

"I'm really sorry to hear that, Jeffrey."

"Yeah, I'm beginning to doubt my own instincts. Maybe they were never here. Maybe they're in Canada. I don't know. If they ever were in New York, they're long gone now. If they *were* here, they were probably around just long enough for Rachel to get to Fifth Avenue to max my credit card out," he said glumly.

A long silence ensued.

Wheaton could tell by viewing Kawakami on the picturephone that some gears were grinding away in his partner's brain. "Penny for your thoughts, T.K."

"I don't know. It's just a shot in the dark."

"Go for it."

"I'll need to uplink the computers. May I?"

"Be my guest."

Back in Philadelphia, Tommy Kawakami inserted a floppy disk into his computer. Then he cold-booted a computer program that linked the computers via the telephone line. In about sixty seconds, the message UPLINK SUCCESSFUL flashed on Jeff's computer screen.

"Okay," Jeff said. "You're uplinked here."

In another moment, another message:

SLAVE MODE

Jeff knew that this message meant Kawakami's screen in Philadelphia would be flashing the message: MASTER MODE. In essence, Kawakami now controlled everything that appeared on Jeff's computer. What appeared on Kawakami's screen would simultaneously flash on Wheaton's screen.

"Okay, Mr. Science," Jeff chided. "Clue me in."

On the picture phone, Jeff could see a mischievous smirk on Kawakami's face. "Your wife. She likes to shop, right?"

"Loves it, yes."

"Now, I'm just thinking out loud here. You said she possesses a credit card?"

"Yes. And it has my name on it."

"Do you think there's a possibility . . . she used it? *Recently?*"

Jeff Wheaton froze.

*Of course she had.*

She wouldn't have been able to help herself.

"Tommy," he said breathlessly. "The answer has to be yes. But what does that mean?"

"I'd like to see if I can't replicate a little trick I'd picked up in my days as a phreak at MIT. Me and a group of other disgruntled computer geeks pulled it on a mean-spirited professor we all despised. I'll have to dial another number. Hold on—"

"Who're you conferencing me in with?"

"Citibank Visa's merchant line. Hold on."

Kawakami punched up the third-party call button. A dial tone came up and he poked in 555-1492. "You still with me?"

"Right here."

"Watch this."

215

A screen came up indicating that Tommy had tapped into the Citibank Merchant Database.

"Ohmigod," Wheaton said, forgetting to breathe.

"Give me your wife's Visa account number and expiration date."

"Don't you need to know a password?"

"No," Tommy replied. "It's an informational database for merchants. It monitors contemporaneous purchases in any account over a given period of time to help merchants combat credit-card fraud. It's not a restricted database because Citicorp *wants* merchants to access this information freely. It's meant to help deter credit-card abuse. Like your wife's."

Jeff Wheaton issued a short laugh and gave Tommy the card number and expiration date.

THANK YOU, the computer screen said. PLEASE WAIT.

They waited.

A screen asked for a field specifying the dates for which data was requested.

"Just make it for today, Tommy," Jeff said.

Tommy complied.

In another moment, a screen came up: 1 OF 12 ENTRIES. The rest of the information appeared in the next instant. BLOOMINGDALE'S—1000 THIRD AVENUE—NEW YORK, NY. PURCHASE APPROVED—12:37 PM. $221.53.

Tommy yelped happily, "Do you see that?"

Wheaton went numb with excitement. "Scroll through all the entries now, Tom—"

Bloomingdale's, a second transaction.

Louis Vuitton. 49 East 57th Street.

Giorgio Armani of Beverly Hills. 47 East 57th Street.

Hermès. 11 East 57th Street.

Escada. 7 East 57th Street.

Chanel. 9 West 57th Street.

Galeries Lafayette. 1301 Sixth Avenue.

Tiffany. 727 Fifth Avenue.

Bulgari Jewelers. 730 Fifth Avenue.

Bergdorf Goodman's. 754 Fifth Avenue.

Susan Bennis Warren Edwards. 22 West 57th Street.

The last one occurred at 16:17. That would have been 4:17 P.M. Less than two hours ago.

"Tommy?" he blurted into the phone. "You still with me?"

"Ten-four." Tommy Kawakami was exuberant. "Listen, I've got a map of Manhattan in front of me, okay? I've plotted all the addresses and with the single exception of Bloomies on Fifty-ninth, if you play connect the dots? Jesus, it's a straight arrow down Fifty-seventh Street."

"Christ, maybe there's a method to Rachel's madness."

"It seems that way. God."

"You know what we're looking at here, Tommy? This is Rachel's final screw-you. She was gonna stick me with this astronomical Visa bill—"

Kawakami laughed. "Yeah? Well, maybe the screwer just became the screwee."

"Maybe, maybe. Listen, I'm signing off. I have to find out if this is another dead-end or the friggin' big enchilada. You're a goddamn genius, Tommy."

"Go get 'em, boss. Go get 'em."

Feverishly, Wheaton disconnected the line. He gathered up his high-tech apparatus and bolted from the table, causing a stir among the kibbitzers at the next table. "I betcha he's a spy for the Russians," one of the elderly men said to his companion as Wheaton raced out of the building toward Fifty-seventh Street.

# 23

It so happens that one of the finest French nouvelle cuisine restaurants in all of Manhattan is located in Le Parker Meridien Hotel at 118 West Fifty-seventh Street. The Provençal-influenced restaurant, Maurice, is a perennial favorite of the Zagat dining survey's Top 20. Since Mitch Myerson and Rachel Wheaton had tickets for the eight o'clock show of *Miss Saigon,* it made sense to enjoy a superb French meal without having the inconvenience of leaving their hotel. They arrived at Maurice at six-thirty sharp and were seated promptly by the maître d'.

The ambience of Maurice was enhanced by handsome, wood-paneled rooms with mammoth mirrors, comfortable banquettes, and inviting upholstered armchairs. Since it would be their last great meal in the United States for a long time (possibly forever), Mitch insisted that they splurge. When the waiter came by, Myerson ordered a half-dozen appetizers for them to share.

He gazed at Rachel over the top of his menu and quipped, "Lifestyles of the rich and famished."

When she laughed lightly at his cleverness, it was music to his ears.

The waiter brought them dish after dish. They sampled each one adventurously. Mitch especially enjoyed the ravioli stuffed with pureed peas in a tarragon, bacon, and butter-laced broth, while Rachel preferred the tiny crab-filled dumplings in an exotic clear soup perfumed with ginger and lemongrass. Also appealing was Chef Salonsky's specialty, a sausagelike arrangement made of calamari, stuffed with salmon and fresh basil, sliced into medallions the size of silver dollars.

As an entrée, Mitch ordered the dish of rosy lamb loin sliced paper-thin, glazed with a drizzle of darksweet sauce and laid on a bed of fluffy, vegetable-studded couscous in a tomato-based broth, served with a side of Moroccan chick-peas and raisins. Rachel opted for the sea scallops with asparagus, which was set off nicely by a tasty saffron and curry butter sauce.

Mitch dominated their dinner conversation, and Rachel let him do so. She looked positively radiant that night and seemed to hang on his every word. What a trophy she was! Mitch recounted his experience at the Hemisphere Bank of Exchange, how Mr. Mahmood hadn't wanted him to count the money, his confrontation with Mr. Mahmood after he learned that Hemisphere had taken a ten-percent cut for itself rather than the five percent he had expected. Mitch had finally threatened to go to St. Germaine with his displeasure, which caused the Middle Eastern banker to quickly see things Mitch's way. It was incredible, the kind of clout the St. Germaine name carried.

"Enough about my adventures. Did you enjoy shopping today?"

She shrugged casually. "With two hundred dollars, the only thing I could buy was a Louis Vuitton suitcase," she lied. "So it was more torture than pleasure."

Myerson flashed her a grin. "Well, with the money we have now, you can buy *anything* your heart desires as soon as we get to Europe. It won't be long now, my little princess."

The candlelight gave her face a rosy glow. He was moved to take her slim hand in his. When his eyes fell on her 3.2-carat engagement ring, he was visibly disturbed. "Must you wear that?"

"I'm not legally divorced yet," she said teasingly.

His brow furrowed. "Don't be cute, Nuffy. The ring *bothers* me. Reminds me that you were once someone else's."

"Until I get a suitable replacement for it, it stays put." She said this with a girlish smile, but the tone of her voice was firm.

What is it with women and diamonds? he wondered. They

were always comparing the sizes of their stones among themselves. Like guys comparing their respective penis sizes. Unlike the guys, however, girls could always move up a size or two. This witticism brought a self-amused grin to his face.

"Very well," he sighed. "In Italy I shall buy you a diamond twice the size of that one."

She smiled and bobbed her head approvingly.

Their waiter came by with a cart full of tantalizing desserts. Rachel picked out the pinwheel of sweet apples over a wisp of a pastry crust with *crème fraîche* and hazelnuts; Myerson ordered cinnamon rice *crème brûlée* and decaffeinated coffee, with the coffee right away, please. After the waiter left with their orders, Rachel politely excused herself to go to the ladies' room. She rose from the table, kissed Mitch on the lips, wiped away the trace of lipstick she left on his mouth, and sauntered off in the direction of the rest room.

Soon, the waiter brought Mitch his decaffeinated coffee. It steamed as the waiter poured it from the small silver decanter into his coffee cup. When he was alone again, Mitch gazed at his new Rolex. Twenty-two minutes after seven. Plenty of time to get to the theater. Mitch Myerson leaned back, settling into the comfort of the upholstered chair, and permitted himself a daydream. Tomorrow, they would be on the 10:55 A.M. Alitalia flight to Rome. The beginning of a great adventure. *Mitch, old buddy, you're the man. You are the man.* He craved a bong of Hawaiian.

Up toward the front of the restaurant, there was some movement that caught his attention. Mitch looked about lazily, sodden with rich food and wine. He glimpsed a guy who reminded him a little of Jeff Wheaton striding briskly in his general direction. Wait a second—it *was* Jeff Wheaton! No—couldn't be—it was *impossible!* The realization that this was indeed Rachel's husband engulfed him in an animal panic. *What was he doing in New York?*

His heart trip-hammered, and an adrenaline-fueled panic swamped him. A hundred frantic thoughts competed in his brain, and he found himself momentarily paralyzed, like a deer in the middle of the highway, frozen by the oncoming headlights of a Mack truck. *It was all over before it had even begun!*

What happened to him next seemed almost Twilight Zone-weird.

*"Sonuvabitch! You sonuvabitch!"* Jeff Wheaton was screaming at the top of his lungs, out of control. Rachel's husband began running directly toward Myerson, causing shocked waiters and patrons to gasp in awe. To them, it appeared that some raving lunatic was attacking an unassuming patron who had been dining quietly among them for nearly an hour.

As Jeff reached the table, Mitch seized the moment. He bolted upright from his seat and chucked the steaming coffee in Wheaton's face. Wheaton howled in agony and confusion. His hands blindly shot out for Mitch, but Myerson ducked and rolled under his adversary's outstretched arms. Myerson cried out, "Help me! Help me someone!"

Jeff Wheaton sputtered and scrabbled desperately at his face to wipe away the sticky fluid, to regain his faculties. Mitch, however, snagged the beleaguered CPA by the lapels, danced him a few steps to the right and hurled him into the dessert cart. The cart toppled onto its side, and ten-dollar desserts splattered on the carpet. In the midst of the confusion, people gasped audibly, but no one moved to intervene, since it was New York City, after all. In his speeded-up sense of perception, Mitch was vaguely aware of a woman's screaming.

"Somebody help me," Mitch yelled. "Somebody call the police, have him arrested!"

Then Mitch turned heel and ran.

Heart thumping, blood pounding, he found that his vision became fogged. *Have to find Rachel and get the hell out of here.* He burst into the ladies' room, yelling her name, the echo in the rest room jangling his already frayed nerves. No response. In hysterical desperation, he checked each stall, finally kicking the door in on a closed stall. No one was there. Where *was* she, oh god, where did she go? Mitch raced out of the rest room. The thought of leaving her behind—the worst-case scenario—flashed in his mind; he hadn't wanted to, but Jesus, survive or die was the operative phrase right now. He was on the verge of racing up to the hotel room and grabbing the money when he spied her on a pay phone. Those goddam 900-number *horoscopes!* "Rachel!" he cried. She turned to him with a startled look on her face. He ran up to her, barely able to sputter out the words. The frenzy in his voice caused a look of alarm on her own face.

"Your husband's *here* in the fucking restaurant!" he hissed. "You gotta get outta here *now!*" He pressed a twenty-dollar bill into her palm and named the first hotel that came to mind. "Get to the U.N. Plaza on the East Side. Wait for me at the Ambassador Grill! Go now!" She began to stammer a response, but he quashed it. "Just *go!*" He pointed her in the direction of the Fifty-sixth Street exit and literally pushed her toward it. She sprinted out of the building.

He turned and raced up the nearest stairwell. In his mind, he paranoically imagined Wheaton and a phalanx of policemen to be right on his heels, guns drawn. The air in the stairwell was choking, reeking of fresh paint. He was almost hyperventilating; amplified by the acoustics of the stairwell, his breathing had the cadence of the sound of the sawing of wood. Gripping the railing with a white-knuckled grasp, he took the steps two at a time, ignoring the cramp in his stomach, pushing himself, racing up the six flights of steps to the floor of their room. Reaching the sixth floor, he burst through the door into the hallway. For a panicky moment, he lost his bearings and couldn't remember his room number. *Think Myerson, think!* Then he remembered the number was printed on the key. He sprinted down the hall toward the room.

His hand trembled so badly, he had difficulty keying into the lock. After what seemed like an eternity, he slid the key in and shoved the door open. The Gucci bag full of the items secreting the currency was hidden between the two mattresses of the king-size bed. With a grunt, he heaved the top mattress, which jounced once off the floor and settled akimbo on the other side of the bed. Myerson yanked the briefcase free from the tangle of sheets and blankets and scurried out of the room, allowing the door to close behind him.

Escape, escape, escape, escape.... The word was repeated in his mind monomaniacally, like an endless sound loop. He was having trouble thinking. Escape, escape, escape. How? He came upon the bank of elevators and jabbed at the down button. Even as he did so, he had his doubts about escaping by elevator. Momentarily, the doors slid open to one of the cars. It was going down. There was a matronly woman with hair the color and texture of steel wool coming out of the elevator, fingering her strand of pearls, preoccupied with her own thoughts. Mitch shoved her viciously, and she listed to one side with a squeal. He stabbed the lobby button as the door skidded shut, muffling the woman's breathless squeal of *"Asshole!"* in Mitch's wake. As the car plunged down toward the lobby, Mitch was seized by a growing panic. *They would be waiting for him in the lobby!* He would be mobbed by a sea of law-enforcement officials as soon as the doors opened, and the jig would be up—

—the elevator plummeted past the fourth floor, and Mitch pushed three at the last second. He crouched in a fighting stance, ready to engage in a struggle. The car lurched to a rocking halt. The door opened, and thank god, no one was there. Mitch bolted out of the car, dizzy with terror. He swiveled around, looking in all directions, trying to devise a means of escape.

On the Fifty-sixth Street side of the corridor, there was a large window. Mitch raced over to it. Maddeningly, he couldn't see out of it: It was frosted glass, translucent only, a cityscape of nineteenth-century Paris etched into it. Nor was there a latch to open it. *Think, man, think!* Cursing, he whirled around, looking for a heavy object. His eyes fell on the freestanding, rectangular cigarette receptacle located across from the elevators some sixty, seventy feet away. He laid the leather bag down beneath the window and bolted over to pick up the receptacle. It was bottom-heavy, maybe thirty or forty pounds, loaded with lead or sand, he guessed. He groaned as he lifted it. Ash and sand and cigarette butts spilled onto the front of his dinner jacket as he struggled to bring the object over to the window.

He closed his eyes tightly and gritted his teeth. Brandishing it as a weapon, he brought the receptacle into a backswing and, with a mighty wail, bashed out the window. The glass exploded outward with a crash, followed by an almost melodic tinkling of small shards, not unlike that of a wind chime. He dropped the receptacle to the carpeted floor, where it landed with a heavy thud. Mitch Myerson quickly plucked out some jagged shards of glass that remained in the frame of the window, widening the gaping opening. Then he gripped the edge of the frame and leaned out as far as he could, looking down.

One and one-half floors beneath him was the massive glass and steel awning of Le Parker Meridien. Another one and a half stories beneath the awning was the sidewalk and Fifty-sixth Street. From the window to the awning below was a considerable distance. He realized that if he lost his footing upon landing, he could be severely lacerated by the shards of broken glass that had fallen onto the surface of the awning. Worse, he realized, if he landed with too much force on the awning, the glass might give beneath his weight, causing him to fall to the sidewalk and risk death. Momentarily, he was overcome by a spell of vertigo, but he willed it away. There was no choice. He had to jump.

Quickly now, he used the Gucci bag to sweep the frame for any remnants of glass. Then he leaned out the opening, holding the bag with both hands, palms-up and at each end. He let the bag fall to the awning below, where it landed with a loud *thwap*. Next, he slipped out of his Italian loafers and dropped them. They bounced onto the slanted surface of the awning, just a short distance away from the bag. Then, gulping a lungful of air, he gripped the jambs of the windowframe and hoisted himself up onto the ledge. Straddling the bottom of the frame, he swung his stockinged feet out, three stories above street level. He eased himself down along the side of the building, almost as if he were slipping his body gradually into a hot tub. Cautiously, he flipped himself around so that he was facing the rough surface of the building. The surface scraped at the skin of his face, but he ignored this annoyance, lowering himself inch by inch, carefully, so as not to lose his grip, extending himself to his full length, closing his eyes, holding his breath, and praying he wouldn't be decapitated should he fall all the way through the glass awning—

—and he let go—

For a helpless moment, he was suspended in nothingness, aware of the wind rushing past him, his hair blowing straight up, the horrible sensation of having utter weightlessness. In an instant, however, his legs absorbed the shock of contact, and he was overcome by a euphoric realization: He had made it! He collected his wits about him and swiftly gathered up the briefcase and dipped his feet into the loafers.

He still had another floor-and-a-half to descend before he was on street level, but this was a piece of cake. He slip-slided along the slanted glass awning, out toward the edge, which jutted over the street. With not an instant of hesitation, he leapt from the edge of the awning onto the roof of a black Mercedes-Benz 420 SEL, a laughably effortless maneuver. Then he stepped down over the windshield and onto the hood of the car. The metal of the hood gave some under his weight, causing him to lose his balance a little.

"Hey, you!" a fat doorman yelled angrily. "What the fuck you doing?" He began to blow his whistle at Mitch.

Myerson ignored him, of course; he hit the ground running. Ironically, it was the four-foot leap from the hood that caused Mitch to twist his left ankle. As the pain shot up through his leg, he ignored it and tucked the bag up under his arm like a football. He ran east, toward Sixth Avenue.

He was aware of footfalls about ten feet behind him. Someone was chasing him. "Hey! Stop! Stop, you!" Mitch chanced a glance over his shoulder. It was the uniformed doorman giving chase, but Mitch instantly knew the guy was way out-of-shape and already tiring. *Eat my dust, you fat fuck*, Mitch said to himself in a moment of wild euphoria, and he turned on the speed, easily outpacing the doorman, whose shouts and whistles grew more distant as Myerson crossed the intersection.

After three blocks, Mitch was reasonably certain that he had escaped Wheaton and the house security. Panting to catch his breath, he waved down a cab on Madison Avenue, yanked open the door, and crawled into the backseat with some effort and slammed the door shut. He commanded the driver to take him south to the Village; there he would take another cab back uptown to the United Nations Plaza. That way, the authorities couldn't trace his whereabouts by consulting the cabbies' logs.

As the vehicle weaved in and out of the evening traffic, Mitch Myerson closed his eyes, struggling to fight off the wave of nausea driving up through his stomach like an iron spike. He could feel the puke rising up in his throat, he could even *taste* it. Only through superhuman effort did he prevent himself from upchucking all over the vinyl backseat. His mind screamed a single thought, over and over. *We were almost caught, we were almost caught, we were almost caught, we were almost caught....*

# 24

"Hey, Ace, you all right back there?" The cabdriver eyeballed McPhillips worriedly in the reflective slat of his rearview mirror.

"I said I'm fine."

"You're not gonna get sick or anything, are you?"

"No, I'm not gonna get sick. I told you, I'm *fine*."

"Last week, a passenger of mine threw up all over the back-seat. Right where you're sitting. Said the same thing as you, that he was feeling fine."

"You want a written guarantee or what?" McPhillips asked, irritated by the driver's monomania.

The driver turned around and tried a reconciliatory, no-hard-feelings smile. "Not necessary. I'll take you at your word."

McPhillips peered about at the unfamiliar cityscape. "Where are we?"

"Park at Seventy-fifth."

"Whoa. You've got to turn us around. Get me to the Grand Hyatt."

"You got it, Ace." The driver obediently U-turned at the next traffic light and nosed into the southbound traffic.

McPhillips lapsed into his own thoughts. Only now had he regained his faculties. Now he rode in the back seat of Henry Wiedemann's 1982 Checker Cab in a state of moderate amazement, replaying the scene that had just gone down at Cafe Iguana. Had he really decked the smug bastard? His reddened, ballooning knuckles throbbed with dull pain, irrefutable evidence confirming the recent series of events. He gazed at them with a sense of awe. Boy, he had cracked Bruce a couple of good ones to the jaw. Payback *with* interest.

The cabdriver piped up again from the front. "Whatever's buggin' you, Ace, it can't be all that bad."

"Oh, yes it can," McPhillips said sullenly. Betrayed by people he considered close friends not once, but *twice*, in less than twenty-four hours. At that moment, he had an impulse to tender his resignation from the human race. Human nature was just too fucked up. Morality in America had gone Chapter 11; no one gave a damn about anyone else. Looking out for number one, that was the only true religion left in America.

The cabbie reached his hand around to the backseat and tapped a printed sign taped to the plastic partition. "You read this, my friend?"

In his agitated state, Brian hadn't noticed it before.

It read: Welcome to Henry Wiedemann's 1982 Vintage Checker Cab. Good Things Are Going to Happen to You . . . If You Only *Think Positive* . . . Your Driver, Henry.

"There's only fifteen of these original babies still in operation in the entire city," Wiedemann informed him. "Your chances of you getting a Checker cab in this city is like the ones in the lottery. You see, this is a *lucky* cab."

McPhillips smiled skeptically. "Lucky. Right."

"Hey, I'm telling you," the driver insisted. "Whatever your troubles, your luck is about to change. You'll see."

When Henry Wiedemann deposited McPhillips at the Grand Hyatt, he handed Brian an "official certificate" that attested to the fact that he had taken a ride in a "lucky" Checker cab. The guy was wacky, McPhillip thought, but he had been kind of amusing in a way. Brian handed Wiedemann a ten on a $6.75 fare and told him to keep the change. You had to give the guy an A for effort.

McPhillips folded the certificate into quarters and stuffed it into his jacket pocket.

As he returned to the hotel room, it was his intention to

simply gather his belongings, leave Jeff a note of apology, and take the next train back to Philadelphia. However, when he slipped the plastic key into the electronic lock of the suite, he heard the phone ringing inside. He hurried through the door and swooped up the receiver before the other party hung up. "Hello?"

Wheaton. His voice was supercharged, frantic. *"Where the fuck have you guys been?"*

For an instant, McPhillips was confounded. "Didn't Mazzola tell you? We were out for a drink—"

*"Never mind that!"* he screamed on the other end. *"Now listen to me very carefully:* I . . . had . . . them—*in my fucking hands!"*

McPhillips felt both his heart and stomach squirm. Breathlessly, he managed: *"What?"*

Wheaton was only able to babble out disjointed phrases, his thoughts coming faster than he could frame them into words. "I found them . . . they were at a restaurant, y'see. . . . Rachel had used credit cards . . . so I traced them down Fifty-seventh . . . and I found them. . . . They were eating at a French restaurant—"

The words hit Brian like a stun grenade.

*"What are you saying?"* he cried.

Wheaton gulped in a breath and simply spat out the news: "McPhillips, they're in New York! Do you understand what I'm telling you? *They're . . . in . . . New . . . York!"*

As McPhillips yelped in disbelief, the visage of Henry Weidemann flashed in his mind's eye, an apparition whose knowing expression all but said, *See, I told you so. . . .*

# 25

Mitch Myerson found her sitting by herself at the Ambassador Grill in the United Nations Plaza Hotel, sipping wine, smoking Dunhill after Dunhill. She looked forlorn and frightened, clearly shaken by the knowledge that her husband was in town, hunting them down like an obsessed bloodhound.

He walked up to her table. She looked up at him with pitiful eyes swimming in teardrops, eyes that could break a heart of stone. Yet he was unmoved. "Don't say a word until I tell you it's okay," he ordered her in a harsh whisper. She knew how grave her offenses were; he had never before used such a hostile tone with her.

The U.N. Plaza Hotel had accommodations available for the night. Praise the lord for small favors. In keeping with his propensity to use the names of geographic regions as aliases, he checked them in as Dr. and Mrs. Richard France of Kansas City, Missouri. He paid in cash. They had no luggage, of course, so when the clerk asked Mitch if he needed a bellhop to take their bags to the room, he concocted a story that the airline baggage handlers had misrouted it.

As they rode the brass-and-mirror elevator up to the room on the sixteenth floor, Rachel opened her mouth as if to speak. Myerson said brusquely, "I didn't say it was okay yet."

She cast her eyes to the floor.

Once they were in the room, Mitch paced back and forth in

a controlled fury. He shoved his fingers through his hair repeatedly in an agitated manner. He fought an irrational impulse to yank out hefts of hair from his head or, better yet, bang his head repeatedly against the wall to quell his anger. Instead, he paced, cursed, and sputtered. His left ankle pulsated with pain from the fall at the Meredien, but he ignored it and continued moving about the room.

"We were almost caught, Rachel," he announced after a while. "Do you realize that?"

Rachel sat on the bed and said nothing; just looked at him.

Myerson whirled on her. "Did you hear what I said? We were almost caught."

"I heard you," she murmured softly.

"Your husband was literally *six feet* away from me at the restaurant. Six feet! He had his hands out like this, reaching for my neck." By way of demonstration, Mitch roleplayed how Jeff had come after him. He groaned aloud. *"Very* unpleasant experience, Rachel."

Rachel simply followed his pacing with her eyes.

"How do you suppose he figured out where we were, Rachel? How do you think that happened?"

"I don't—" She trailed off and cast her eyes to the carpet. "I don't know."

*"Think,* Rachel, think," he implored her. "How is it that your husband very nearly caught us?"

"I told you, I don't know," she said in a trembly voice.

"Well, you can kiss our plans goodbye. We're not going to Rome now. I'm not going anywhere *near* that goddamn airport. It'll be crawling with feds now." He squinched his eyes shut and pinched the bridge of his nose. "How did it happen, goddammit? Think!"

"I'm *thinking!*"

"Did you leave him a note at home?"

"No!"

"Did you make a phone call that could be traced?"

"No. Mitch, stop it! You're *scaring* me—" Her voice went blurty with emotion.

Myerson paced some more, his mind racing to make some sense out of this. Suddenly, he froze in midstep. He turned toward her, very slowly. He spoke in a measured tone. "Did you use a credit card at Bloomingdale's today?"

She said nothing.

"Rachel! I asked you a question: *did you use a credit card?*"

"No!" she wailed.

He stared at her and whispered: "I don't believe you."

She began hugging her elbows, rocking back and forth a little. When she started to cry, crying then, his worst fears were confirmed. His shoulders sagged. *Oh, God, she had used a credit card! How could she do that? How could she expose us like that? It was so . . . selfish of her.*

"Oh, Mitch," she wept, "I'm so, so sorry. I just wanted to hurt him. I didn't want *this* to happen."

He wanted to remain angry with her, but involuntarily, the white-hot anger he had felt began to seep away. An overriding protective instinct swept over him. How it tore him up inside to see her like *that*, feeling any sort of pain. He gazed at her remorsefully, feeling guilty, feeling an impulse to rush over to her, to console her.

"Can you ever forgive me?" she sobbed.

*God, she cries so beautifully*, he thought. He had never known it to be possible for a woman to turn the act of crying into such a thing of beauty. Myerson moved to the bed and took her in his arms. "Of course, Nuffy," he mumbled. "I'm so sorry I made you cry."

"Oh, Mitch, please, please tell me that everything is going to be all right."

He sighed, "I swear it will be all right, Nuffy." He truly believed that. Yes, they had *almost* been caught just under an hour ago. But *almost* was the key word. They were safe and secure now. Still standing. New York was a big city. He made a vow that he wouldn't permit Wheaton to get that close to them again. "I'll protect you, Nuffy, I promise."

She hugged him and whispered, "Please, please, please let me make love to you, Mitchell. Let me prove my love to you—"

They quickly undressed.

Then she made love to him with a passion and an urgency he had never experienced with her before, not even the night previous. It was the best sex he ever had; he moaned in mind-burning ecstasy when she brought him to a prolonged orgasm.

Hours afterward, as they lay entwined in each other's arms, Mitch Myerson realized that this woman loved him every ounce as much as he loved her. They were perfect for each other. The thought that fate had somehow brought them together caused his eyes to well up with tears of blissful gratitude. *Thank you, God.*

# 26

A New York City police officer by the name of Leonard Warnke escorted McPhillips upstairs to the sixth-floor hotel room Mitch and Rachel had occupied a few hours before. The cop was casually eating an apple as they rode the elevator wordlessly. Warnke was a florid-faced cop with hair the color of wet coal. He sported a button on the lapel of his uniform that said, DINKINS MUST GO, quite probably in violation of NYPD regulations.

"This is it," Warnke said around a mouthful of chewed apple pulp, ushering Brian inside the room with a gesture of the half-eaten core.

As soon as McPhillips set foot in the hotel room, he felt an eerie prickle of déjà vu. There was no sense of euphoria that they had come oh-so close. Instead he felt a vague sadness that the couple had eluded them once more. Were they forever doomed to remain just one step behind the people who had stolen from them?

The crime scene was populated by three FBI agents and Jeff Wheaton. Agent Al Johnstone dusted for prints; Agent Jennifer Pearce sorted through their clothing for clues; Agent Wil Wiggins stood next to Wheaton, who was having a telephone conversation with Philadelphia Bureau Chief Newby.

Newby's angry voice crackled over the speakerphones. "Hey, with all due respect, Mr. Wheaton, I want to know what the fuck you're doing in New York City?"

"Yeah?" Wheaton shot back. "And I want to know what the fuck *you're* doing in Philadelphia when the sons-a-bitches are here in Manhattan."

"You ever hear the old saying about how private citizens aren't supposed to take the law into their own hands, Mr. Whea—"

"Spare me the vigilante speech," Wheaton said, impatiently. "I tracked our man down to a single restaurant, which is a lot more than I can say for the fibbies. I *actually* had the guy in my hands for a brief instant—"

Newby's voice softened. "Yeah, so I heard. What happened?"

"Bastard escaped."

Agent Wiggins leaned over toward the phone and spoke toward the microphone. "Guy busted out of a window on a lower floor of the hotel and jumped. Got away."

"All right," Newby said. "All right, listen to me. Mr. Wheaton, you there?"

"Yeah. I'm here."

"New York is an entirely different jurisdiction, Mr. Wheaton. Our branch is cooperating with their branch. Would you please back off and let these good people do their jobs?"

"Hey, me and my team came *this* close—"

Newby interrupted him with a belligerent bellow. "I said, *let them do their job*, Mr. Wheaton! We're widening the sweep now that we've . . . now that *you've* pinned them down to midtown Manhattan. We'll canvass the airports and make inquiries at the hotels—"

"Just what *we've* been doing all along—" Jeff muttered.

"—and if they try to leave town, we'll nail their asses faster than you can say 'convicted felon.' Do you *hear* me, Mr. Wheaton?"

Wheaton frowned miserably. "Loud and clear," he mumbled.

"Marvelous. Put Wiggins back on the phone. Agent Wiggins, are you there?"

"Right here, sir," Wiggins said.

"Take me off the goddam speakerphone. I *hate* speakerphones."

As Agent Wiggins picked up the receiver and punched the call off speakerphone, Brian called to Jeff and motioned him over.

"Where are the others?" Jeff asked him.

"Long story." Brian shrugged, not wanting to get into his brawl with Bruce right then. Later.

"Just think of it, Brian," Jeff said excitedly. "Myerson and my wife were in this room no more than *two* hours ago. No doubt dolling themselves up for a lovely dinner, a top-ticket Broadway show, maybe some dancing later at the Rainbow Room. Right *here*. You can still smell Rachel's perfume in the air. She wears Byzance. Jesus, I can still smell it in the air. Do you smell it?"

"Tell me what happened, Jeff."

"It started out as just a lark, a real fluke. Tommy hacked into a credit card database and identified a string of purchases Rachel had charged along Fifty-seventh Street. The final fuck-you, I guess." He shrugged. "We marked the stores on a city street map and just played connect-the-dots. Her purchases stopped at Fifty-seventh and Sixth Avenue, so I went to the hotel at that intersection—Le Parker Meridien."

McPhillips was suitably impressed by the detective-work. "That's smart thinking, Jeff."

"Anyway, while I'm there, I get this *hunch* that maybe, just maybe they're dining at the hotel's French restaurant, Maurice. Rachel loves French food, you know. Also, in the past, she'd once mentioned Maurice as a place she wanted to try during our next trip to New York City. She mentions a lot of restaurants, mind you, but I figure, why not, what harm could there be in taking a peek?"

"And they were *there?*"

"Yeah. They were there all right. Brian, you got to picture it. I tell the maître d' I'm looking for a friend, and he lets me take a look. So I start casing the joint, looking around at all the beautiful people, when suddenly my eyes fall on Mitch."

"Jesus," McPhillips whispered.

"I knew it was him the second I laid eyes on him. He was just sitting there, by himself, with this god-awful smug look on his face."

"Where was Rachel? Wasn't she there with him?"

"No. She was in the bathroom, I think. I don't know. But there were two sets of plates with half-eaten desserts on 'em."

"What happened then?"

"Well," Jeff said, a sheepish look coming over his face, "what should've happened next is me calling the cops. But . . . it didn't happen like that." Jeff licked the corner of his mouth. "Ah, Christ. I don't know if you can understand, but when I saw him sitting there, up on his high horse, something inside me *snapped*. I mean literally snapped. I just totally lost it, Brian. I start screaming at him, cursing him out, and running the length of the restaurant toward him, seriously ready to kill him. And I might've killed him too, if I'd got my hands on him. You should've seen the look on his face."

"I can picture it," McPhillips said with gentle humor.

Wheaton gave a short laugh to this. "Yeah. I suppose I was a terror."

"Go on," McPhillips urged.

"Nothing much left to tell. He started screaming for help and everyone there thought I was the lunatic psycho killer after a nice quiet guy enjoying his dinner, minding his own business. Who could blame them? I must've scared the shit out of every patron there, let alone Myerson."

"So he escaped out of the restaurant?"

"Yeah."

"How?"

"The fuck threw scalding coffee in my face and pushed me into a dessert cart, all the while yelling, 'Help! Help!' When I got up to go after him, I was restrained by three or four waiters while the maître d' called the police. By the time I managed to convince everyone that *Mitch* was the bad guy, he had already escaped." Wheaton looked at his open hands incredulously. "Slipped right through my fingers, Brian."

"Yeah," McPhillips said ruefully. "Slime will do that."

They were silent for a while. Then Brian said, "Well, you were right. They were in New York."

Wheaton corrected him. "They still *are*."

They hung around the crime scene for another forty minutes until Wiggins and Pearce took their respective statements. The FBI agents' search of the room had turned up two one-way tickets for a flight to Rome departing out of JFK at 10:55 A.M. the next day. This discovery verified Jeff's initial hypothesis that his wife had insisted on taking her dream trip with the stolen money, and that the world tour would begin in Italy. McPhillips was amazed at his friend's prescience, but Jeff shrugged it off. "Elementary," he said, without the slightest trace of Doylesian humor.

The agents discovered a Louis Vuitton suitcase crammed with brand-new, high-ticket items. Clothing, shoes, beautification products. Each item still had its price tag intact. Wheaton informed the agents that these were the goods his wife had purchased that afternoon during her telltale shopping spree. He notified the agents that he wished to file a specific claim against these goods, to satisfy the debt now owed on his credit card. Pearce duly made a note of his request.

Discouragingly, there were no clues among the clothing, toiletries, and other personal effects that would suggest where the couple was at this moment. They could be anywhere in the city, Wiggins told them with a shrug.

Johnstone assured them that the FBI would have four or five undercover agents on the lookout for the fugitives at the international airports for the next forty-eight hours.

"What if they take a bus out of the Port Authority?" Wheaton challenged.

Johnstone thought it over. "We can't stake out the bus terminals, Mr. Wheaton. There must be a thousand departures a day out of the Port Authority. Christ, it's a *weekend,* and we're short-staffed as it is."

"So what happens if they decide to take a bus to, say, Cleveland?" Wheaton pressed. "You're telling me they're home free?"

"I wouldn't worry about it," Johnstone chuckled. "Would *you* go to Cleveland if you didn't have to?"

But Wheaton was ill-humored at the moment and scowled at Johnstone's lame Cleveland-bashing. Johnstone thanked them for their cooperation and sent them away with the solemn promise that the Bureau would call if anything turned up.

In the cab back to the Hyatt, Jeff stared straight ahead. "We're not going to get a second shot at them," he said in a morose monotone. "We've lost the element of surprise. Myerson won't be so sloppy next time."

Though McPhillips said nothing, he was inclined to agree with his sullen companion. This time, they were gone. There could be no doubt about that.

*God, what a strange twenty-four hours it had been!* McPhillips said to himself.

# 27

"Underground sex clubs?" Chuck Beekman gave an incredulous laugh. "In Manhattan?" He had never heard of such a thing.

"Oh, yes," Mazzola assured him. "They certainly do exist. *Believe me, they exist.*"

There was something emphatic in Mazzola's tone—something *knowing*—that gave Beekman pause. He leaned back in his chair, swirling the ice cubes around in his cocktail, allowing himself to be consumed by his own imagination. *Underground sex clubs!*

It was nearing one in the morning and both men were exceedingly drunk. After the physical confrontation between McPhillips and Mazzola, it had taken every ounce of Beekman's powers of persuasion to deter Mazzola from chasing after Brian and thrashing him to within an inch of his life. As a diversionary tactic, Beekman had proposed a pub-crawling excursion throughout lower Manhattan. One drink per bar, like the old days at Penn. Never one to turn down a cocktail or two, Mazzola agreed.

As the night wore on, a purplish mouse had swollen up nastily beneath Mazzola's left eye, a throbbing memento of the ugly and brutal fistfight between two one-time friends. It took several hours of hard drinking for Mazzola to finally tire of ranting about what scum McPhillips had become since he was married with children. In fact, Mazzola's upswing in mood over the last several hours was nothing short of dramatic. He now appeared near ebullient as they shared a wobbly wooden table in the Peculier Pub, a legendary Irish bar in the Village near Washington Square Park, belting back a few stiff drinks. Bruce speedrapped animatedly, spouting forth juicy *bons mots* from his seemingly endless catalogue of sexual conquests over the last ten years.

When Mazzola casually mentioned that he had frequented some underground sex clubs with his business clients a few years back, Beekman's ears had pricked up in interest.

Now Beekman licked his lips and leaned forward. "Okay okay okay. Let's take it from the top. You're telling me that there's such a thing as 'sex clubs' in Manhattan."

"That's correct."

"Where strangers have sex with each other? In public?"

"That's what sex clubs *are*, Chuckster."

"That's wild, man. How come I've never heard of 'em before?"

"They're *underground*, Chuck. They don't exactly take out ads in the Bell Atlantic Yellow Pages."

"So what happens at these places?"

"Whatever you want, Chuck. Voyeurism. Fantasy. B & D. S & M. Gay. Bi. Masturbation. Anything goes."

"That's incredible."

Bruce leered. "Yeah. It is."

"These sex clubs, have they been around for a while?"

"Oh sure. Since the early seventies." Bruce then delivered a learned colloquy on the secret history of Manhattan's underground sex-on-premises clubs. The phenomenon of public sex among consenting strangers occurred first in the gay bathhouses, porn theaters, and bookstores of the early seventies. Sex clubs followed, the inevitable commercial evolution of the Sexual Revolution sweeping the nation at the time. The first real hetero sex-on-premises enterprise was Plato's Retreat, a mate-swapping marketplace. It was hardly original, what with the Roman orgy motif and all, but it was an enormously popular place to find strangers willing to fuck and suck in huge bubbling mineral baths.

Disco music put an entirely new spin on the phenomenon. Again, it was the gay community of Greenwich Village that pioneered the cutting edge clubs. Clubs like 12 West, Anvil, The Locker Room, the Hangout, Shooting Stars—they were establishments that pushed the envelope—the lips-below-the-hips joints. One of the most noteworthy entries in the annals of sex clubs was The Hell Fire Club, a self-contained gay S & M theme park that was most definitely not for the faint of heart.

The concept of sex clubs was too good for the gays to keep all to themselves. The cocaine-fueled decadence of the mid-eighties led to widespread public promiscuity among heterosexuals in the ultrahip, internationally famous discotheques of the Jay McInerney decade: Limelight, Area, Xenon, and, of course, Studio 54. Though it was a certified to-die-for thrill merely to be *permitted* to enter the premises of one of these clubs, it was truly a superhuman accomplishment to wangle an invite from a Eurotrash club owner to party in one of the private rooms away from the huddled masses of the common people. In these rooms, cocaine flowed as freely as the champagne, and a quick bunny-fuck with someone you'd known scarcely five minutes was a distinct possibility if you played your cards right.

"God, those were the days," Mazzola sighed parenthetically to his enraptured companion. "Anyway—"

During this glorious era, a number of very chi-chi but hush-hush sex-on-premises clubs came and went. These clubs, both straight and gay, bore names like the Rubber Room and the Crisco Disco, and became *the* in places for sex aficionados. They invariably cropped up in bad neighborhoods where even the vice cops rarely went: Hell's Kitchen, Alphabet City, and the meat-packing district.

Chuck Beekman laughed delightedly at the wonderful irony of the *meat-packing district* being a hotbed for sexual activity. But Mazzola frowned at the interruption and continued his discourse.

The sex-on-premises clubs of this time were known to be extremely mobile. A sex-club owner never knew when a bribe to a city official would backfire or when the overexcited scumbag the bouncer had to thrash last Saturday night happened to be the younger brother of a member of the NYPD. Operating without liquor licenses, tax certificates or any other indicia of commercial legitimacy was the *modus operandi* of these illegitimate joints that depended upon word-of-mouth. But they were incredibly lucrative businesses. A former New York City Commissioner was rumored to own a club called Mine Shaft that cleared $5 million profit in a single year. In fact, it was the success of these sex clubs more than anything else that led to the last great exploitation of the concept: Before it reinvented itself as a—quote-unquote—*family resort*, Club Med was the ultimate—an open-air sex club situated in a tropical paradise.

That so many places of illicit pleasures existed without his knowledge boggled Chuck's mind. "Have you been to . . . a lot of these places?"

Bruce Mazzola fired his companion a severe look. "Chuckster, you're looking at a borderline, if not *over-the-line*, sex addict. What do *you* think?"

Beekman bit his fingernail thoughtfully. "I imagine the arrival of AIDS put an end to the fun, huh?"

"Au contraire, Voltaire. Reports of the death of recreational sex clubs in the nineties are greatly exaggerated."

"Seriously?"

"You think that just because there's AIDS, people don't get *horny* anymore?" Mazzola began ticking off the existing clubs on his fingertips. "You got La Trapeze for downtown swingers. The Clit Club for lipstick lesbians. The Vault for major S & M fetishes. Second Avenue Affair for fantasy sex."

"In-fucking-credible. With all this talk of safe sex—"

"Hey, there're plenty of clubs that specialize in safe sex."

"There are?"

"Of course. In fact, I happen to know of the hottest safe-sex club on the East Coast. It's uptown, on the West Side."

"You're yanking my crank, man."

"I kid you not. It's called Club X."

"Club *what*?"

"Club X." Mazzola withdrew his billfold from his jacket pocket and produced a purple plastic card with a red 'X' slashed across it. "So happens, I'm a lifetime member."

Beekman blurted out a laugh. "Figures."

Mazzola showed his teeth and said, "You know what, Charlie

Three-Sticks? Night's still young. You feelin' sexually adventurous?" He jiggled the Club X card.

Beekman felt the breath rushing out of him. *An underground sex club.* The prospect of checking out Club X filled him with equal measures of euphoria and trepidation. It would be the ultimate sexual frontier for a sexually frustrated man. *But what if something happened?* He assured himself that nothing would happen. He didn't *have to do anything.* He could just . . . check it out. What was the harm in that? No purchase necessary, right? *Hey, Chuck, it's been a rough weekend. Live a little.*

"Sure," Chuck Beekman said. "Let's go."

At Mazzola's instruction, the cab sliced through the gentrified neighborhoods of midtown Manhattan and plunged into the industrial section of town on the West Side. In about ten minutes, the driver arrived at the address Mazzola had provided, Fifty-third Street between Eleventh and Twelfth avenues. Chuck Beekman peered out the back window and felt a chill rising up his spine. There was a ghost-town stillness that left him unsettled. Zoned for industrial use, the area appeared to be comprised mostly of automobile-related businesses. S & A COLLISION. PALKENDO TIRE & BATTERY. DEWITT BODY & REPAIR. The north side of the street was comprised of bombed-out buildings boarded up with sheets of rotting plywood or secured by rusting plates of slatted-iron armor. Most of the streetlights were burned out. Beekman had bad vibes about this place.

As if reading his thoughts, the cabbie piped up in his thick Brooklynese, "Jesus, Joseph, and Mary. You guys *sure* you want me to leave you here?"

Mazzola said, "You got a problem with that?"

"Hey, no skin off *my* ass. But were I you, I wouldn't expect a cab coming back."

"Well, that's *our* problem then, isn't it?" Mazzola thrust a ten-dollar bill at the driver. They disembarked and the cab lumbered off into the night. Off in the distance, they could hear the vague rumble of the traffic on the West Side Highway. Other than that, the atmosphere was graveyard-still. Beekman's uneasy feeling intensified. *A guy could get killed around here.*

"This way," Mazzola said, guiding Beekman by the arm.

They started across the street to a three-story warehouse that looked like a hulking shell long-abandoned by its owners. Most of the windowpanes were broken. Sworls of unintelligible graffiti obscured the face of the building. Nevertheless, as they approached, Beekman could make out the faint thump of dance music emanating from inside the building. His initial trepidation was replaced by a prickly sensation of anticipation.

Mazzola led them to a metal door that had a giant red X spraypainted across its length. A simple red sign with white letters stated: YOU MUST SHOW YOUR CARD.

"X marks the spot," Beekman said. A giddiness had crept into his voice.

Before pressing the buzzer, Mazzola stared at his companion's hand disapprovingly. "You know what they say about those things."

"What things?"

"Wedding bands."

Chuck Beekman's eyes dropped self-consciously to the gold band on his ring finger. "No."

"They're actually homing devices that transmit radio waves to wives. The frequency can only be picked up by a wife's female intuition. You dig?"

Beekman yanked the ring over his knuckle and stashed it in his front pocket.

Mazzola smirked approvingly. "You're a good man, Charlie Brown." Mazz stabbed at the buzzer. Momentarily, the steel door opened and light spilled out from within. A scowling uniformed security guard filled the doorway. The guard was a menacing Irishman with a putty-featured face and a big roast-beef of a body. An off-duty police officer, Beekman guessed. The guard looked imposing enough that the notion of turning tail and getting the hell out of there struck Beekman as a capital idea. Then he noticed the Tanqueray-and-tonic in the Irishman's hand.

"Help you gentlemen?" the guard said.

"We're here for the club," Beekman said.

Mazzola immediately fired him a shut-up look.

The guard, meanwhile, tilted his chin up and reacted with a

heavy-lidded expression of indifference. "Club? No club here. This is a cable-and-wire distribution company. A warehouse." The heavy thump of dance music from several floors above belied this statement.

Mazzola wordlessly flashed the X card. The guard's expression softened noticeably. "This way," he said, indicating the direction by jutting his chin.

"Never leave home without it," Mazzola muttered, sotto voce.

The Irishman escorted them across the nondescript lobby of the commercial building to the freight elevator. The guard pushed an illuminated button, which caused a loud buzzing to echo throughout the elevator shaft. In the next instant, there was a loud mechanical clatter, the grinding of some ancient gears and the creak of steel cables. When the freight elevator arrived, the metal grille parted and a breathtakingly beautiful woman straight out of the slick pages of Victoria's Secret greeted them. She had emerald eyes and her hair was a silken shawl of gold. "Welcome to the Club, gentlemen. My name is Tiffany. It will be fifty dollars apiece tonight."

Mazzola pulled out a wad of bills and covered them. He and Beekman stepped into the elevator. "Have a good time, fellas," the guard chuckled after them. In a knowing singsong, he said, "Don't forget to wrap that rascal."

On the way up to the fifth floor, Tiffany informed them, "It's Live Your Fantasy Night, gentlemen. Your waitress will provide you with a menu of tonight's girls."

*A menu?* Beekman mouthed to Mazzola.

They arrived on the fifth floor and Tiffany threw open the elevator door.

Chuck Beekman stepped out into a cavernous male-fantasyland. Immediately upon walking into the expanse of Club X, he was set upon by a swarm of a dozen drop-dead gorgeous sex kittens decked out in bikinis, thongs, and teddies. They congregated around him and Bruce, murmuring and cooing, running their hot hands over his face, his body, through his hair. An electric charge zipped through his genitals.

"C'mon, Romeo," Mazzola laughed, as he pulled Beekman

away from the gaggle of semi-nude models. "Plenty of time for that later."

"Good god, the girls here are so *friendly*."

"No shit, Sherlock. It's a sex club."

A surprisingly clean-cut man in an exquisitely tailored tuxedo introduced himself to them. "I'm your host for the evening," the man said in a Crocodile Dundee accent. "The name's Ian, mates." Beekman nodded, as he stared at the man. Though he never once thought himself gay, Beekman had to admit he was entranced by the guy working the door. Perfectly white teeth like Chicklets, flowing blond hair, chiseled face. Guy looked something like Bo Derek, except of course, he was a *dude*. Guy had to be a male model, had to be.

"Follow me, mates," Ian said.

As Prince's "U Got the Look" pulsated over the sound system, they followed Ian to their table. Charles Beekman craned his neck around, gathering in the incredible spectacle of a sex club. In a cage suspended from the ceiling, two major slices of cheesecake in fishnet bodysuits, going at it in a suggestive tussle. On the large stage, five model-perfect pinups, doing erotic dances, two of them kissing each other. Chuck gaped in awe. This place was completely different than what he had expected. For one thing, it didn't have the makeshift feel he had associated with the fly-by-night sex joints Mazzola had described; this place had the aura of permanence, of legitimacy. There were tasteful erotic nudes adorning the walls and silk backdrops, Romanesque figures engaged in various forms of sexual activity. Mirrors everywhere. The lighting was just subtle enough to enhance the ambience and the sparing use of neons and strobes worked to heighten the eroticism of the activity onstage. This place, Beekman decided, exuded pure sex.

The club was packed with about 150 young, urban professional types who didn't appear any different from Mazzola and Beekman. The yuppies were all Ivy League types, well-dressed, each wearing his aura of confidence like body armor. Everyone seemed to enjoy being clued in on the secret of Club X's existence. Although there were mostly guys in their twenties and thirties, he spied an occasional gray-hair in the crowd.

Once they were seated, Bruce placed a drink order with Ian—

Stoli rocks for Bruce, a martini for Chuck—and requested their "menus" right away. Ian disappeared and Mazzola said, "See those guys over there?"

Beekman followed his stare across the room. Two humungous black guys were taking turns enjoying a fully nude lap dance from a full-breasted Asian girl. "Yeah?"

"They used to play backfield for the New York Giants."

The drinks came presently. Swizzling his excellent martini, Beekman cast his eyes about the place. He locked eyes with a statuesque blonde in a black teddy. Girl was a Heather Locklear lookalike, straight out of Westwood Village. She smiled and blew him a kiss. Beekman nearly yelped in euphoria. All around him, yuppies were drinking, smoking cigars, and ogling the beautiful women as they came on stage, one after another, in skimpy outfits. It was like some glorious bachelor party, Beekman thought. He was stunned by the consistent beauty of the "hostesses" as they struck poses for the patrons, teasing them, priming them for the main event—balling for dollars, as Mazzola once called it.

"I can't believe the police haven't come in and shut this place down," Beekman said.

"You kiddin' me?" Mazzola frowned. "The NYPD has a helluva lot better things to do than worry about victimless crimes involving consensual sex. Besides, ain't their job to be the orgasm police."

Ian brought menus. Chuck picked his up and gave it a cursory glance.

His mouth fell open in surprise the moment he laid eyes on it.

The menu was a listing of the women available for the night. By name, by nationality, and by sexual inclination. They had names like Dominique, Epiphany, Felicity, Amber Lynn. They were identified as Swiss, black, Hawaiian, Chinese, Russian. They were described with lines such as "hot frosty blonde, eager for mutual pleasure" and "long lithe Island girl, ready to reveal her tropical paradise to you" and "submissive Oriental girl, wanting to share ancient Chinese secrets of ecstasy." In all, there were thirty choices. The reverse side of the menu was a schematic laying out the locations of the so-called fantasy rooms on the two floors above them. There were twenty rooms in all, some of them no doubt already occupied. The pricetag for forty-five minutes in heaven: $195.

Mazzola watched the contortions on Beekman's face with vast amusement. "Didn't I tell you this place was great? Huh? Huh?"

Up onstage, the emcee-slash-bouncer named Ian grabbed the microphone and boomed out, "Welcome to Live Your Fantasy Night, mates." The throng cheered. "For your consideration for the fantasy rooms upstairs, Club X gives you—*the girls of the house!*"

Beekman watched, transfixed, as thirty-some semi-clad wannabe models, moonlighting coeds, former soap-opera actresses, and professional prostitutes, strutted onstage, engaged in suggestive poses, tussling and writhing, taunting the all-male audience, driving them into a cheering, testosterone-fueled frenzy. It was downright *primal*, Beekman thought deliriously. Beekman zeroed in on the long-legged blond in the dental-floss thong. She had big beestung lips and almond-shaped eyes that made his muscles go slack. What a piece of eye candy. *Such* a flat belly on that hardbody of hers, curving so softly into her panties. His craving for her was inarticulable.

Mazzola picked up on Beekman's apparent fixation.

"Sproutin' a chubbie yet, Chuckie?" Mazzola taunted.

"This place is great! This place is great!" Beekman yelled.

"It gets even better."

"Awww right, mates," the Australian emcee roared, milking the Crocodile Dundee shtick for all it was worth, "Club X presents—AUDIENCE PARTICIPATION TIME!"

As Guns N' Roses' "Welcome to the Jungle" blasted out, the girls streamed offstage in a tidal wave of suntanned flesh, dispersing among the frenetic audience of wildly cheering men. Couples paired off in a weird, orgiastic ritual that sent tables tumbling, chairs flying, drinks spilling. Sexually crazed New York attorneys, bankers, brokers, pro athletes, and doctors knocked into each other, scrambling desperately for a partner to fornicate with. Just when it seemed certain that one of the former New York Giant halfbacks was about to snag Charles Beekman's dreamgirl, Mazzola lunged in front of him and yanked her cleanly away. "Hey-y-y-y, sweetcakes. I'd like you to meet a really, really good friend of mine—"

*Twenty minutes later, Beekman found himself alone with the girl. They were together in one of the fantasy rooms on the seventh floor.*

*Mazzola had most graciously covered the $195 fee.*

*What a guy.*

*She said her name was Heather. As in Locklear.*

*Beekman knew it was a fake. Had to be.*

*She told him she was a second-year law student at NYU. Just earning herself some book money for the fall semester. She laughed at the notion.*

"Do you like law school?" he asked.

"It sucks," she said cheerfully. "I'm in it for the money."

"I always thought I should've applied to law school," he said, chattily. *Having second thoughts about the impending sexual encounter, he believed he would have been content just talking to the girl for the entire forty-five minutes. He could just lie to Mazzola afterward. Tell him it was phenomenal. It'd be a lot easier than lying to his wife.*

*But Heather was on to his game. She cupped his face in her hands and cooed in a honey-coated whisper,* "You've got to relax, sugar. You're way too uptight."

*Beekman smiled weakly and nodded.*

"It's going to be okay. We're going to have fun together."

"Okay."

"Don't you like what you see?" *She stepped away from him, stepped out of her panties and arched her back in order to give him a full view of her tight body. She twirled around, affording him a 360-degree assessment of her wares. The fog of alcohol shrouded his perception, as if he was viewing everything through a Vaseline-smeared lens, but he knew the girl before him was uncommonly striking. Not as beautiful as Jeff's wife Rachel, perhaps, but drop-dead attractive in her own right. He realized sex with her was an inevitability. He sighed.* "You are very beautiful, Heather."

*She leaned over him, pushing her breasts into his face. "Now tell me, sugar—who am I?"*

*He was confused by what sounded like a philosophical question. "I don't understand."*

*She laughed softly. "Do you want me to be someone? A secretary? A lady boss? A nurse or a princess? What's your fantasy?"*

*"Could we pretend . . . we just got married? And we're on our honeymoon?"*

*"Anything you want, sugar."*

*"Can I . . . can I call you Phoebe?"*

*"Phoebe?"*

*"Yes, Phoebe." He locked eyes with the woman before him. "You remind me of a woman I know named Phoebe."*

*"Is this someone you've wanted for a long time?"*

*"Phoebe is my wife, actually."*

*The hooker drew back and blinked at him in disbelief. "Oh."*

*"You remind me of her," Beekman said, "when I first fell in love with her."*

*"Whatever gets you off, sugar," she said, her enthusiasm somewhat diminished. She tore open a red foil packet and withdrew the rubber O of a latex condom. She set about unrolling the condom over his semi-erect penis.*

*"Ouch," Beekman winced.*

*"Sorry, baby. Did I hurt you?"*

*"It's okay."*

*"You want me, don't you?"*

*"Yes."*

*"Are you ready for me?"*

*"Yes."*

*"It's going to be really good, I promise you."*

*He nodded numbly. Then he closed his eyes tightly, as if he expected to experience pain instead of pleasure. No turning back now.*

*Heather doused the lights and went to work on him. He fully surrendered himself to her. He tried to enjoy it, but in his mind's eye, he was haunted by a vivid apparition of his wife, a vision he couldn't shake. Guilt overcame what little pleasure he felt. When he came a few minutes later, his orgasm was so weak, so ungratifying, he scarcely felt it. Shame rushed in.*

Pale and shaken, Chuck Beekman staggered back to the table at just before 2:30 A.M.

Mazzola greeted him with a luminous smile. "Well, well, well. That was quick."

Beekman slumped into his chair and closed his eyes.

"So tell me," Bruce said. "How was it? Spare me no riches."

Beekman shook his head slowly from side to side. His sense of equilibrium was depleting quickly and the entire room was awhirl. He was absolutely certain he was going to be sick.

"C'mawwwwn," Mazzola coaxed. "You don't want to make your Uncle Bruce *beg*, do you? Lemme live vicariously, you stud."

Beekman managed to mutter, "It was horrid."

"Come again?"

"Horrible. It was horrible."

"Ah, how bad could it have been?" Mazzola burbled. "You had a Heather Locklear lookalike doing your bidding. A hardbody with silky legs straight up to her shoulders. A *model*, for chrissake." Mazzola issued a throaty chuckle.

"I can't believe I did that," Beekman said. "I can't believe I let that happen."

"Easy, big guy."

"I can't believe it," he kept repeating. "I can't believe it."

"Jesus, Chuckie," Mazzola said with mock sympathy. "Look at you. You're shaking like James Brown on a caffeine jag. What happened in there?"

"Bruce—"

"It's okay. Your Uncle Bruce is right here."

"It's *not okay!* How'm I gonna face my wife again?" Chuck Beekman leaned forward and tucked his chin into his chest, hoping the nausea would pass.

"Piece of cake, Chuckster. Game plan is, you don't tell her *squat*."

"I can't believe it," he moaned. He lifted his head and faced Mazzola. "How could I let you talk me into that?"

The joviality on Mazzola's face disappeared. Mazzola eyed

Beekman evenly. "Because it was what *you* wanted, Chuck. What *you* wanted. Remember that."

*No.* This was not what he wanted. *Not at all.*

Neither man spoke for awhile. Beekman cradled his stomach hoping to subdue the sickly feeling rising up in him again.

"Tell you what," Mazzola said, suddenly grinning once more. "Why don't I buy you a shot of Kentucky confidence? One for the road."

Beekman shook his head. "No. I just want to go back to the hotel now."

"Uncle Bruce insists." The grin was frozen on Mazzola's face. "It'll soothe what ails ya."

Mazzola stood up and thrust his hand into his jacket pocket to withdraw his billfold. As he tugged it out, however, something got snagged in the folds of the leather: a packet of papers or something. As Beekman watched, Mazzola cursed and fumbled to catch the bundle as it popped free of the jacket pocket. Bruce was deeply intoxicated though, and, by swiping hamhandedly at it in mid-air, he actually batted it away with the side of his hand. The bundled packet bounded across the table, falling closest to Beekman.

Chuck Beekman's eyes dropped to the packet before him.

It was two blue passports bound together against the sleeve of some airline tickets by a pair of rubber bands. The sleeve had fallen face up. The Alitalia trademark was in plain view. A notation of a flight to Rome with tomorrow's date was handwritten in neat block letters.

Both men stared at the bundle for a long moment. Neither one moving, neither one speaking.

Then, without a word, Beekman picked the bundled items up off the table and handed them to Mazzola. Mazzola's eyes never left Beekman's face as he replaced the packet back into his blazer pocket.

After a time, Chuck Beekman said, "You're going to Italy, Bruce?"

"Yeah," Mazzola said, adjusting his Hermès tie, visibly unsettled. "I was going to tell you. I was going to invite you actually. Let's get those drinks and talk about it."

Mazzola collared a passing hostess and ordered double shots of Jack Daniel's. Beekman made no protest. He continued to stare at Bruce.

"I didn't want to say anything to the others," Mazzola said, locking up Beekman's eyes with his. "But goddammit, we can't let Mitch get away with this, we just can't." Bruce ran a hand through his hair and his eyes flitted about the room. "I want to . . . to *find them* if it's the last thing I do. So, this afternoon, on a whim, I got two plane tickets to Rome, to check around the hotels there. And I want to know if you'll come."

Chuck Beekman said nothing as the hostess returned with their two drinks. Mazzola paid her. When she went away, he asked, "When did you buy those tickets?"

"When? Yesterday."

"Yesterday?" Beekman looked confused. "How did you know?"

"How did I know what?"

"How did you know to buy tickets to Italy?"

"How did I know? Jeff said that's where his wife would probably go, that's how—"

"But he didn't tell us that until this morning. You said you bought them yesterday."

Mazzola froze for an instant. Then he snarled, "You're givin' me a fucking migrane with this cross-examination, Beekman. Let's go over it one more time. Right now, it's two o'fucking clock in the morning on Sunday, right? So when I say 'yesterday,' I mean Saturday. Today to you. You followin' me now?"

Beekman blinked. "Why do you have two passports there?"

Mazzola floundered, gestured, then spat, "What is this, the fucking Spanish Inquisition? Just drink your motherfucking drink and let's get you back to the hotel."

"I don't want it. I don't feel well."

"Have it anyway. It'll clear the clutter in your brain."

"I really don't want another drink, Bruce."

Mazzola eyed him menacingly. "It's already bought and paid for. So down the hatch."

"I just want to go back to the hotel," Beekman moaned.

Mazzola shook his head slowly from side to side, like a stern parent dealing firmly with a precocious child refusing his vegetables. "You're not leavin' till you've polished off the last drop."

Bullied, Chuck picked up the double shot with trembling fingers. He stared at it queasily.

"That's my boy," Mazzola said. "One, two, three: *go!*"

Beekman tilted his head back, opened his throat and poured the drink straight down, hoping not to taste it. But the aftertaste and the burn of the alcohol made him gag. His face screwed into a grimace. His stomach protested, acid heat spreading along the lining of his stomach. He fought to will away the roiling waves of nausea cascading through his innards. His eyes teared. He scrubbed at them, trying to clear his vision.

When the fog lifted, the first thing he saw was Bruce Mazzola sitting across from him, holding his undrunk drink between his thumb and forefinger. A wolfish grin spread across his face.

"Fooled you," Mazzola said in a taunting singsong. He upended the drink onto the floor.

Charles Beekman, Jr., stared blankly at his companion.

"We can go now," Mazzola announced. "Let's get you to bed."

Somehow, Chuck Beekman made it outside without blowing chunks. Once outside, he was encouraged by a cool breeze whipping off the Hudson River that eased his queasiness some. He cared about one thing only: crawling into the bed back at the hotel.

A group of a half-dozen boisterous men had come down the freight elevator with them. They spilled out onto the street in a drunken amoeba. They began moving toward Ninth Avenue in search of a cab. Mazzola, however, was beating a brisk pace in the opposite direction, toward Eleventh Avenue. Beekman staggered to catch up with Bruce. Though his first steps were taken with legs of pudding, he managed to shore up his remaining strength and lurch forward in uncertain locomotion.

"Let's go to Fifty-first Street," Mazzola said tersely. "We can probably catch a cab there."

Beekman nodded. Whatever.

When they reached Fifty-first Street, they found it completely deserted. In the dead of the night like this, the neighborhood seemed to Beekman as lifeless and alien as a lunar landscape.

Various thoughts swirled in his mind: fear of being stranded in the depths of this godforsaken urban nightmare; anger at Mazzola, for talking him into Club X, goading him into sex; there was also confusion, guilt, and, of course, nausea. Beekman was a tangle of drunken emotions. He was a mess.

He prayed they would find a cab at this hour somewhere before a street gang showed up and sliced them up with switchblades. He didn't want to wind up the front page story of the *New York Post*.

Abruptly, Mazzola stopped short, startling him.

"What is it?" Beekman asked, alarmed.

"Fuck," Mazzola spat. "We should've gone toward the West Side Highway. Let's go this way."

Mazzola steered him down Fifty-first Street, heading west. Beekman could hear the sounds of traffic on the West Side Highway growing closer. This section of the neighborhood, too, was utterly bereft of any signs of life.

"Almost there," Mazzola asked soothingly. "How do you feel? You feel okay?"

"No," Beekman said. "I feel like I'm going to puke."

"What I mean is, what's going through your mind right now? I'm being serious: what are you thinking?"

The tone of Bruce's voice had taken on an odd timbre. "Bruce, please. I just want to get home."

Mazzola nodded and put a reassuring hand on his companion's shoulder. "That's just what I'm trying to do, chief. Get you home. There'll be a bunch of cabs on Twelfth Avenue."

Beekman nodded. Twelfth Avenue was still about five football fields away, but Beekman could see cars in the distance if he squinted. So distracted was he in searching out passing cabs in the distance, he never saw Bruce Mazzola lunging for him. He never fully realized what was happening even after Bruce had surged forward and wrapped his hands around Chuck Beekman's neck with viselike pressure.

The force propelled Beekman backward, causing him to backpedal into the chain-link fence of a junkyard with a ringing clatter. Mazzola had managed to get a firm grip around his throat and savagely pressed both thumbs against Beekman's thyroid cartilage, choking off the supply of oxygen to his lungs and his brain. Beekman's unseeing eyes bulged forth in shock, glistening in the pale moonlight, as if to burst free from their sockets. Short sucking noises emanated within him as he struggled with all his might to draw in a breath. In another instant, his shock gave way to self-preservation instinct: Beekman clawed desperately at Mazzola's ramrod-straight arms, trying to break free of the deathgrip. It was close to ten seconds since oxygen had been cut off and his energy was waning, consciousness was ebbing.

With all his remaining strength, Beekman managed to land a blind blow in the crook of Mazzola's right arm, causing Mazzola to loosen his grip for a split-second. Beekman's lungs heaved, trying desperately to suck in some precious oxygen; he managed to get a wisp. Mazzola cursed loudly, sidestepped around Beekman, and positioned himself behind his victim. He applied an eight-finger chokehold against the windpipe. Beekman, drunk and dying, clawed and thrashed like a wild animal, scrabbling to get at Mazzola, but he could not reach him. The deathgrip tightened its lethal circle around his trachea. In a few more seconds, the light dimmed in Beekman's world and gave way to nothingness.

Only when Bruce Mazzola felt Beekman's body go slack in his hands did he relax. Satisfied he was dead, Bruce Mazzola relaxed his grip on his companion's neck and took a step back. The corpse slumped to the litter-strewn asphalt. An empty Old English Malt Liquor bottle squirted out from beneath the dead body and skittered into the gutter with a clatter.

Then there was nothing but dead silence.

Mazzola leaned over and tried to catch his breath. He was trembling from the exertion killing Chuck had required. After a moment, he allowed himself to glance at Beekman's prone form.

*Good news, bad news.* The good news was that Chuck didn't have to face his wife about his infidelities now. . . .

Mazzola stared at his hands. His fingers were tingling; *no*, they were actually *vibrating*. He was stunned at how easy it had been. An expert at calculated risk-taking, he had often found making a killing on Wall Street to be hard. Killing Chuck, by contrast, had been a piece of cake.

\* \* \*

He wanted to make it look like a robbery-murder, so once he dragged the corpse into the nearby junkyard, he stripped the body of its wallet, watch and all identification. Then he disposed of the wallet in the dumpster of a run-down establishment called F & S Auto Salvage, some fifty yards further down the block. The identification cards were deposited down a sewer grate on the next corner.

Then Bruce Mazzola sprinted the rest of the way down Fifty-first Street to Twelfth Avenue. Once there, it seemed like a fucking eternity until a taxi came along. He commanded the driver to take him to Loew's New York Plaza at Fifty-first and Lexington. The cabbie asked him pointedly what the hell he had been doing, risking his neck in such a bad neighborhood at such an ungodly hour. "Car trouble," Mazzola told him in a pissed-off tone. He and the driver lapsed into a companionable silence for the remainder of the trip. The traffic at three in the morning was sparse, and the taxi made good time across Fifty-seventh Street into the East Side.

In the lobby of Loew's, Mazzola approached the desk and checked in. He signed the name Mike Schwartz and paid for the room with a counterfeit American Express card that had been forged with that name two weeks before. Mazzola thought this was a nice touch. Mike Schwartz was the alias used by Dennis Levine for his secret bank account in the Bahamas in the mid-eighties, when Levine was making millions from his insider trading schemes. Once the formalities of check-in were completed, the bleary-eyed clerk handed him a key and two messages on pink paper, then returned to his corned-beef on a deli roll.

Mazzola waited until he was secluded in his room before he read the messages. He found himself laughing aloud at their content.

Afterward, he walked into the bathroom, where he crumpled the messages into wads and flushed them away, into the labyrinthine sewer system of New York City. He splashed cold water on his face and allowed himself an exhilarated laugh. Club X was *always* so much fun.

But tomorrow was a big day. Much to be done.

He turned in for the night and immediately fell into a fitful sleep.

# PART SIX

## SUNDAY MORNING
## JUNE 28, 1992

# 28

Sunday morning broke. She woke with the dawn and was wide awake for several hours, waiting for him to break the membrane of sleep.

Finally—*finally!*—he began stirring on his side of the bed. The glowing red digits of the bedside clock put the time at nine-fifteen. He'd had almost ten hours of sleep.

She must've really worn him out last night. She mulled this thought over with a considerable degree of pride.

When he whispered her name, she pretended to be asleep. She knew he would never try to wake her. He knew how much she valued her beauty sleep. He knew that as a practice, she enjoyed staying in bed until the better part of the morning was killed off.

With a rustling of bedsheets, he got up and padded to the bathroom. From behind the closed door, she could hear the clank of the toilet seat as it was lowered. Moments later, she heard him grunting, then flatulating wetly into the bowl.

French food did that to him.

*Okay, now.*

Feeling the first ripples of excited anticipation, she slipped out of bed. She knew precisely what she had to do.

First things first: what to wear? There were only two choices: the evening gown she wore last night to the restaurant or the white terrycloth bathrobe with the hotel's emblem stitched on the breast pocket. Decisions, decisions.

She chose the bathrobe. The evening dress would have been much too much this early in the morning.

Then she slipped into her only pair of shoes—Ferragamo pumps! Jesus, Joseph, and Mary! She would be some sight, parading around the hotel in a bathrobe and evening shoes. She smiled. Okay, so she would look dreadful. So be it. It wasn't like this was a fashion show or something.

She waited until Myerson turned on the shower. He started crooning an off-key version of Frank Sinatra's "New York, New York." Talk about *dreadful!*

Knowing this was now her window of opportunity, she crept stealthily out of the hotel room in her crested bathrobe.

She glided down to the lobby in the elevator.

There he was, waiting for her at the entrance. Smoking a cigar, of course. He stood there casually, aloof and dangerous, like he didn't know he was gorgeous. Looking hot enough to melt mascara a mile away, as always. Her heart leapt at the mere sight of him.

What a major-league babe he was!

She rushed into the expanse of his chest and threw her arms around him. "My hero," she sang. "I missed you so much!"

They broke the clinch.

"Glamourpuss," he crooned. He lovingly cupped her chin in his hand. But she was surprised; his affectionate gesture became a viselike pinch that *hurt.*

"Ouch," she yelped.

"Glamourpuss, I saw that lovely video you and scumboy made back in Philly. Tell me, what the fuck was going through your pretty head, huh?"

She batted his hand away and stepped back. She glared at him evenly, a defiant smile on her face. "Whatever it takes, remember? We both agreed. That was the plan." She shrugged. "That's what it took."

Bruce Mazzola nodded, smirked. "Yeah, but maybe you took it a little too literally. Tell me, did you enjoy it?"

Rachel paused long enough to let him squirm. "It was purely business."

Bruce Mazzola stared hard at Rachel Fairweather Wheaton. A smile spread over his face as well. Mazzola loved her and hated her at the same instant; it was a tremendous turn-on. "You're a bitch with ice water for blood, you know that?" He meant it affectionately.

"Omigod!" Her face softened with compassion. "What happened to your eye?"

He ignored the question. "C'mon," he said. "We got business to attend to."

He took her arm and guided her toward the elevators.

From across the lobby, the hotel's Argentinean concierge had watched this exchange between the two young lovers with a dispassionate curiosity. Something about the woman. . . . He couldn't quite place his finger on it.

It took a good half-minute for the connection to register. When it did, it went off in his mind, a brilliant flashbulb of cognition. His heart racing, Roberto Esperanza scooped up the phone and dialed.

# 29

Over breakfast, Brian told Jeff Wheaton of his tangle with Bruce Mazzola at Cafe Iguana the previous night in all its inglorious detail.

After a thoughtful pause, Jeff said, "Well, I guess that explains why he and Beekman didn't come back to the hotel last night."

Brian sipped his coffee thoughtfully. "Don't you think it's odd that they left their weekend bags in the room? And their toilet kits?"

Wheaton shrugged. "Knowing Bruce, they probably hooked up with a pair of bimboids at some skeevy bar and shacked up for the night."

"Probably," McPhillips said. Still, something didn't ring right. Wouldn't Beekman have at least called them? McPhillips kept this thought to himself.

They worked on their eggs in silence.

Then Wheaton said, "You know, it doesn't surprise me that Bruce mixed it up with you last night. The guy's been about as volatile as nitroglycerine lately, just a total rage-ball."

Brian rolled his eyes. "Yeah, tell me about it."

"I mean, you know about his legal troubles, right?"

*Bruce has legal troubles?* This was quite a newsflash.

"What, from Drexel?"

"Yeah. There's a major lawsuit in the works against his LBO firm, FYM Group."

McPhillips' eyebrows shot up. "This is the first I've heard about it."

Wheaton stared at him incredulously. "You mean to tell me you don't know about *Falcon-Myers Steel Workers v. Bruce Mazzola, et al.?*"

"No."

"Hoo boy! And you call yourself a bankruptcy attorney?"

McPhillips was annoyed. "Why don't you enlighten me?"

"Well, as it happens, when Drexel went out in 1987, Mazzola didn't miss a beat. He whipped out his Rolodex and assembled maybe a half-dozen other newly unemployed young investment bankers, each man as hungry as Bruce. Started his own LBO boutique on Wall Street."

McPhillips said, "Right. It was called FYM Group."

"Right." Jeff pointed his fork at him. "Do you know what FYM stands for?"

"I know the M stands for Mazzola, but who were F and Y?"

Wheaton shook his head. "You're wrong. The M doesn't stand for Mazzola. FYM is an acronym for 'fuck-you money.'"

That made perfect sense. Bruce was always talking about accumulating enough money to tell the world to screw itself. Fuck-you money, he called it. Perfect acronym for Bruce's own firm. "Go on," he said.

"Like everyone else on Wall Street in those days, Mazz was supremely confident of his own ability to succeed. He manages to convince three New York banks to extend his firm these wildly excessive lines of credit. He proceeds to purchase expensive artwork, a new penthouse condo on Madison Avenue, a Lamborghini, the whole schmear. Deals himself a six-figure bonus in the first quarter.

"Within three months, he's tapped out all his credit. The only problem is, he has no deals in the hopper. With the junk market in disarray, the LBO business is in the toilet. Then, one day in 1988, Bruce is thumbing through the *Wall Street Journal* when he spots his salvation—Falcon-Myers Steel Foundry."

"I've heard of it. Aren't they Chapter Eleven?"

"They are *now*. But they weren't before Bruce got his hands on 'em."

McPhillips rolled his eyes. "Oh, boy. Go on."

"Falcon-Myers is this steel plant in West Virginia; makes tools and dies and other parts for a bunch of American factories. It's one of those places where several generations of families worked. You know the kind of company I'm talking about?"

"Yeah. The whole town lives and dies by the plant's fortunes."

"Exactly. Well, the *Journal* piece says that the competition from the Japanese was just too fierce, and modernizing the plant to stay competitive was just not feasible. Management couldn't find anyone to buy the plant from them, so they announced plans to shut doors by the end of the year. Obviously, it was just going to devastate this poor West Virginia town.

"So reading this article, Mazz has a brainstorm. Why not have the workers buy the plant and run it themselves? Just cut out management altogether."

"Actually, on paper it's not a bad concept," McPhillips pointed out. "There've been a lot of successful LBOs in which the workers bought the company and ran it themselves. Avis Rent-A-Car is a prime example."

"Well, that's exactly what Mazzola told the workers of Falcon-Myers. Now you got to picture it. Broadway Bruce, gold collar studs and all, flying down to this tiny West Virginia plant and making a killer presentation to a bunch of blue-collar working stiffs. And these are union guys, in love with the idea of owning a piece of their own company. And Bruce just slays 'em with technical jargon. 'Boys, we'll just do an ESOP-linked LBO with an IPO to follow ASAP.' "

McPhillips laughed. "Right. All the alphabet soup they love so much on the Street."

"Bruce realized that the key to doing the deal was to tap into the employee pension plan, which, at the time, was worth $175 million. Bruce got wind of that, and he started drooling like a real estate developer at Walden Woods."

McPhillips laughed again.

Jeff Wheaton continued. "When it looked like the deal was

going to get the green light from the union workers, Bruce Fed-Ex'ed me a copy of the numbers and asked me to tell him what I thought."

McPhillips looked at him incredulously.

"Why do you look so surprised?" Wheaton asked, irritated. "Think I couldn't handle a bit of number-crunching? I'm a Wharton-educated CPA, remember?"

"It's not that I doubt your ability. It's just that I didn't think of you as a gun-for-hire in the LBO game."

"I wasn't." Jeff smiled bitterly. "Turns out Mazzola didn't pay me a red cent. Probably because I didn't give him the answer he wanted."

"What answer did you give him?"

"To scrap the deal, of course. Brian, it was totally undoable. The company's cash flow was too anemic. Falcon-Myers' market share was plunging. Moreover, the debt-to-equity ratio on this deal would've been a hundred to one. Bri, this was a company that was going straight to hell in a handbasket. It was so obvious—I mean, they had the company on the block for two years, and no sane buyer would go near it. I warned Bruce in the strongest terms possible that if he used the ESOP to buy this company from management, he was opening himself up to some big-time breach of fiduciary responsibility."

"Apparently, he didn't listen."

"Hell, no! The smart thing to do would've been for Bruce to let the plant go out of business, then buy it for pennies on the dollar in bankruptcy proceedings."

"If he was representing the workers, why didn't he do that?"

Jeff Wheaton lowered his voice. "Because he was secretly paid a kickback by the management team to be certain the deal was closed before that happened."

McPhillips whistled. Double-dealing in the midst of a change in corporate control was a major-league no-no. A federal court would string you up by the gonads for screwing around with that kind of conflict of interest.

"So, to make a long story short," Wheaton said, "the deal gets done. The workers end up gambling every penny of their retirement money on the stock of Falcon-Myers. Management, of course, cleans up. Every one of the corporate officers buys a second home in Hilton Head. Mazzola's firm gets a golden shower of fat fees. And the workers? They get screwed. Bri, that company was so overleveraged, they didn't have a thin dime left over to modernize. The LBO died stillborn."

"Went Chapter Eleven."

"Yep. Belly-up within five months after the papers were signed. Needless to say, the blue-collars running the factory went apeshit. Not only were they put out of work *anyway*, but now their pensions were completely wiped out in an eye-blink. Class-action suits were filed. Lawyers swooped in."

"The workers are suing him, I guess."

"*Suing him?* Brian, they *burned* Bruce in effigy in West Virginia a couple of weeks ago. Chanting 'yuppie scum, yuppie scum.' Hell yeah, they're suing him. But I'm afraid the blue-collars have to get in line behind the banks and all the other creditors nipping at his heels. He was evicted from his Upper East Side condo and had his Lamborghini repo'ed. I mean, why do you think he's puttering around in Philadelphia again? He's avoiding service of process."

"Christ," McPhillips breathed. "I had no idea."

"Wait. It goes from bad to worse. About two months ago, the government announced a federal investigation of the Falcon-Myers deal. Department of Labor's looking into it."

"Yeah," McPhillips nodded ruefully. "You can't futz with a company's pension fund without getting Uncle Sam's dander up. Sounds like there was a possible fraudulent conveyance there as well."

"So, yeah, Bruce is caught in a veritable shitstorm without an umbrella." Wheaton sighed. "If Mitch didn't go and electronically steal all of Bruce's money, this lawsuit would've wiped him out anyway."

*No wonder Mazzola thinks all attorneys are scumbags*, McPhillips thought. He frowned. "Y'know, there's something here that bugs me."

"What's that?"

"Mazz told the FBI that Mitch embezzled over two million bucks from him, right?"

"Yeah. So?" Wheaton made a motion to the waitress for the check.

"And yet, you said they repossessed his condo, his car. I don't get it. Why didn't they attach the money in that account?"

"Maybe they had," Wheaton said.

"No. If it was frozen, Myerson wouldn't've been able to lay his paws on it."

"Maybe he managed to hide it from the banks in a Philadelphia account, and the lawyers couldn't find it."

McPhillips shook his head. "Lawyers *always* find it if it's there."

"What are you driving at?"

"Something doesn't quite add up. First Bruce told us that he had $2 million in his account. Another time he said it was three. I'm beginning to wonder whether he had *any* money in that account at all. . . ."

The portable phone twittered. Wheaton answered it. "Yes, hello . . . Oh, hello, Lisa." To Brian, he silently mouthed the words, "Your wife." McPhillips nodded, his mind still awhirl with Mazzola's Byzantine legal troubles. "How are you? Yes, I'm okay. Yes, I'm doing fine." A pained look crossed his friend's face, as McPhillips sensed that his wife was overdoing it with the sympathy bit on the other end of the line. "I know. Yes, I know. Thank you very much. You don't know what that means to me. He's right here. Good talking to you. Hold on."

Jeff Wheaton handed him the telephone and worked to finish off his eggs Benedict.

"Hello, honey," Brian said.

"Guess who called this morning," Lisa McPhillips said in a mock-cheery singsong.

"The FBI?"

"Nope."

"The police?"

"Not even close."

He drummed his fingers impatiently on the tabletop. He was in no mood for guessing games. "Who, then?"

"Samantha C. Powell."

"Who is Samantha C. Powell?"

"A metropolitan reporter for the *Philadelphia Inquirer.*"

"Ah, Christ," he muttered softly.

"Brian, they're calling for details about the Myerson affair."

"Did you tell them anything?"

"Nothing at all, of course. I figured you wanted to do that."

"Perfect. I'll put them off until Monday, until I can talk to someone at the firm about the bank's obligation to us. Maybe I can turn the publicity to our advantage."

There was a long silence on the other end. "Brian?"

"Yes?"

"Are you coming home this morning?"

"Yes. I'll probably be on the next train, Lisa."

"Good," she sighed. "I'm depressed."

"Oh, honey—"

"I was good about it all along, wasn't I? About losing our house, I mean?" She sighed again. "I guess I could just use some husbandly TLC right about now—"

—at that moment, it was as if the telephone line hiccupped, swallowing her words—

Brian realized that it was the call-waiting signal.

"—when you come home." Lisa's voice finished the end of the sentence.

McPhillips covered the mouthpiece and asked Wheaton, "You have call-waiting on this thing?"

"Yeah."

"You've got another call coming through." McPhillips turned back to the phone and told Lisa he'd call her right back; there was another call waiting on the line that could be important. When she rang off, he clicked the other call onto the line. "Hello?"

On the other end an excited voice asked for Mr. Wheaton.

McPhillips handed the phone to Wheaton. "Guy said it's extremely urgent," he told him.

"This is Wheaton," Jeff said into the mouthpiece.

The call lasted less than a minute. Mostly, Wheaton just listened; after a half-minute, his face became flushed, his speech became agitated. "Wait! Are you positive? . . . You're *not* positive . . . Fifty-fifty chance, would you say? . . . Less? Okay . . . No, you're right. Let's not call the police yet, not if you can't be sure . . . All right, then . . . Yes, we're on our way. Thank you *so much*, Mr. Esperanza."

Wheaton hung up the phone and stared numbly at McPhillips. "The concierge at the U.N. Plaza isn't positive—and I stress the phrase *not positive*, but—" Wheaton stole a breath "—but he thinks he might have spotted Rachel in the lobby just a few minutes ago."

"Jesus! How far are we from the U.N. Plaza?"

"By cab, maybe five, six minutes."

They barreled out to the street in search of one.

# 30

As Brian McPhillips and Jeff Wheaton raced across town toward his hotel, Mitch Myerson bent forward in the shower and fully rinsed the shampoo from his hair. Then he wrenched the faucet to the right, turning off the water. The stream dwindled to a trickle.

Myerson was still plagued with guilt about last night. Never, ever did he intend to hurt Rachel, to make her cry. The events of last night were most unfortunate. He was eager to tell her of his plans to make it up to her. He wanted to buy her a diamond the size of a walnut.

He drew back the shower curtain and stepped out of the tub. Snapping the towel from the rack, he dipped his dripping-wet head into it and vigorously massaged his hair dry.

A new plan of escape was being formulated in his mind.

If the heat was on at the airport, well, so what? They could just stay here in New York for a few days, until things cooled off a bit, then lam out of town. Maybe go west somewhere. California or Arizona—either one appealed to him. Maybe they could even live on a ranch in Montana. When you had a briefcase full of one hundred thousand dollars (just for starters!), then the whole world was simply bursting with possibilities.

As Mitch swathed himself in a terrycloth bathrobe, he noted that he and Rachel were together, and that was the most important thing. They would get through this as long as they toughed it out together. They were fugitives of love.

He was about to light himself a jay, when he heard Rachel rapping lightly on the door. His spirits soared.

"Come in, Nuffy. It's unlocked!" He said this happily, awash in the sweet anticipation of seeing her cheerful face appear around the edge of the door.

The door swung open.

He saw Bruce Mazzola's face, instead.

Mitch Myerson's jaw dropped. Shock immobilized him. His eyes blinked, uncomprehendingly, and he moved his mouth to say something, but no sound came.

Mazzola smiled ferociously. All in a fluid motion, he took a step toward Mitch, his shoulder dipped, and his arm blurred in a sidearm swing. Myerson's clouded mind formed one clear thought before the impact: *God, he's gonna hit me—*

—then Myerson was vaguely aware of his face jolting violently to one side. His world was rocked by an explosion of sparks and colors and pain going off behind his eyes. Dimly, as if he were under water, he was cognizant of Mazzola's voice, addressing him with a venomous sarcasm—

"Thought I'd never see you again, Mitch. Such a *pleasure* to see you. I trust you feel the same way seeing *me* again, old chum?"

Mazzola struck him again with a more savage blow to the face. This time, the punch split Myerson's lower lip. Blood splashed forth, a staggered scarlet scrawl against the antiseptic white tile of the bathroom wall.

"Here's your *Anatomy* Award for best new actor in a porno flick," Mazzola snarled, bashing him a third time.

Myerson felt his legs wobbling underneath him. He feared he was going to lose his footing. But Mazzola didn't let it happen. He grabbed two fistfuls of the bathrobe, supporting Mitch's sagging weight. Mazzola then backed out of the bathroom, dancing Myerson out to the main area of the hotel room. Mitch staggered like a marionette, too woozy to put up any resistance.

Rachel was sitting on the edge of the bed in her bathrobe. Her legs were crossed, her gleaming thighs revealed. Her arms were folded and she had a lit Dunhill clipped between the slim fingers of her right hand. She watched the scene with a cool, detached disinterest.

Piteously, Mitch cried out his pet name for her. "Nuffy!"

She turned her gaze away from him with pure disgust. "Ugh! I always *hated it* when you called me that name. It's so *asinine.*"

Mazzola shook him menacingly. "Shut up," he commanded. "If you make another sound, I swear I will kill you. And I'm not fucking around, either."

Mitch refused to tear his eyes away from the woman who had betrayed him so completely. "Why, Rachel?" he whined desperately. "You've got to tell me *why.*"

She sighed as if the question rendered her supremely bored and refused to meet his eyes.

"Why? Let me count the reasons for you. One, because you're a real fish in bed, a lousy lay. Two, because I love Mazzola. And three, because you were so pathetically gullible." Then she looked at him and smiled sweetly. "Need I go on?"

Myerson howled in his brokenhearted agony.

Mazzola grabbed Myerson's face in a viselike grip, silencing him. "Shut up," he barked. Then to Rachel, he said, "Get a glass of water from the bathroom."

With Mitch's lip split and streaming blood, his mouth had become an ugly smear of cherry red. Blood had filled the gaps between his teeth. He looked like a hideous clown. "What're you gonna do to me?" he sputtered.

Mazzola ignored the question.

Rachel brought the glass of water. Turning to face Myerson, Mazzola said in a throaty rumble, "Open up your hand."

When he did, Mazzola forcefully shoved four black capsules into Mitch's sweating palm.

"Put these in your mouth and swallow," Mazzola demanded.

Mitch Myerson looked down at the mysterious capsules in his hand with sheer terror. He began crying. "Oh, god, you're gonna *poison* me, Bruce? *Please* don't do this. *Please, please, please*—"

"Ah, Christ, you're so pathetic and weak," Bruce sighed. "Swallow them all, or I'll kill you, I swear it."

Terrified, Mitch put them in his mouth as ordered.

Then Mazzola forced his mouth open and poured the full glass of water down his throat, every drop, until he was certain that Myerson had consumed all four tranqs.

Afterward, Mitch Myerson coughed and sputtered, blood and spit dribbling from his mouth. "Oh, god," he wept. "Oh, god."

"Now you're gonna calm down for your Uncle Bruce, aren't you, Mitchie?"

"What're you gonna do to me, Bruce?"

"Have you take a little dictation." He turned to Rachel. "Get your boyfriend a piece of hotel stationery and a pen."

Rachel obliged.

Mazzola brutally steered Myerson over to the desk. "Take a letter, asshole."

"Please don't hurt me—"

"Shut up. Write the following. 'I am truly sorry . . .'"

"Please, Bruce. I've got money. I'll give you money."

"Shut your yap and start writing. 'I am truly sorry . . .'"

Mitch Myerson wept softly as he wrote down what Mazzola said.

". . . for what I have done . . . to my friends and my clients . . . They put their trust in me . . . and what I did was terribly wrong . . . I cannot live with myself after doing something so terrible to so many innocent people. . . ."

Myerson finished. The tears of terror streamed down his face, yet he dared not utter a word.

Mazzola inspected the letter. He nodded with approval. "Looks like it was written with a very shaky hand. Perfect." He turned back to Mitch. "Time for your next dose of medication, Mitchster."

"No," Myerson wailed. "I did what you wanted—please, Bruce. After *all* we've been through—"

Mazzola forced Myerson to consume sixteen more tranquilizers.

"Sock," Bruce said to Rachel.

Rachel reached into the bag Mazzola had brought with him and pulled out a pair of new, white athletic socks with a Nike logo. Mazzola had purchased them from the hotel sundry shop less than a half-hour before. Rachel coolly strided over to the two of them and placed the socks in Mazzola's hand. Mazzola swiftly plucked the socks apart, discarded one to the floor, and balled up the other into a tightly bound wad. He stuffed the wad into Mitch's mouth. The sock was a most effective gag; Mitch's pathetic sobs were muffled to insignificant whimpers.

As Mazzola waited for the pharmaceuticals to take effect, he put his face within an inch of Mitch's. "You're not very bright, Myerson. Not very bright at all. You fell for the whole enchilada, hook, line, and sinker. Man, did you really think she *loved you?* That was *acting,* you dummy. She *faked* it, Myerson, faked every word, every gesture, every *orgasm.* You were such an easy mark, *so* easy to fool, so easy—"

The tranquilizers rapidly dulled Mitch's consciousness. His eyelids began to flutter with drowsiness; his legs swayed beneath his weight. His body felt leaden, and the light was dimming. Myerson felt himself sliding inexorably into the black hole of a tranquilizer-induced sleep.

Bruce Mazzola could feel the fight flagging from Myerson. When he was convinced that Mitch was on the verge of passing out, Mazzola cocked his arm back and threw one last punch to the face. It sent Myerson staggering, tumbling backwards like a rag doll. His limbs thrashed about as if made of rubber. Mitch collapsed onto the carpet, dead to the world.

Mazzola regarded his prone body with a poisonous contempt. He was tempted to spit on him.

"Did you give him a lethal dose?" Rachel asked, massaging her lover's back.

"Pumped him with enough Xanax to kill a horse."

"How long should it take?"

"An hour. Probably less."

"With that sock in his mouth, couldn't he upchuck and choke on his own vomit?" She posed this question with an almost clinical disinterest.

"Good for him," Mazzola muttered. "All right, babe. Make the phone call so we can rock 'n' roll."

Rachel went back to the edge of the bed. She picked up the phone and called the front desk. In her sexiest voice, she informed the clerk that she and her husband were newlyweds, and they wished to make their honeymoon stay at the United Nations Plaza an especially memorable one—that is, if he *caught her drift*, giggle, giggle. They wished to be completely alone for the next twenty-four hours. This meant no maid service, no complimentary champagne, no phone calls, no disturbances of *any* kind whatsoever. Could he be a dear and make the proper arrangements?

The clerk cheerfully assured her that he would personally see to it that she and her new husband would have complete privacy during their stay. He conveyed his congratulations on their recent nuptials.

Rachel hung up the phone and smiled. "Taken care of," she said, stubbing out the Dunhill.

"Excellent." Mazzola stepped forward and snapped the telephone line out of the wall with a mighty tug. "Now get dressed. I bought you a Nike warm-up suit at the hotel shop. There's some cheap tennis shoes in there also. Sorry I couldn't get you any Ellesse."

As Bruce proceeded to move Mitch Myerson's prostrate body into the bathroom, Rachel swiftly got dressed in the nylon warm-ups. She looked in the mirror and made a face of distaste. *Ugh!* Neon green and purple weren't her colors, but they would simply have to do until they got overseas.

Bruce Mazzola dragged Mitch Myerson into the bathroom. He picked him up and struggled to throw him into the bathtub. Myerson's slack body was deadweight, like a lumpy sack of potatoes or flour, difficult to maneuver. Ultimately, Mazzola all but rolled him roughly over the edge of the tub. Then Bruce locked the bathroom door from the inside and closed it. He jiggled the knob, testing it. Door was locked all right. They'd have to bust the door down to get at him.

He found he whirled around to find Rachel on the bed, gazing at him. Her seductive eyes were burning with a superheated lust.

"I want you to fuck me right now," she breathed.

He was plenty tempted to take her, right then and there. But cool reason prevailed, and he fought off the temptation. "Plenty of time for that later," he told her. She shrugged indifferently.

He clapped his hands together happily. So far, so good.

"All right, Mrs. Wheaton," he chided, as he spanked her tushie. "Let's get that shapely little ass of yours off into the friendly skies." She grabbed the Gucci bag full of lira and off they went.

# 31

It took ninety-five seconds for Bruce and Rachel to reach the lobby from the sixteenth floor.

On the way down, they looked at each other and, without so much as a word, broke into peals of ringing laughter. Myerson had been so pitiful back there, they just *had to* laugh.

The elevator jolted to a halt on the ground floor. Rachel took his hand in hers and gave it a squeeze. They stepped forth and walked at a brisk pace toward the gleaming metal-frame doors that led to East Forty-fourth Street.

Without warning, Mazzola stopped short. He grabbed Rachel's arm and roughly yanked her backward several feet. She cried out in pain, "Hey!"

"Shh!" he hissed.

"What is it?" she whispered, suddenly alarmed. "Police?"

Mazzola didn't answer her immediately. Cautiously, he craned his neck forward and peered around the corner to take a second look, just to make certain his eyes weren't playing tricks on him. Then he drew back, flattened himself against the wall and turned his face skyward as if to castigate the heavens for his bad luck. He muttered, "I can't fucking believe it, I can't *fucking* believe it."

"What's wrong?" she demanded.

"Of all the fucking lousy luck. *Those guys* are here."

"Which guys?"

"Your *husband,* that's who. And that douchebag McPhillips."

"Omigod! How the fuck does he keep finding me?" She said this with genuine awe.

"I don't know, but he's *here.*"

"What're we going to do?"

"Stay calm, that's what." Mazzola crept judiciously forward and stole another look toward the concierge's desk. There they were, all right, jawboning with the concierge. Bruce figured them to be a good fifty, sixty feet away. In-*fucking*-credible. It occurred to him that the concierge might have recognized Rachel in the lobby and tipped off her husband. Jesus!

One thing emboldened him, though. Those two rummies were so engrossed in playing sleuth, they paid no attention to the comings and goings of the guests. That was good, very good. So long as they called no attention to themselves, it was highly likely that he and Rachel could slip out unnoticed, right under their noses.

"Here's the game plan," he whispered. "We wait here until some other people come off the elevator; then we walk with them out the exit. We don't walk too slow; we don't walk too fast. Just normal pace, so that we blend in with the others, okay? Then ver-rry nonchalantly, we walk to that first cab there at the curb. Got it?"

She took a deep breath. "Got it."

They waited there quietly for some others to come out of an elevator. Mazzola squinted toward the curb. He guesstimated that the walk across the driveway to the taxi stand was a solid seventy-five yards. *Well, one thing was certain.* It would be the longest fucking seventy-five yards he ever had to walk.

The young concierge ran a hand through his hair in exasperation. "I'm sorry," Roberto Esperanza said softly, as he pushed the photographs away. "I just can't be sure."

Wheaton tapped the photograph of his wife with a forefinger. "How did the woman you saw differ from the woman in this picture?"

"Mmm . . . The woman I saw this morning looked kind of like

this one, but her hair was up in a bun." Esperanza used his hands to suggest the woman's hairstyle. "Also, the woman I saw wore no makeup. And she was in a loose-fitting bathrobe." He shrugged. "That's why I can't say for sure."

McPhillips said, "But the guy who was with her, you say he definitely *was not* the man in this picture." He pointed to the photo of Mitch.

"That's right. He was not."

"You're positive about that?"

"Yes. As sure as I'm standing here."

McPhillips grunted. Well, that clinched it for him. If the guy in the lobby wasn't Mitch, then the woman couldn't have been Rachel. It was as simple as that.

"Roberto," Wheaton persisted, "You said earlier you thought the woman was a guest of the hotel."

"Yes." He bobbed his head.

"Why do you say that?"

"The woman came down to the lobby wearing a bathrobe with the house crest on it."

"How about the man? Was he a guest?"

"No. He came from outside. Met her here in the lobby."

"Hmm." Wheaton looked thoughtful. More to himself than anyone else, he said, "Wish we knew what floor she was on."

"Sixteen," the concierge said.

They both gaped at him in disbelief.

"How did you know that?" Brian asked him.

The concierge permitted himself a smile. "I followed them to the elevator and watched the display to see what floor they got off on."

Wheaton laughed, slapping his palm sharply on the marble surface of the desk. "If you ever decide to become a private detective, Roberto, I'd love to write you a letter of recommendation."

Just then, a thin, elderly Jewish woman who was a guest of the hotel came to the desk for directions to the Ellis Island Immigration Museum. Esperanza politely excused himself from the discussion to attend to the guest.

"Of course," Jeff said. "You've been most helpful."

Then Wheaton took McPhillips aside and said, "How do you want to handle this?"

McPhillips frowned. "Handle what?"

"This new information."

"Quite frankly, Jeff, there's not enough here to go to the police."

"Agreed." Jeff Wheaton shrugged. "So instead, we'll hang here a couple hours ourselves. Watch people as they get off the elevator."

McPhillips shook his head in disbelief. "Oh, c'mon, Jeff. For chrissake, you heard what the concierge said about the guy the woman was with."

"Yeah, so?"

"It *wasn't* Mitch. That's the only thing he can say for certain, remember?"

Wheaton grasped Brian's arm urgently. "Brian, there's a good shot this is her. I just *know* it."

"Jeff," McPhillips said quietly. "I don't want to see you get your hopes up for nothing. I'm telling you—it's not her."

In the end, Bruce Mazzola and Rachel Wheaton would have escaped were it not for a single lapse in judgment. They effectively slipped past Jeff and Brian, concealed amidst a pack of seven West German tourists who had just poured forth from the elevator. Though Bruce and Rachel were a mere thirty-three feet away from the concierge's desk, not once did McPhillips or Wheaton glance in their direction.

Rachel kept her eyes closed the entire distance, as if to ward off evil spirits. "I can't believe this is happening," she whispered several times.

"Just keep walking," Mazzola muttered under his breath. "We're almost to the promised land."

And then: they were outside.

"Home free," Mazzola breathed.

But Bruce Mazzola couldn't resist the temptation to steal one last peek over his shoulder, just to see if they were coming after him.

And that was his fatal error.

He locked eyes with Roberto Esperanza through the smoked plate-glass front of the hotel. Each man held the other's gaze for no more than an instant, but in that instant, something passed between the two men: an exchange of some sort, a communication, a transfer. A mutual flash of cognition.

Inside the lobby, the concierge's quiet dignity dropped away and he burst out, "That's them!"

His exclamation startled Wheaton, McPhillips, and the guest who had inquired about Ellis Island.

"Where?" McPhillips yelped, whipping his head around to scan the lobby.

"Out there!" Esperanza pointed outside, to the curb beyond the driveway. "By the cabs!"

Wheaton saw them before McPhillips did. "My god!" he cried in elation. "You see that, Bri? Fuckin' Bruce Mazzola nabbed her! Bruce found Rachel!"

But McPhillips saw it for what it was.

"It's not what you think, Jeff," he said gently. *"He's* in on it."

In that awful moment, Wheaton knew Brian was right, and his face froze into a collage of pain and shock. "Sonuvabitch," he breathed.

McPhillips instructed the concierge to call the police; then he and Wheaton burst into motion, giving chase.

# 32

At that moment, there were four cabs idling at the curbside taxi stand. The first cab in line was a 1988 schoolbus-yellow Chevrolet Impala belonging to a Polish émigré named Jacek Krzleszowski, who had been leaning against his front fender and serial-smoking unfiltered Camels for seventeen minutes while waiting on his next fare. Krzleszowski was an unrepentant four-pack-a-day smoker and was exceedingly grateful to have found himself in a country where cigarettes and vodka were priced solidly within the reach of the average laborer.

Krzleszowski had arrived in the United States less than four years ago and, like many foreign-born cabdrivers operating in the metropolitan area, his English was scarcely on the third-grade level. Despite his limited vocabulary, however, even Jacek Krzleszowski knew the term used to describe the young couple rushing toward his car. They were called *yuppies*, the American word for prodigiously spoiled youth.

*Yuppies.* He turned the word over in his mind with no small measure of distaste. Krzleszowski had come to despise yuppies in the last four years, especially those whose bread was buttered on Wall Street. Krzleszowski hated their perpetual aura of arrogance as much as he envied the vast universe of opportunities that came to them at such an early age. The yuppie man coming toward him was almost certainly a Wall Streeter, all right—always in such a rush, the Wall Streeters—and he was accompanied by a *piekna dziewczyna*, a strikingly beautiful woman. Ah, that's the way it always was with the yuppie men. Their yuppie wives were so infuriatingly beautiful, so deliciously slim-waisted, so unlike the *gruba zona* who was mother to his four children in Elizabeth, New Jersey.

Almost certainly, Jacek knew, the yuppies would stiff him on the tip. Even worse, they would disapprove of his cigarette and demand that he extinguish it immediately. Well, *niech ich diabli wezma*, he thought, which was Polish for "screw them." If they weren't going to the airport, he would feign complete ignorance of English and gesture them toward the black cabdriver in line behind him.

In the next instant, the couple reached Krzleszowski. Up close, he was stunned by the perfection of the woman. She was a woman whose presence he would enjoy in his cab—if not his bed.

"Where you going to?" Krzleszowski demanded.

The man ignored the question. Instead, he swept his eyes over Krzleszowski. The man had a wild look that sent a chill through the cabdriver.

The yuppie was on drugs, Jacek thought.

"Rachel, get in the front seat," the yuppie man snapped to his companion. *"Now."*

She moved around the front of the cab toward the passenger door.

"Hey, hey!" Krzleszowski sputtered in protest. He didn't want any drug-crazed yuppies in *his* cab. He moved to block the driver's side. But in the next instant, he felt himself losing equilibrium, as the man shove-tripped him roughly, clipping Jacek's legs out from beneath him at the same time the man's forearm crashed forcefully into Jacek's breastplate, hurtling him backward. For an instant, Krzleszowski was suspended in midair. Then he crashed heavily to the asphalt, landing painfully on the nub of his coccyx, the impact knocking the breath from him. His half-smoked cigarette struck the ground in a small burst of sparks and ash, then skittered out of sight beneath the cab.

The yuppie leaped over him, behind the wheel of the car. Jacek Krzleszowski could only watch helplessly as his Impala gunned away from the curb with a high-pitched squeal and the stink of burning rubber in its wake.

Scrambling to his feet, Krzleszowski shouted, *"Matko boska! Matko boska! Zkodzieje ukradli mi taksowke!"* The thieves have stolen my cab!

The name of the driver of the next cab in line was Jamelle Childs. Jamelle was an aspiring hip-hop recording artist from the Bronx who had created an entirely new genre of rap called "hip-roll," in which he took the *hip* from hop, the *roll* from rock and came up with some bitchin' mixes. His day job was driving a cab, at least until a major record label recognized his enormous talent and signed him to a three-record deal. He lowered the volume of his Arrested Development cassette, adjusted his shades and gaped in disbelief as the stolen cab disappeared east down Forty-fourth Street. Now *that* was something you didn't see every day, not even in New York. A cab hijacked in broad daylight.

Jacek Krzleszowski's mustachioed face appeared in Jamelle's open window. *"Czy widzieliscie?"*

"Word up, homey. Talk English."

"Did you see? Did you see?" Krzleszowski sprayed Jamelle with spittle. "Bastards thieved my cab—"

Childs shook his head and shrugged. "Yo, do I look like a *po*-liceman to you? Call nine-one-one." Shit, what was *Jamelle* supposed to do about it? Chase the motherfuckers for this guy?

It proved to be a prophetic thought.

Next thing Jamelle Childs knew, two fifty-dollar bills had been thrown onto the seat next to him. Jamelle whirled around in time to see two white guys scrambling into the back of his taxi.

One of them barked, "Hundred dollars to chase that cab, another hundred if you catch 'em."

"The price is *right.*" Jamelle grinned as he slapped the gearshift down into drive and stuffed the bills into his pocket. He turned to the beleaguered Polish cabdriver and said, "Yo, yo, c'mon, homey. You want your wheels back or not?"

Jacek Krzleszowski raced around the front of Jamelle's Dodge Diplomat and inserted himself in the passenger seat. He braced himself with a white-knuckled grip on the edge of the dashboard and nodded grimly to Jamelle. *"Zatrzymajcie tych zkodzieji,"* he said, which meant *stop the thieves.*

Jamelle Childs stomped on the accelerator and the Diplomat surged forward. In a few heartbeats, the cab hit First Avenue and careened wildly on Childs' hard left turn. The hip-hop artist narrowly averted sideswiping a gunmetal gray BMW in the next lane, drawing a cacophony of outraged horns in the process. Jamelle ignored the fist-pumping and cursing of the other drivers, focusing intently on the ass-end of the car he was pursuing and the hundred-dollar bounty he was determined to get.

The mighty monolith of the United Nations world headquarters tilted into view on First. A block-long row of flagpoles flying the flags of its member nations whipped past on their right.

The lead cab fishtailed left again onto Forty-fifth Street, its rear skidding wildly to the right with the squealing protest of rubber against asphalt. Its rear bumper slammed into the side of a parked commercial van marked BEACON SERVICES, crumpling the side panel of the van and denting the backside of Krzleszowski's cab. Krzleszowski threw his hands up to his head and wailed in horror. For his part, Jamelle Childs took the turn more judiciously, retaining control of the vehicle, flooring the accelerator only when the course turned straightaway once more. It had become apparent that the Diplomat had more horsepower beneath its hood than the Impala. They now trailed Krzleszowski's automobile by just eight car lengths.

Jamelle felt elation. *Hey, this was fucking fun.*

He peered over the top of his wraparound shades and eyed his passengers in the rearview mirror. "This your first time in Fun City, fellas?"

Jeff Wheaton fired him a Clint Eastwood scowl and snapped, "Stop being cute and catch that fucking cab."

Jamelle shrugged. "Whatever you say, *kimosabe*. It's your nickel."

Wheaton and McPhillips were perched on the edge of the vinyl seats in the back, leaning forward and hugging the headrests for ballast. It was a veritable wind tunnel in the back, gusts whipping their hair about wildly. Wheaton massaged his temples and shouted over the growl of the engine, "My world has been blown completely to pieces."

"Mine too."

"I mean, is this *really happening* or is it a hallucination? Is that really—I mean—that's—Jesus Christ, Brian, that's not *Myerson* with my wife. That's *Mazzola* with my wife. Are they *all* in it together or what?"

"No. Mitch was double-crossed," McPhillips shot back, his eyes fixed on the cab ahead. "Set up."

"Unfuckingbelievable."

McPhillips nodded.

"Tell me," Jeff shouted over the wind, "what will we do if we catch 'em?"

"Cross that bridge when we come to it. *Faster*, driver."

The two cabs rocketed westbound down Forty-fifth Street. The street was lined on both sides by solid walls of skyscrapers, creating the illusion that they were traveling along in the gully of some deep urban canyon. Fortunately, since it was a Sunday morning in midsummer, most Manhattanites were weekending at their country homes and traffic was exceptionally light. But Forty-fifth Street was narrower than the broad avenues of Manhattan, making traveling at a high velocity far more treacherous.

The Dodge Diplomat began gaining on its quarry, gradually, yard by yard. McPhillips silently urged Jamelle Childs on.

Green lights made for smooth sailing through the intersections at Second and Third Avenue. But then the light blazed yellow as the Impala thundered across the intersection at Lexington Avenue.

"Make this light!" Wheaton urged.

The light turned red before they reached the intersection. Nevertheless, the traffic on Lexington had not yet lurched into motion, so Jamelle Childs pushed the pedal to the floor and blazed through the red light. The cab hit the speed bump at the outer grid of the intersection at such velocity that it was momentarily airborne. It impacted jarringly on the other end of the intersection, causing the front end of the Diplomat's undercarriage to scrape against the street with a harsh, metallic sound. The four men jounced about the cab like crash-test dummies. McPhillips and Wheaton bumped heads.

But they had made the light.

The high-speed chase continued, taking them past Vanderbilt and Madison Avenues, with the Pan Am Building looming into sight on the left, then rapidly disappearing from view. The two cabs sped past Fifth Avenue, through the retail electronics district, heading towards Sixth, now just five car lengths apart. McPhillips was praying the chase would attract the cops.

Just ahead, at Sixth Avenue, a solid red light glowed. Krzleszowski cheered. The yuppie bastards had come to the end of the line—and he for one was ready to roll up his sleeves and whack the spit out of the thief.

But to the dismay of all, the Impala pushed brazenly into the cross-directional stream of traffic, honking and flashing its lights as if signaling some sort of emergency. The vehicles cruising down Sixth Avenue returned the honks at the Impala and drivers leaned out their windows to hurl curses. Nevertheless, Bruce and Rachel managed to successfully ford the flow of traffic, reaching the other side of the avenue and continuing west with renewed speed.

"Fuck me!" Jamelle yelled, slapping his palms against the steering wheel in a tattoo of frustration.

"Do it!" Jeff Wheaton commanded.

"I'm doin' it," Jamelle wailed. He reached Sixth Avenue and nosed his vehicle gingerly into the string of five-lane traffic. As he threaded through the jagged gridlock, an elderly pedestrian approached the cab and kicked a manhole-sized dent in the back door of Jamelle's cab, proclaiming him an "asswipe." Jamelle cursed, but he too eventually crossed to the other side and the pursuit resumed.

The high-voltage gaudiness of the Great White Way came into view. The two cabs bulleted past Times Square where gargantuan billboards advertised the brand names of superior, foreign-made products: Canon, Suntory Whisky, JVC, Reebok, Minolta, Samsung and Daewoo; past the Minskoff Theatre on the left, then Shubert Alley; past the giant blowup of the sad-faced urchin from *Les Misérables* at the Imperial and the string of famed Broadway eateries—Puleo's, Sam's, Barrymore's and the Stage Door Canteen.

At a red light on Eighth Avenue, the stolen cab wheeled sharply to the right, spewing gravel and dirt in its wake. It was headed north. Closing in, Jamelle Childs spun the wheel and followed the lead cab's move, nosing closer to the bumper of the fleeing vehicle. "Gettin' there. Gettin' there." The cars jockeyed through the five lanes of light traffic as X-rated movie houses, beer-and-a-shot taverns and pawnshops whipped past outside the windows.

Where was it going to end? McPhillips wondered.

They crossed Forty-sixth Street.

Then Forty-seventh Street.

Forty-eighth Street.

Forty-ninth Street.

But before reaching Fiftieth Street, Jamelle Childs fell victim to a spectacular fake-out. The Impala unexpectedly swerved left, cutting off two lanes of traffic and thudding into the back bumper of a Honda Prelude with Jersey plates. A half-dozen horns erupted. Cars locked up their brakes and careened out of their lanes, the drivers desperately jerking their steering wheels to avoid collision. Childs was forced to veer to the right, his front wheel thumping up on the sidewalk and toppling over a rubbish can.

Meanwhile, the stolen Impala continued forking off to the left, crossing Fiftieth Street and heading suicide-straight for the brick wall of an abandoned building on the west side of the street.

Krzleszowski screamed, "He's going to crash my car!"

Krzleszowski was right. Mazzola hopped the curb at the northwest corner of Fiftieth Street and Eighth Avenue and deliberately smashed the cab into the brick wall at thirty-five miles per hour. The front of the Impala crumpled on impact, folding back like an accordion. Krzleszowski wailed in agony as mushroom clouds of steam began to billow out from beneath the hood. The four men watched helplessly as the front door on the driver's side of the Impala burst open and Bruce Mazzola and Rachel Wheaton spilled out of the totaled automobile, briefcase in tow, and disappeared down a set of stairs leading to the underground subway platform. It was then that Brian realized that Mazzola had intentionally crashed the vehicle so that the steaming wreckage sealed off the only entrance to the downtown A and C subway trains. *Scheming bastard.*

"Stop the car!" McPhillips commanded.

Jamelle Childs slammed on the brakes and came to a squealing halt some twenty yards past Krzleszowski's wreck. Pure adrenaline kicked in: McPhillips exploded out of the cab and hit the ground running. He weaved in and out of the moving cars, through the gridlock of rubbernecking motorists, moving swiftly toward the barricaded subway entrance. *Have to stop them.* Reaching the demolished cab, he scrambled up onto the trunk of the Impala and bounded over to the other side. He leaped down onto the second step of the stairwell, landing badly and nearly falling into a seventeen-year-old Vietnamese heroin addict who was huddled on the steps in a yellow nylon jacket caked in the addict's dried saliva and vomit. McPhillips skipped around the junkie's slack form and raced down the stairs, taking them three at a time.

He felt the unpleasant heat of the subway hit him in the face, thick and turgid. He blinked his eyes repeatedly, willing his vision to adjust to the faint illumination here beneath street level. The ramp leading to the subway trains was encrusted with decades of soot, filth and grime, and the air possessed the omnipresent tang of stale urine. McPhillips sprinted down the ramp of this urban purgatory, the slap of his footfalls echoing in the vast underground expanse of the station.

After a hundred yards, he reached the row of turnstiles and the token booth. The booth was closed. The hand-scrawled sign taped to the window said, simply, SORRY. He hesitated for a moment, gathering lungfuls of fetid air. He scanned the platform. There. He glimpsed Mazzola and Rachel as they scampered into the last car of a downtown-bound C train. *Shit!* McPhillips leapfrogged over the thick bar of the turnstile and dashed toward the last car at breakneck speed. Over the sound of the wind rushing past his ears, he heard the flat warning gongs ringing out from inside the train and then the mechanical voice: *"Please stand clear of the closing doors of the train—"*

He was going to lose them.

Goddammit!

As the doors began to clatter with movement, McPhillips lunged forward. He threw forth an extended left arm, hoping to keep the doors wedged open. His left arm sunk into the interior of the subway car up to the meat of his shoulder. *Gotcha!* But the doors slapped shut, the hard rubber-lined edges pressing firmly, painfully, against his flesh. . . .

He was alarmed to discover that the safety sensors in the closing mechanism had failed to instruct the doors to open automatically. He clawed at the narrow crack between the stainless-steel doors with his free hand, but the mechanism resisted his efforts.

Through the two rectangular windows of the doors, McPhillips could see Mazzola stepping forward, coming toward him. Mazzola firmly grasped Brian's left arm with both hands, preventing him from extricating himself from the doors. A malevolent grin came to his former college friend's face.

Brian McPhillips was trapped between the double doors as if wedged in the unyielding jaws of a mechanical beast.

Then the subway train began to move.

McPhillips cried out in alarm, but no one could hear him over the clatter of the train as it pulled out of the station. He felt the platform moving beneath his feet, slowly at first, but rapidly gaining velocity. He tried to keep pace with the accelerating speed of the train—it was now beginning to pick up velocity, gathering momentum—five miles per hour became ten, which became fifteen—and McPhillips struggled like a wild animal. From within the car, Bruce's voice, muffled but audible, "You shouldn't've followed us, fuckhead—" Then everything began to flicker before him in superfast motion; the steel support girders whooshed past him at horrific speed, like a speeded-up motion picture. He was no longer able to work his legs fast enough to keep pace. The train began dragging him. In the numbing fog of his terror, he perceived that he was a few seconds away from plowing into the wall at the far end of the station—

—a few seconds away from death—

In an act of animal desperation, he brought his free arm around in a whipcrack arc and slammed his forearm against the Plexiglas window of the subway-car door with all his might. The force of the blow fractured the Plexiglas with a tremendous snap audible over the roar of the hurtling train. The sharp report exploded like a rifle shot in Mazzola's face; he leaped back, startled, releasing his clasp on Brian's arm for but an instant.

—and Brian McPhillips went into a freefall. McPhillips instinctively collapsed into a ball and rolled away from the train, spinning end over end at twenty miles per hour, narrowly missing a collision with a steel girder. He finally tumbled to a halt near a row of benches, just as the subway train bulleted out of the Fiftieth Street Station, whisking Bruce and Rachel off to freedom.

Wheaton yelled his name, rushed over to him. Dropping to his side, Wheaton hovered over him, repeatedly asking: "You all right? You all right?"

Brian McPhillips *was* all right, but was too shaken to respond. Everything in his world seemed to be vibrating wildly. The ringing in his ears had become a deafening roar.

The aspiring hip-hop recording star and full-time cab driver Jamelle Childs ambled over to the two of them, thumbs hooked in his front pockets. He stood by, rocking back and forth on his heels, as he waited patiently for the appropriate moment to ask the dude about the other hundred-dollar bounty. Hey, man, if you cared to get technical about it, Childs lived up to his end of the bargain; he *did* catch up to the runaway Chevrolet Impala.

After all, a deal was a deal.

# 33

Bruce and Rachel's cab arrived at the west wing of John F. Kennedy International Airport at 10:17 A.M. The unforeseen circumstances had caused them to cut it extremely close to their flight time of 10:55 A.M.

Bruce and Rachel hurriedly walked to the Alitalia facility to check in. Since most of the passengers had already checked in, the line was mercifully short. At the *accettazione*—check-in—counter, a plump Italian woman with the improbable name of Maria Buongiorno gently scolded them for arriving at the airport so late; their seats could have been given to someone else on standby. They checked in as Mr. and Mrs. Mike Schwartz, proffering authentic-looking but fraudulent passports provided to them by someone who knew St. Germaine. Maria promptly checked them in and provided them with boarding passes. She directed them to the *sala d'attesa*—the waiting room—for ticketed passengers. Flight 611 to Rome was on time and would be leaving from Gate 32.

At the duty-free shop, Mazzola purchased a pair of moronic sunglasses with lenses in the shape of the Statue of Liberty. At another shop, he found a foolish-looking I ♥ NY softball cap. He instructed Rachel to put these on and to tuck her hair up underneath the hat.

After she did so, she protested. "I look ridiculous."

"That's the point," Mazzola said. "Your husband's been spreading pictures of you all over New York. We have to de-beautify you."

She clung to his arm and put her chin on his shoulder with a girlish pertness. "Tell me such a thing is not possible."

Mazzola smiled. Rachel was tireless when it came to fishing for compliments on her beauty. But at this moment he wasn't nibbling.

He looked at his watch. He felt reasonably confident that those two bastards wouldn't catch up with them now. Between the airport traffic and the tolls, there was no way they could get out here in time. Not unless they sprouted wings and flew.

The rotor blades whirled with an ear-splitting intensity as the helicopter lurched skyward. New York Helicopter, Flight HD-236 took off from the East Thirty-fourth Street Heliport at 10:22 A.M., two minutes behind schedule. It was expected to arrive at JFK at 10:32.

McPhillips looked out the window and watched the skyline of Manhattan shrink into toy-like miniature. Just when the twin-rotor chopper seemed as if it was going to clip the needle of the Chrysler Building, it wheeled around over the East River, heading toward Queens. Behind them, the twin towers of the World Trade Center receded until they were a pair of mere crackerboxes.

Wheaton consulted a computer printout of Sunday departures. "The first flight leaving JFK for Italy is an Alitalia flight, number 611. That leaves at 10:55."

"That's the flight Mitch had tickets for," McPhillips said.

"Yeah. We should check that out first." Wheaton lowered the printout and gazed at the urbanscapes sprawled out beneath them. "All this defies explanation, doesn't it?"

"At least we now know why Mazzola was such a spoilsport about our chances of finding Mitch and Rachel."

"Yeah, he came along so we *wouldn't* find them. That would've screwed up his doublecross." Almost wistfully, Jeff murmured, "God, how I wish to Christ I had a *gun* right now."

"Oh no you don't," McPhillips said softly. "Believe me, you'd only live to regret it."

"Maybe you're right," Wheaton said wryly. "Killing Mazzola with my bare hands will be so much more satisfying."

The helicopter landed at the helipad behind the TWA Terminal. Good tailwinds pushed up the arrival time by a minute; they disembarked from the chopper at 10:31 A.M.

It was a four-minute jog to the International Terminal. At the entrance, Wheaton said, "We can cover more ground if we split up. Why don't you go into the main concourse and look around at the food court and the duty-free shops? I'm going to check out this flight at Alitalia."

They agreed to reconnoiter at the Ground Transportation desk at 11:15 A.M. With that, they went separate ways—McPhillips into the main entrance of the International Terminal, Wheaton to the West Wing of the terminal, where the Alitalia facilities were located.

As the minutes crawled at a maddening pace, Mazzola and Rachel waited in the lounge area near Gate 32. Mazzola had a copy of *Barron's* in hand, while Rachel scanned the models in *Elle* with a critical eye. Mazzola was unable to concentrate on the printed words before him. He couldn't shake the sense that he was forgetting something important.

What was it?

The moment it occurred to him, he snapped his fingers. "I forgot, I have to call St. Germaine."

"Bruce," Rachel sighed irritably. "They'll be calling us for boarding any minute now."

"I know, I know. But I've got to call him. It was part of the plan. Jesus H. Christ!" He seethed. "If I don't call him, he assumes the worst and freezes the money. That happens, then everything'll get royally fucked up."

Rachel bit a nail and cast her eyes up toward the clock.

"Here," Bruce said, handing her a ticket, a boarding pass and the leather bag full of lira. "If they call us for boarding, just go ahead and get on board. I shouldn't be more than five minutes, okay?"

"'Kay," she said, uncertainly.

He wet-kissed her, a flash of tongue, then left the waiting area. He trotted through the long and wide corridor that connected the west wing of the International Terminal to the central concourse. The call would be short and sweet, but it simply had to be made. Otherwise, St. Germaine would fly into a panic and do something stupid.

John F. Kennedy Airport was in the midst of an ambitious $3.2 billion renovation project called JFK 2000 that was scheduled for completion, appropriately enough, at the turn of the century. It seemed that more than half the tunnel was undergoing reconstruction. Everywhere Brian went, he had to detour around scaffolding, newly erected drywalls, and cordoned-off construction areas. The signs said PLEASE PARDON THE TEMPORARY INCONVENIENCE—THE PORT AUTHORITY. The officials at JFK had even gone so far as to have set up a gallery of *New Yorker*–style cartoons lampooning the terminal's disarray, a bit of comic relief to soothe any disgruntled air traveler.

Brian jogged around another large construction site, scanning the terminal for a sign of the couple. His fruitless search covered the cafeteria, the cocktail lounge, and the currency exchange, and still had two levels to go. Fortunately, the number of passengers in the International Terminal was surprisingly light that Sunday morning in June. McPhillips knew from experience that most international flights departed in the afternoon. It was a plus that he didn't have to deal with hordes of faces. Made his job a bit easier.

Brian passed a toteboard listing arriving flights and some rotating placards for Marlboro cigarettes and *Time* magazine. A sign caught McPhillips' attention.

AIRPORT CHAPEL →

A chapel? In the airport? A place to go before your international flight to pray you didn't drop out of the sky to your death? Out of curiosity more than anything else, McPhillips walked the twenty paces to the open door of the chapel. He poked his head inside. Another sign indicated that the chapel was a multidenominational house of worship, Roman Catholic, Jewish, and Protestant. Surprisingly, there was not a soul to be found inside the simple, non-ornamental chapel. The sight of an empty house of worship on a Sunday was a depressing one to McPhillips, who still felt the guilt of becoming a lapsed Protestant. He hurried back into the hallway.

McPhillips then moved away from the chapel down the length of a long corridor, expecting it would lead him to the West Wing of the International Terminal. However, as he neared the other side, he saw that the corridor had been sealed off for the construction of a new retail shop. A sign proclaimed that BONGIOVANNI-CDC CONSTRUCTION CORP., BROOKLYN, N.Y. was the general contractor on the site. Sheets of yellowing plywood had been nailed up against the facade to close off the passageway to the general public. Nothing of interest here. McPhillips hastened past the construction site toward the elbow bend of the corridor.

Fortunately for Bruce Mazzola, the AT&T Telecommunication Center was located not too far away from the Alitalia waiting area, near the food courts and the core of the main concourse. There was only one other person in the dozen or so semi-secluded carrels: a Middle Eastern businessman speaking in a feverish Arabic. Mazzola dropped into one of the seats, swiped his AT&T Calling Card through the slot, and punched up The Saint's special number in Zurich.

Bruce had known St. Germaine since his days on Wall Street. The Saint had been an avid participant in hostile takeover deals, which had proven highly lucrative to Hemisphere Bank. Occasionally, Mazzola had provided inside information on some pending deals that had made the Saint's personal account hundreds of thousands in illicit profits. The Saint was only too happy to repay the favor by helping Mazzola and Rachel engineer the double-cross scam that would send them jetsetting around the world. Bruce waited for Raoul to answer.

"Yes?" St. Germaine's irritated voice was distorted by the snap-crackle-pop of intercontinental static.

"London? This is Soldier of Fortune calling." Bruce lapsed into codespeak, as per the plan. One never knew who might be eavesdropping. "Everything is good to go."

"Glad to hear from you, Soldier," St. Germaine said tartly.

"You left your man in London dangling on the precipice. More than once he considered scrapping the whole thing and going to Plan B."

"No need for that, London. Just a few complications that have since been worked out. Smooth sailing from here on out."

"Bloody good to hear it. The third party is out of the picture I presume."

"Yes. No need to concern yourself with that. London, I must be going."

"Indeed. Make contact when you're ensconced in your next destination."

"Will do." Mazzola hung up and breathed a little easier. Plan B would have been a fucking nightmare.

Mazzola stood up and sidled out of the carrel.

He was flabbergasted to encounter McPhillips face to face, no more than a hundred feet away.

McPhillips, for his part, went wide-eyed in surprise.

Neither man made a move.

McPhillips spun through his options. He could retreat; head back down the sparsely populated corridor from whence he came. Or he could try to barrel past Mazzola, through the AT&T center, yelling for Airport Security . . .

Remembering a security phone fifty yards behind him, he chose the former. He began retreating.

Mazzola charged after him.

Before McPhillips could make the turn down the corridor, Mazzola caught up with him, dipped his head and shoulder, and rammed into McPhillips' solar plexus with a savage force that drove Brian violently into the unyielding cinderblock wall of the construction site. Brian's head lashed back, slamming against the wall. The impact rendered him semiconscious.

As McPhillips saw stars, Mazzola wedged his fingers underneath one of the plywood sheets and pried it back from the wall. It peeled back easily, yielding access to the sealed-off area of the construction site. Since it was a Sunday, the union crewmen were off and the site was utterly abandoned. Mazzola grabbed the dazed McPhillips roughly about the collar and shoved him inside.

Brian tumbled to the filthy floor, sending a cloud of plaster dust into the air.

Mazzola stepped in over the cinderblock barrier and let the plywood sheet slap shut behind him. They were completely isolated from the rest of the airport.

"You lookin' for *me*, asshole?" Mazzola's voice thundered, amplified by the acoustics of the confined area. "Well, here I am."

Though his head throbbed badly, McPhillips had largely regained his faculties. He glared up at Mazzola from a bent-knee crouch. His mouth was filling with blood; he had bitten open the side of his tongue when he impacted against the cinderblock wall. He dispelled a large crimson glob of blood and saliva, not for an instant taking his spiteful glare from Mazzola's face.

It was cool and dank in the concealed room; the air was thick with plaster dust. It was hard to see in there as well; the only illumination was provided by several bare bulbs dangling from the ceiling. The construction project was in its earliest phase. The ceiling was completely exposed, revealing a skeletal structure of metal slats and support beams, thick black electrical cables, copper piping, and billowy wisps of fiberglass insulation. The floor itself was cluttered with construction tools and gear: cinder blocks, scraps of metal, wheelbarrows, dumpsters, plastic buckets, paint, chunks of plaster, refuse carts, stepladders, rubber cones in fluorescent orange, and empty wooden spools.

McPhillips cast his eyes about wildly, scanning the area for a weapon of some sort. There were many possibilities—hammers, chains, screwdrivers, and metal bars—but not one was within reach. It would do no good to yell for help; no one would hear. While escape was always a viable alternative, Mazzola stood in the way of the room's only exit—and he outweighed Brian by a good twenty-five or thirty pounds.

"Where's Wheaton?" Mazzola demanded. His voice boomed in the expanse of the site.

"Give it up, Mazzola. You're not gonna get away with it."

"Shut up!" he thundered. "I asked you where Wheaton was."

"He went to get the cops."

"Bullshit!" Then Mazzola touched a finger lightly to the black eye McPhillips had given him the night before. "You know, I still owe you one for the shiner. I figure this is my last chance to settle the score."

As McPhillips rose to his feet, Mazzola made a show of rolling up his shirtsleeves.

"Yeah," Mazzola growled around a ferocious smile. "Just you'n me, mano a mano. No more of your chickenshit sucker punches."

"What'd you do it for, Bruce?" McPhillips said in a throaty rumble. "Why'd you screw us all over?"

"Riddle me *this*, boy wonder. Why does a dog lick his balls?"

Brian knew the answer. *Because he can.*

"You never had the balls to hit the big time, McPussy." Mazzola took a step toward him. "You got a pair of cocktail onions between your legs."

"Damn shame about your legal troubles, Mazzola," McPhillips said.

"Yeah, no biggie." Mazzola fired him a twenty-tooth grin. "Shit happens. But you know what? Cream *always* rises to the top."

"Yeah? So does scum."

Mazzola hurtled toward him again. McPhillips crouched in anticipation of it this time, but Mazzola's twenty-five pounds over him made a critical difference, and he was able to overpower Brian, slamming him backward into a pile of discarded scrap metal and iron grating. McPhillips managed to get a solid punch in, another to Mazzola's face, which caused his adversary to bellow in pain and surprise. Mazzola recovered quickly and pinned McPhillips against the floor; then he bent McPhillips' left wrist back at an impossibly sharp angle, as if to snap it off and pinion it against his forearm. McPhillips roared in white-hot pain.

McPhillips' self-preservation instinct surfaced and he thrashed himself into a better position, kicking viciously upward. But Mazzola anticipated the move and rolled away from the thrust, off to the side. McPhillips scrambled away from his adversary and got to his feet, where he coughed wrackingly having inhaled a lungful of plaster dust.

Mazzola beckoned. "C'mon, slimdick. Let's go at it, you 'n' me."

McPhillips' heart pumped wildly.

"C'maaaawn!" Mazzola stood between him and the passageway like a nose tackle eager to thrash the quarterback one more time. "C'mon, candyass. You gonna go for it?"

They glared at each other for several moments. Then Mazzola charged him again, a bull bearing down on a red cape. Mazzola ducked down and flipped Brian over his shoulder viciously. McPhillips crashed heavily into a pile of cinderblocks and metal slats. He landed off-kilter, his ankle screaming in pain. Something popped and his leg went numb.

*I broke my ankle*, he realized.

A few yards away, Mazzola breathed heavily, shaking his head angrily. He stooped to the ground and picked up a solid length of lead pipe. "Nothing personal, Brian. It's just that I have a plane to catch and, well . . ." He smiled balefully. "I've really come to hate *your guts.*"

He began stalking toward Brian with the pipe.

McPhillips moved his hands about, scrabbling for a weapon of some sort before Mazzola put his lights out. His right hand dropped to the bed of a wheelbarrow that was positioned next to the pile of scrap. Brian's fingertips touched the cool, smooth contours of the wooden handle of a hammer of some sort. It was a mallet-sized sledgehammer used for bashing out unwanted plasterboard. The leaden head weighed about ten, fifteen pounds. His hand closed around the handle and he gripped it tightly. Played possum until Mazzola loomed above him.

Mazzola brought the lead pipe into a backswing, his face contorted by murderous intent.

Summoning every ounce of energy he had left, Brian shifted his weight so that he slipped from the pile and fell to his knees. Simultaneously, he gripped the hammer with both hands and, with a scraping of metal-against-metal, lifted it from the bed of the wheelbarrow. He brought it around in full swing, aiming it at Mazzola's kneecap—like a tomahawk. Then Brian heard the satisfying crunch of the cartilage shattering completely beneath the mighty blow of the mallet.

Mazzola bellowed in a primal scream, collapsing to the floor as if gunshot. He clutched his mangled mash of connective tissue and bone fragments and reeled about in the filth and the dust. His world had been reduced to a hell of excruciating agony, and he bellowed out nonsensical gibberish as he experienced the unspeakable pain.

McPhillips somehow forced himself to his feet, hobbled across the room toward the opening that was sealed off by the plywood. His energy sapped by the effort of battle, he summoned up the strength to fall against it with all his weight. The plywood sheet ruptured outward, clattering to the floor of the corridor. McPhillips fell to the floor with it.

He picked himself up and hopped to the red security phone, one painful step at a time.

"Security," the dispatcher answered.

McPhillips closed his eyes and allowed a moment of triumph to block out the throbbing pain. "I think," he said, "I've captured one of America's Most Wanted. . . ."

His heart slamming against his chest, Jeff Wheaton raced frantically up the escalator toward Gate 32, hoping he wasn't too late.

When he arrived, his heart dropped. He *was* too late. There was not a single passenger in sight. *It must've just finished boarding.* All that remained were two lone attendants in Alitalia uniforms, standing at the checkpoint facility, shuffling carbon copies of boarding passes and softly conversing in Italian.

Wheaton approached the men. Breathlessly, he informed them, "I've got to get on board that plane."

Both men looked up from their paperwork. To Wheaton, the two of them resembled something of a neapolitan Laurel and Hardy. From their ID plates, he learned that the one who resembled Laurel was named Marcello di Firenze; his Hardy-like counterpart was Mario Ricci. At the moment, he had only one objective: *to get on that plane.*

Di Firenze peered up at a digital clock. His face crumpled into an expression of annoyance. "I'm afraid you've arrived too late, sir. Flight 611 has finished boarding."

"It can't be!" Wheaton wailed.

In a soothing voice, Ricci said, "There will be another flight to Rome later this afternoon. Our agent will help you transfer your ticket to that flight at no additional cost—"

"You don't understand," Wheaton snapped. "It's an emergency."

Di Firenze sighed as if he had heard that line before. "They have already closed the door of the plane. It is cleared for takeoff."

"You've got to stop it!"

Ricci put his hands up to calm Wheaton down. "Let's see what we can do. May we see your boarding pass, passport and ticket, please?"

Wheaton closed his eyes and pressed his fingertips to his forehead. "I don't have a boarding pass or my passport."

The two men stared at him.

Wheaton battled the iceberg of panic rising within. He *had to* find out if they were aboard Flight 611. Had to think straight. "It's not my flight. I believe my wife is on board that plane and I need to find out."

Ricci said, "Perhaps if you tell us her name, we can verify whether she is on the flight. But we cannot hold up the flight. What is your wife's name?"

"Rachel."

"Her surname, please?"

"I don't know that."

"You don't know your wife's last name?" di Firenze asked.

"What I mean is, I don't know what name she's traveling under. She's using . . . an assumed name. The truth is, she's a fugitive from the law."

"I see," di Firenze said, giving Ricci a sidelong look.

"It's the *truth*. You can check it out with the FBI. Ask for Special Agent Newby, Jack Newby. He's in charge."

"Perhaps it would be prudent to verify what you're telling us," di Firenze said. "Perhaps we should first take it up with airport security."

"Then, you're saying you'll hold this flight?"

"Oh, no. I'm afraid that would be impossible," di Firenze said. "But not to worry. If what you're saying is true, then perhaps the Italian authorities will apprehend her."

"In Rome?"

"Yes."

The notion of Bruce and Rachel leaving the country did not seem like a viable option to Wheaton at that moment. "What would happen then?"

Di Firenze shrugged. "Then, perhaps they will extradite her."

*Perhaps.*

Fuck perhaps. Perhaps wasn't good enough.

Before he himself could realize what was happening, impulse had taken control of Wheaton's actions. He charged past the pair of startled checkpoint Charlies and plunged into the corridor leading to the plane.

He heard the men cry out angrily behind him, heard Laurel roar, "Somebody get Security and the Air Marshals, *now!*"

In the back of his mind, he knew that he had committed a federal offense of some sort and that he would have to answer for that. He also knew that Airport Security would be hot on his heels within a matter of seconds. That was either good news or bad news, depending upon whether Rachel and Mazzola were on the goddamn plane. But he couldn't sweat that. Not now.

He blocked out these thoughts and sprinted blindly for the entrance to the jetliner, the hollow thunder sounding beneath his feet, the blood thumping through his brain with the cadence of a bass drum.

He whipped around the elbowbend of the L-shaped corridor and caught the flight attendant just as she was about to secure the entrance of the plane. His abrupt appearance caught her off-guard.

"Oh, I apologize, sir. I was told they had finished boarding the flight."

He blew past her, brushing her to the side.

She let out a startled cry, more in surprise than in pain.

# PART SEVEN

### THREE WEEKS LATER

# EPILOGUE:
## Cinque Terre, Italy

Since the crime was international in scope, the release of the victims' money was ensnarled in reams of diplomatic red tape. Despite Interpol's announcement that both the Swiss and British banking authorities had pledged full cooperation, release of the funds to the rightful owners would not occur for sixty to ninety days—at the earliest. The recent intervention of the U.S. Department of Commerce promised to delay the disbursements even further.

Resultingly, the McPhillips family lost their opportunity to buy the home in Chestnut Hill despite the capture of all the principals involved in the scam.

As something of a consolation, Brian McPhillips took his wife and children on a two-week vacation to Italy. McPhillips was gratified by the irony that Rachel Wheaton's dream trip around the world had become a splendid family vacation for one of her victims. Perhaps there was such a thing as poetic justice.

Italy was a *wonderful* country. Rugged and provincial, it was an alluring blend of lingering old-world traditions and modern, trend-setting sensibility. The Italians themselves were a lively and impassioned people who cherished excellence in food, sports, style, and beauty. Best of all, McPhillips found, they treated American tourists with a respect and hospitality that the standoffish French would do well to emulate.

On the ninth day of their trip, the McPhillips family arrived at Cinque Terre, a string of five remote fishing villages carved out of the craggy black cliffs that loomed above the Ligurian Sea. Cinque Terre was accessible only by sea or by train; there were no roads for motor vehicles to access Vernazza, Monterosso el Mare, Corniglia, Manarola, or Riomaggiore. Indeed, the most popular means of passage to the five hamlets was an ancient goat trail that had been chiseled into the terraced face of the cliffs by industrious Etruscans some twenty-five hundred years ago. McPhillips had to bypass this attraction because he was recovering from the injury to his ankle. But Lisa enjoyed the forty-minute journey from Vernazza to Riomaggiore wound through vineyards of sweet grapes, fragrant acres of lemon trees and olive trees, and patches of vibrant roses, with its spectacular panorama of the turquoise sea crashing against the rocks below. McPhillips had to give Wheaton's ex-wife credit—Cinque Terre was spellbinding.

At the instant the telephone rang in their hotel room, the family was gathering up provisions to head to the beach for the morning.

McPhillips knew immediately who it would be.

"I'll get it," he said to Lisa. "Why don't you take the kids down to the beach, and I'll join you shortly."

"C'mon, Josh," she said, holding out her hand for him. "We're going to go outside to the water." To her husband she mouthed the words, *Don't be long.*

From a continent and an ocean away, Jeff Wheaton's chipper voice crackled over the wire. "How's Italy?"

"*Molto bene,*" McPhillips replied. "You know, it's absolutely impossible to find a bad meal in this country."

"That's what they say. Tell me, did you get the faxes of newsclips I sent to the hotel?"

"Yes I did. All twenty-seven pages of them." McPhillips laughed. "Seems to be quite a bit happening."

"Oh yeah. That guy St. Germaine? It looks like Britain's going to let him walk. He claims he didn't know his books were being used as a conduit for stolen funds and there's no substantive evidence to the contrary. There's some speculation he used a touch-tone telephone from prison to hook into his computer and shut down access to damning information, but nothing solid."

"All in all, it appears to be your typical media feeding frenzy."

"That's the perfect description of it. My phone's ringing off the hook."

"I can imagine."

"In fact, movie producers are starting to call from Hollyweird. Inquiring about the rights to my story."

"You don't say."

". . . Y'know, it so happens I'm in the market for an attorney to deal with all these offers. What do y'say, counselor, you my man?"

"Let's do lunch," McPhillips said, around a grin. "Just promise me you won't sign anything until I get back, okay?"

"You got it."

After that, the two friends lapsed into an intercontinental silence. It wasn't for a lack of things to say about the scam. Quite the contrary, there was a multitude of topics one or the other could have brought up, but both left untouched. Not a word was spoken about the death of Charles Beekman; nor about Mitch Myerson, whose life had been saved by Esperanza and the U.N. Plaza hotel security, but who had been released from the hospital only to go directly to jail; nor about the pathetic plea-bargaining ploy Rachel Fairweather Wheaton and her defense lawyer were attempting, calling Bruce Mazzola a suave Svengali; nor about the recent murder-one indictment the Manhattan D.A.'s office had lodged against Bruce Mazzola: These were topics they were not yet ready to discuss, to contend with, to make sense out of. Least of all over a transatlantic phone call.

Instead, Brian McPhillips asked, "How're you doing, buddy? Everything okay on your end?"

He heard Wheaton exhale. "Things are . . . good. I met someone, Brian. Someone really good for me, I think. Her name is Alicia, Alicia Moretti. I'd really like for you to meet her when you get back."

"I look forward to it," McPhillips said, feeling happy for the guy.

Jeff sighed, "I should really let you get back to your family . . . There's just one thing before you go."

"Sure." McPhillips waited.

"After . . . all this," Wheaton said. "After all the betrayals, the greed, the frigging *evil* I witnessed throughout this whole damned episode? . . . Well, the only good thing to come out of it was . . . was that you and I came out of it better friends than ever before. I want you to know that means a lot to me."

"Likewise, Jeff."

"You were there when I needed you. I'll never forget it."

"I appreciate that."

Shortly thereafter, they rang off.

McPhillips replaced the phone on its cradle and immersed himself in his thoughts.

Jeff had called the entire affair *evil*. McPhillips reflected upon this. *No. This was something else,* he decided.

It was Brian's belief that every individual was affected to some degree by what he called the Big Hungry. The Big Hungry was that infinite chasm which resided in every soul, the haunting obsession to extract some sort of *meaning* out of life. In a sense, it defined drive, ambition—which in turn, imbued one's existence with some semblance of significance.

To feed the Big Hungry was a lifelong endeavor, articulated in any number of ways. Some climbed mountains. Some built empires. Some sought to collect as many sexual encounters as humanly possible. Others sought to maximize personal wealth, as if such a measure was in direct proportion to the significance of one's time on earth. Most frequently, however, lives were defined by the inarticulable passion to accumulate more worldly possessions than any other.

People like Mitch and Bruce sought to live life at full throttle; if doing so came at the expense of others, then so be it. *Whoever steals the most toys wins.* The truth of the matter was that the Big Hungry could not be sated by the frenzied quest to accumulate . . . *things*. Such a solipsistic pursuit was, in the end, unalloyed futility. How immense must one's mansion be before it became no more than a temple of solitude?

McPhillips rose from the side of the bed and drifted out to

the balcony. There, he leaned over the railing and gazed down upon the miniature figures of his wife and two children, Josh and Ashley, as they splashed about in the roiling surf. Josh leaned down to pick up a seashell, a discovery which he proudly exhibited to his mother and the video camera.

*The only way to outstrip your mortality,* he thought, *is through your children.* A man's progeny were his legacy, the true measure of his wealth. Though Brian McPhillips was not one to quote scripture, a Biblical phrase came to him now: *Go forth and multiply.* Within those four words, perhaps, one could decode the enigma of existence. The purpose of life was to . . . procreate. Keep mankind going. End of story.

Below him, Lisa panned the video camera around, capturing the seaside panorama surrounding them. Eventually, she tilted the lens up in his direction. He waved. Lisa nudged Josh and pointed toward McPhillips on the balcony. In the next moment, his entire family was waving to him, beckoning for him to come down, to join them.

He was heartened to discover that this modest spectacle filled him with a sense of belonging and a sense of purpose.

*Without family,* he realized, *all else was meaningless.*